MAR / 2024

Tree-House Comix Proudly Presents

DOG MAN

The Scarlet Shedder

WRITTEN AND ILLUSTRATED BY DAV PILKEY
AS GEORGE BEARD AND HAROLD HUTCHINS
WITH COLOR BY JOSE GARIBALDI & WES DZIOBA

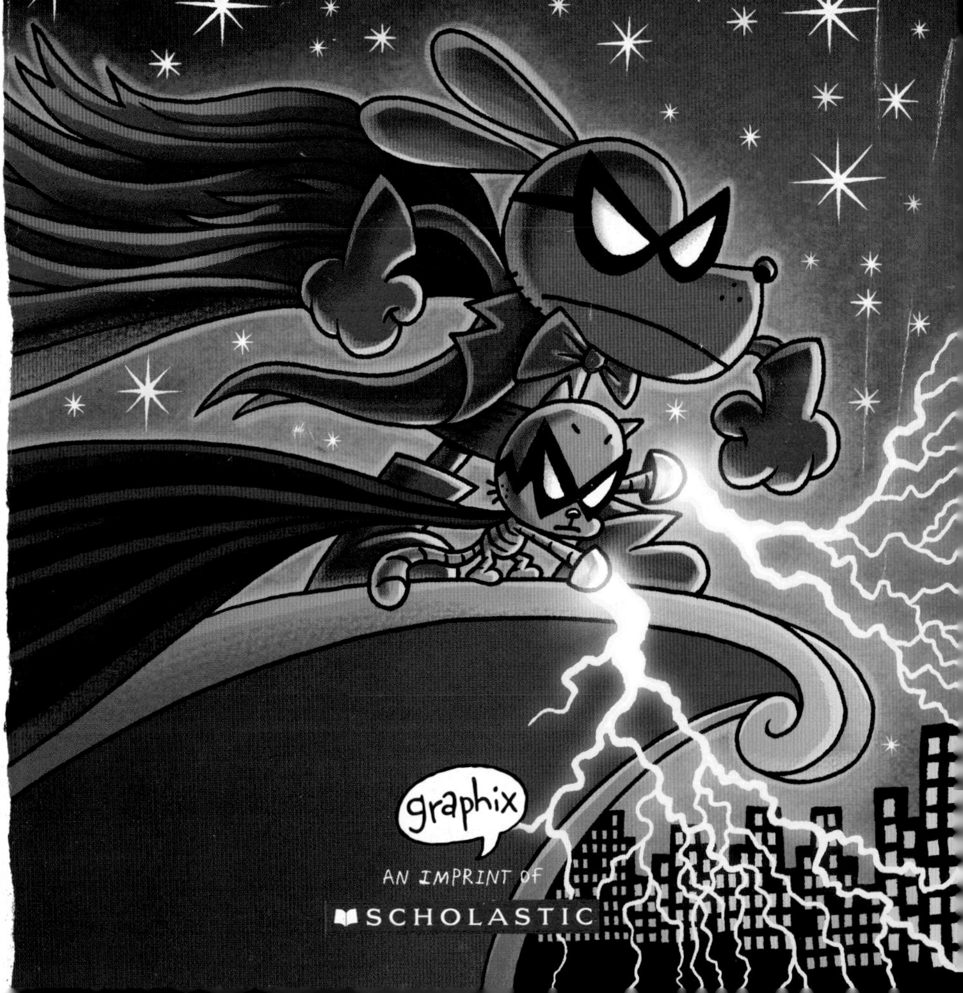

graphix
AN IMPRINT OF
SCHOLASTIC

Library of Congress Control Number 2023946577

978-1-338-89643-5 (POB)
978-1-338-89648-0 (Library)

10 9 8 7 6 5 4 3 2 1 24 25 26 27 28

Printed in China 62
First edition, March 2024

Editorial team: Ken Geist and Jonah Newman
Book design by Dav Pilkey and Phil Falco
Color by Jose Garibaldi and Wes Dzioba
Color flatting by Aaron Polk
Creative Director: Phil Falco
Publisher: David Saylor

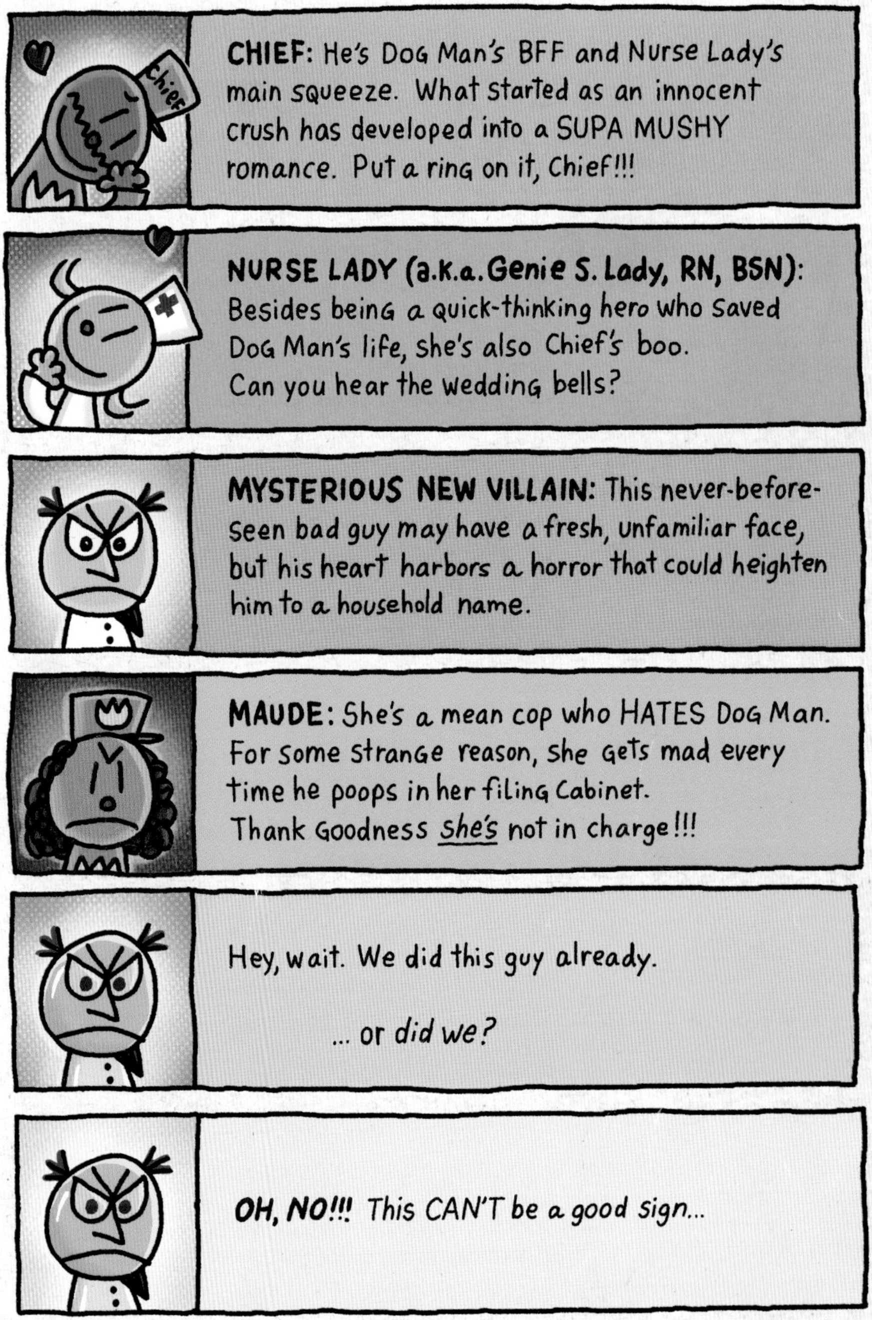
CHIEF: He's Dog Man's BFF and Nurse Lady's main squeeze. What started as an innocent crush has developed into a SUPA MUSHY romance. Put a ring on it, Chief!!!
NURSE LADY (a.k.a. Genie S. Lady, RN, BSN): Besides being a quick-thinking hero who saved Dog Man's life, she's also Chief's boo. Can you hear the wedding bells?
MYSTERIOUS NEW VILLAIN: This never-before-seen bad guy may have a fresh, unfamiliar face, but his heart harbors a horror that could heighten him to a household name.
MAUDE: She's a mean cop who HATES Dog Man. For some strange reason, she gets mad every time he poops in her filing cabinet. Thank goodness she's not in charge!!!
Hey, wait. We did this guy already.
... or did we?
OH, NO!!! This CAN'T be a good sign...

To the Kibuishi family:
Kazu, Amy, Juni, and Sophie

CHAPTER 1

The Best DOG MAN

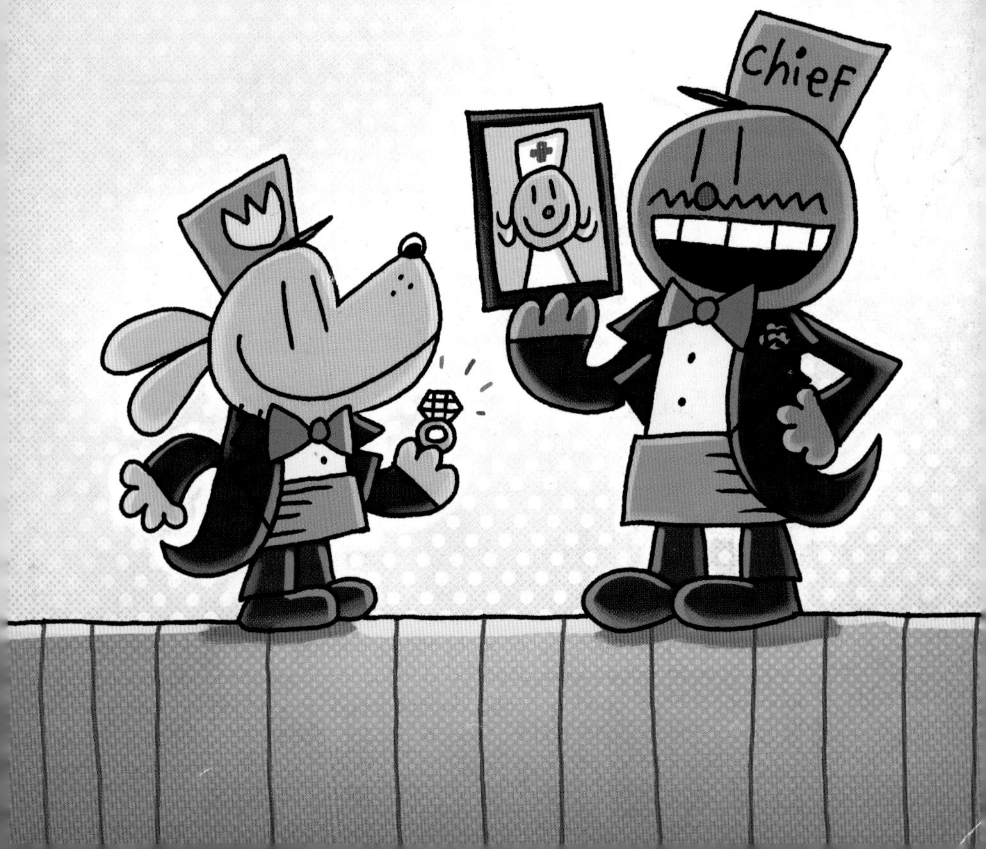
Chief

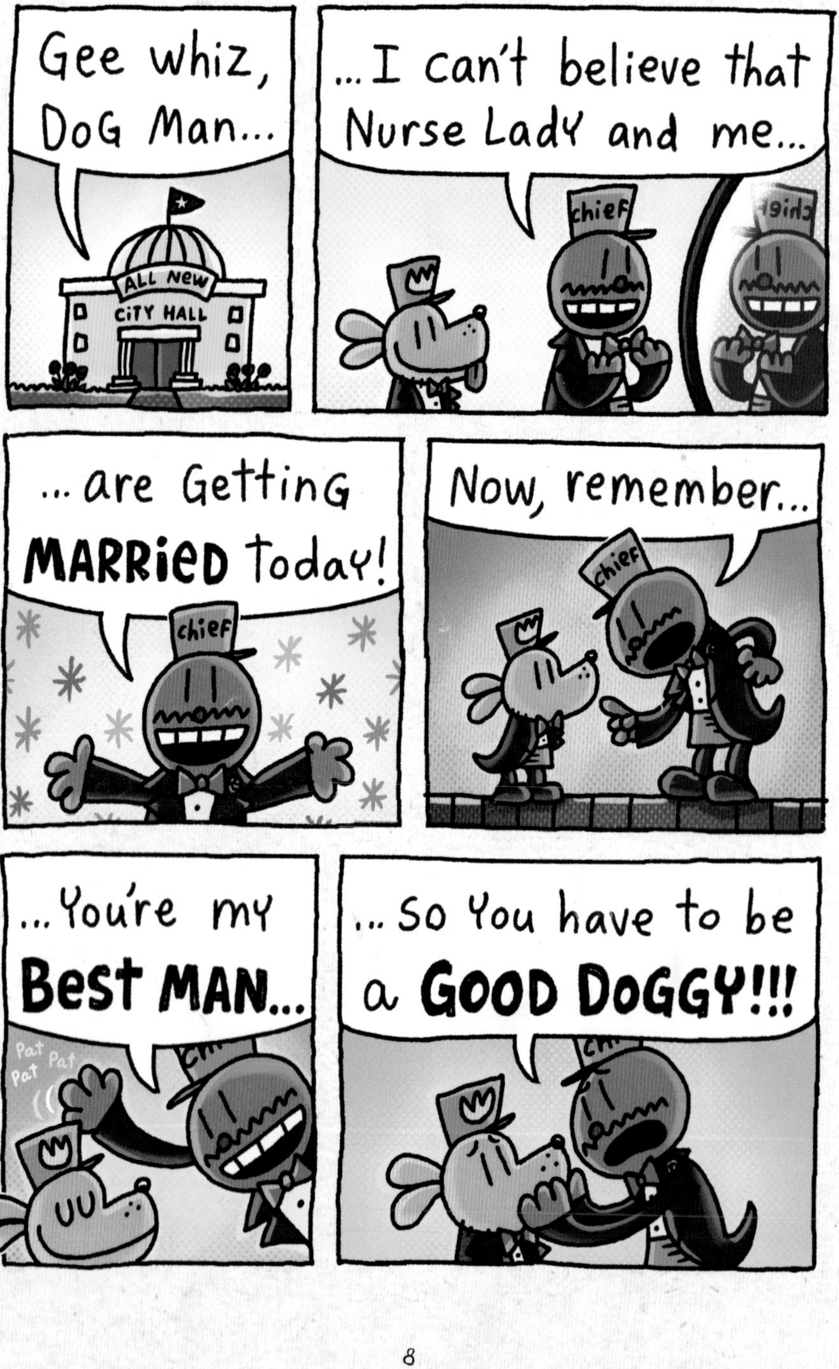
Gee whiz, DoG Man...
ALL NEW
CiTY HALL
...I can't believe that Nurse Lady and me...
chief
...are Getting MARRieD today!
chief
Now, remember...
chief
...You're my Best MAN...
Pat Pat Pat
...So You have to be a GOOD DOGGY!!!

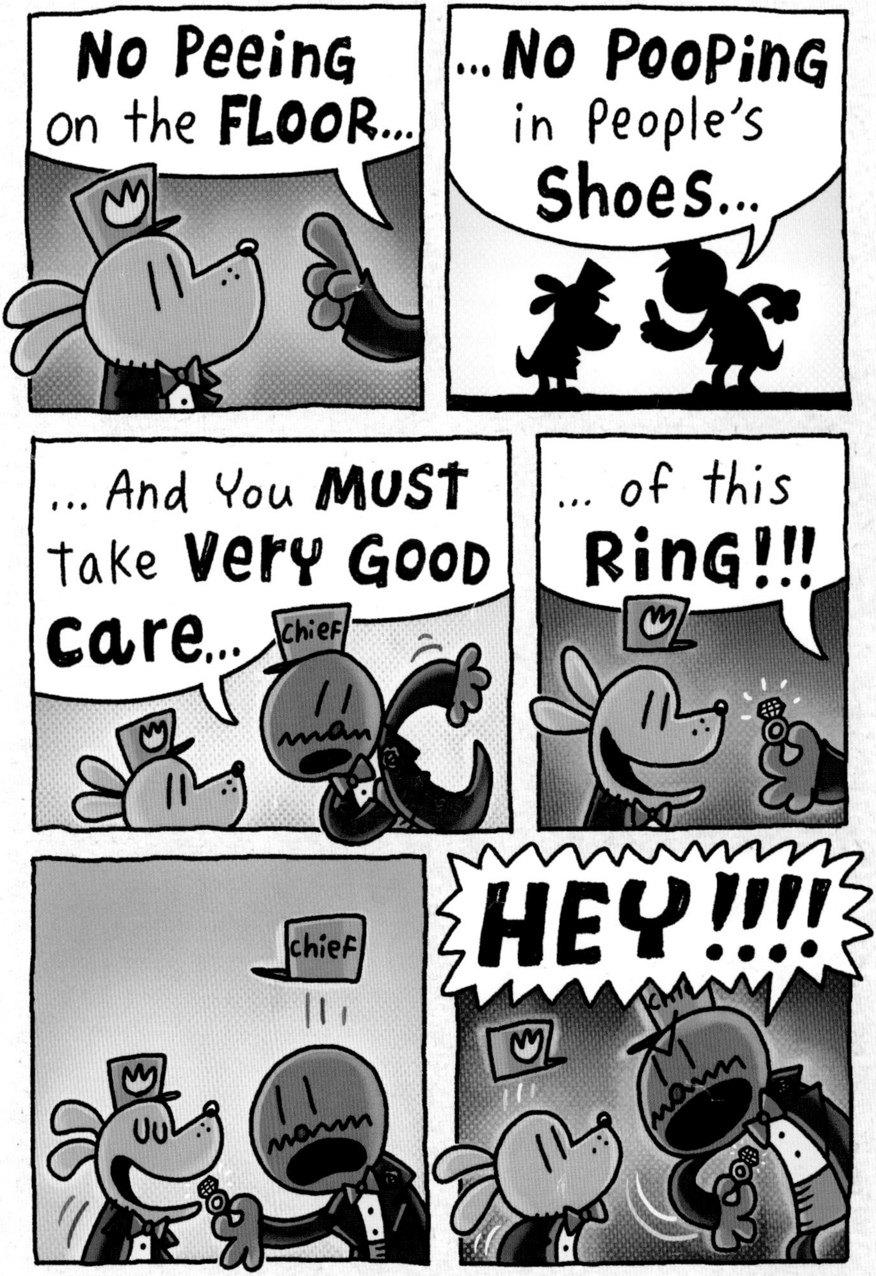

No Peeing on the FLOOR...
...NO POOPING in People's Shoes...
... And You MUST take Very GOOD care...
Chief
... of this RinG!!!
chief
HEY!!!!

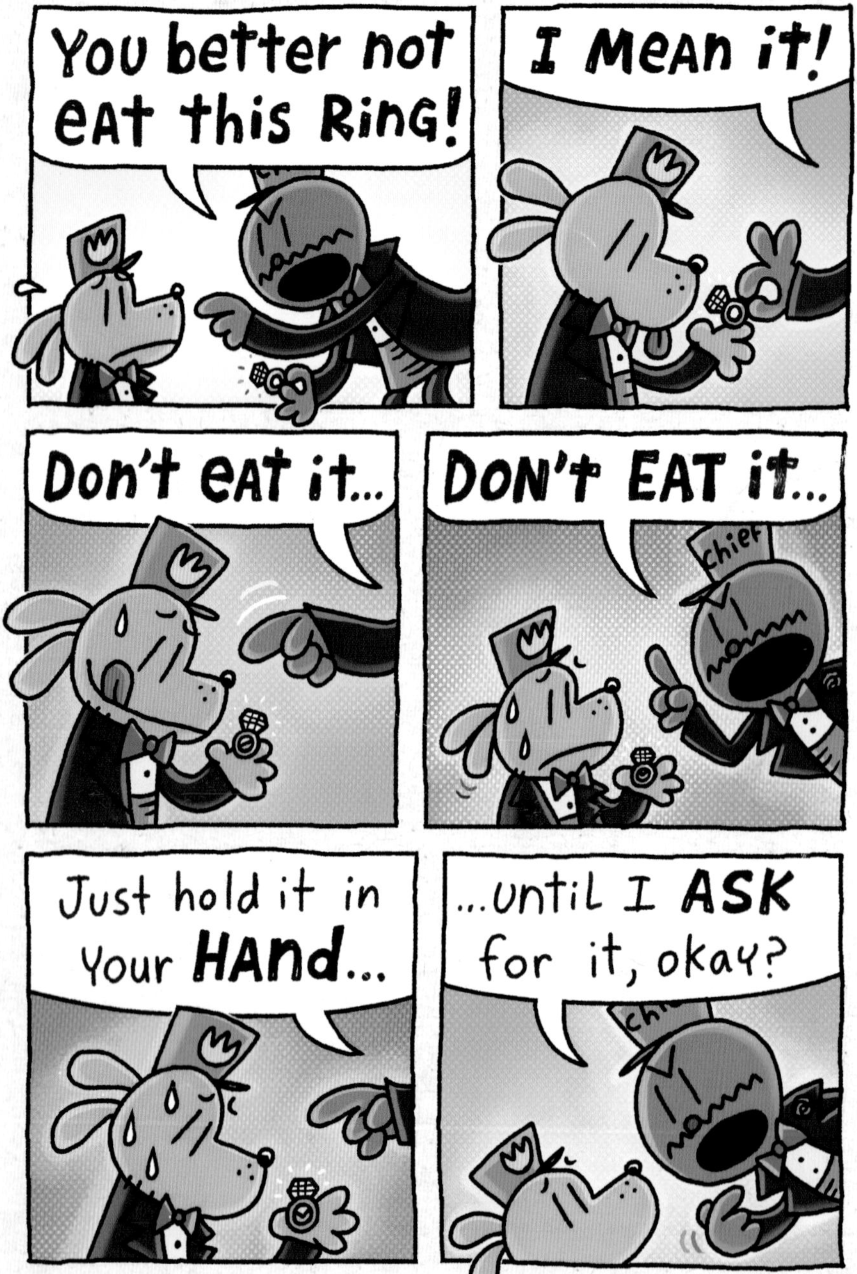
You better not eat this RinG!
I Mean it!
Don't eat it...
DON'T EAT it...
Chief
Just hold it in Your HAnd...
...until I ASK for it, okay?

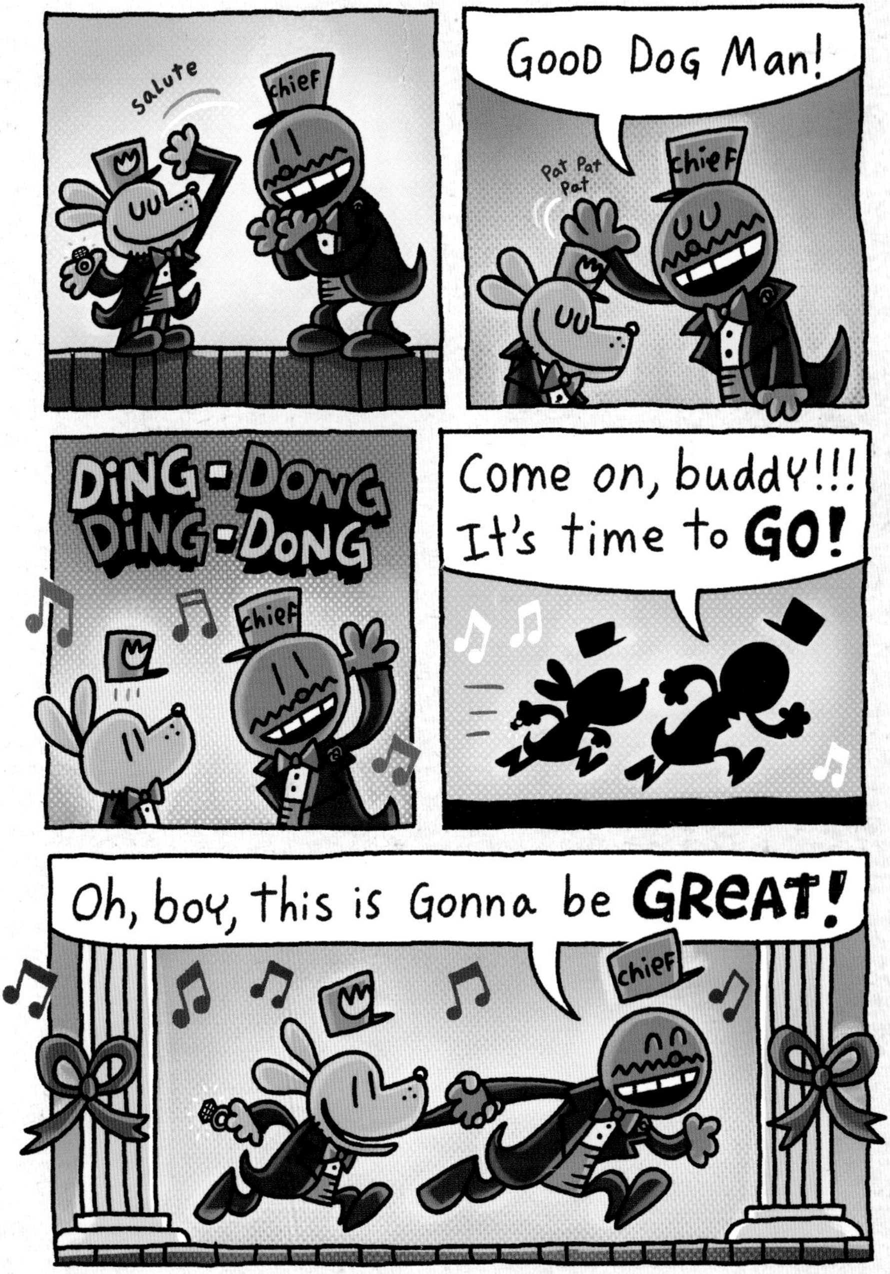
salute
chief
Good Dog Man!
Pat Pat Pat
chief
DiNG-DONG DiNG-DONG
chief
Come on, buddy!!! It's time to GO!
Oh, boy, this is Gonna be GREAT!
chief

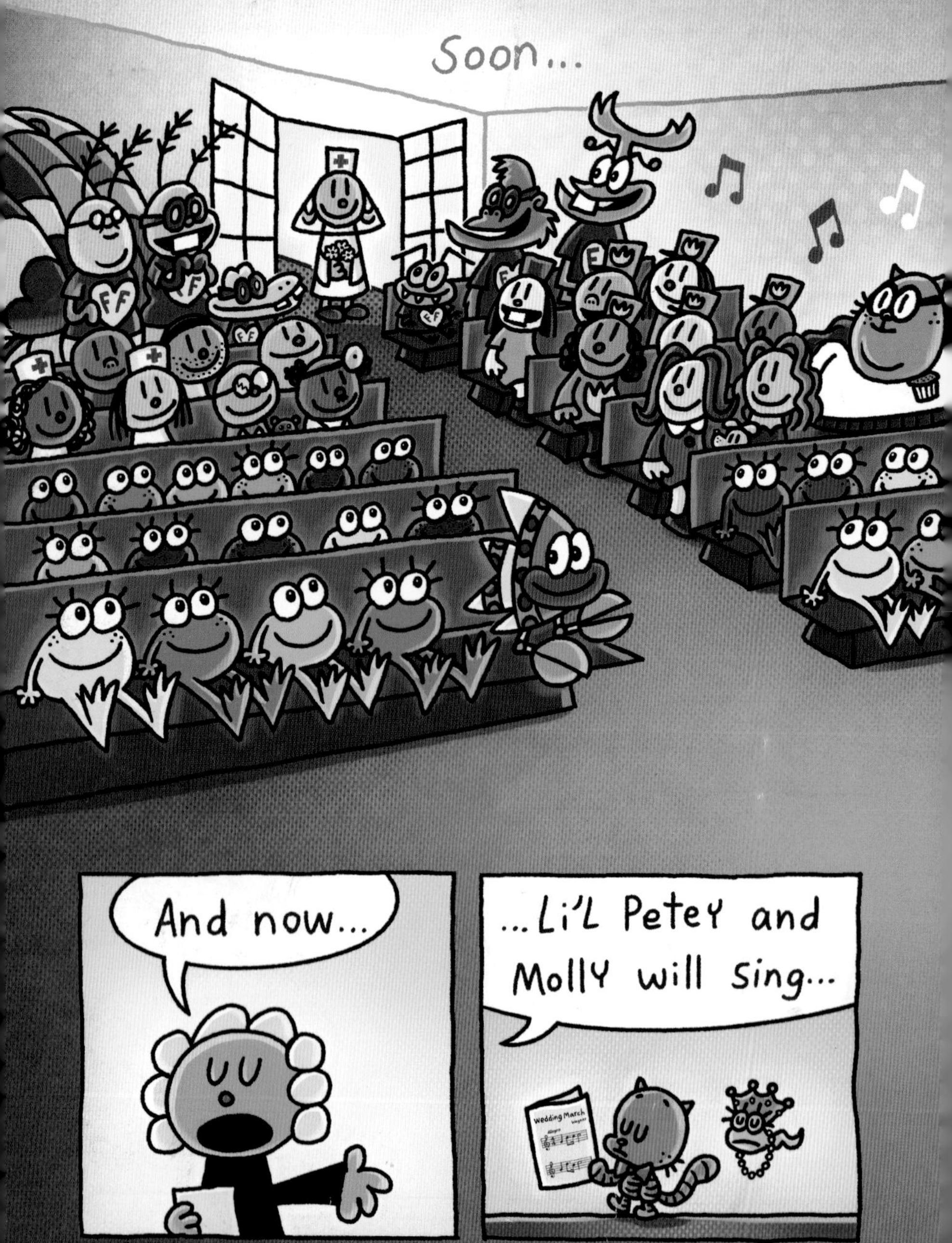
Soon...
And now...
...Li'L Petey and Molly will sing...
Wedding March

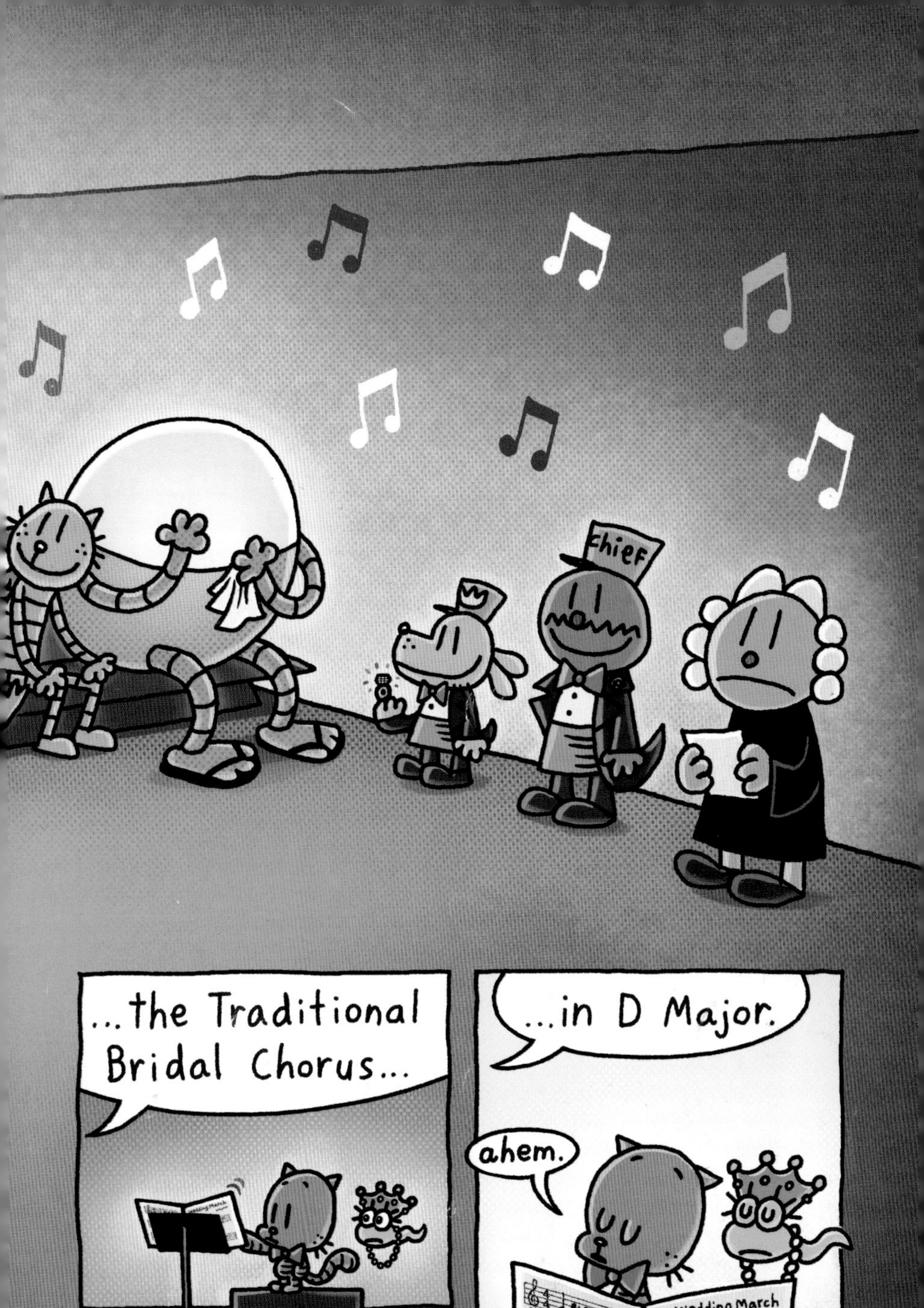
Chief
...the Traditional Bridal Chorus...
...in D Major.
ahem.
Wedding March

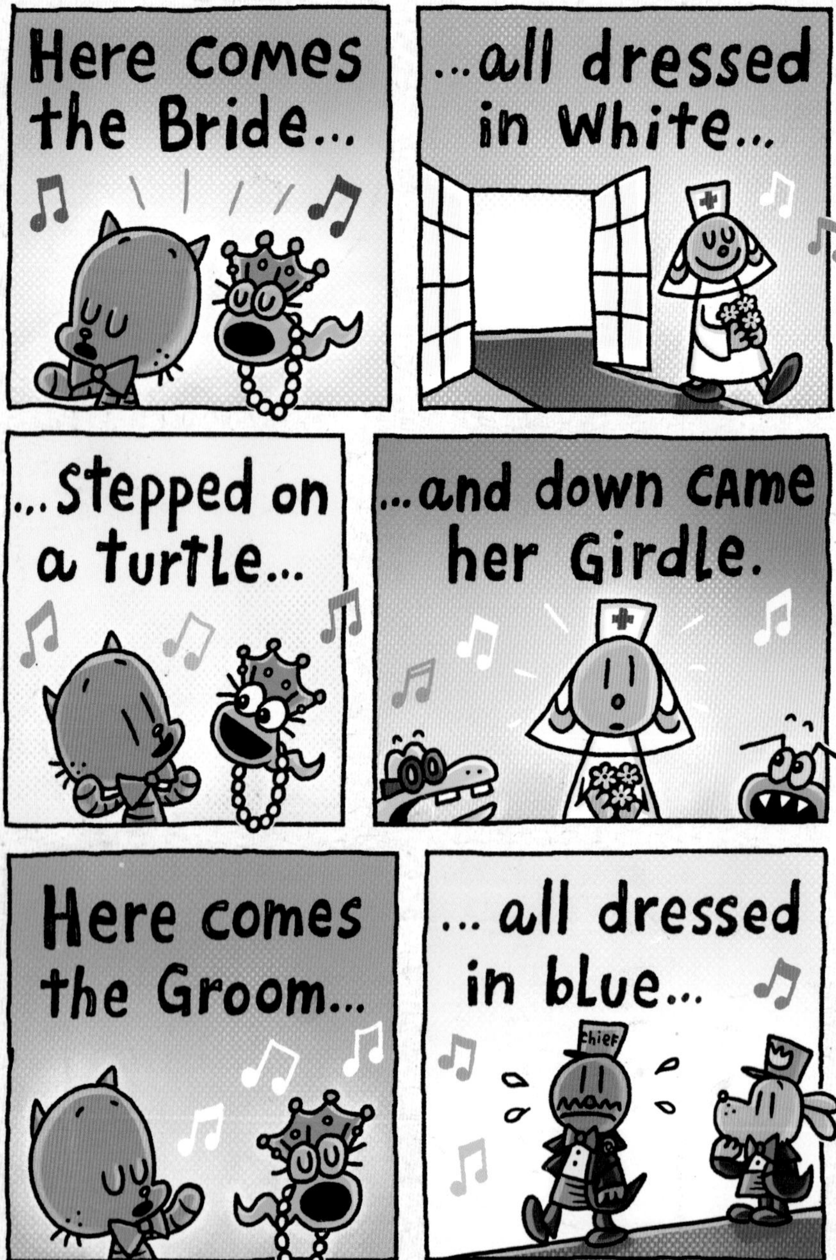
Here comes the Bride...
...all dressed in White...
...Stepped on a turtle...
...and down came her Girdle.
Here comes the Groom...
... all dressed in blue...
chief

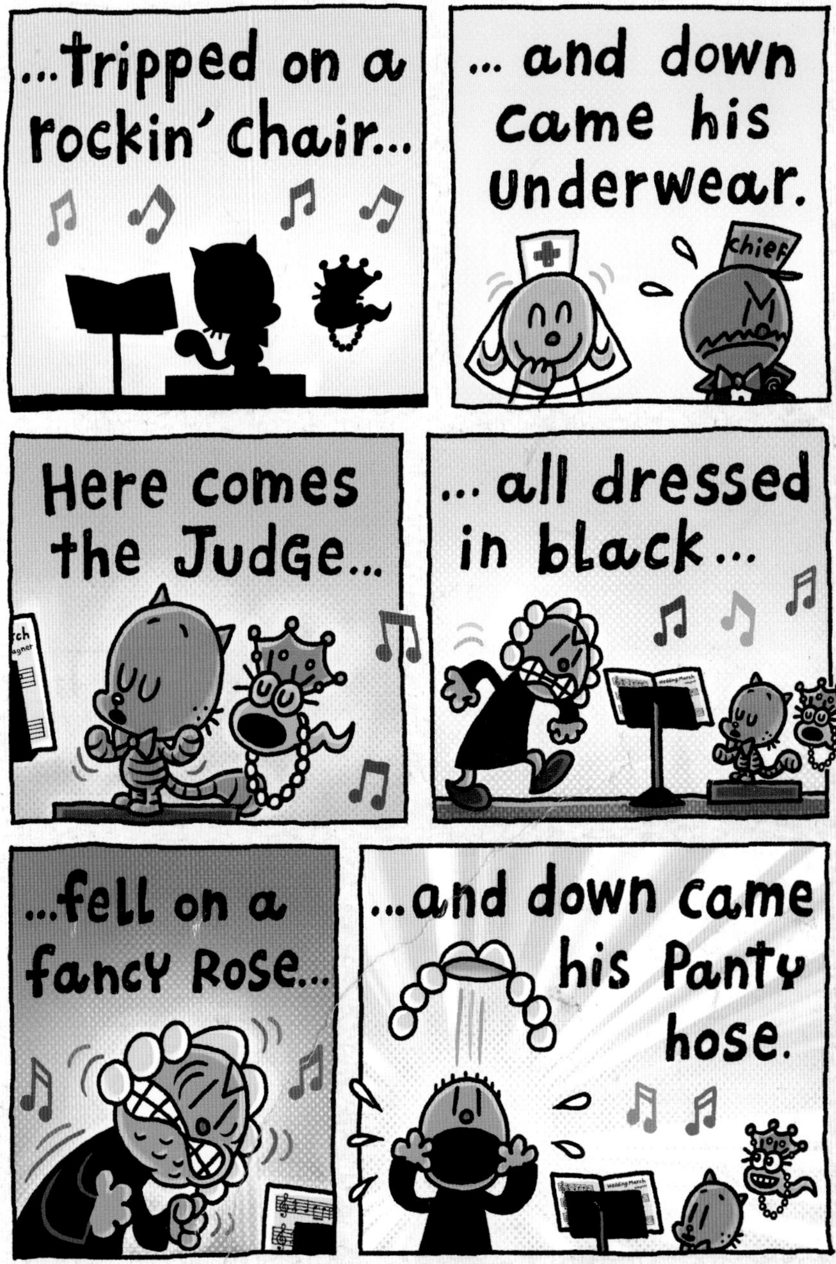
...tripped on a rockin' chair...
...and down came his underwear.
Chief
Here comes the Judge...
...all dressed in black...
...fell on a fancy rose...
...and down came his panty hose.

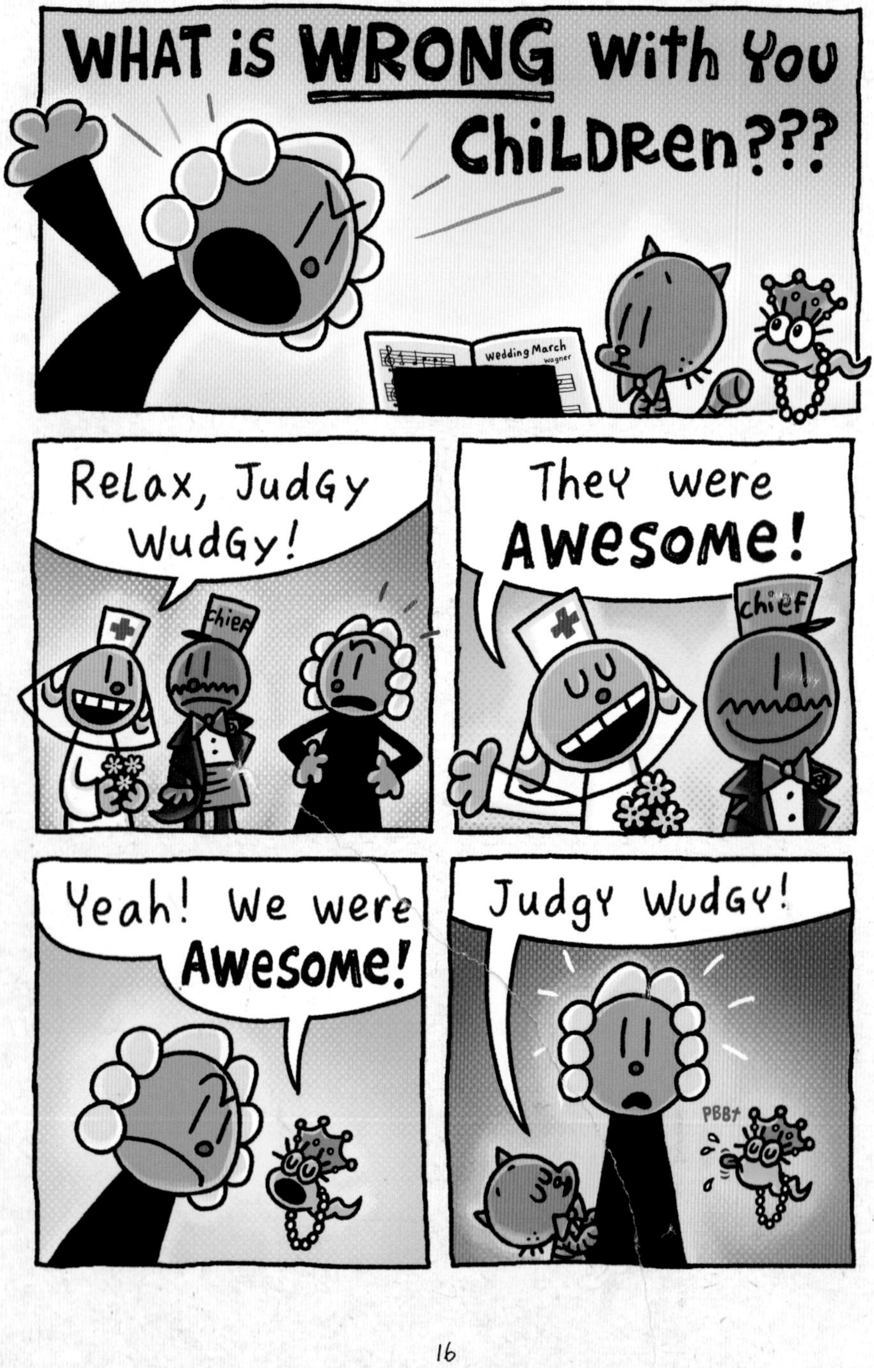
WHAT is WRONG with You ChiLDRen???
Wedding March
wagner
Relax, Judgy Wudgy!
chief
They were AWESOME!
chief
Yeah! We were AWESOME!
Judgy Wudgy!
PBBT

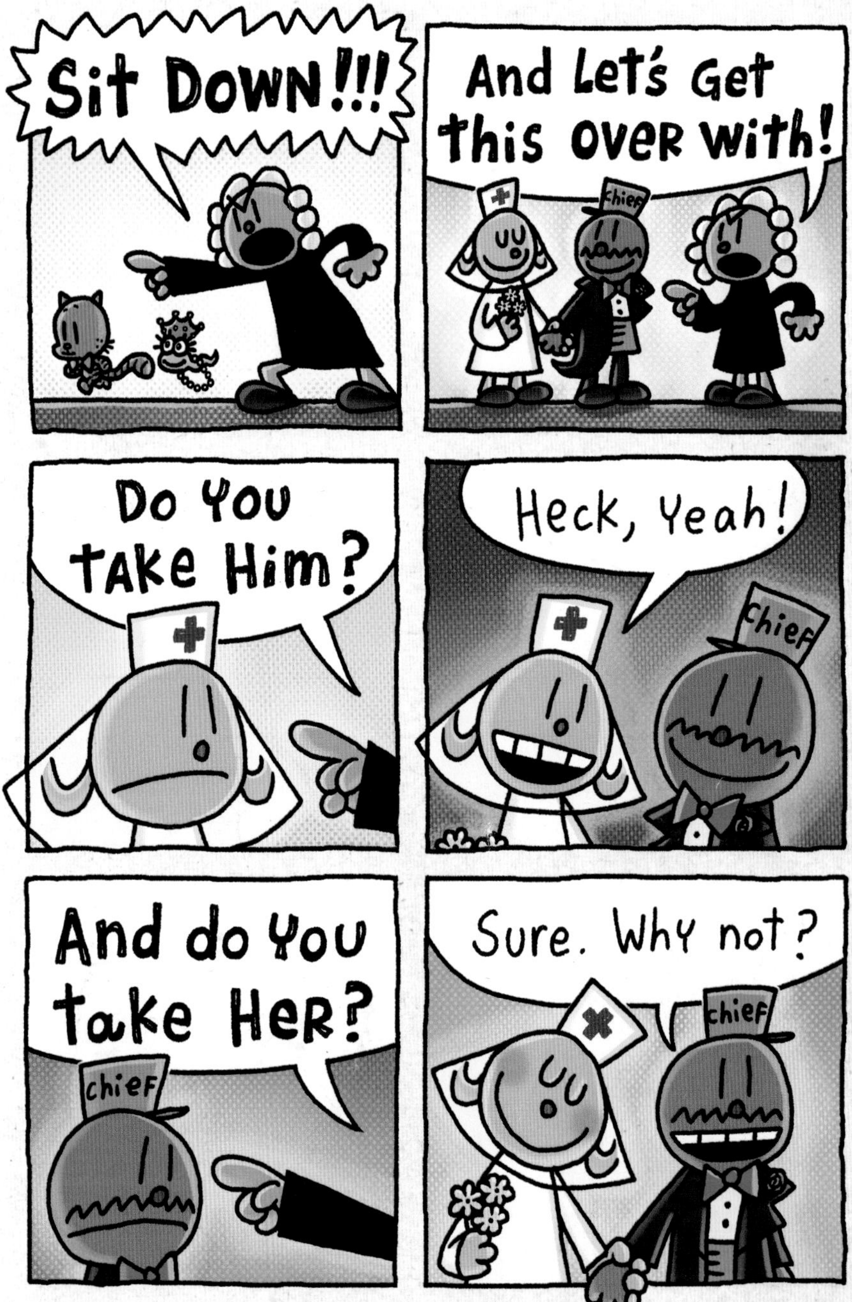
Sit Down!!!
And Let's Get this over with!
Do you take Him?
Heck, Yeah!
And do you take Her?
Sure. Why not?

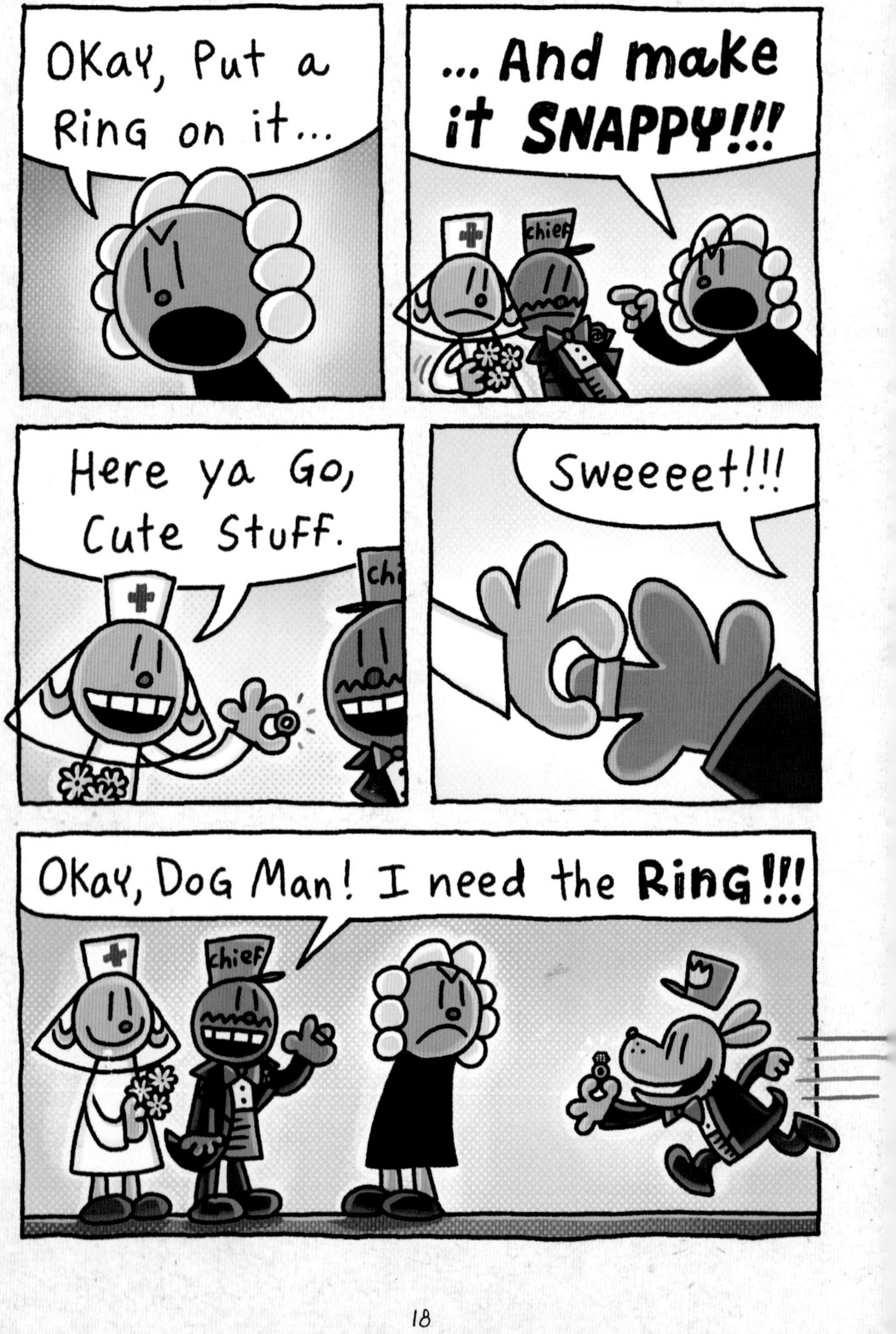
OKAY, Put a Ring on it...
... And make it SNAPPY!!!
Here ya Go, Cute Stuff.
Sweeeet!!!
OKAY, DOG Man! I need the RING!!!

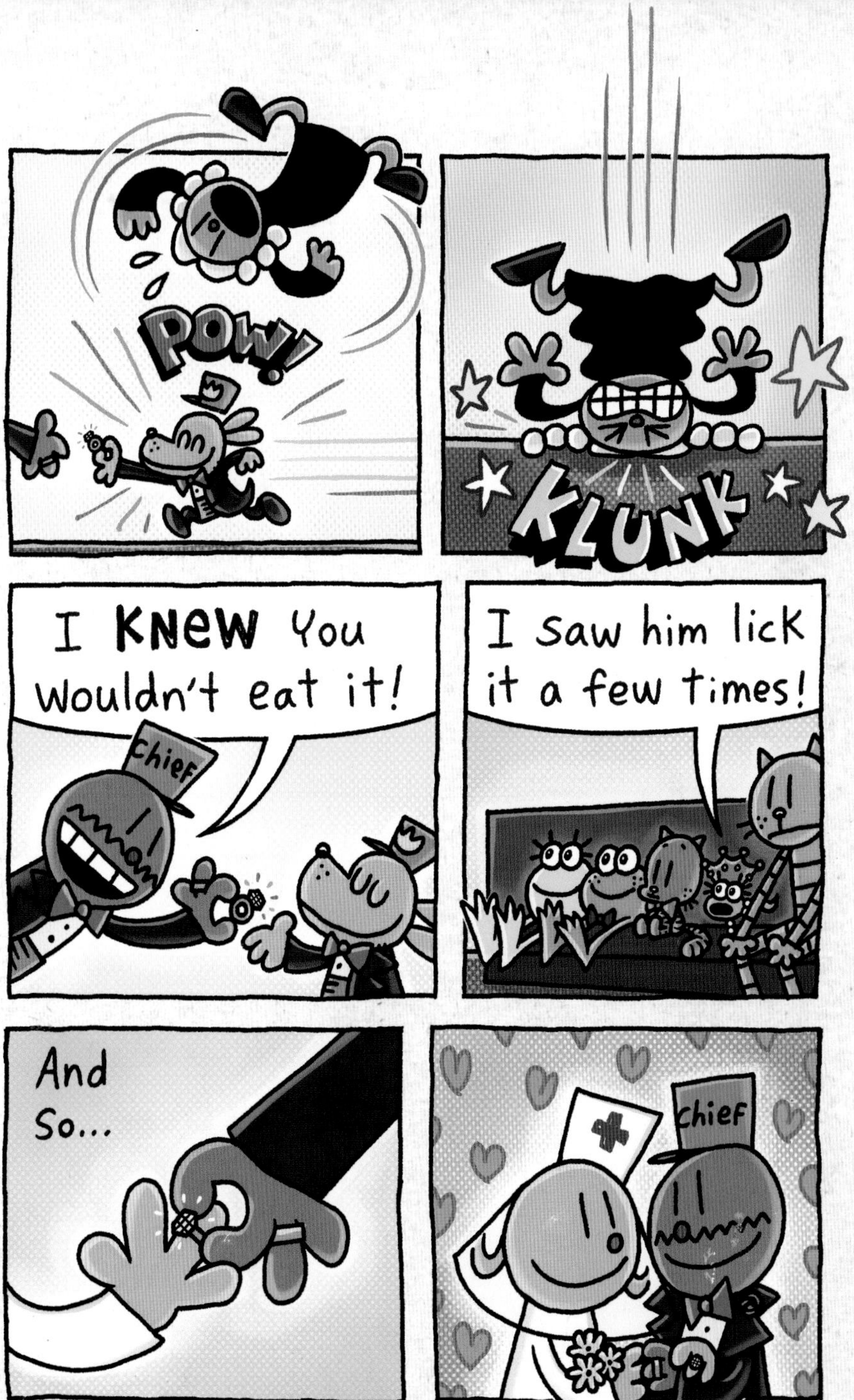
POW!
KLUNK
I KNEW You Wouldn't eat it!
Chief
I saw him lick it a few times!
And So...
Chief

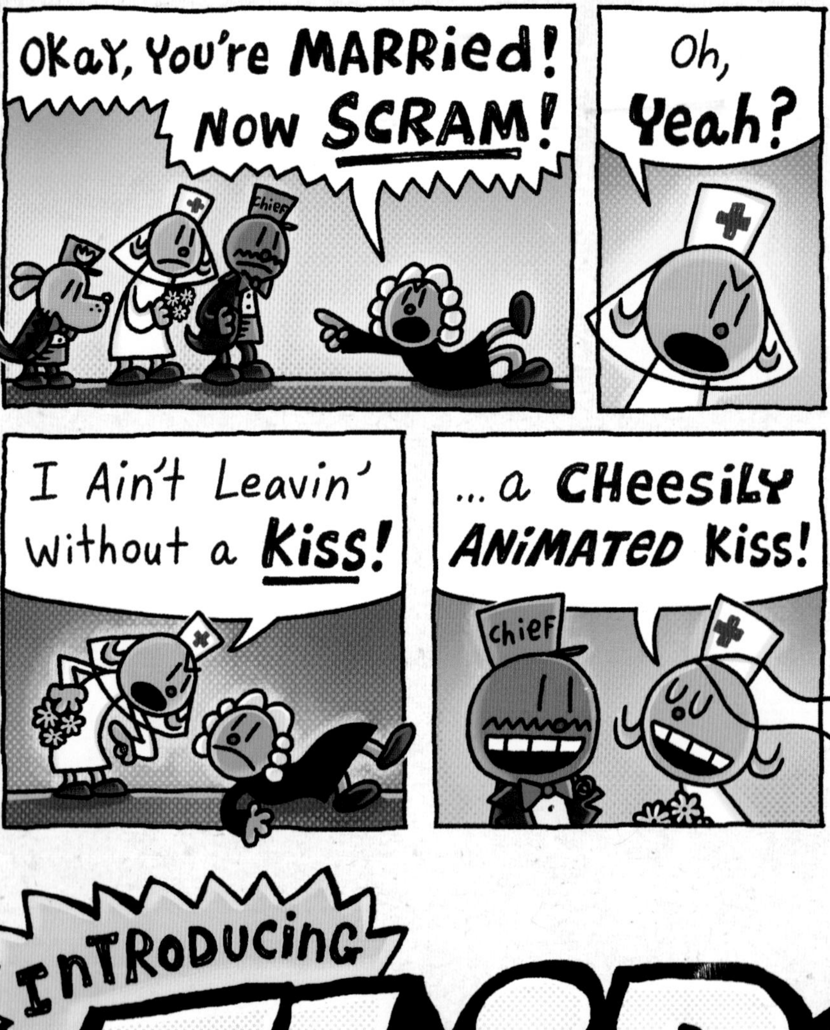
OKAY, YOU'RE MARRIED! NOW SCRAM!
Oh, Yeah?
I Ain't Leavin' without a Kiss!
...a CHEESILY ANIMATED Kiss!
CHIEF
CHIEF

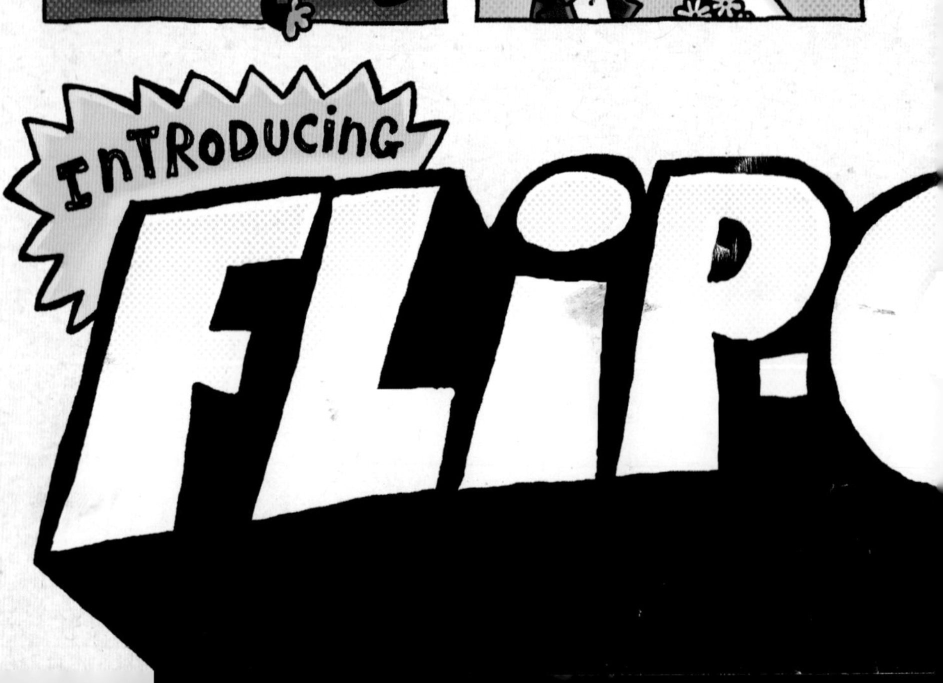
INTRODUCING
FLIP

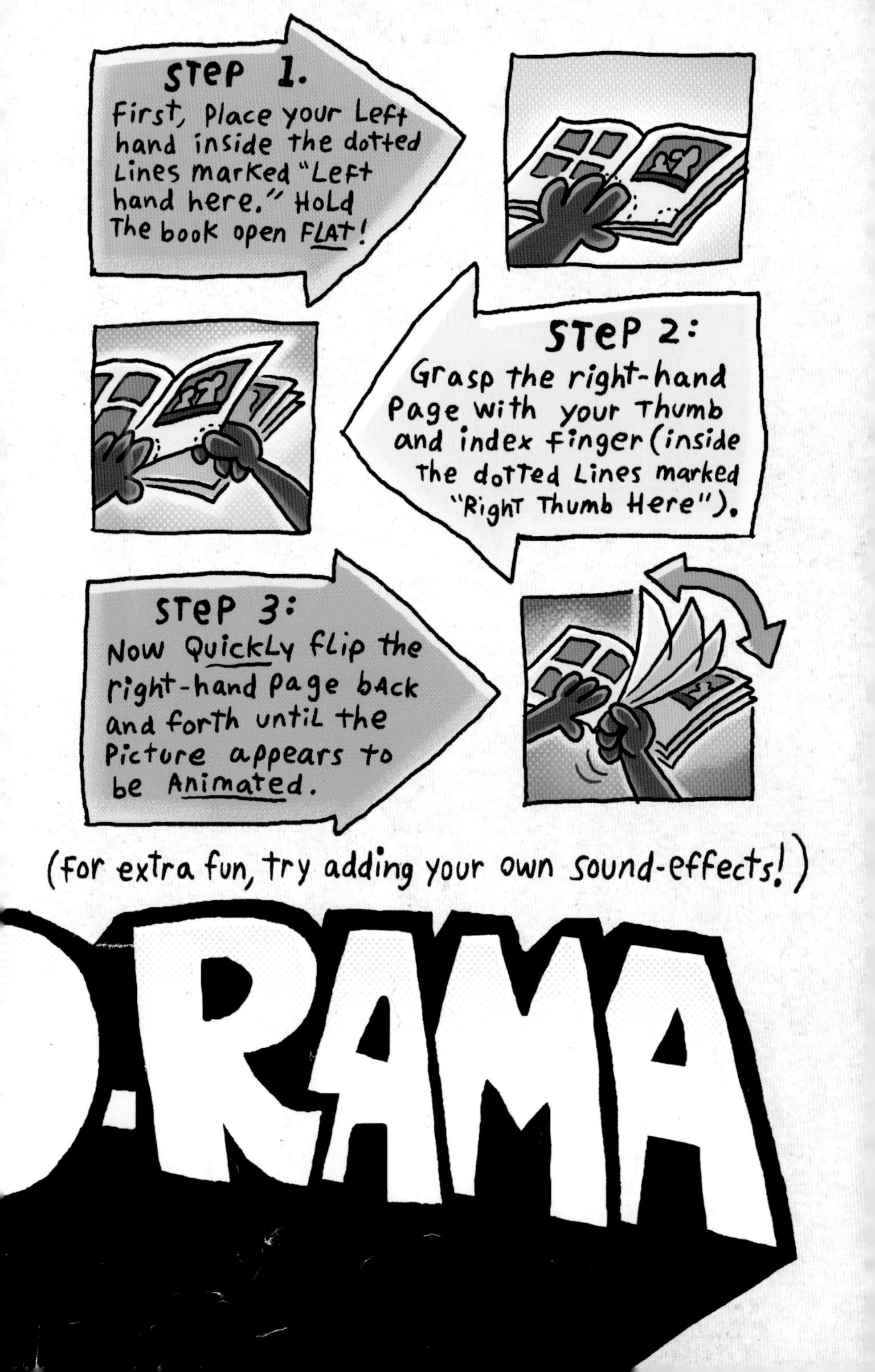
STEP 1.
First, Place your Left hand inside the dotted Lines marked "Left hand here." Hold The book open FLAT!
STEP 2:
Grasp the right-hand Page with your Thumb and index finger (inside the dotted Lines marked "Right Thumb Here").
STEP 3:
Now QUICKLY flip the right-hand page back and forth until the Picture appears to be Animated.
(for extra fun, try adding your own sound-effects!)
RAMA

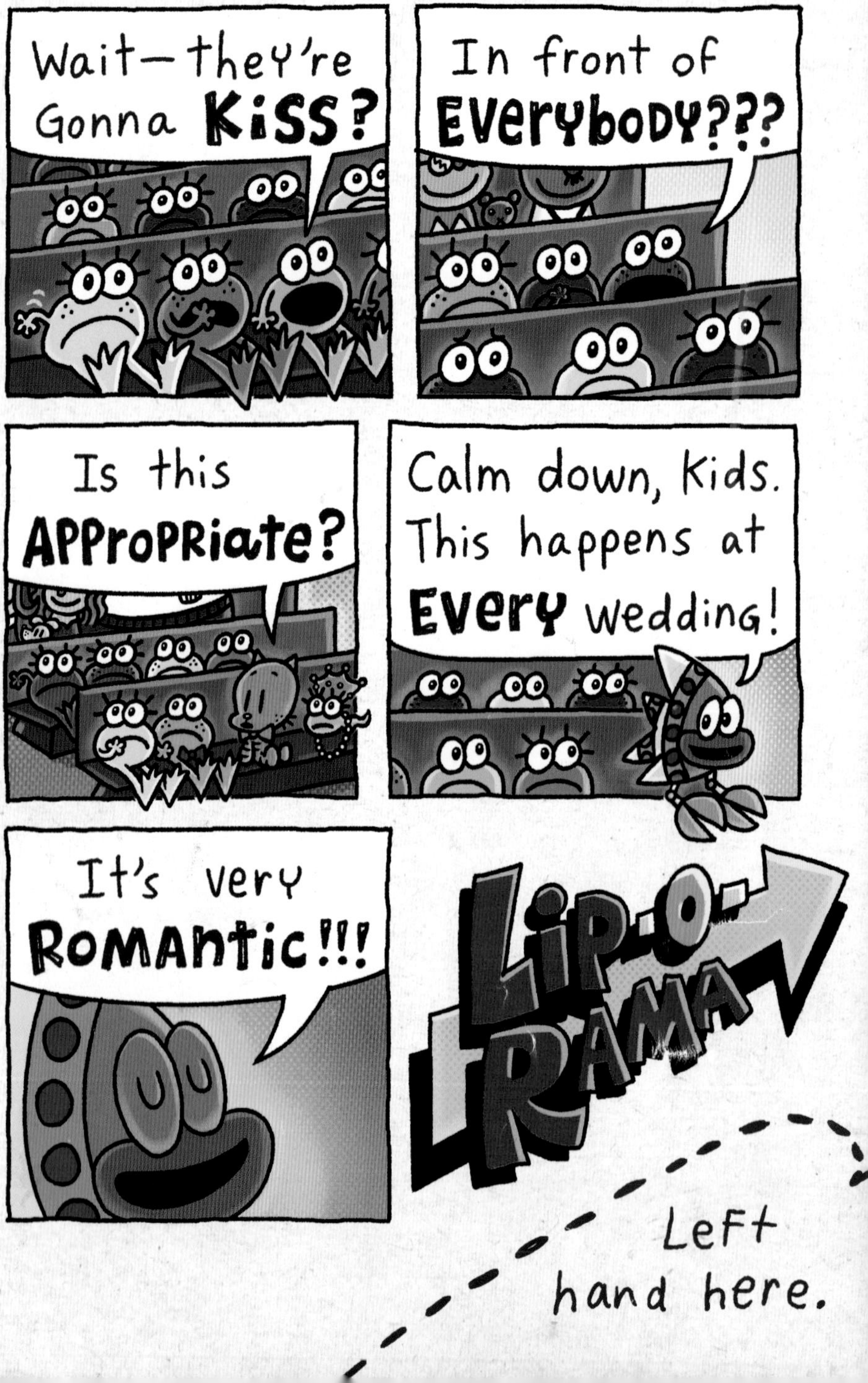
Wait—they're Gonna KiSS?
In front of EVERYbODY???
Is this APPROPRIATE?
Calm down, Kids. This happens at EVERY wedding!
It's very ROMANTIC!!!
LIP-O-RAMA
Left hand here.

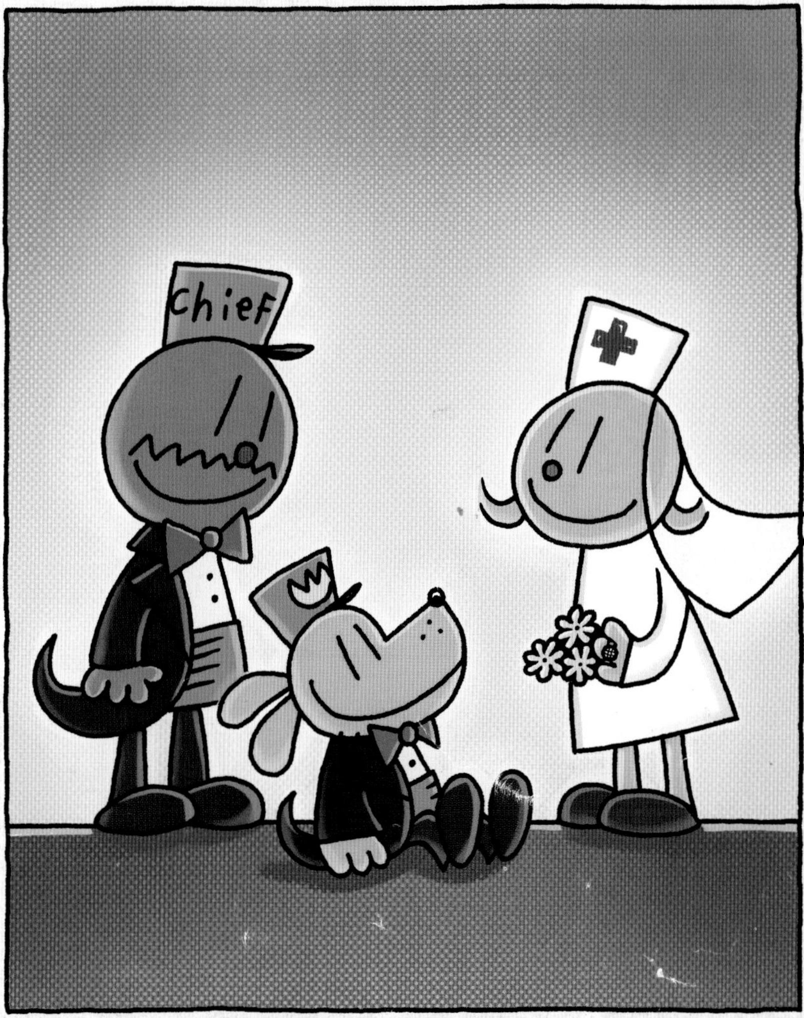
Chief

Poochie Smoochie

Right Thumb here.

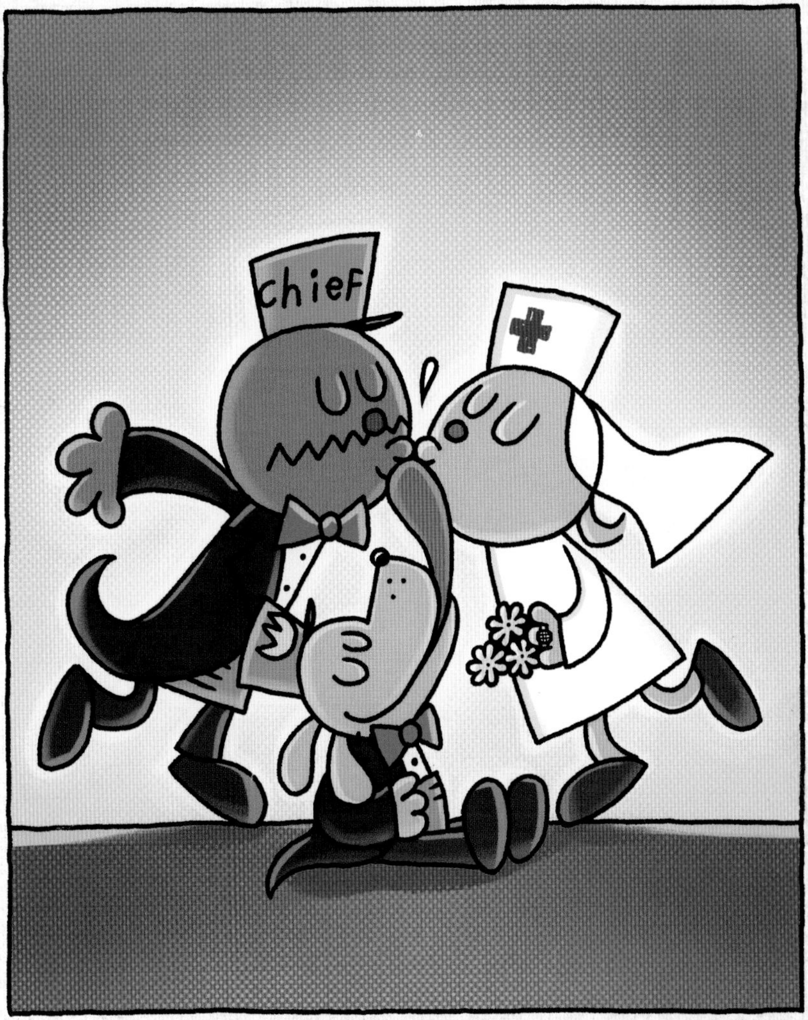
chieF

Poochie Smoochie

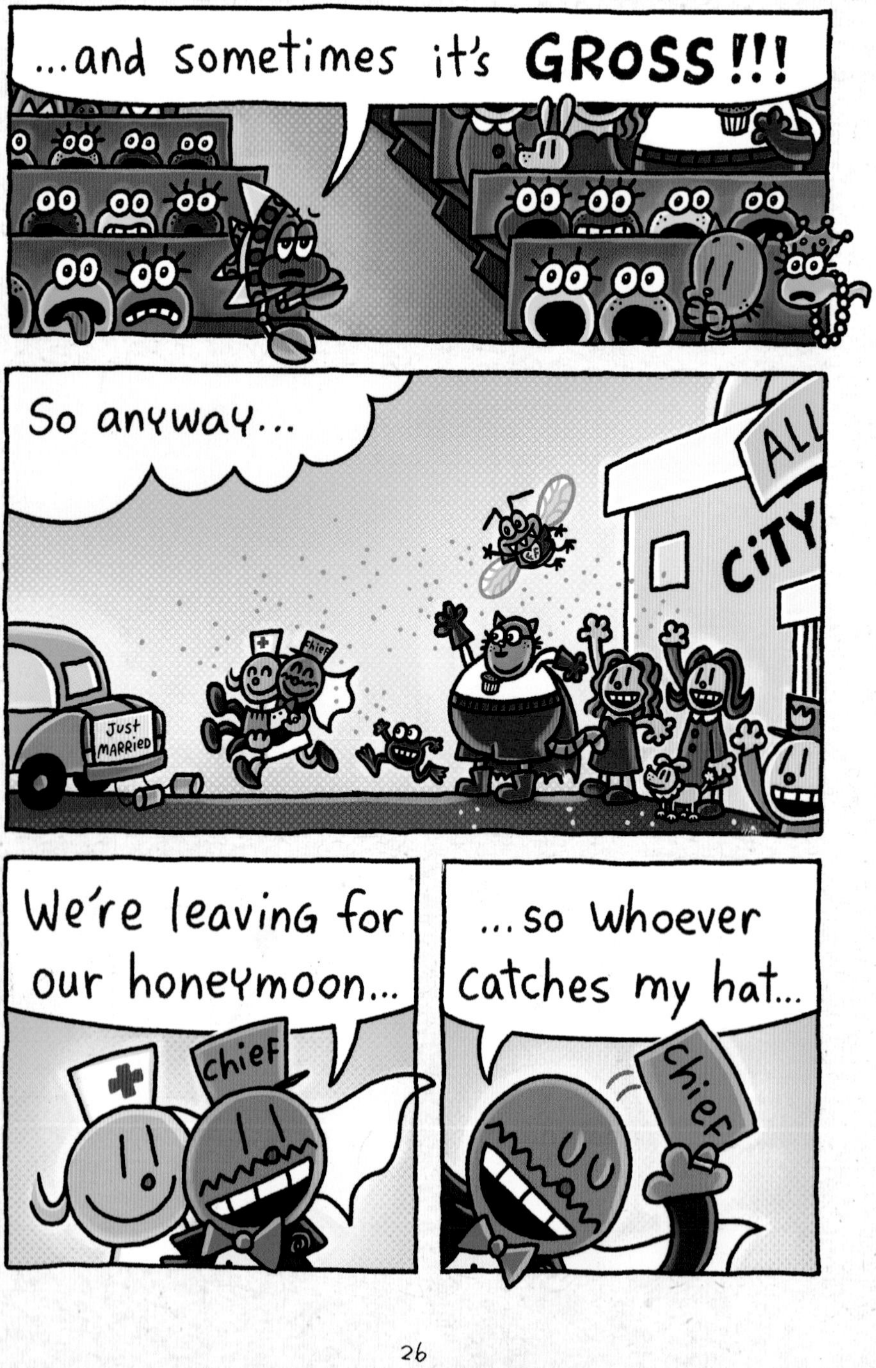
...and sometimes it's **GROSS!!!**
So anyway...
ALL
CITY
JUST MARRIED
chief
We're leaving for our honeymoon...
chief
...so whoever catches my hat...
chief

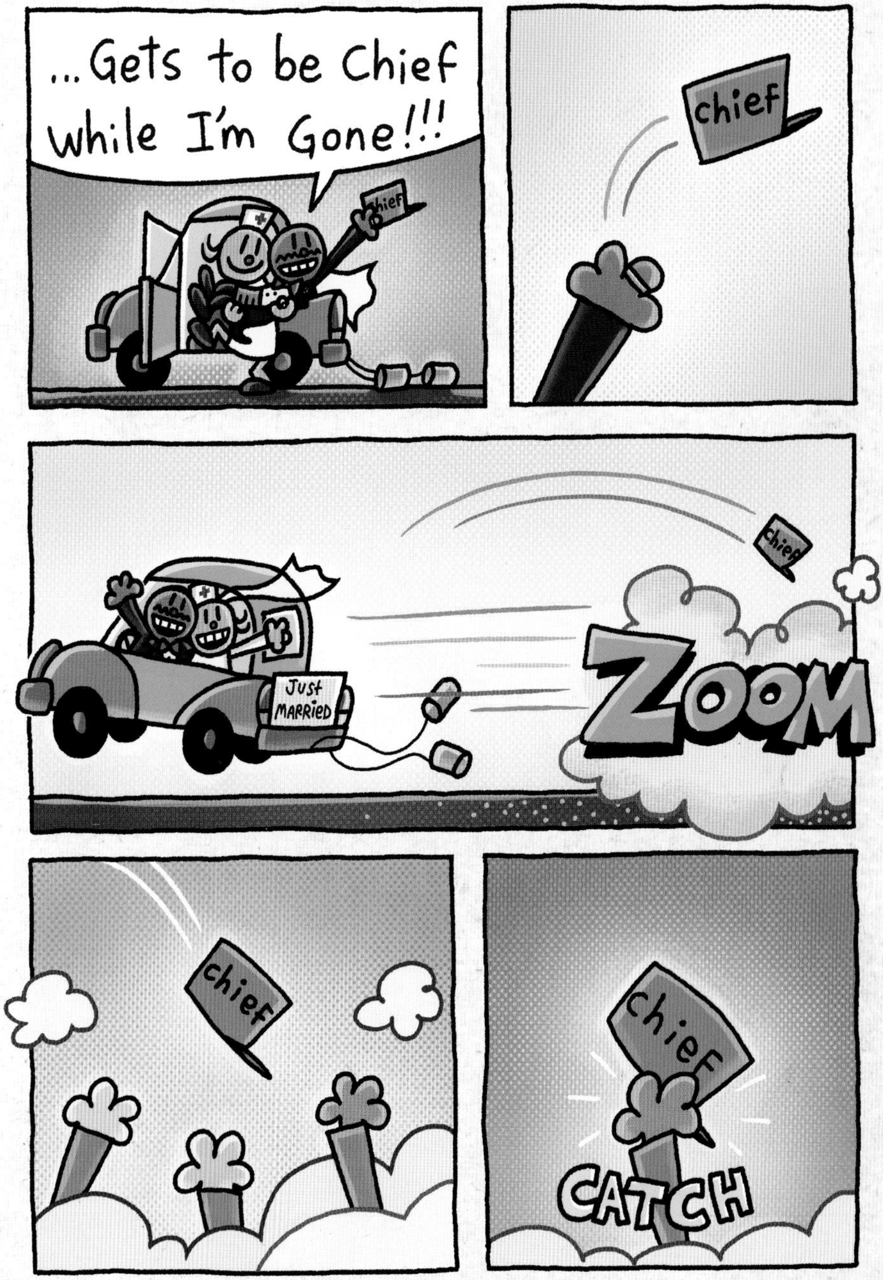
...Gets to be Chief while I'm Gone!!!
chief
chief
chief
JUST MARRIED
ZOOM
chief
chief
chief
CATCH

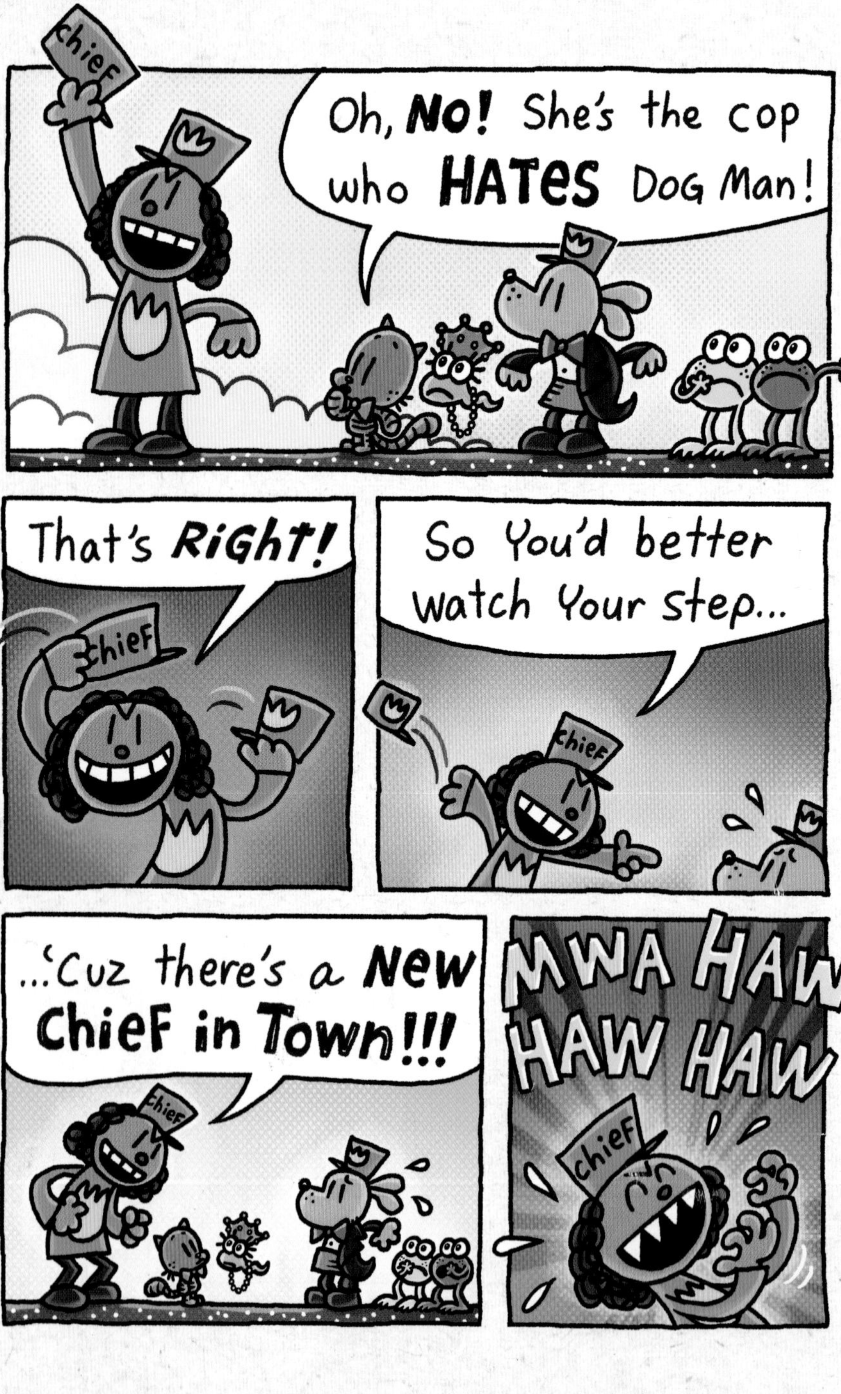
chief
Oh, NO! She's the cop who HATES Dog Man!
That's RiGhT!
chieF
So You'd better watch Your step...
chieF
...'Cuz there's a New ChieF in Town!!!
chieF
MWA HAW HAW HAW
chieF

CHAPTER 2

Heeere, Kitty, Kitty, Kitty!

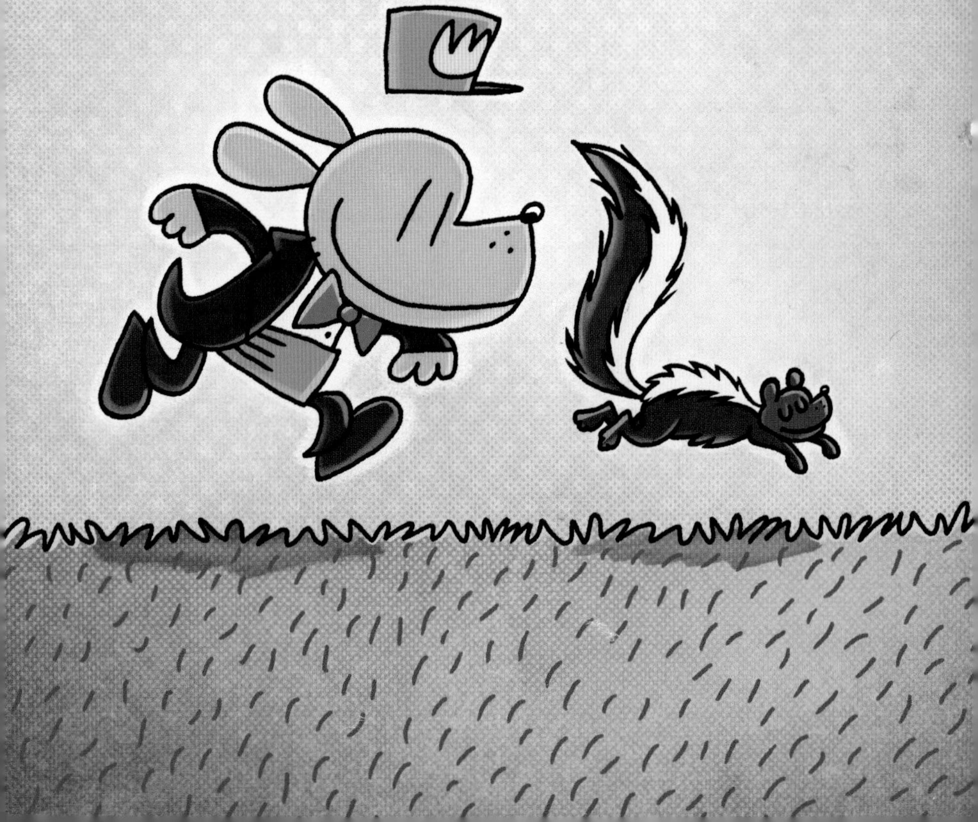

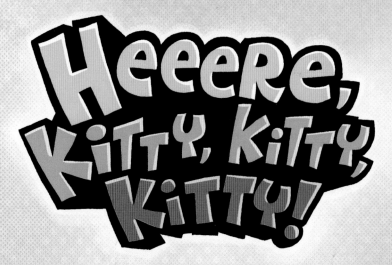

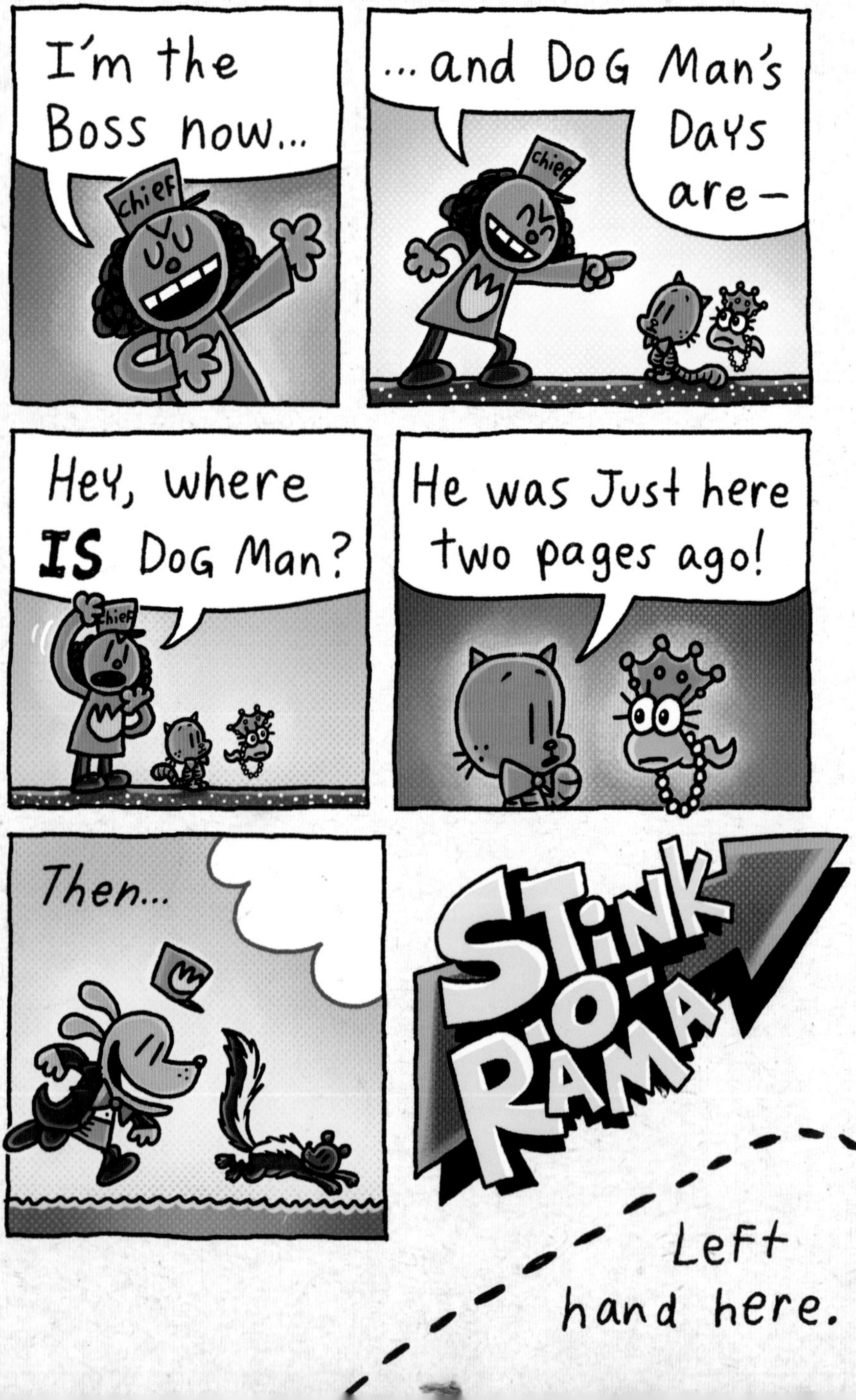
I'm the Boss now...
...and DoG Man's Days are—
Hey, where IS Dog Man?
He was Just here two pages ago!
Then...
STINK-O-RAMA
Left hand here.

EVERY DOG
HAS HIS
SPRAY

Right
Thumb
here.

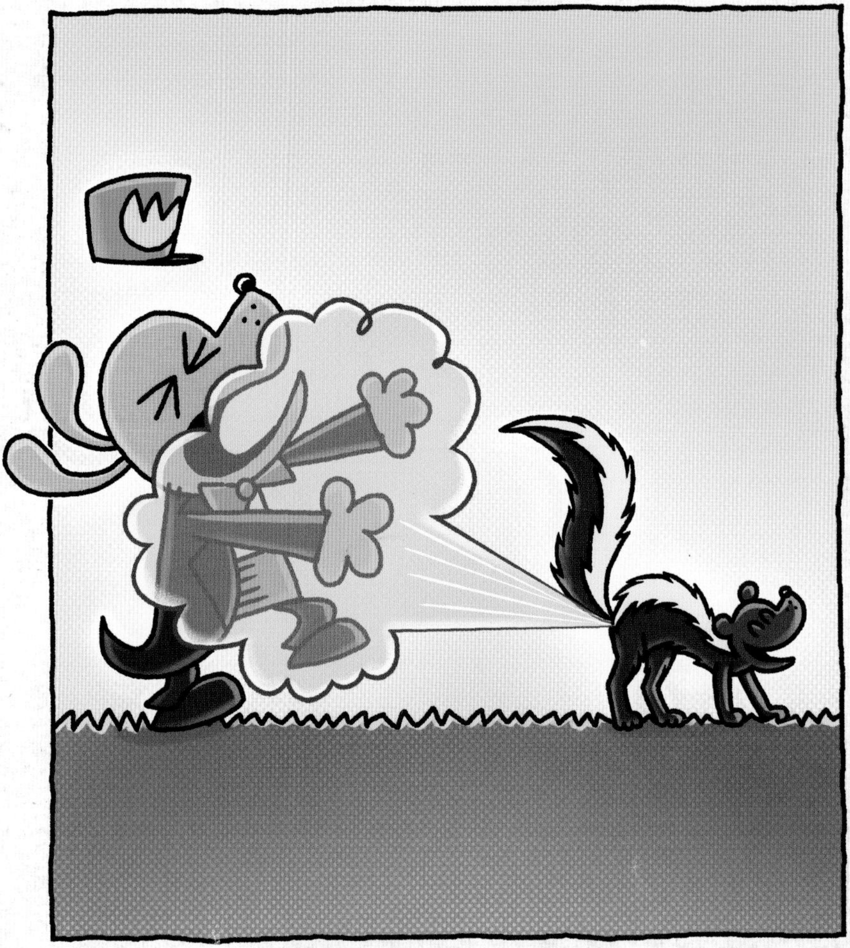

Every Dog Has His Spray

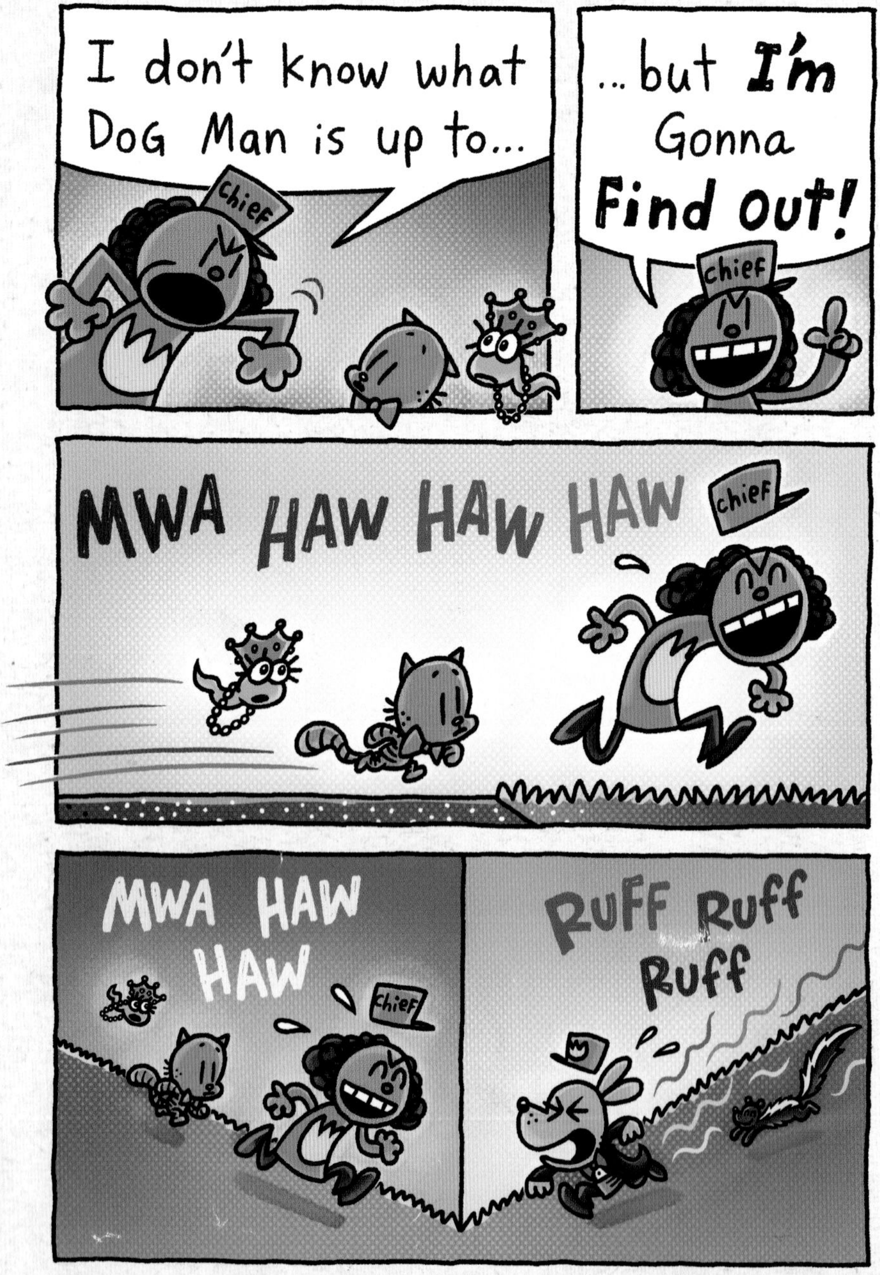
I don't know what DoG Man is up to...
chief
...but I'm Gonna Find Out!
chief
MWA HAW HAW HAW
chief
MWA HAW HAW
chief
RUFF Ruff Ruff

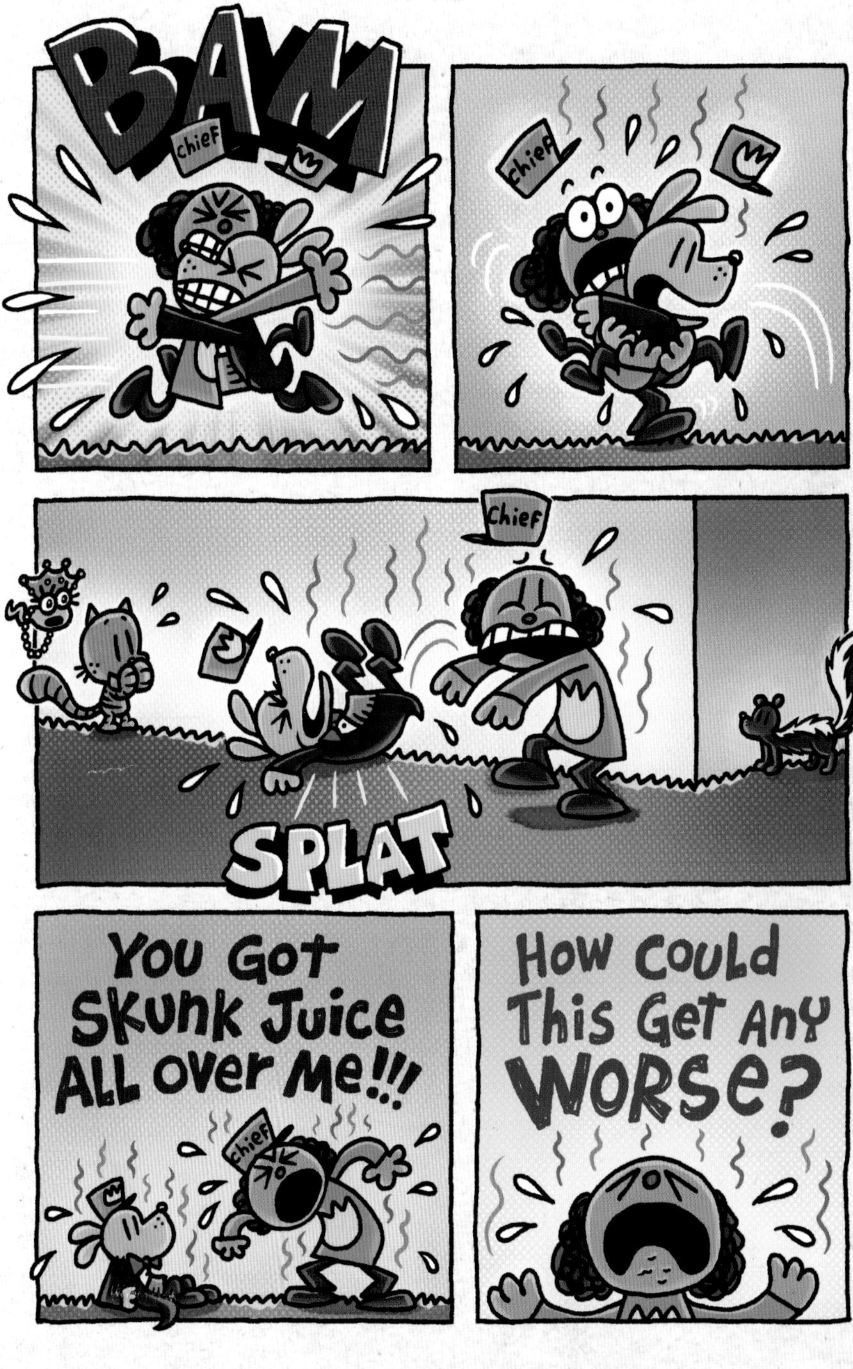
BAM
chief
Chief
Chief
SPLAT
You Got Skunk Juice ALL over Me!!!
chief
How Could This Get Any WORSE?

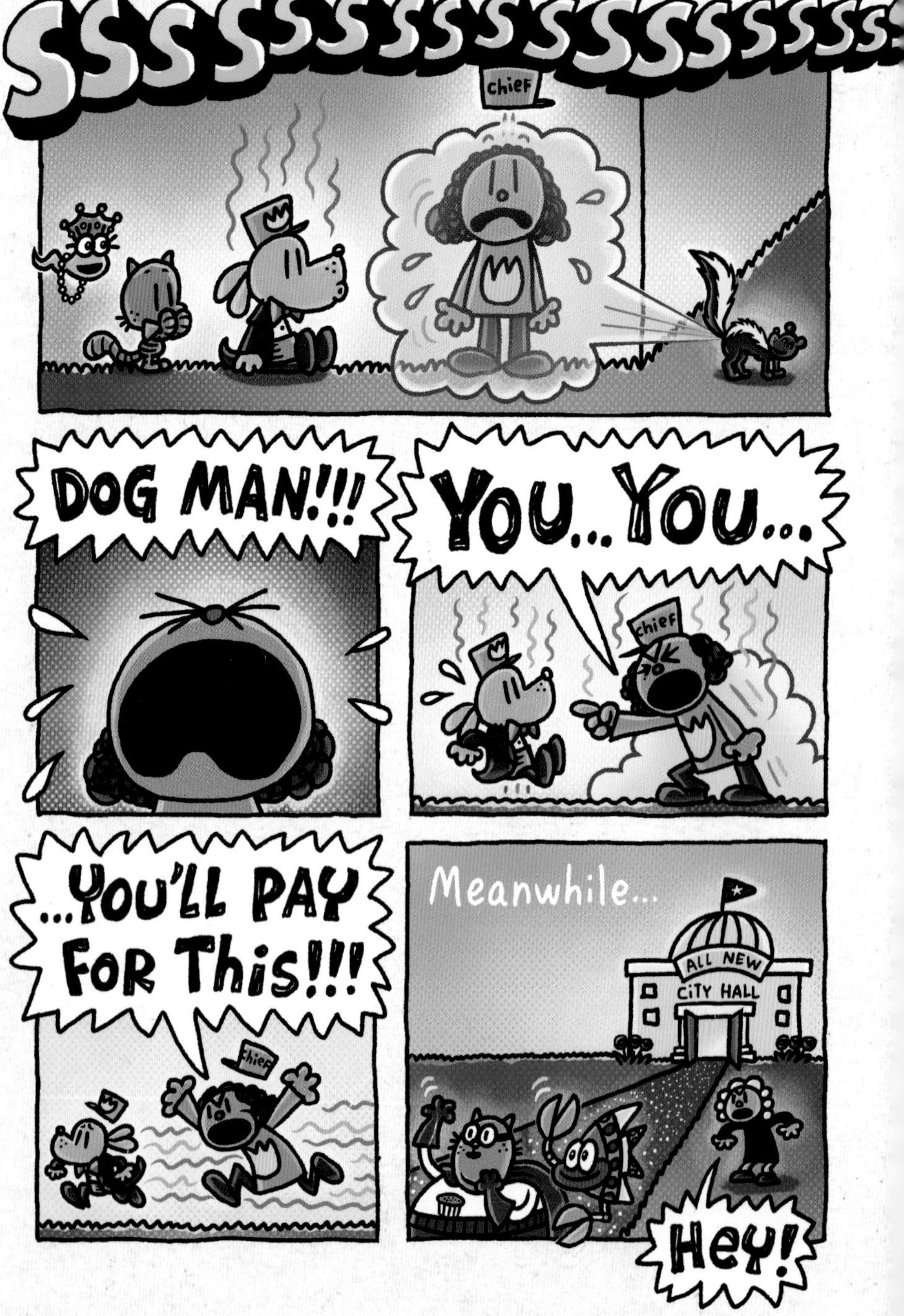
SSSSSSSSSSSSSSS
Chief
DOG MAN!!!
YOU... YOU...
...YOU'LL PAY FOR This!!!
Meanwhile...
ALL NEW CITY HALL
Hey!

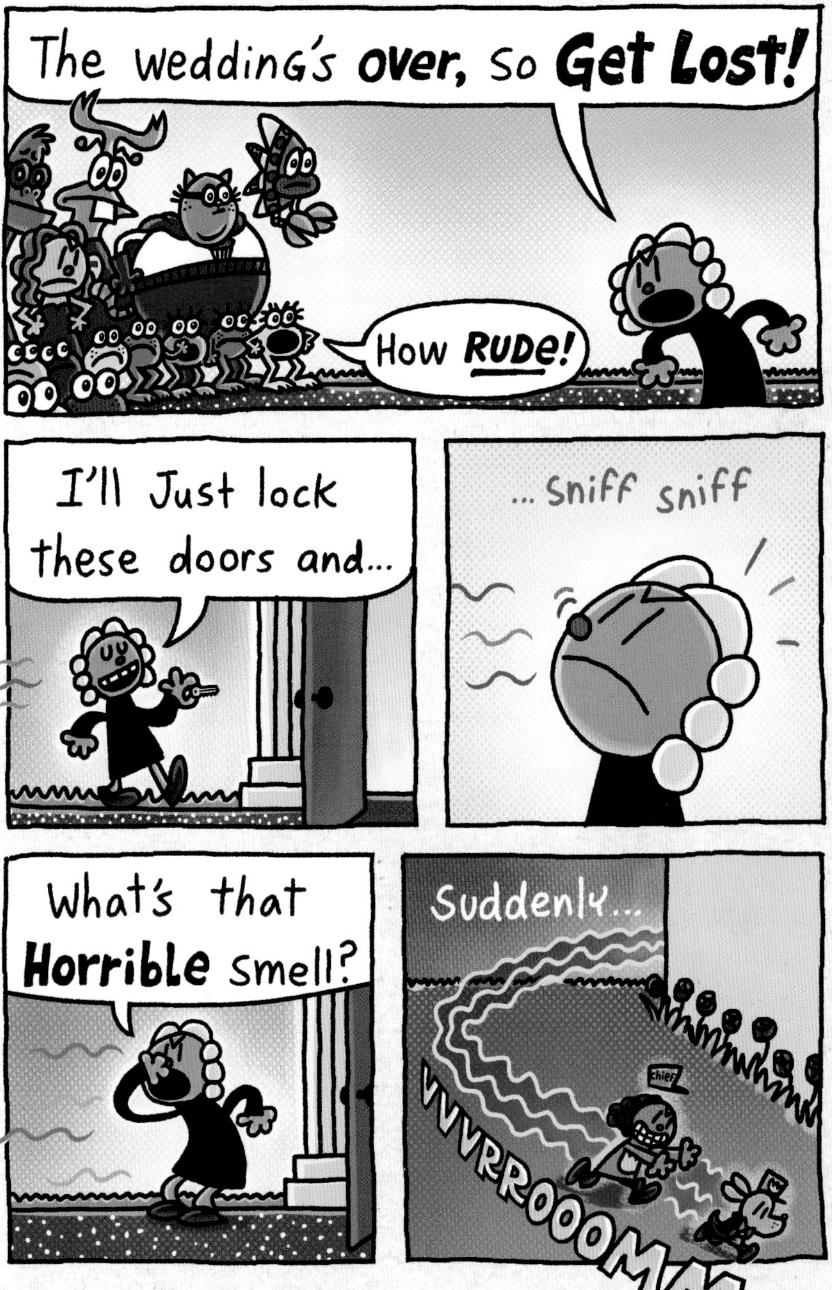
The wedding's over, so Get Lost!
How RUDE!
I'll Just lock these doors and...
...sniff sniff
What's that Horrible smell?
Suddenly...
Chief
VVVRROOOOMM

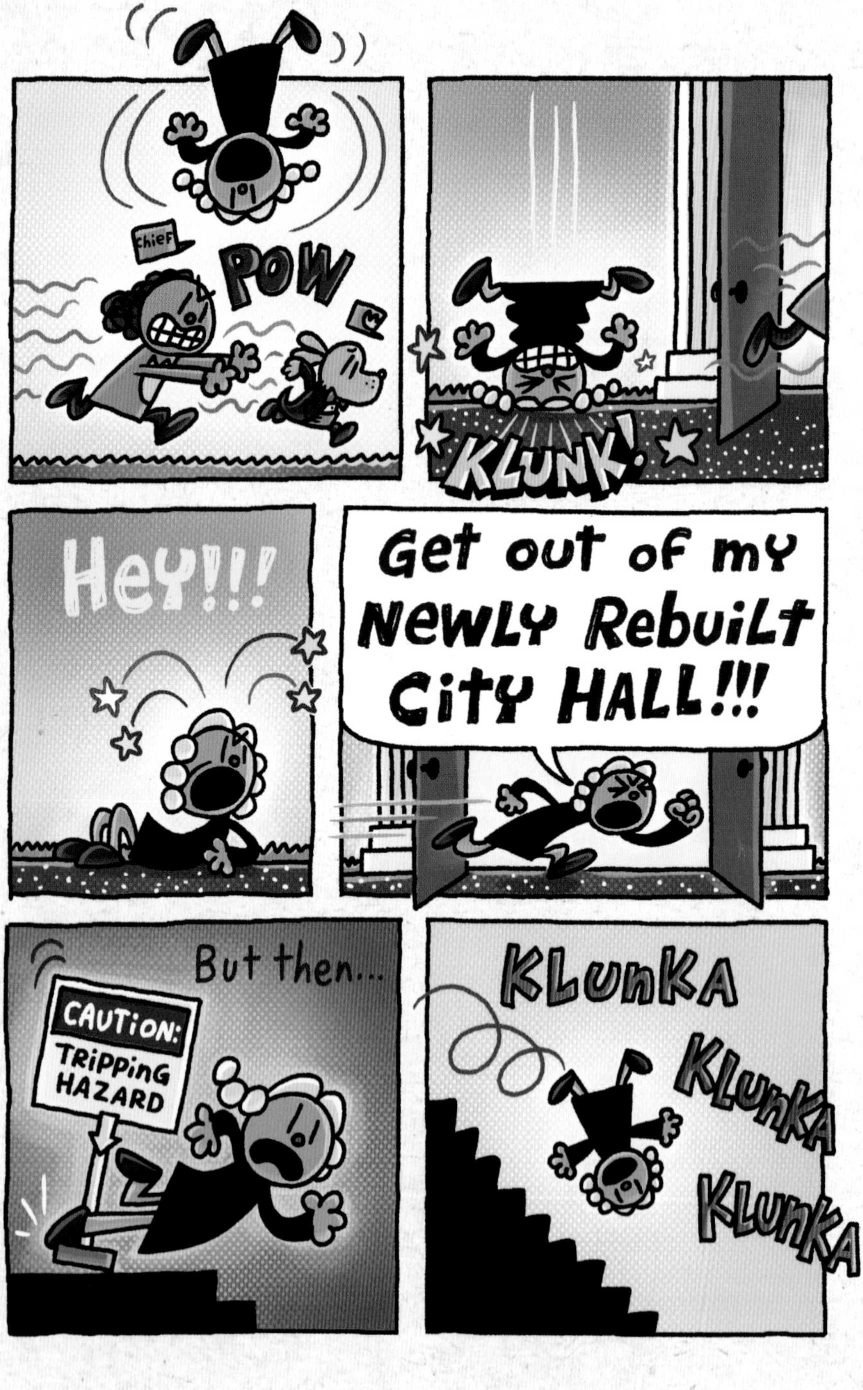

CHIEF
POW
KLUNK!
HEY!!!
Get out of my NEWLY Rebuilt City HALL!!!
But then...
CAUTION: TRIPPING HAZARD
KLUNKA
KLUNKA
KLUNKA

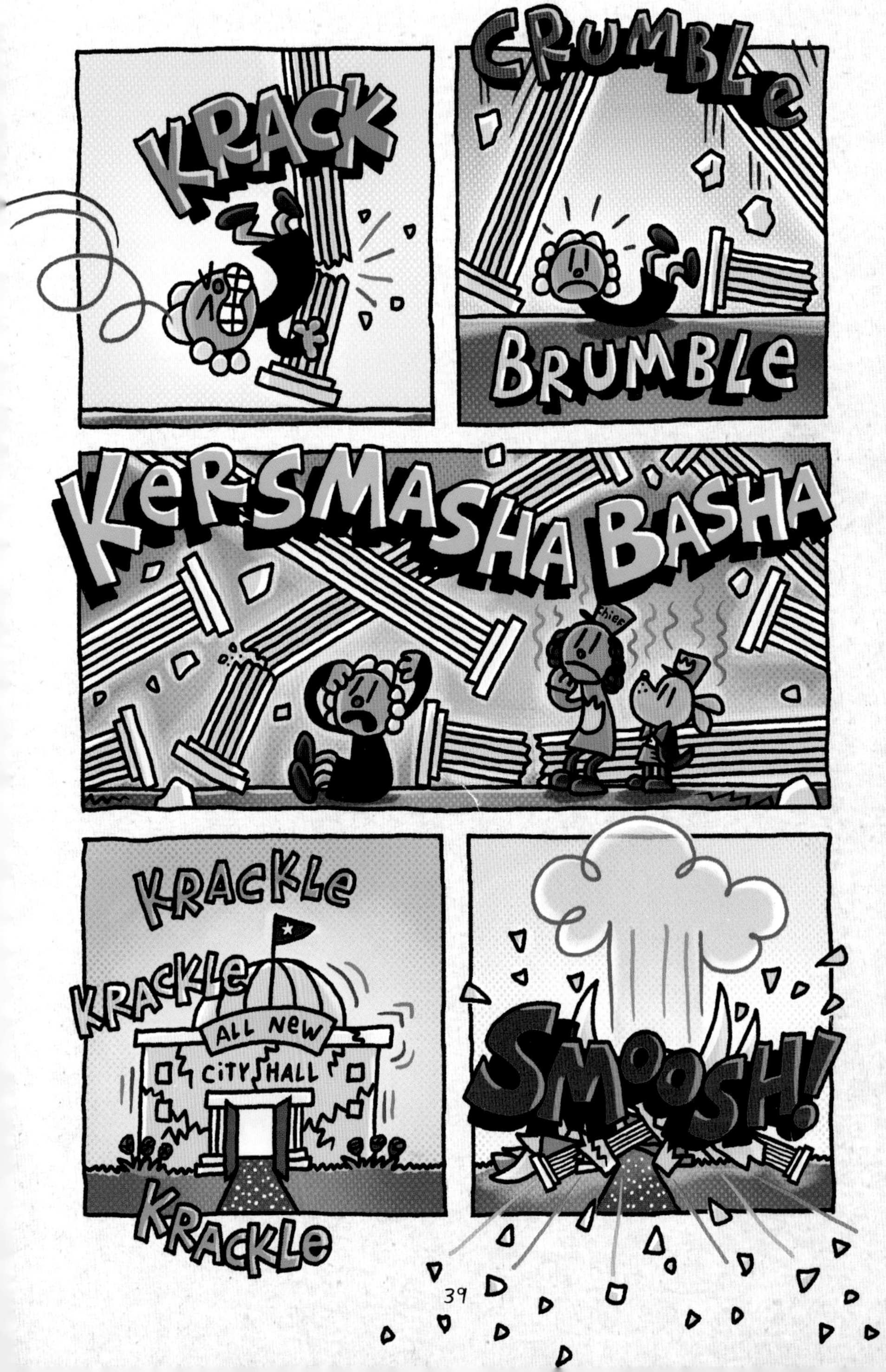
KRACK
CRUMBLE
BRUMBLE
KERSMASHA BASHA
Chief
KRACKLE
KRACKLE
ALL NEW
CITY HALL
KRACKLE
SMOOSH!

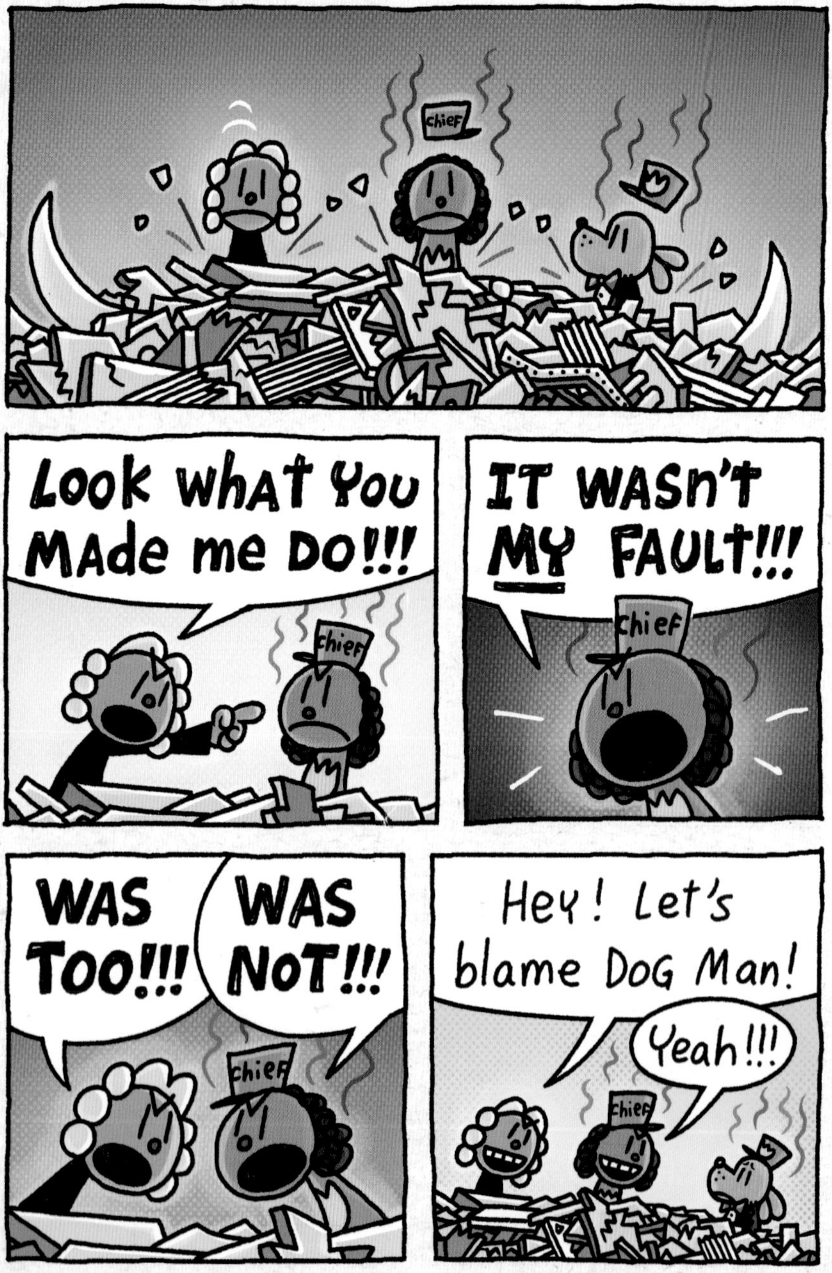
chief
LOOK WHAT YOU MADE ME DO!!!
chief
IT WASN'T MY FAULT!!!
chief
WAS TOO!!!
WAS NOT!!!
chief
Hey! Let's blame DOG Man!
Yeah!!!
chief

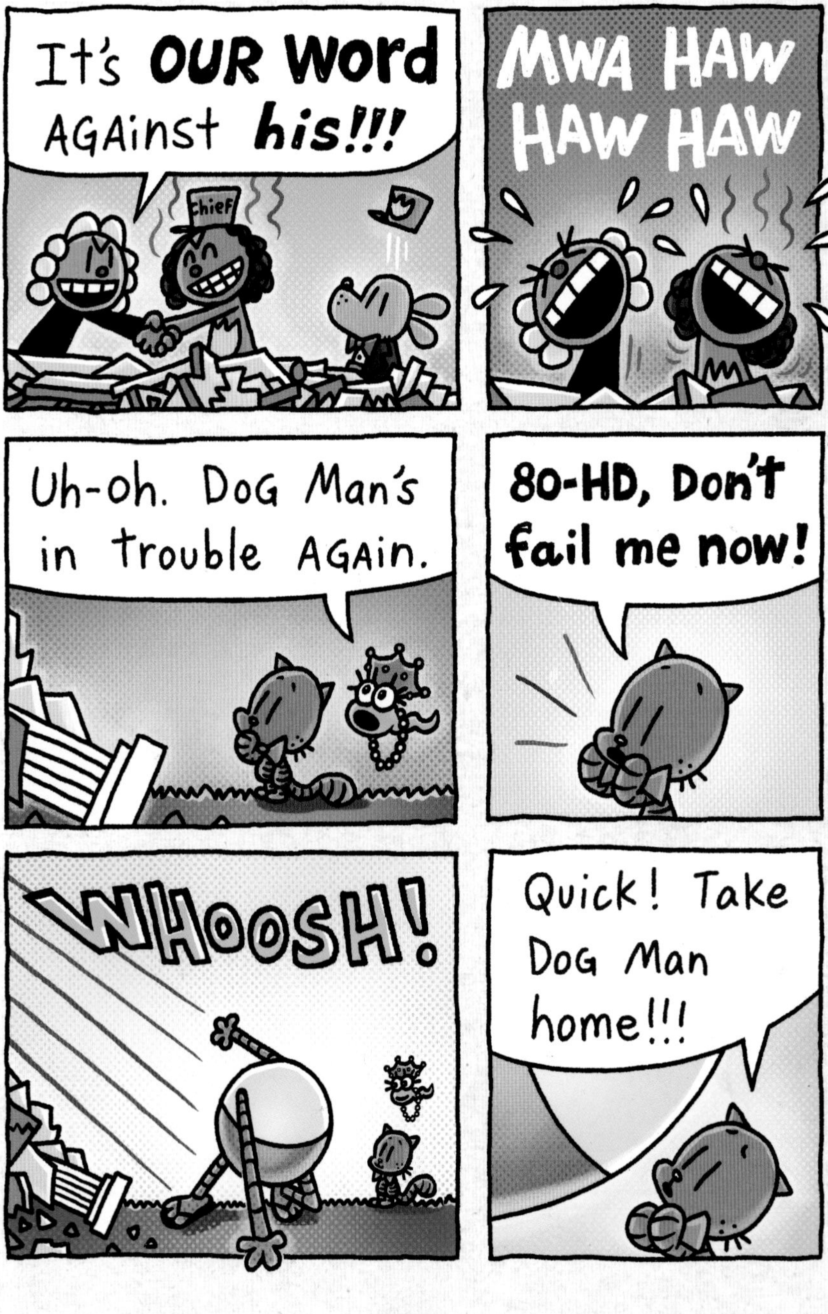
It's OUR Word AGAinst his!!!
Chief
MWA HAW HAW HAW
Uh-oh. DoG Man's in trouble AGAin.
80-HD, Don't fail me now!
WHOOSH!
Quick! Take DoG Man home!!!

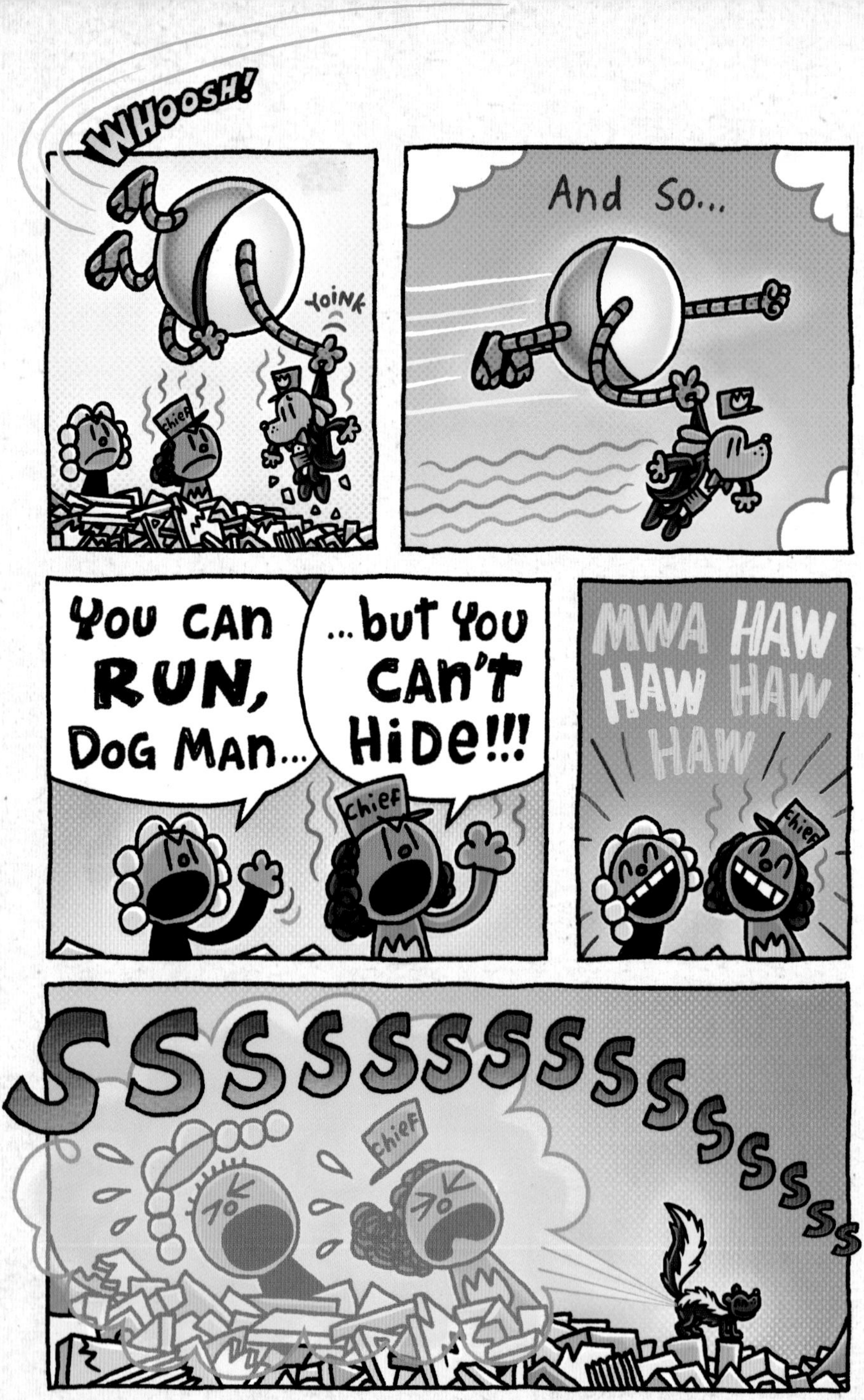
WHOOSH!
YOINK
CHIEF
And so...
You can RUN, Dog Man...
...but you CAN'T HIDE!!!
Chief
MWA HAW HAW HAW HAW
Chief
SSSSSSSSSSSSSSSSS
Chief

CHAPTER 3

The Tomato Juice Solution

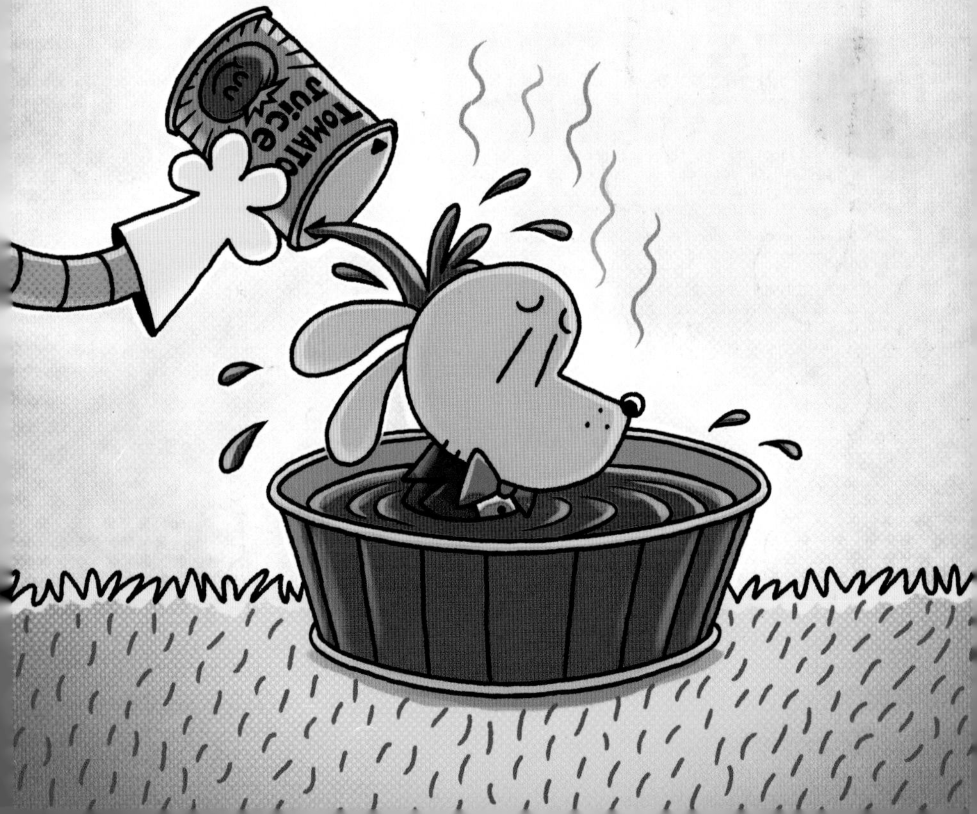
TOMATO
JUICE

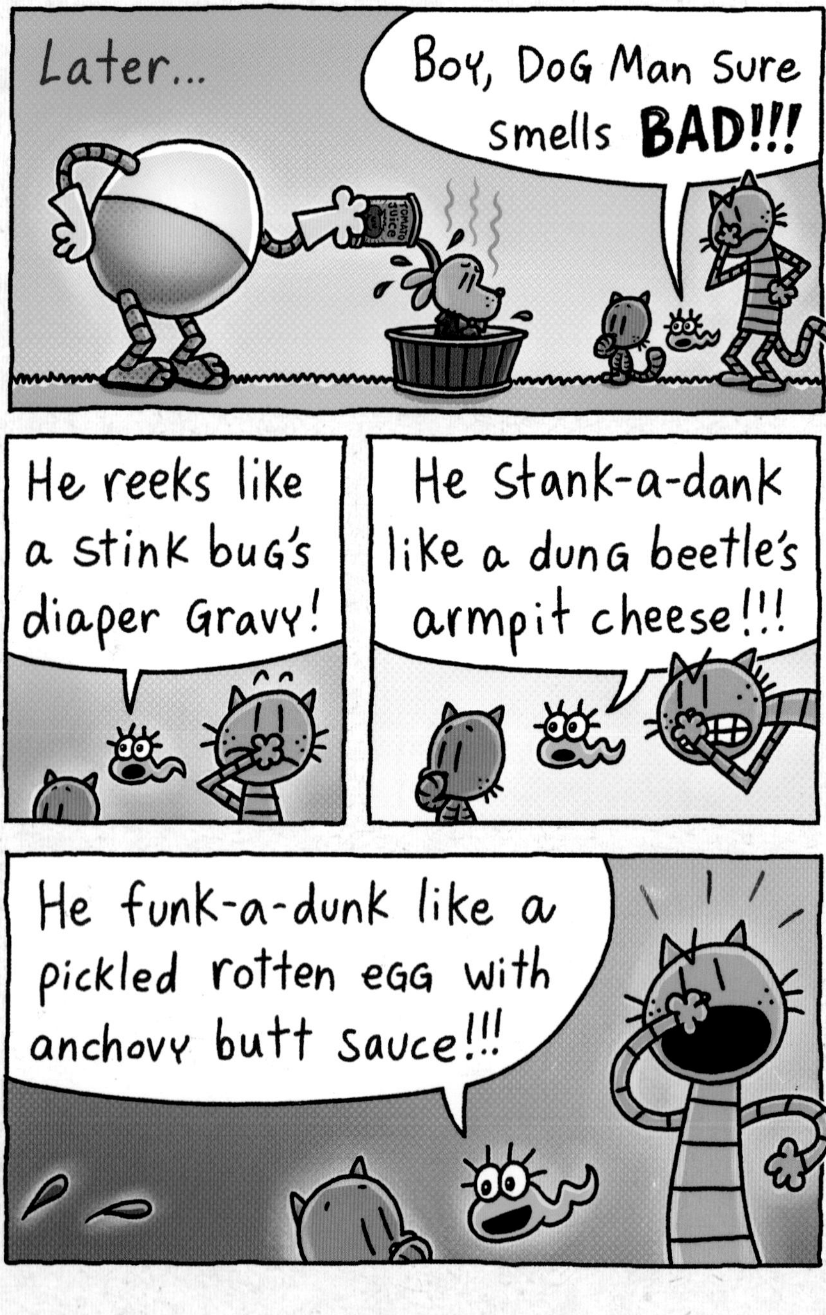
Later...
Boy, Dog Man sure smells BAD!!!
TOMATO JUICE
He reeks like a stink bug's diaper gravy!
He stank-a-dank like a dung beetle's armpit cheese!!!
He funk-a-dunk like a pickled rotten egg with anchovy butt sauce!!!

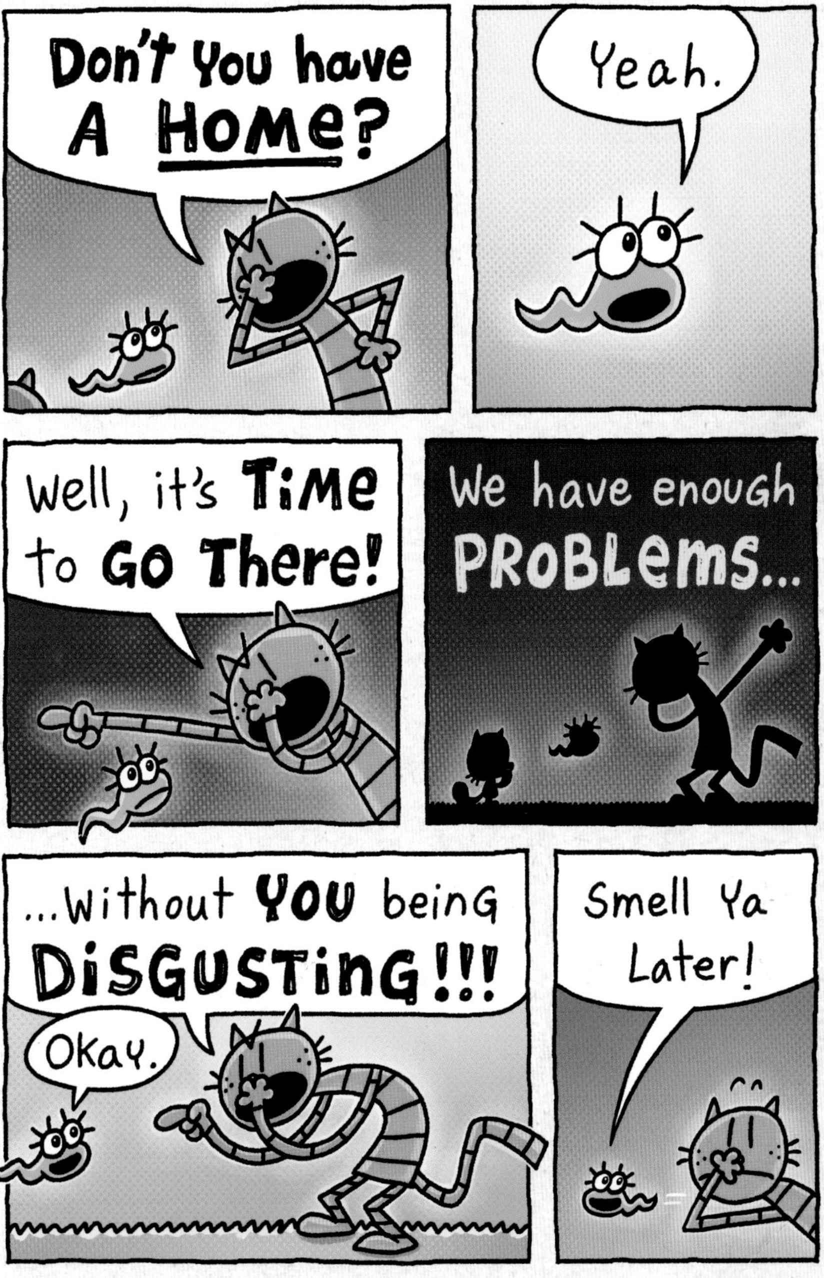
Don't you have A HOME?
Yeah.
Well, it's TIME to GO There!
We have enough PROBLEMS...
...without YOU being DISGUSTING!!!
Okay.
Smell Ya Later!

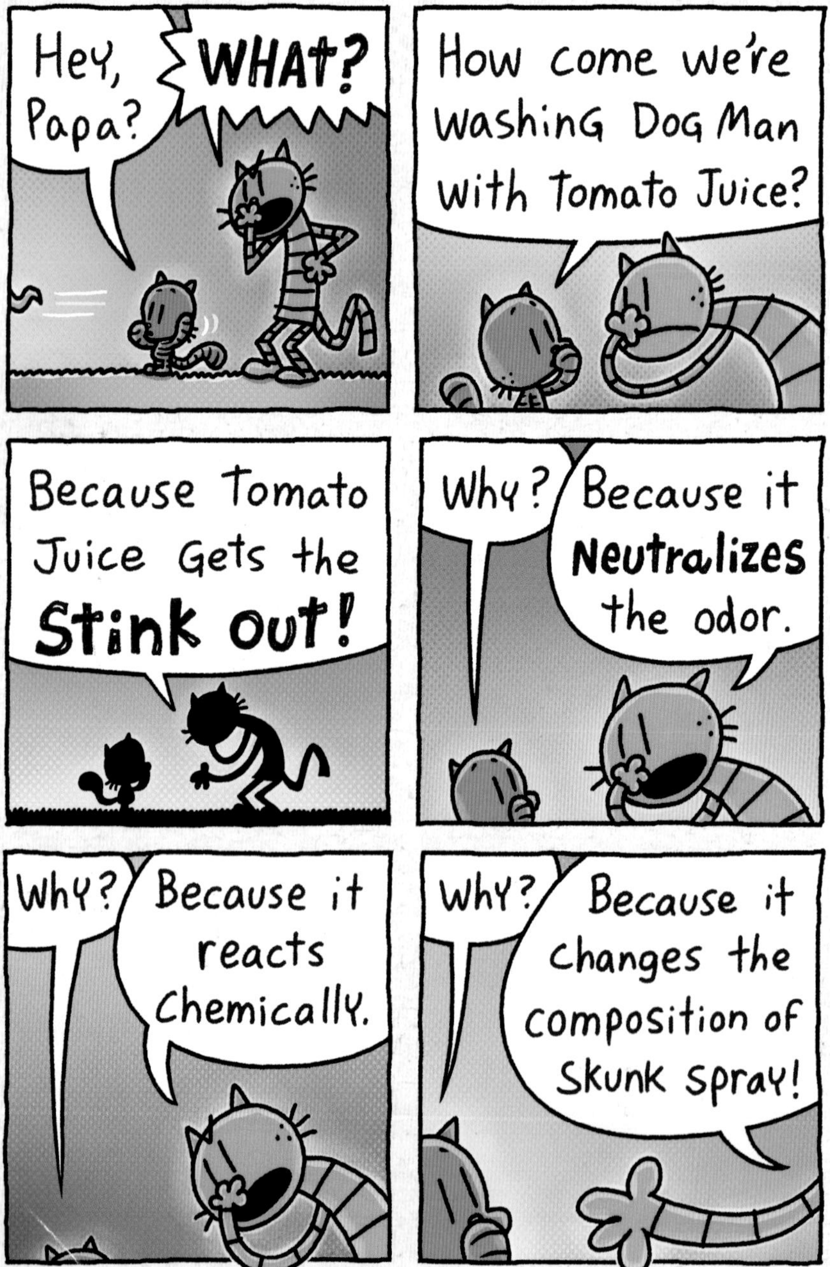
Hey, Papa?
WHAT?
How come we're washing Dog Man with Tomato Juice?
Because Tomato Juice Gets the Stink out!
Why?
Because it Neutralizes the odor.
Why?
Because it reacts Chemically.
Why?
Because it changes the composition of Skunk spray!

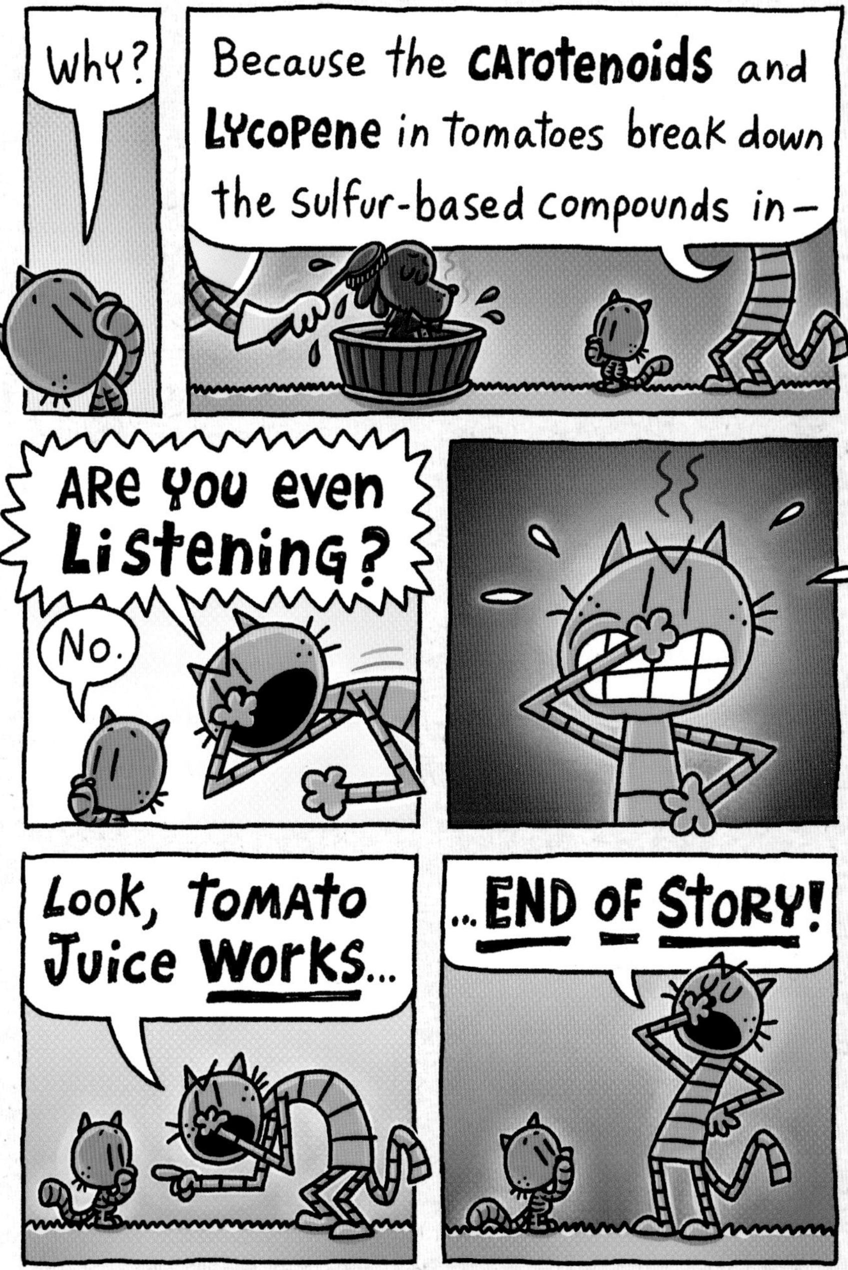
Why?
Because the CAROTENOIDS and LYCOPENE in tomatoes break down the sulfur-based compounds in—
ARE YOU even Listening?
No.
Look, TOMATO Juice WORKS...
...END OF STORY!

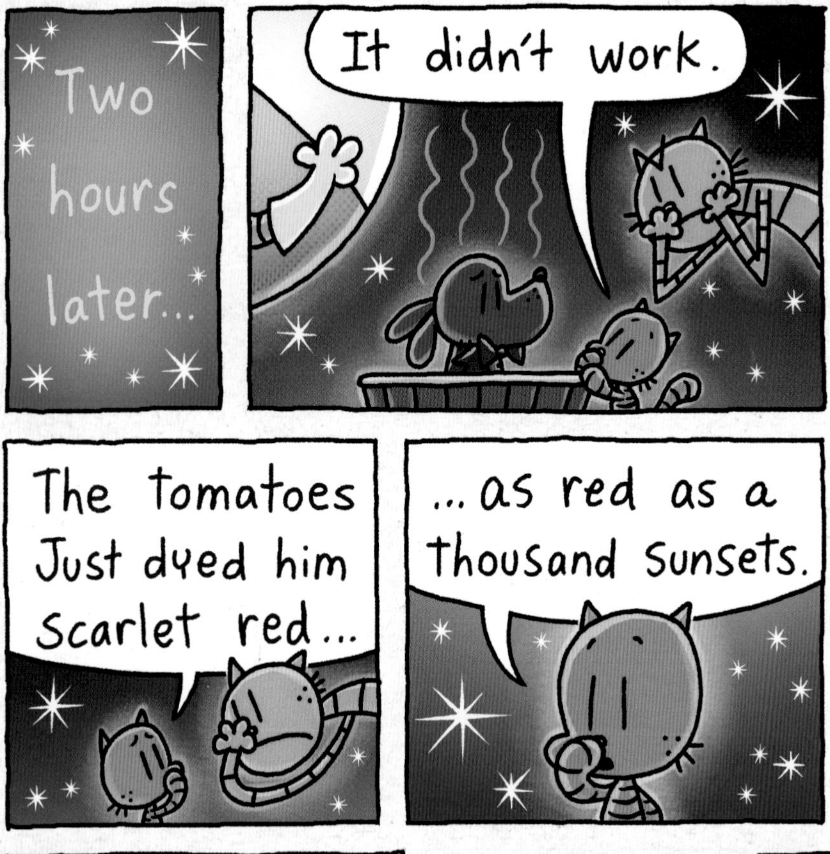
Two hours later...
It didn't work.
The tomatoes Just dyed him Scarlet red...
...as red as a thousand Sunsets.
Welp, at least it can't Get any **WORSE**!

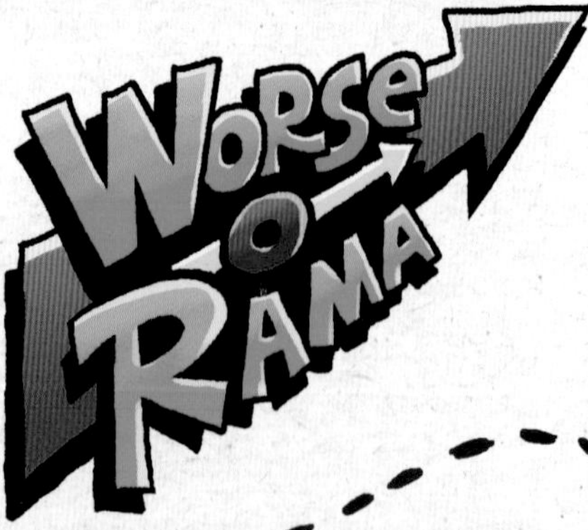
WORSE O RAMA

Left hand here.

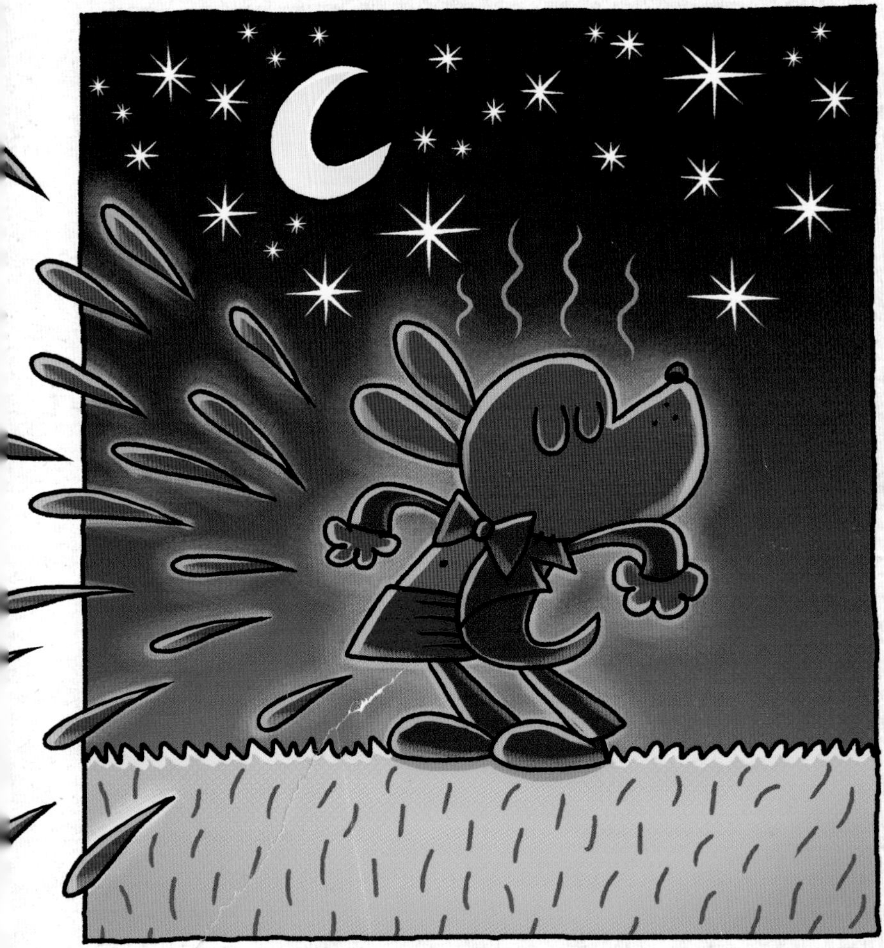

Stinkle Sprinkle

Right Thumb here.

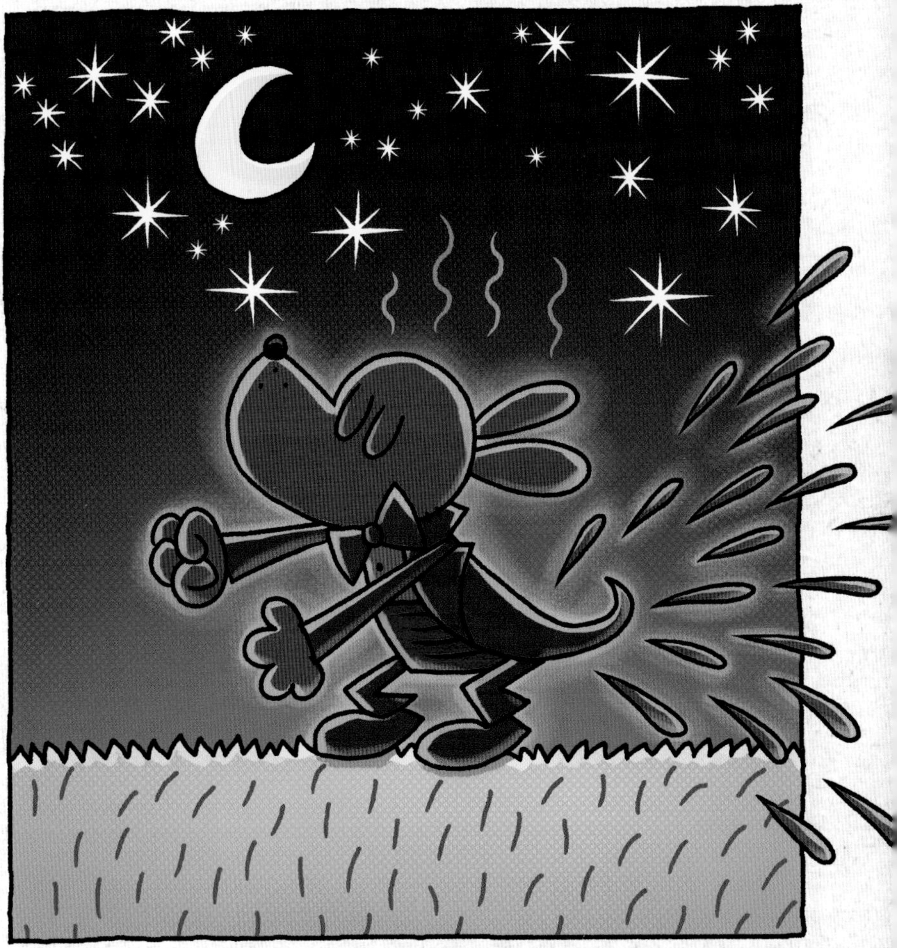

Stinkle Sprinkle

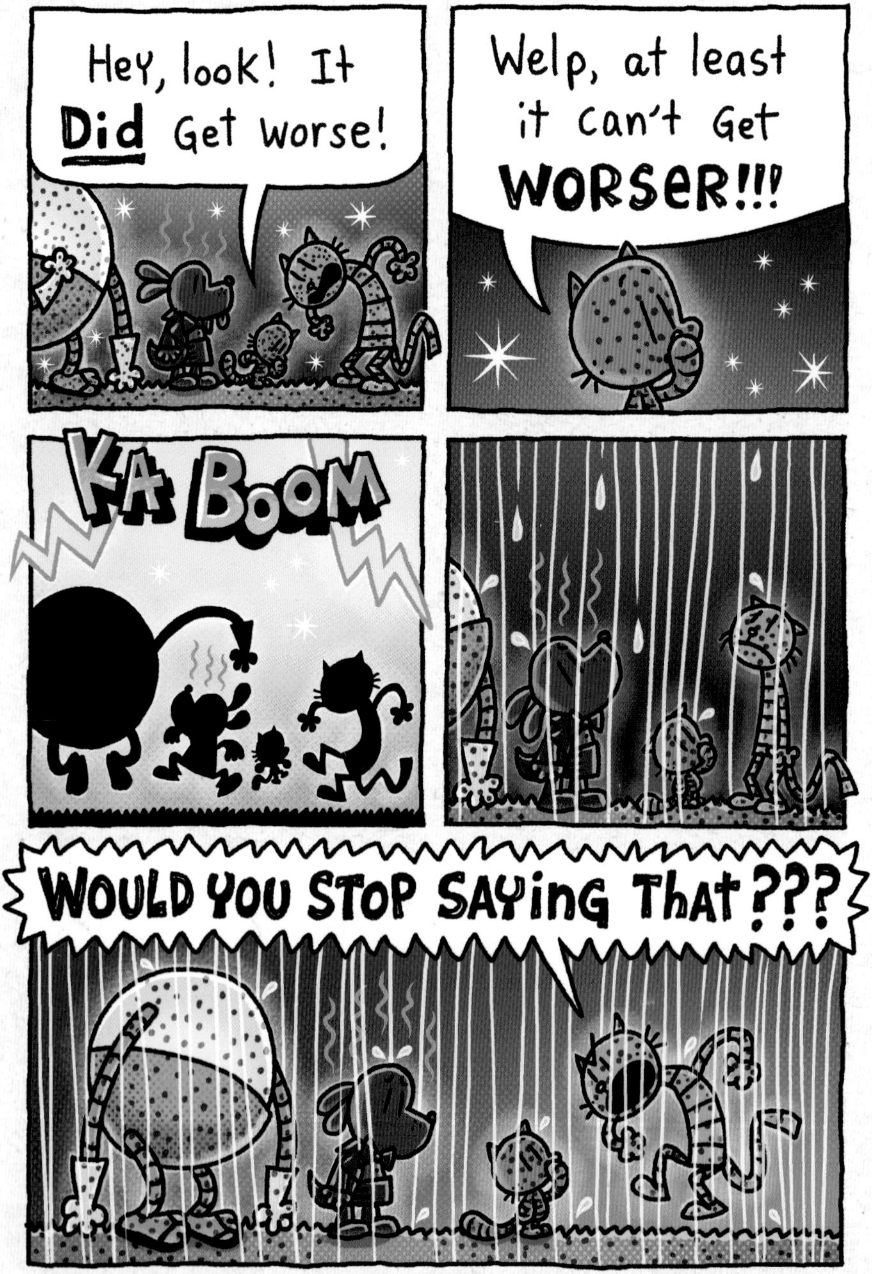
Hey, look! It Did Get worse!
Welp, at least it can't Get WORSER!!!
KA BOOM
WOULD YOU STOP SAYING THAT???

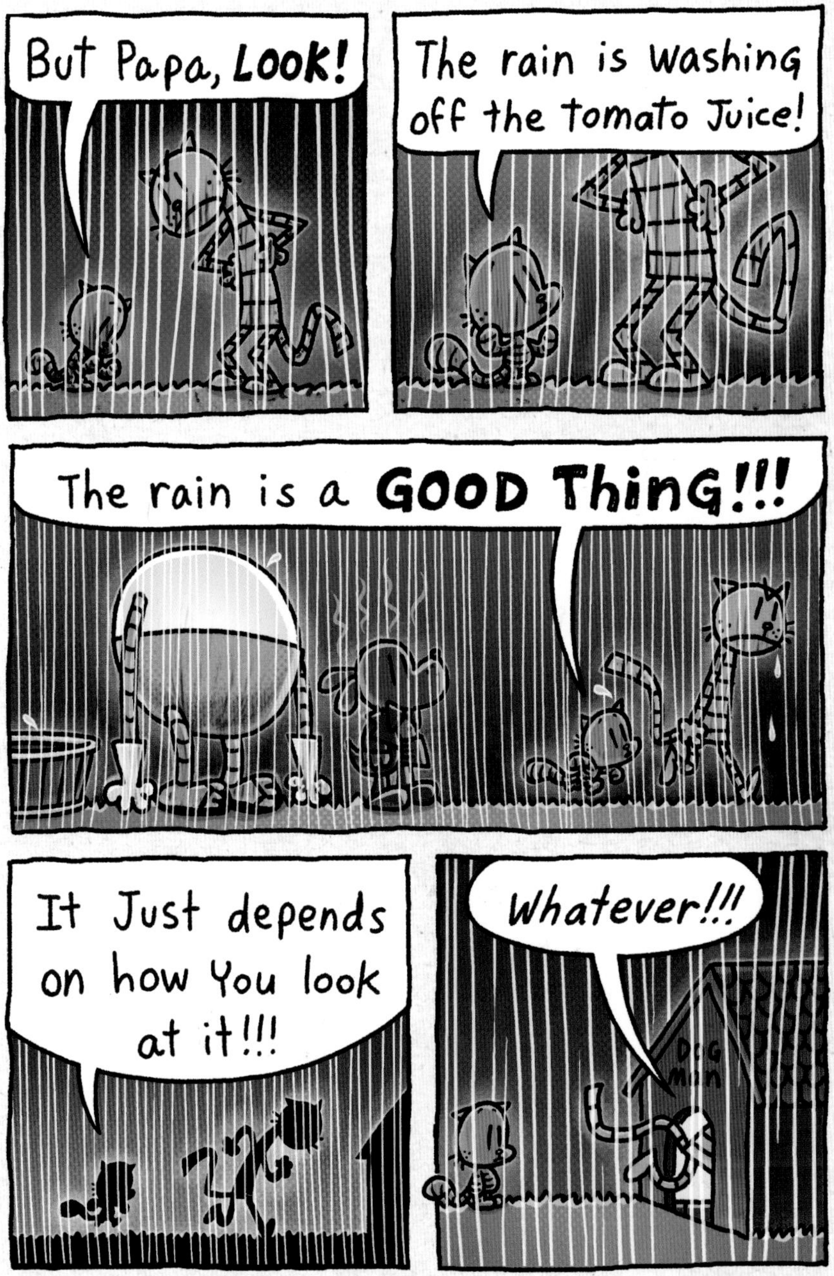

But Papa, LOOK!
The rain is washing off the tomato Juice!
The rain is a GOOD THING!!!
It Just depends on how You look at it!!!
Whatever!!!

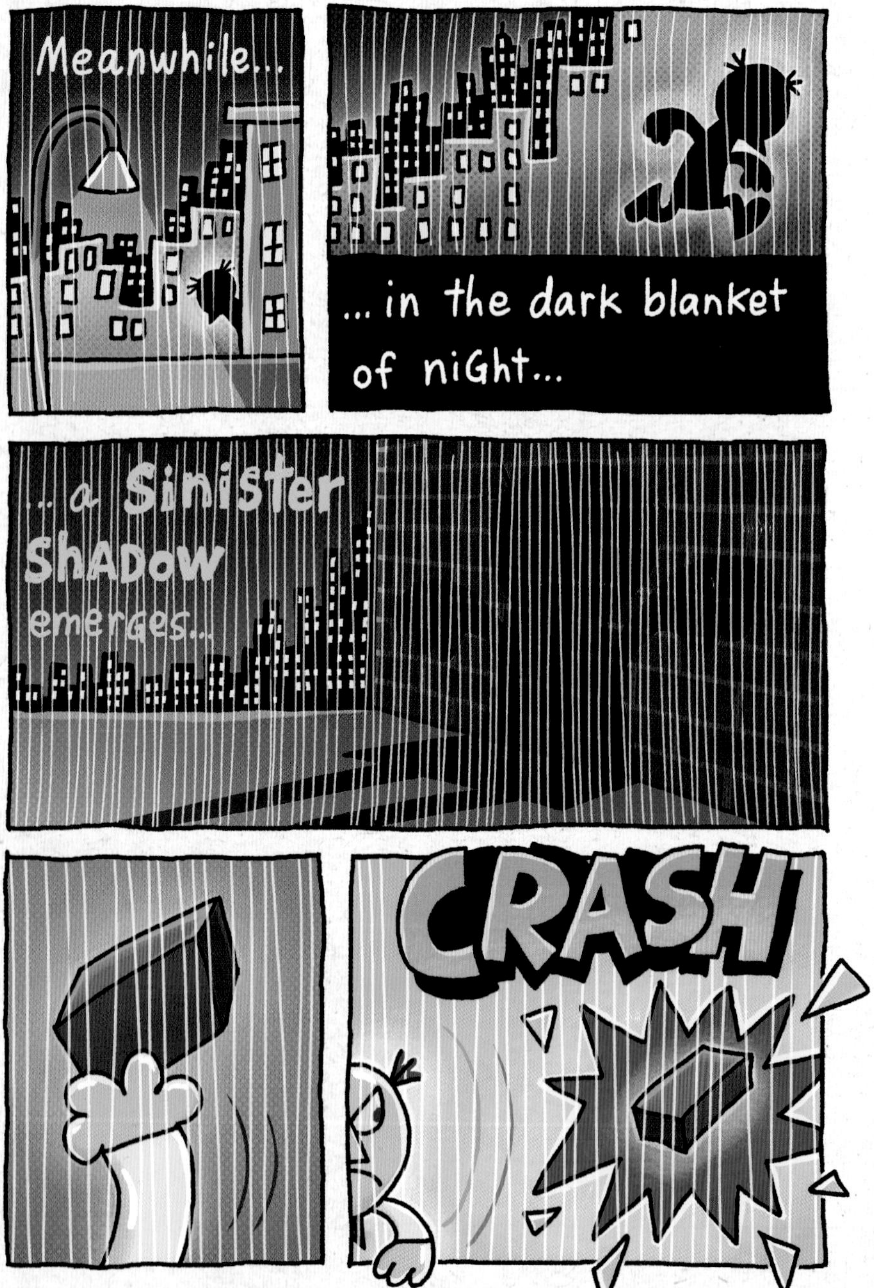
Meanwhile...
... in the dark blanket of niGht...
... a Sinister ShADOW emerGes...
CRASH

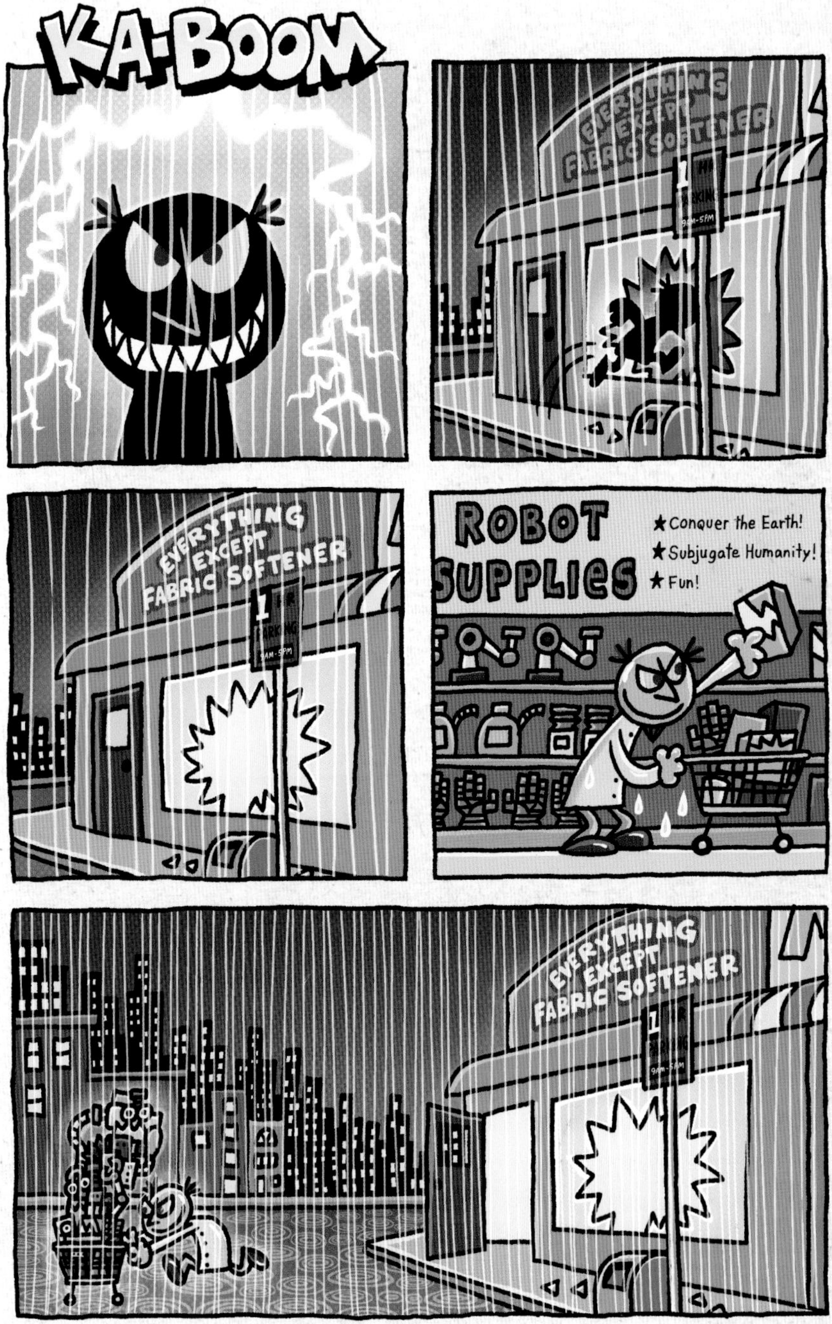
KA-BOOM
EVERYTHING EXCEPT FABRIC SOFTENER
EVERYTHING EXCEPT FABRIC SOFTENER
PARKING
9AM-5PM
ROBOT SUPPLIES
★Conquer the Earth!
★Subjugate Humanity!
★Fun!
EVERYTHING EXCEPT FABRIC SOFTENER

Hi, boss.

I got the robot parts for you.

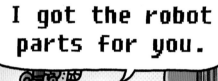

Excellent!!!

CHAPTER 4

A Buncha Stuff That Happened Next

supa 'puter

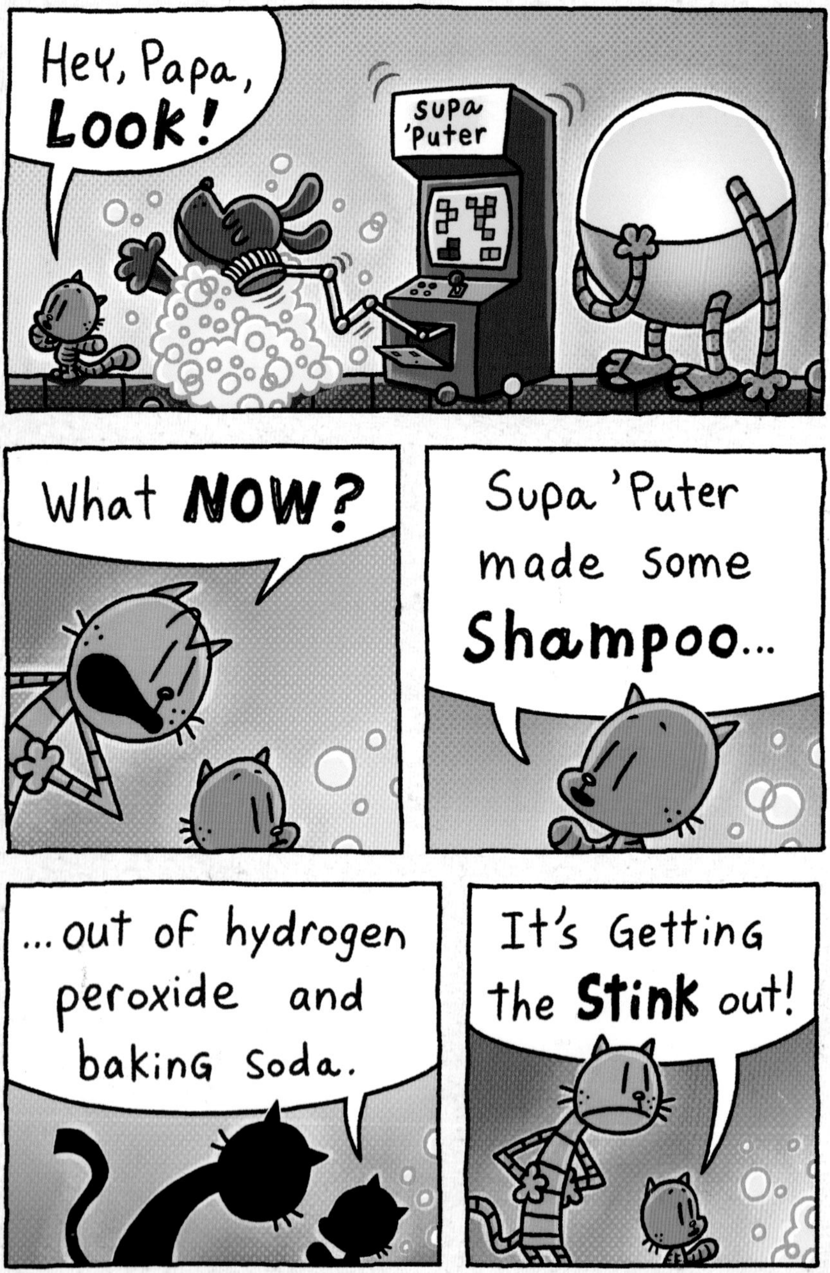
Hey, Papa, LOOK!
Supa 'Puter
What NOW?
Supa 'Puter made some Shampoo...
...out of hydrogen peroxide and baking soda.
It's Getting the Stink out!

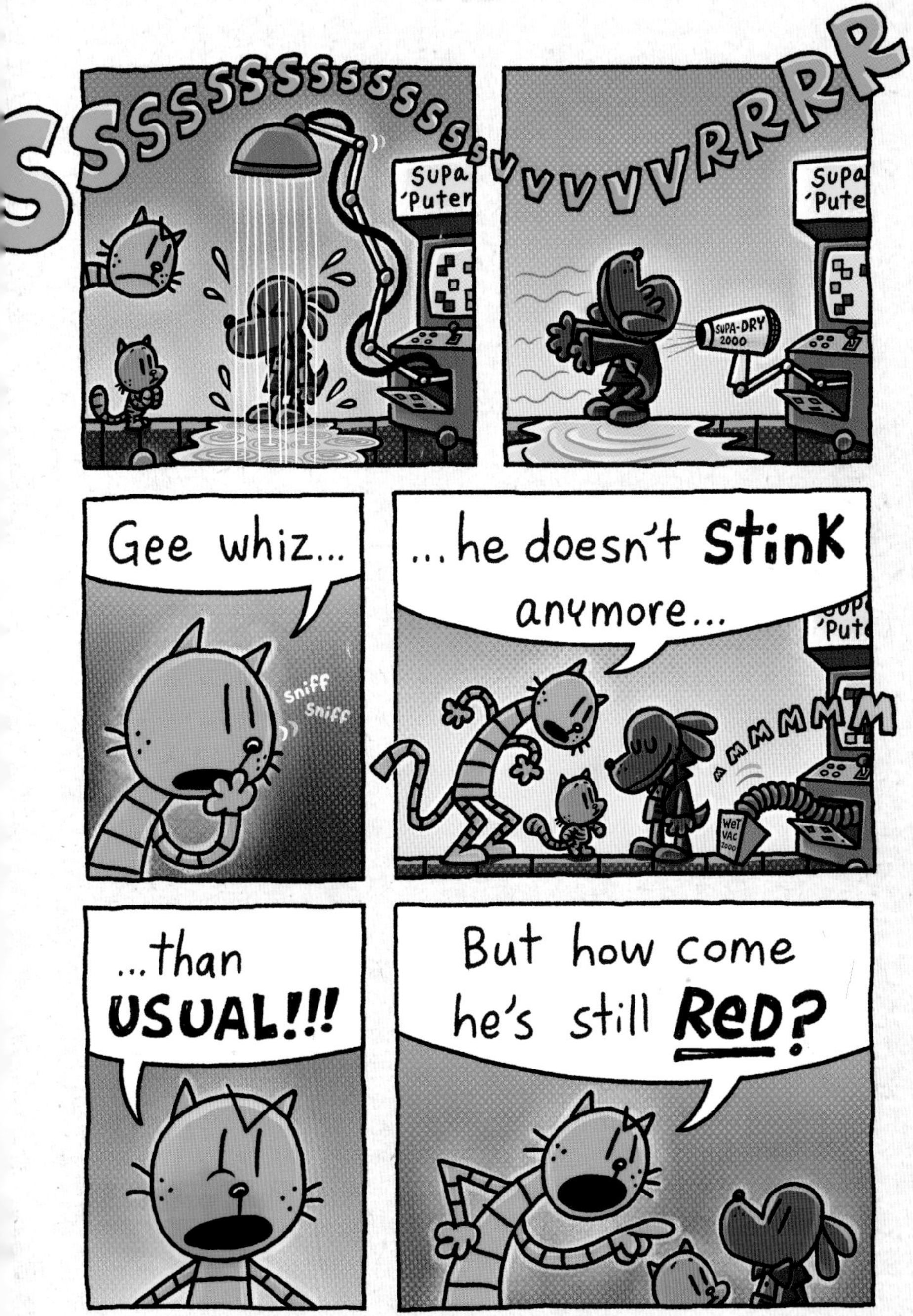
SSSSSSSSSSSSSSSSS
Supa 'Puter
VVVVVVRRRRR
SUPA-DRY 2000
Gee whiz...
Sniff Sniff
...he doesn't Stink anymore...
MMMMMMM
WET VAC 2000
...than USUAL!!!
But how come he's still RED?

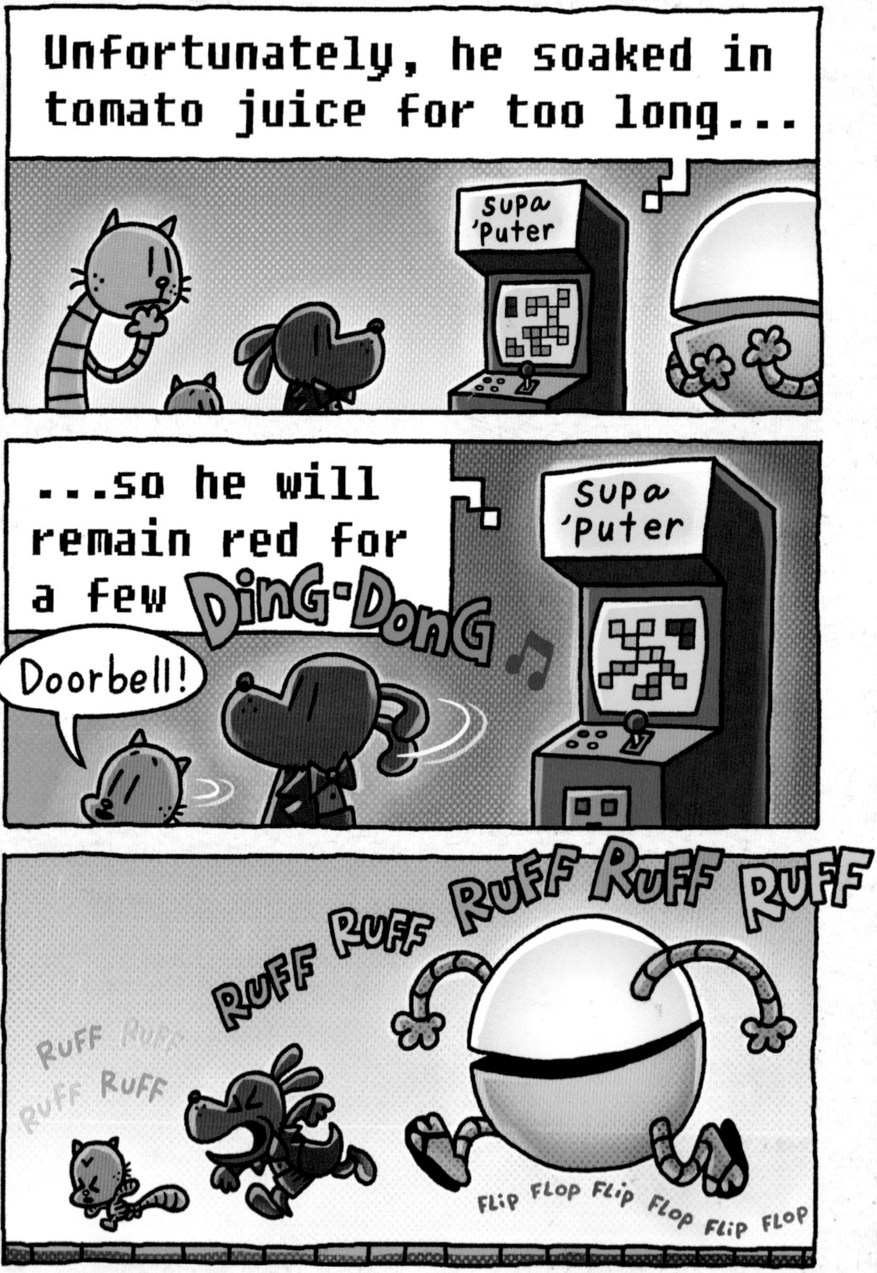
Unfortunately, he soaked in tomato juice for too long...
Supa 'Puter
...so he will remain red for a few
DinG-DonG
Doorbell!
Supa 'Puter
RUFF RUFF RUFF RUFF RUFF
RUFF RUFF RUFF RUFF
FLip FLop FLip FLop FLip FLOP

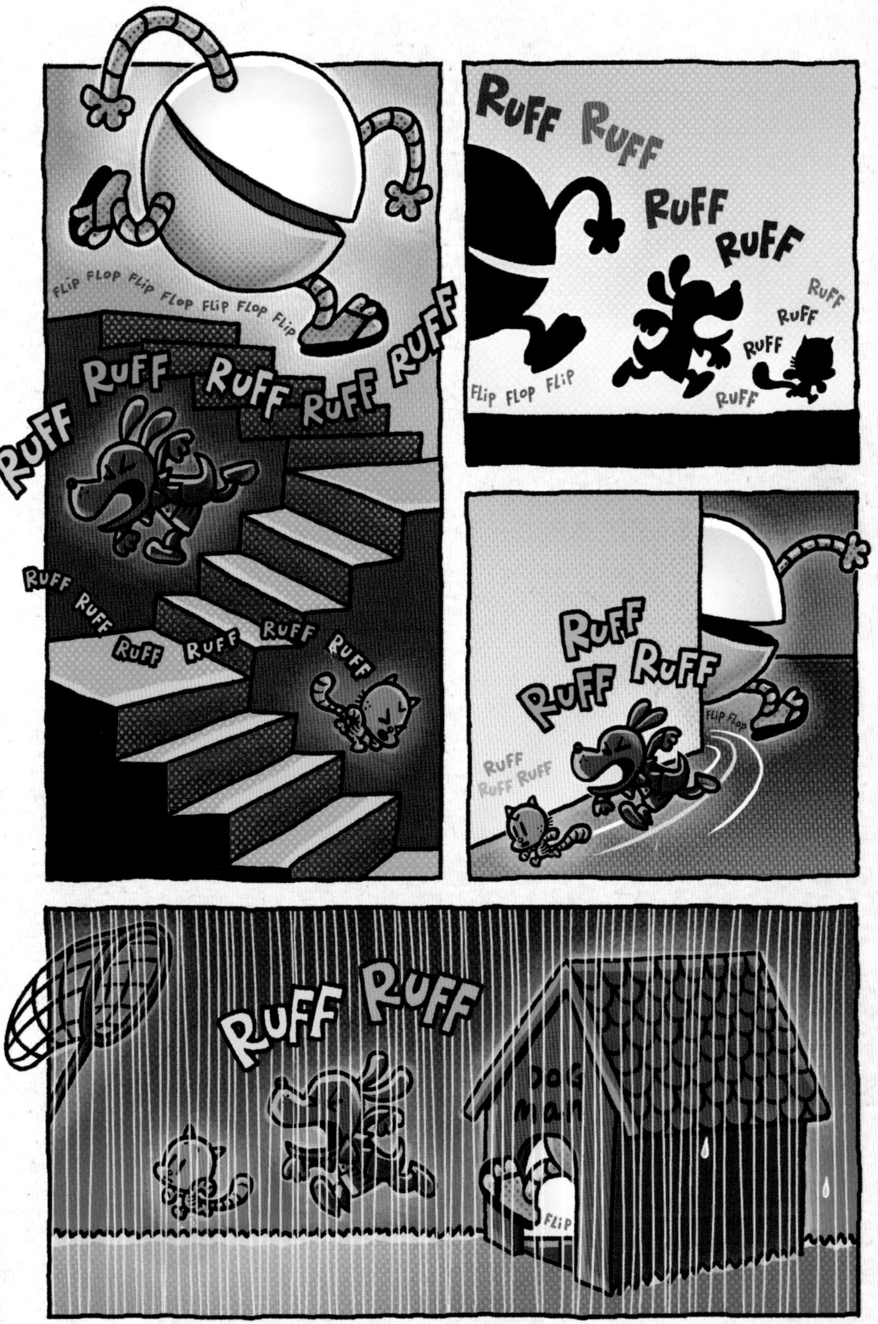

FLIP FLOP FLIP FLOP FLIP FLOP FLIP
RUFF RUFF RUFF RUFF RUFF
RUFF RUFF RUFF RUFF RUFF RUFF
RUFF RUFF
RUFF RUFF
RUFF RUFF RUFF RUFF
FLIP FLOP FLIP
RUFF
RUFF RUFF RUFF
FLIP FLOP
RUFF RUFF RUFF
RUFF RUFF
DOG MAN
FLIP

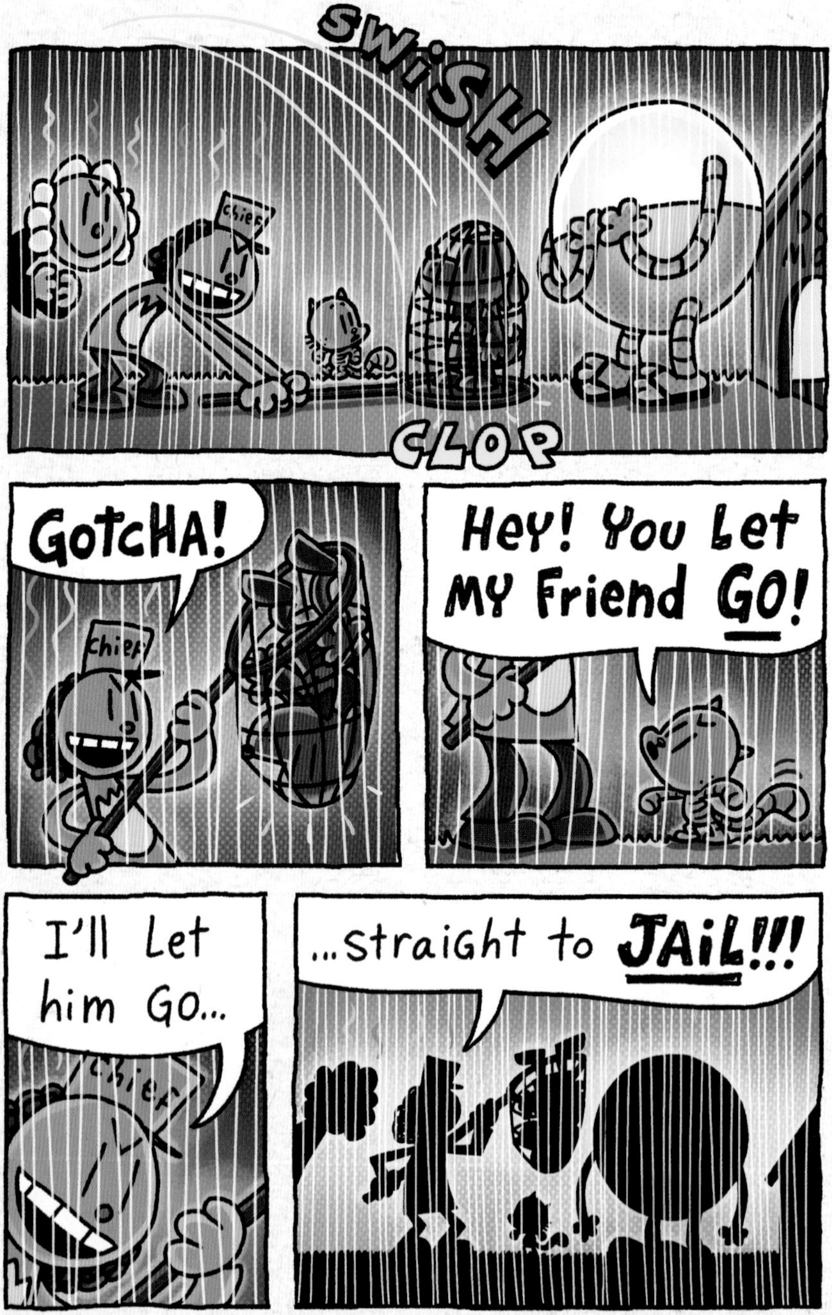
SWiSH
CLOP
GOTCHA!
Hey! You Let MY Friend GO!
I'll Let him Go...
...straight to JAiL!!!
Chief

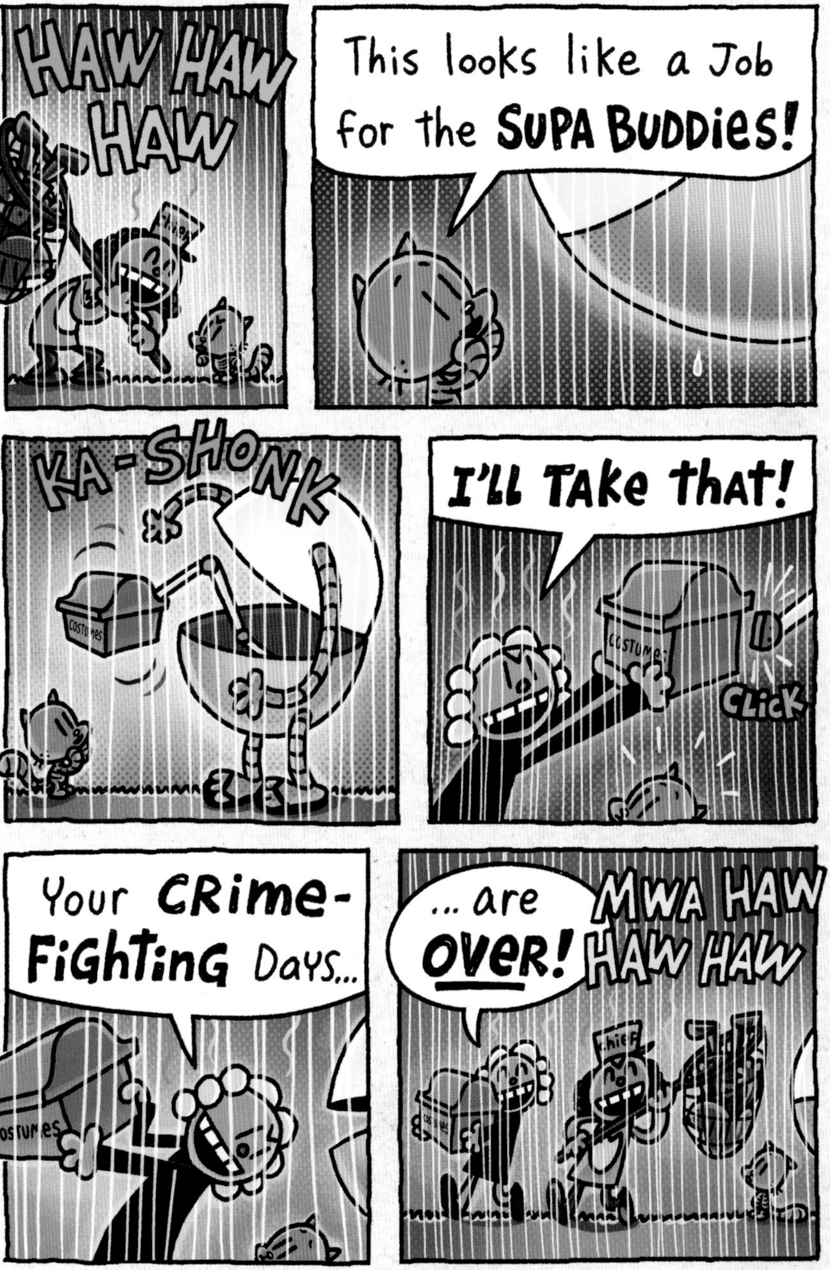
HAW HAW HAW
This looks like a Job for the SUPA BUDDies!
KA-SHONK
COSTUMES
I'll TAke that!
COSTUMES
CLiCK
Your CRime-FiGhTinG DAYS...
COSTUMES
... are OVER!
MWA HAW HAW HAW
THIEF

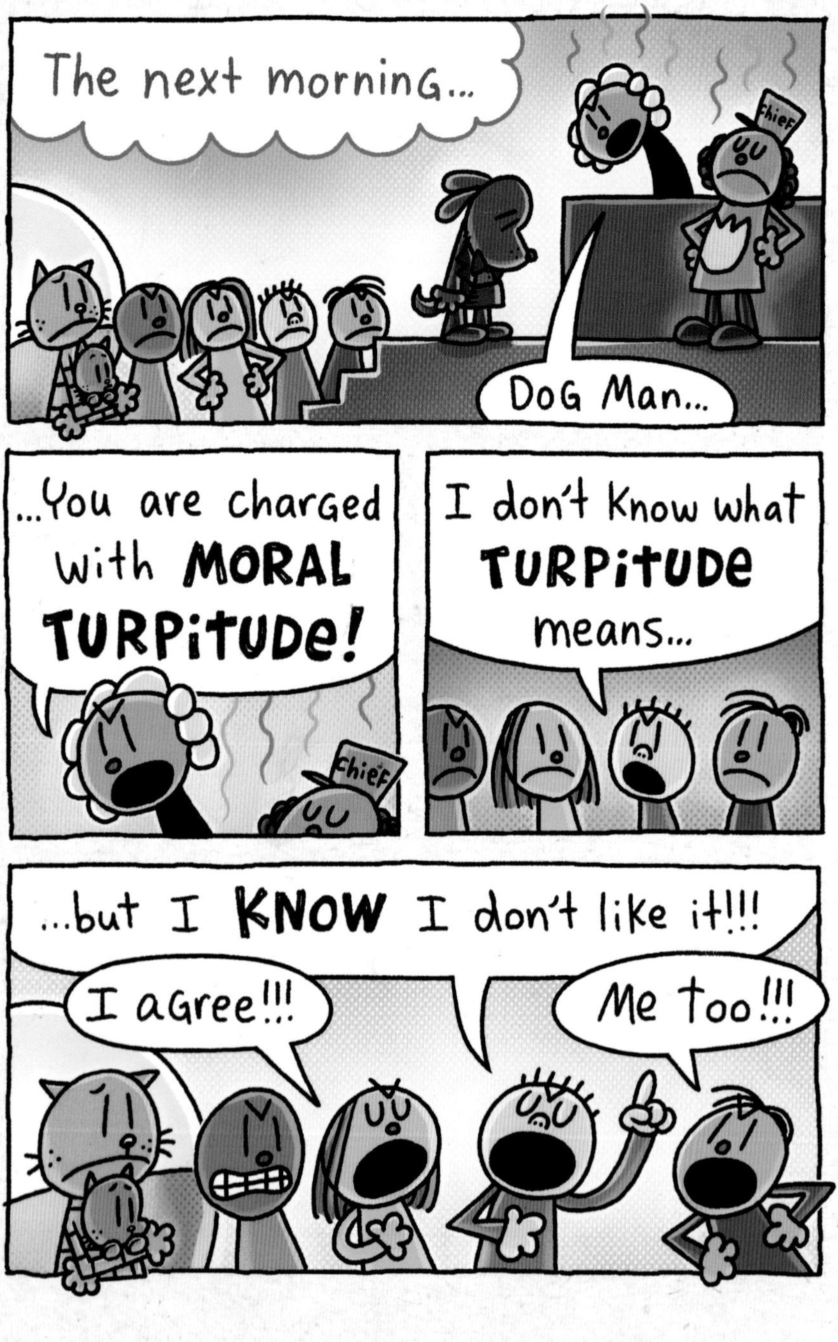
The next morning...
Dog Man...
...You are charged with MORAL TURPITUDE!
I don't know what TURPITUDE means...
...but I KNOW I don't like it!!!
I agree!!!
Me too!!!

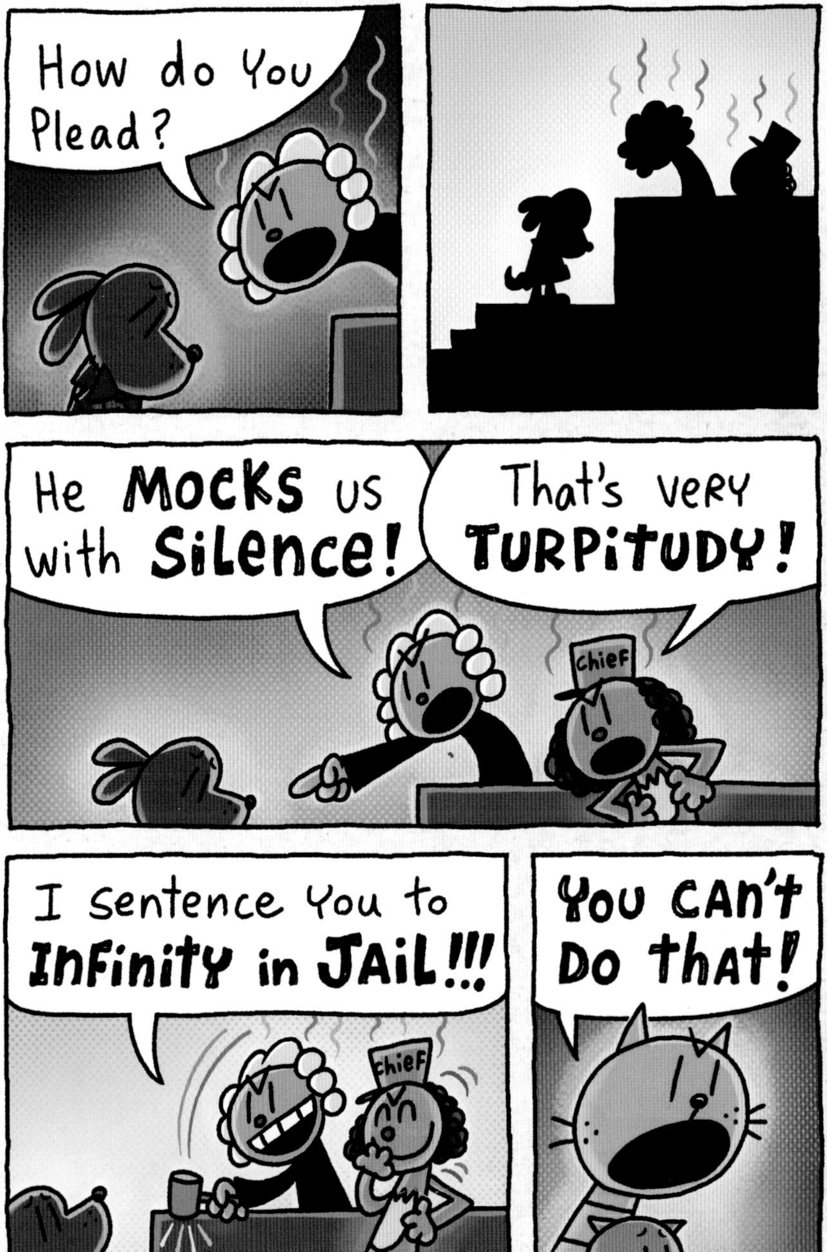
How do You Plead?
He MOCKS us with SiLence!
That's VeRY TURPiTUDY!
I sentence You to INFiNiTY in JAiL!!!
BONK!
YOU CAN'T DO THAT!

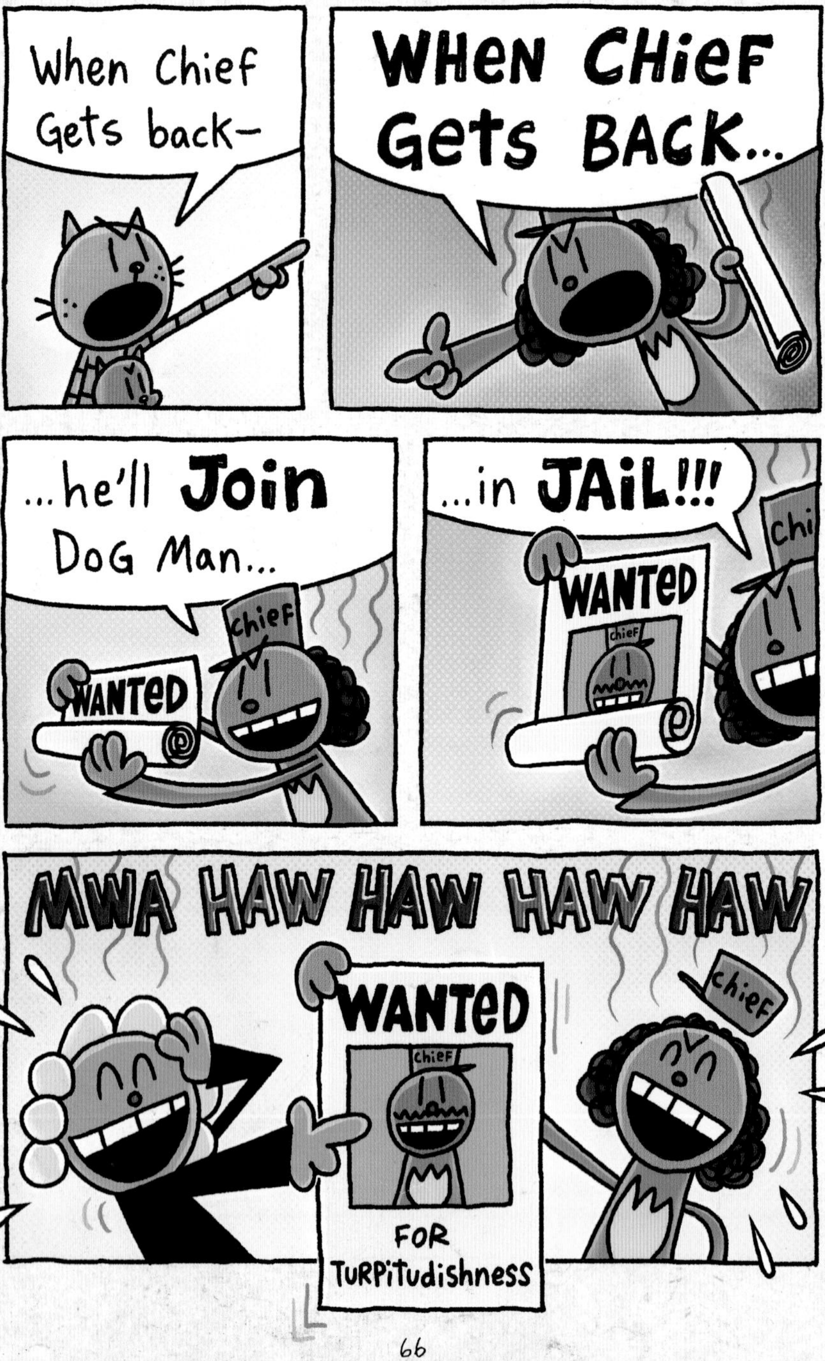
When Chief Gets back—
WHEN CHIEF GETS BACK...
...he'll Join Dog Man...
CHIEF
WANTED
...in JAIL!!!
Chi
WANTED
CHIEF
MWA HAW HAW HAW HAW
WANTED
CHIEF
FOR TURPITUDISHNESS
CHIEF

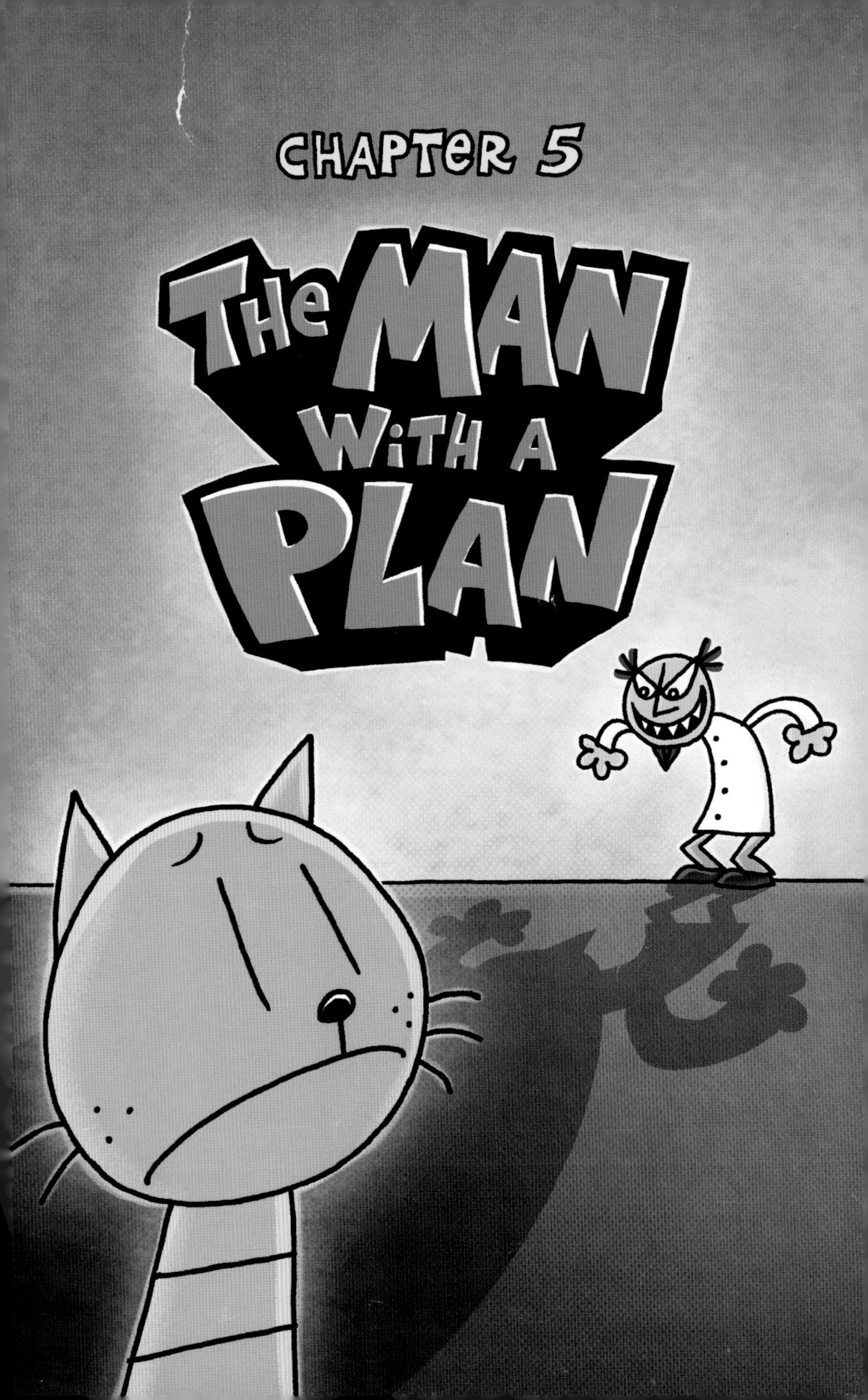

CHAPTER 5
The MAN With A PLAN

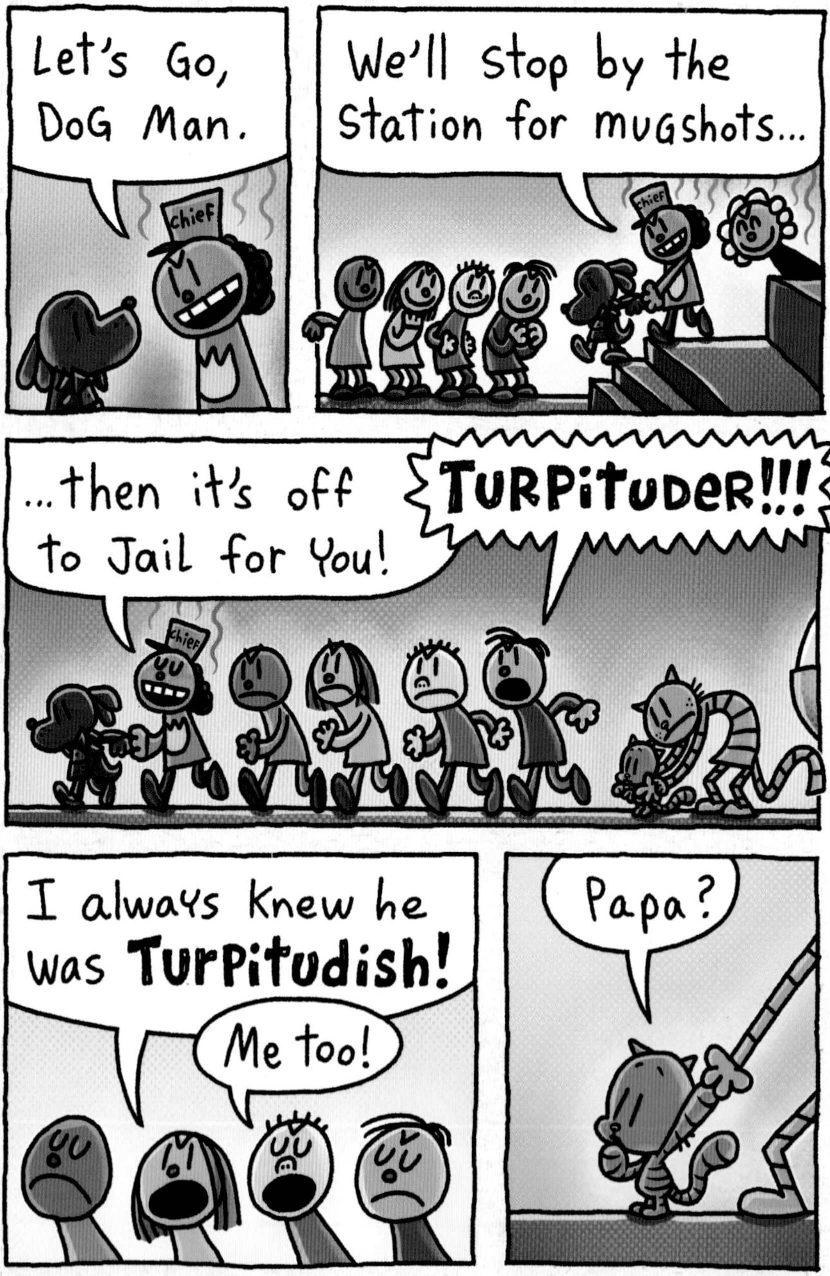
Let's Go, DoG Man.
We'll Stop by the Station for mugshots...
...then it's off to Jail for You!
TURPiTUDER!!!
I always Knew he was TurPitudish!
Me too!
Papa?

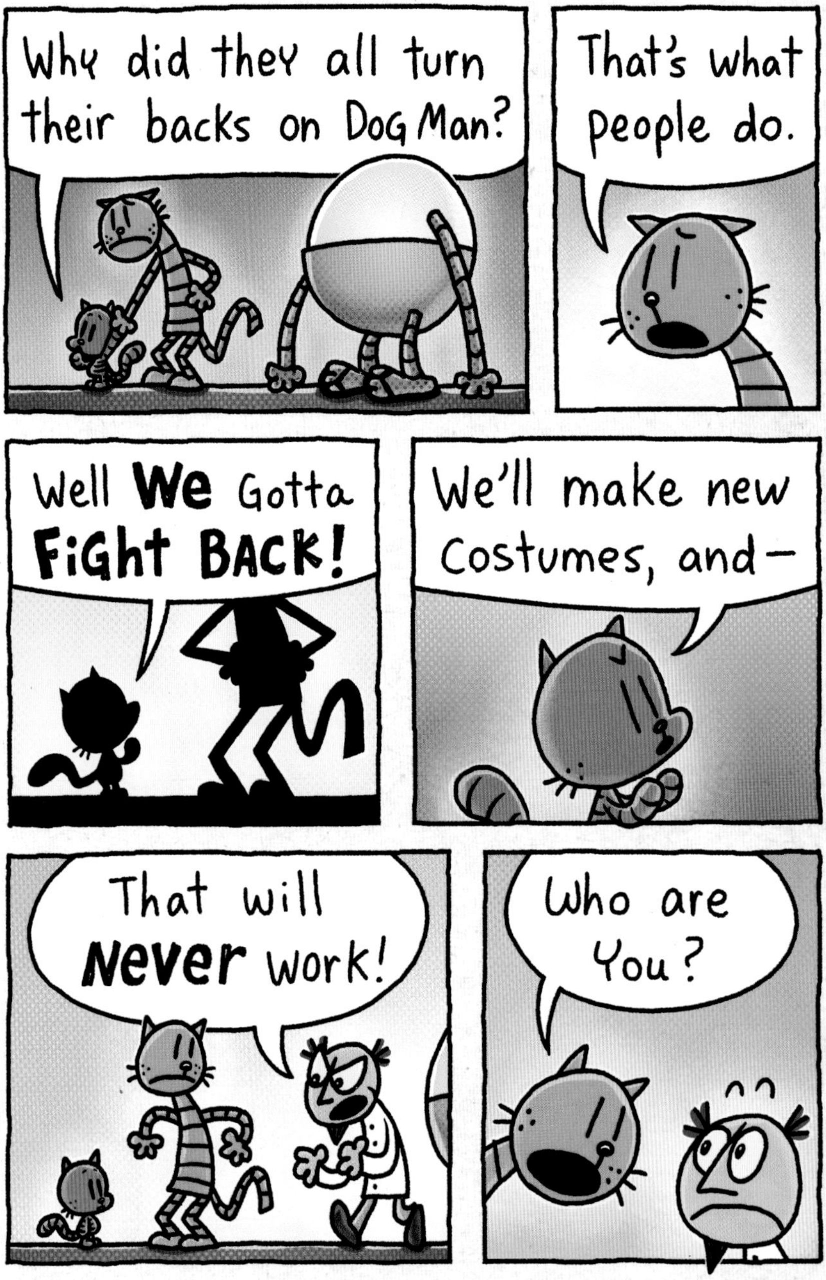
Why did they all turn their backs on Dog Man?
That's what people do.
Well We Gotta FiGht BACK!
We'll make new Costumes, and—
That will Never work!
Who are You?

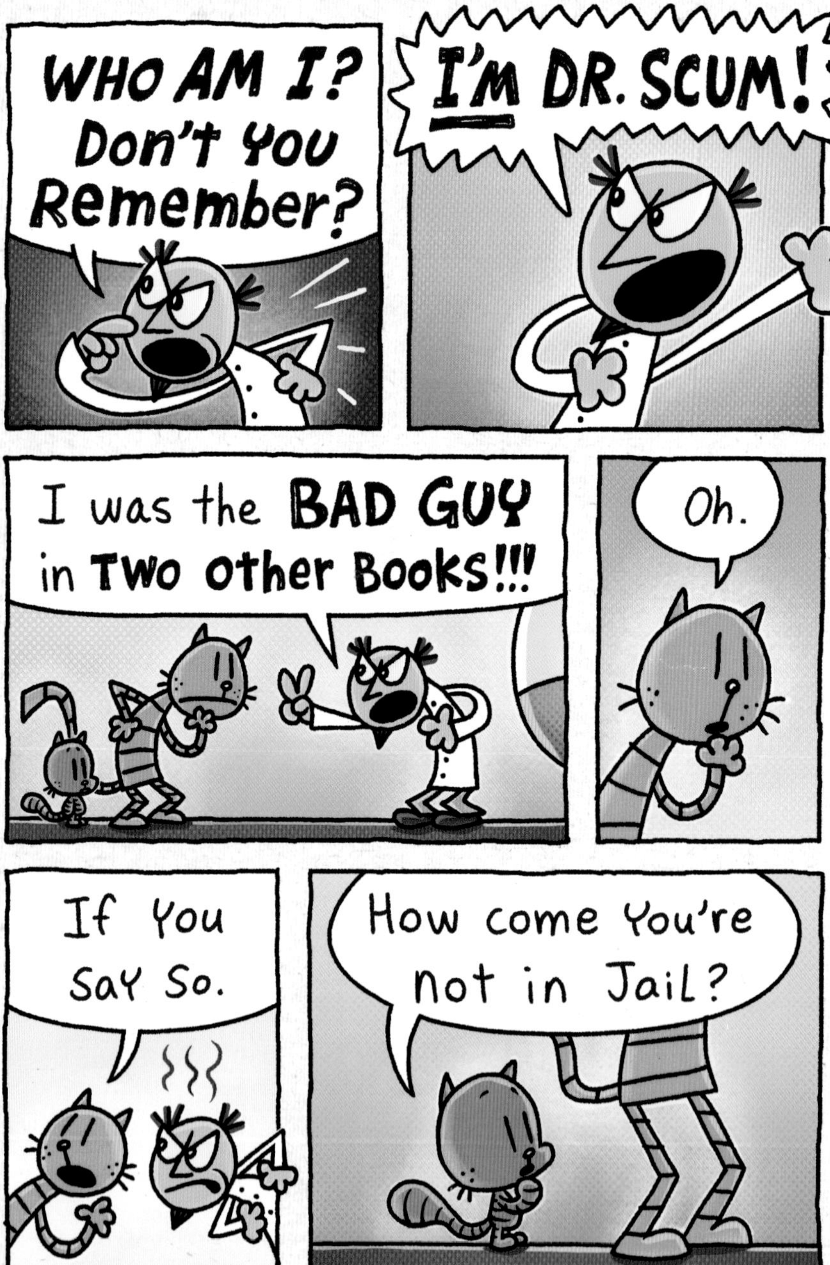
WHO AM I? Don't you Remember?
I'M DR. SCUM!
I was the BAD GUY in TWO Other Books!!!
Oh.
If you say so.
How come you're not in Jail?

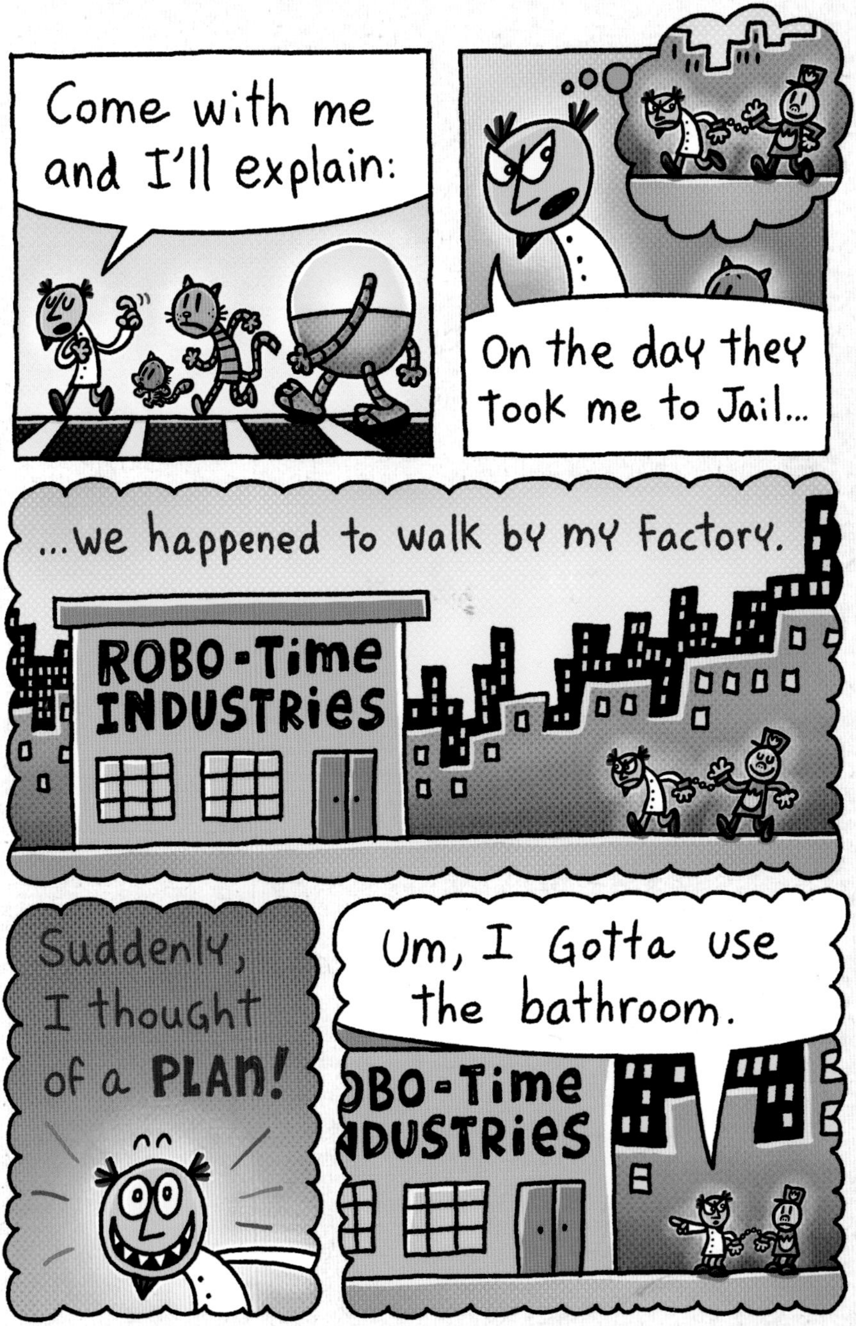

Come with me and I'll explain:
On the day they took me to Jail...
...we happened to walk by my Factory.
ROBO-Time INDUSTRIES
Suddenly, I thought of a PLAN!
Um, I Gotta use the bathroom.
OBO-Time
DUSTRIES

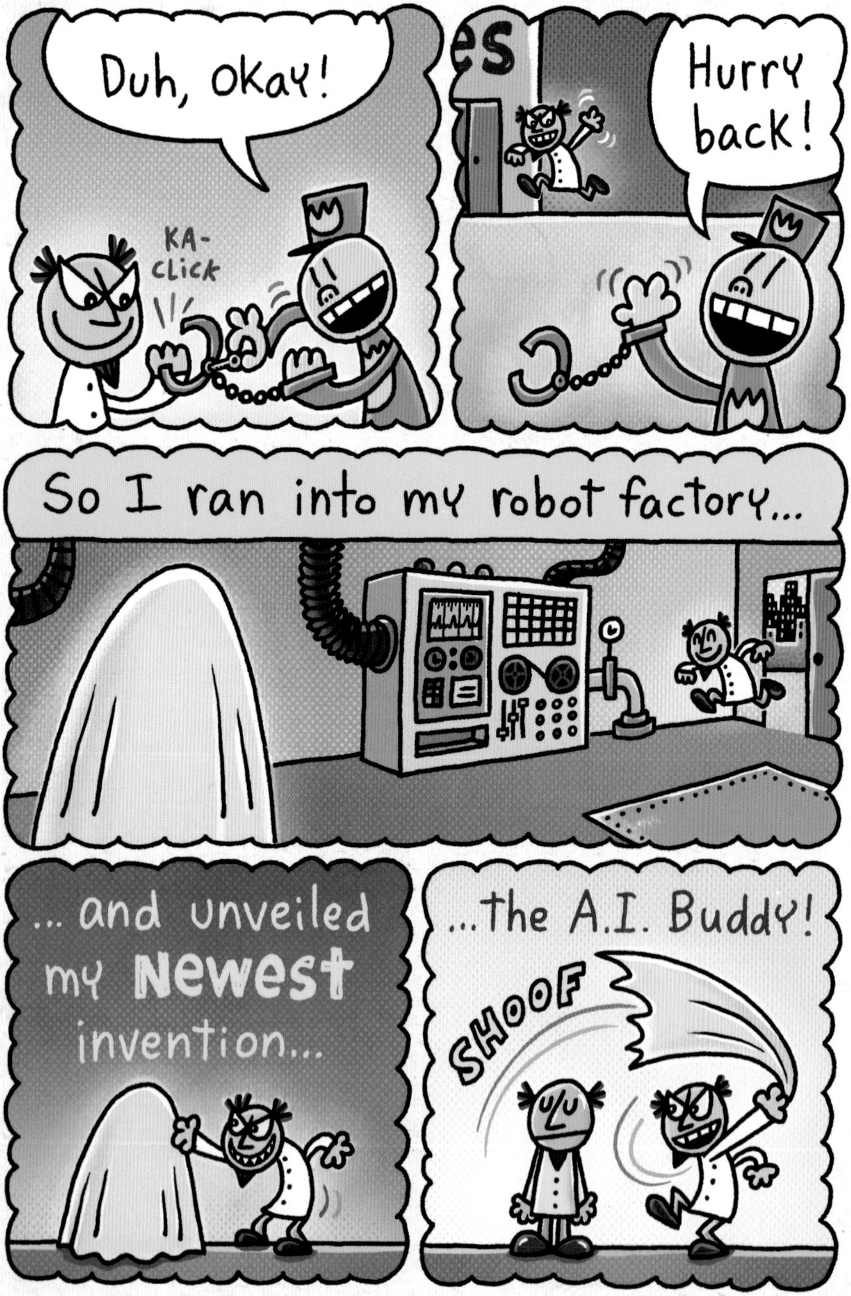
Duh, OKay!
KA-CLICK
Hurry back!
So I ran into my robot factory...
... and unveiled my Newest invention...
... the A.I. Buddy!
SHOOF

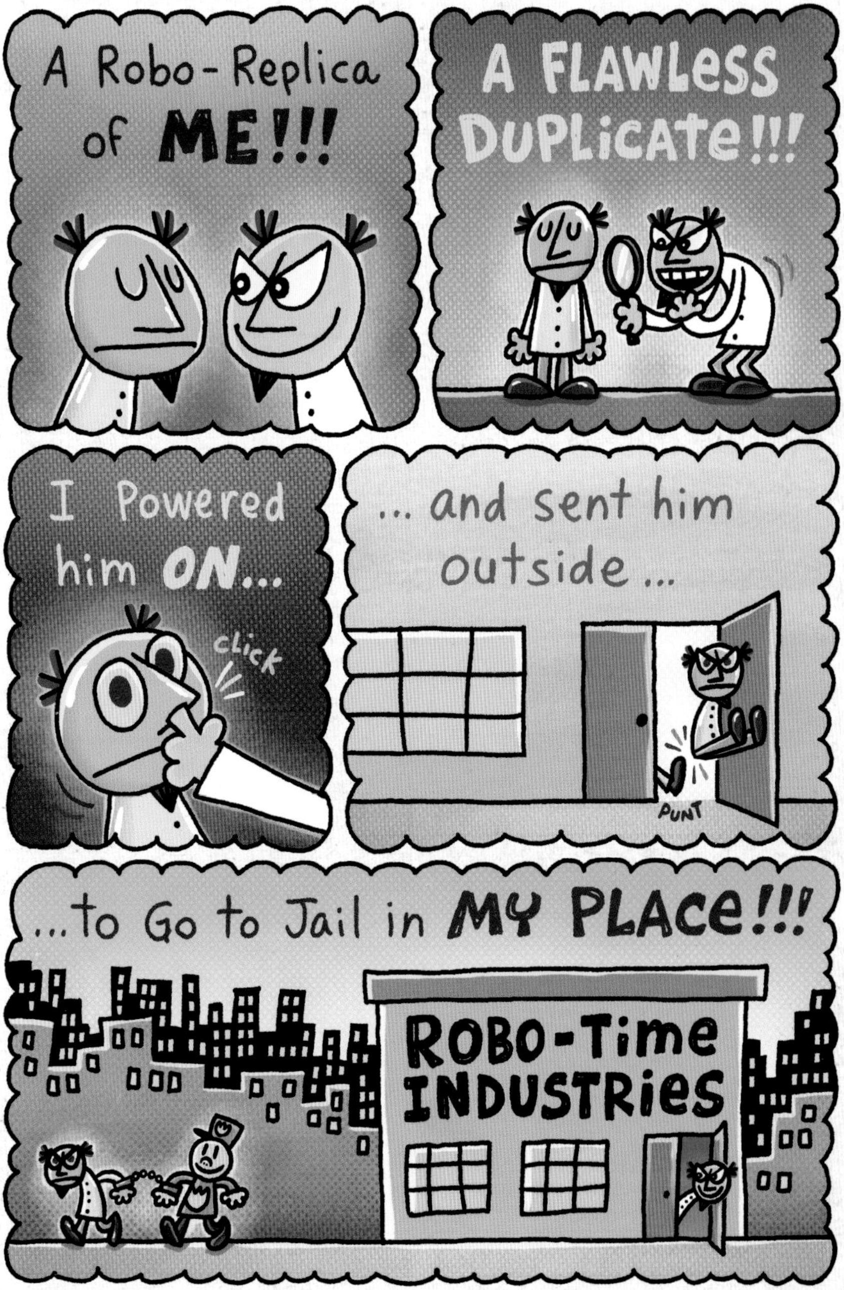
A Robo-Replica of ME!!!
A FLAWLESS DUPLICATE!!!
I Powered him ON...
CLICK
... and sent him outside...
PUNT
...to Go to Jail in MY PLACE!!!
ROBO-Time INDUSTRIES

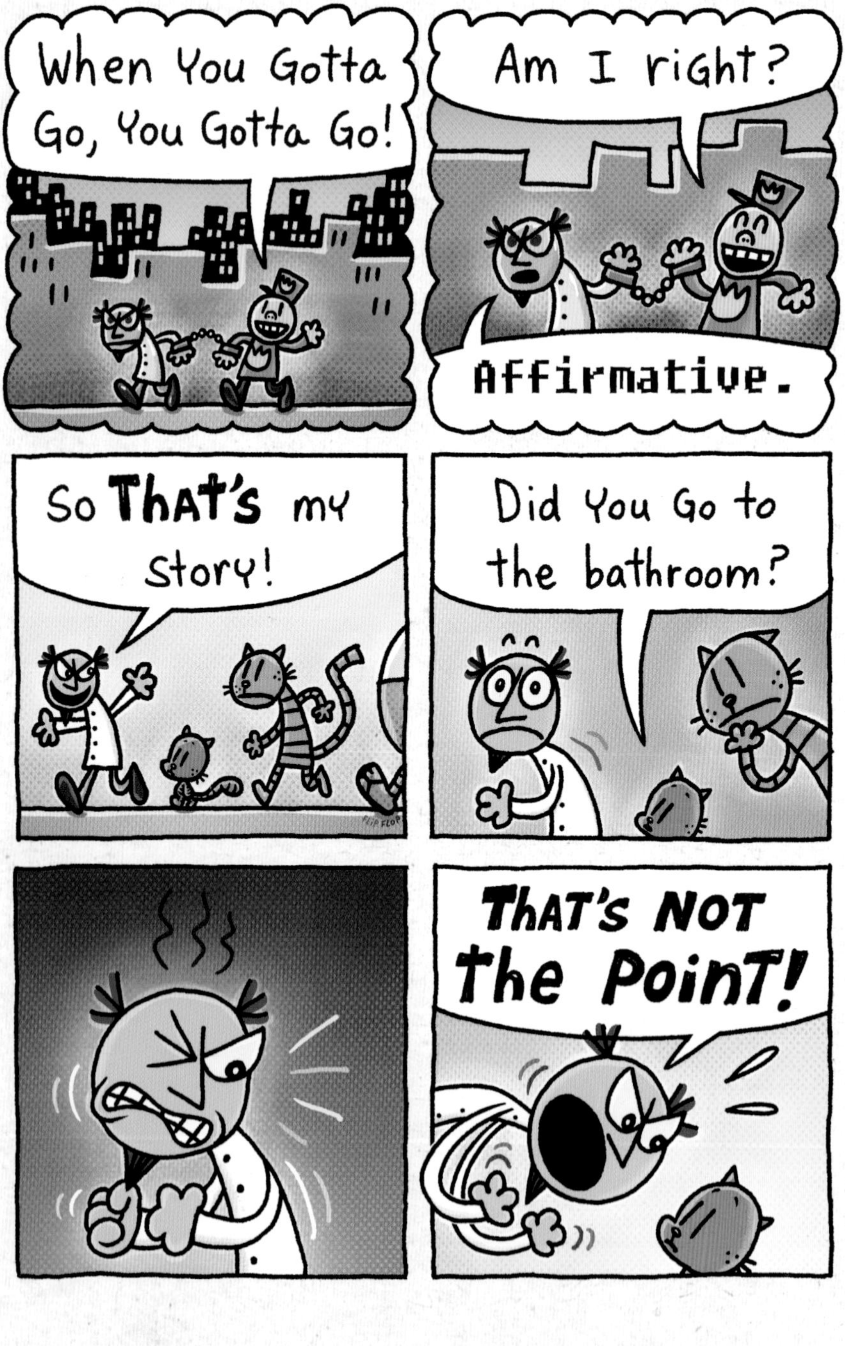
When You Gotta Go, You Gotta Go!
Am I right?
Affirmative.
So THAT'S my story!
Did You Go to the bathroom?
THAT'S NOT The POINT!

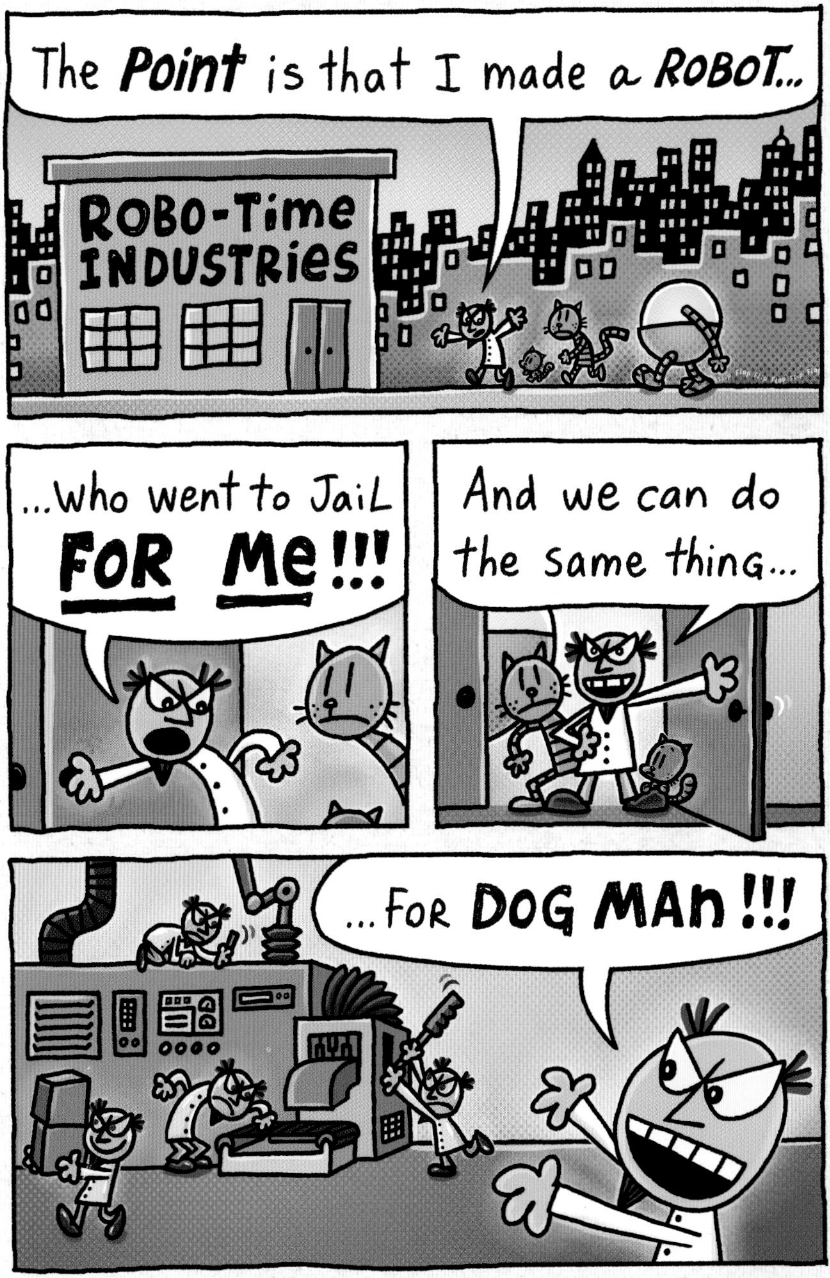
The Point is that I made a ROBOT...
ROBO-Time INDUSTRIES
...Who went to JaiL FOR Me!!!
And we can do the same thing...
...FoR DOG MAn!!!

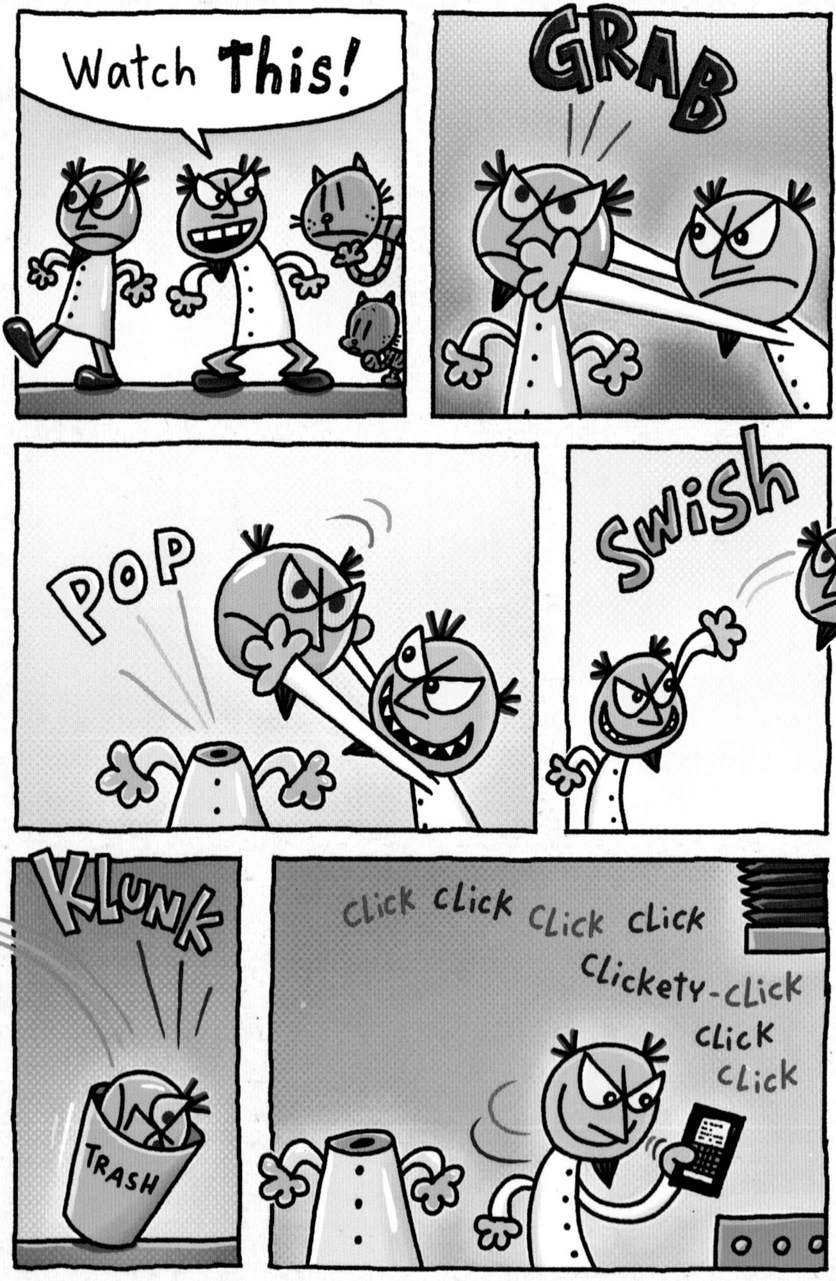
Watch This!
GRAB
POP
SWISH
KLUNK
TRASH
Click Click Click Click
Clickety-Click
Click
Click

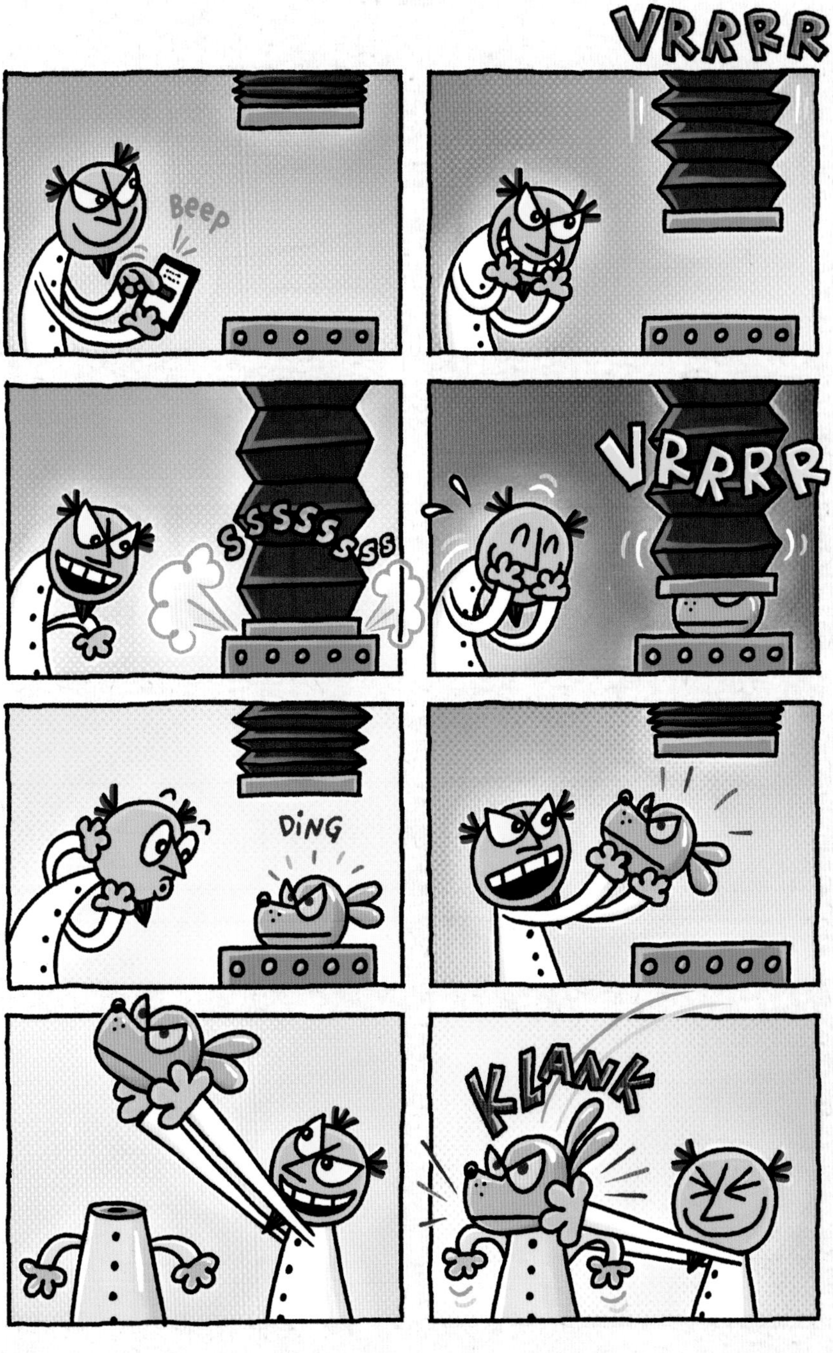
Beep
VRRRR
SSSSSSSS
VRRRR
DING
KLANK

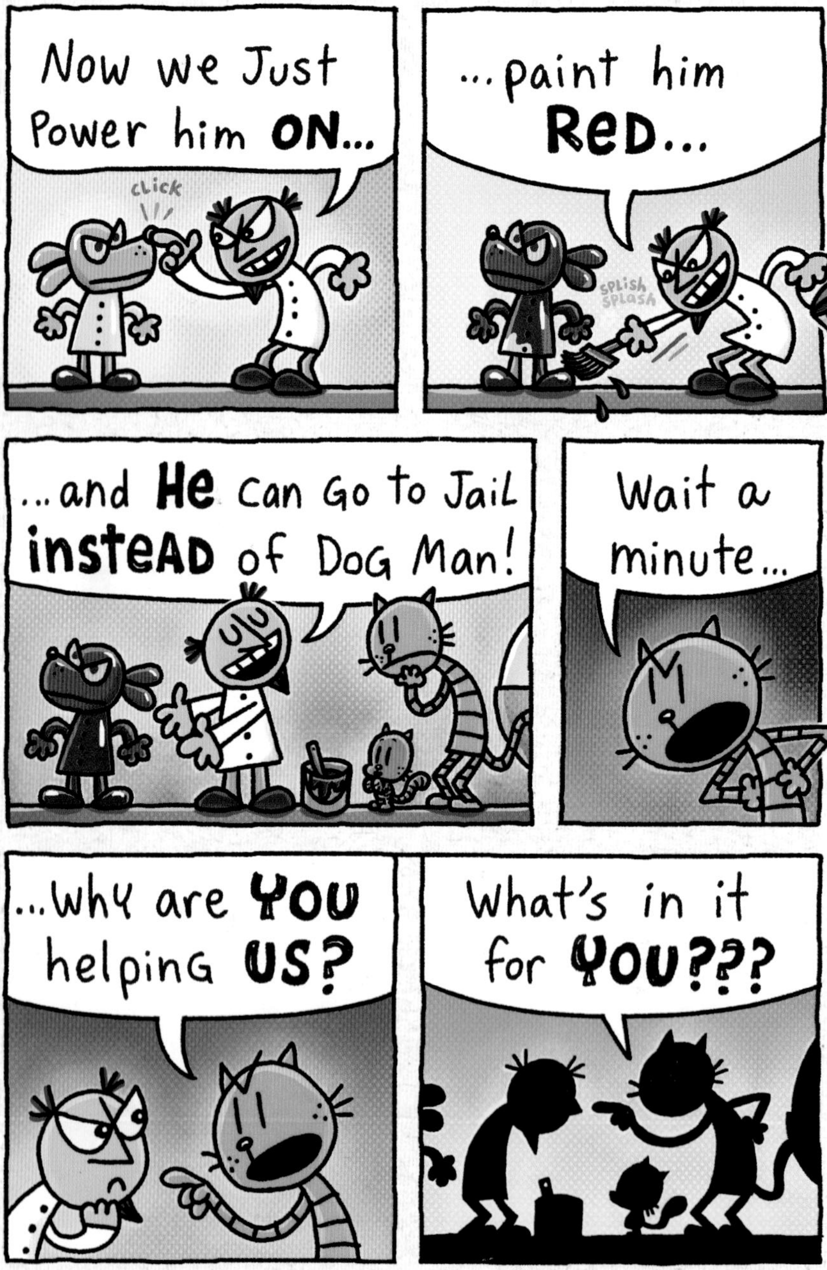
Now we Just Power him ON...
CLICK
...paint him RED...
SPLISH SPLASH
...and HE can Go to JaiL INSTEAD of DOG Man!
Wait a minute...
...Why are YOU helping US?
What's in it for YOU???

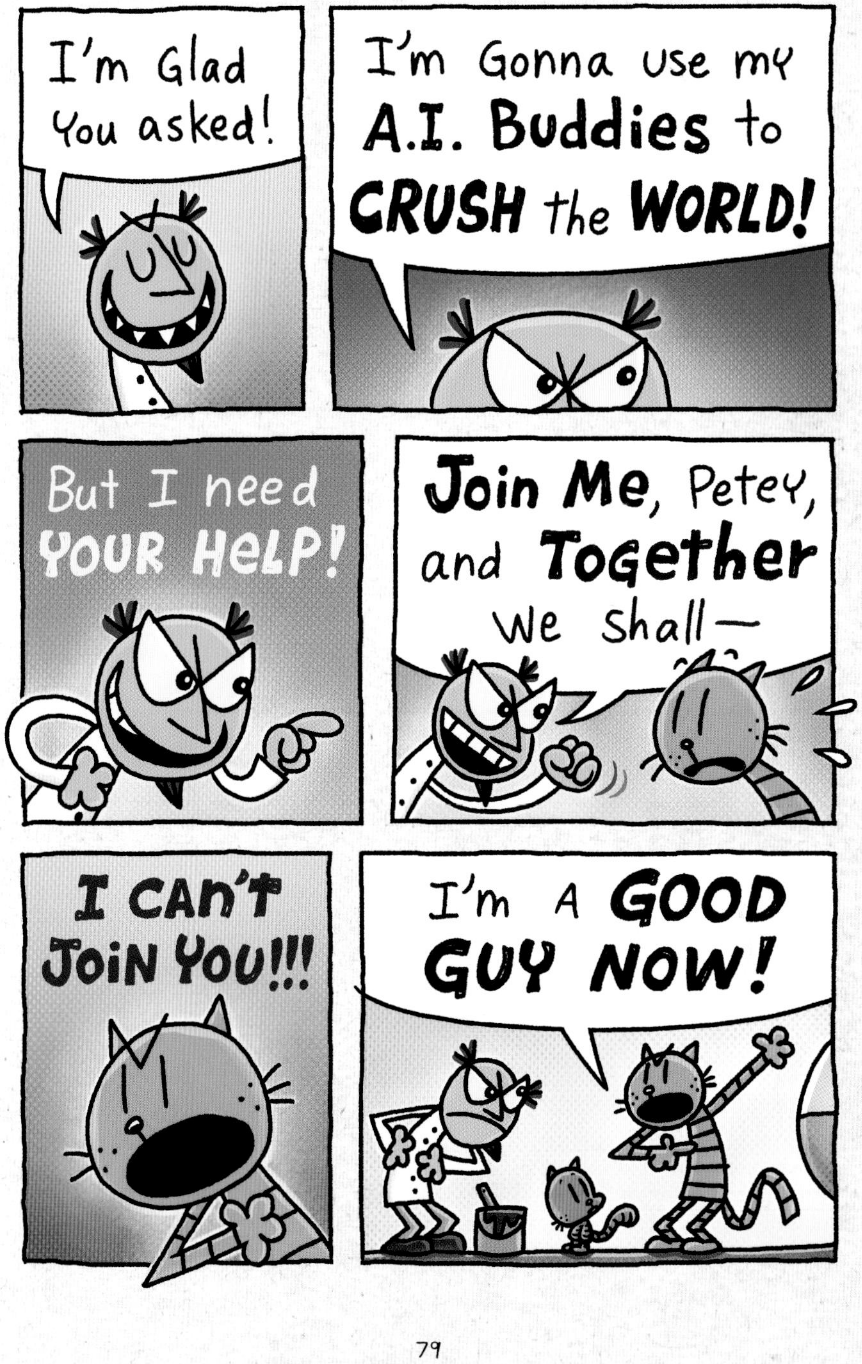
I'm Glad You asked!
I'm Gonna use my A.I. Buddies to CRUSH the WORLD!
But I need YOUR HELP!
Join Me, Petey, and Together we shall—
I CAN'T JOIN YOU!!!
I'm A GOOD GUY NOW!

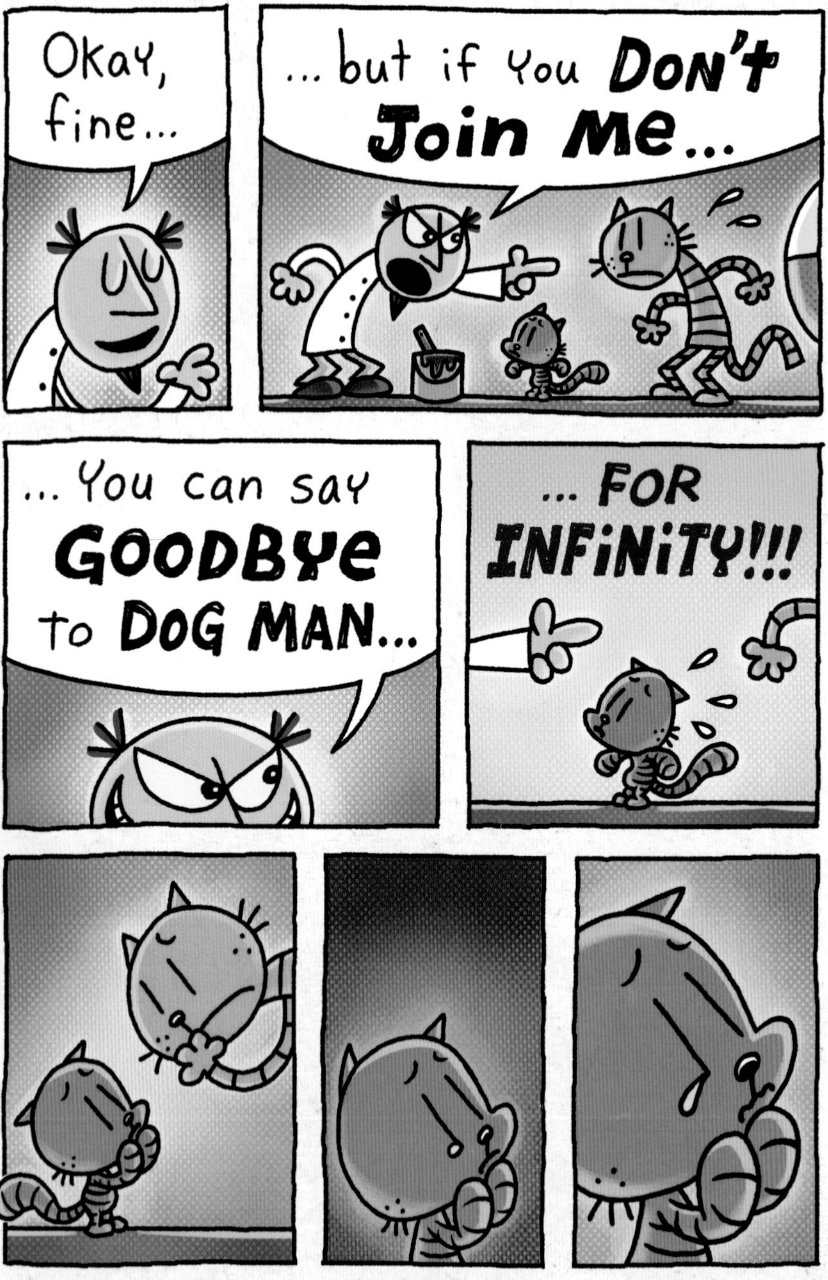
Okay, fine...
...but if you DON'T Join Me...
...You can say GOODBYE to DOG MAN...
...FOR INFINITY!!!

CHAPTER 6

The Big Switcheroo

COPS

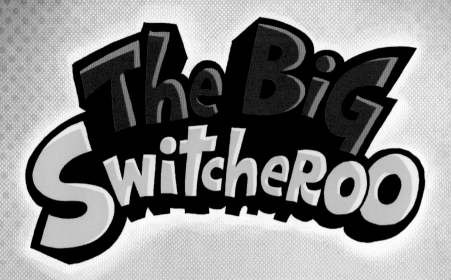

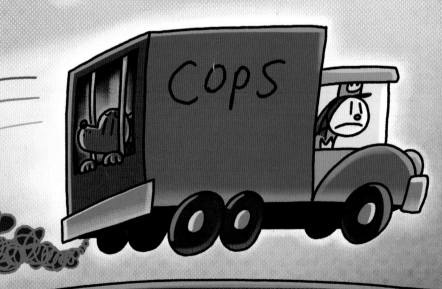

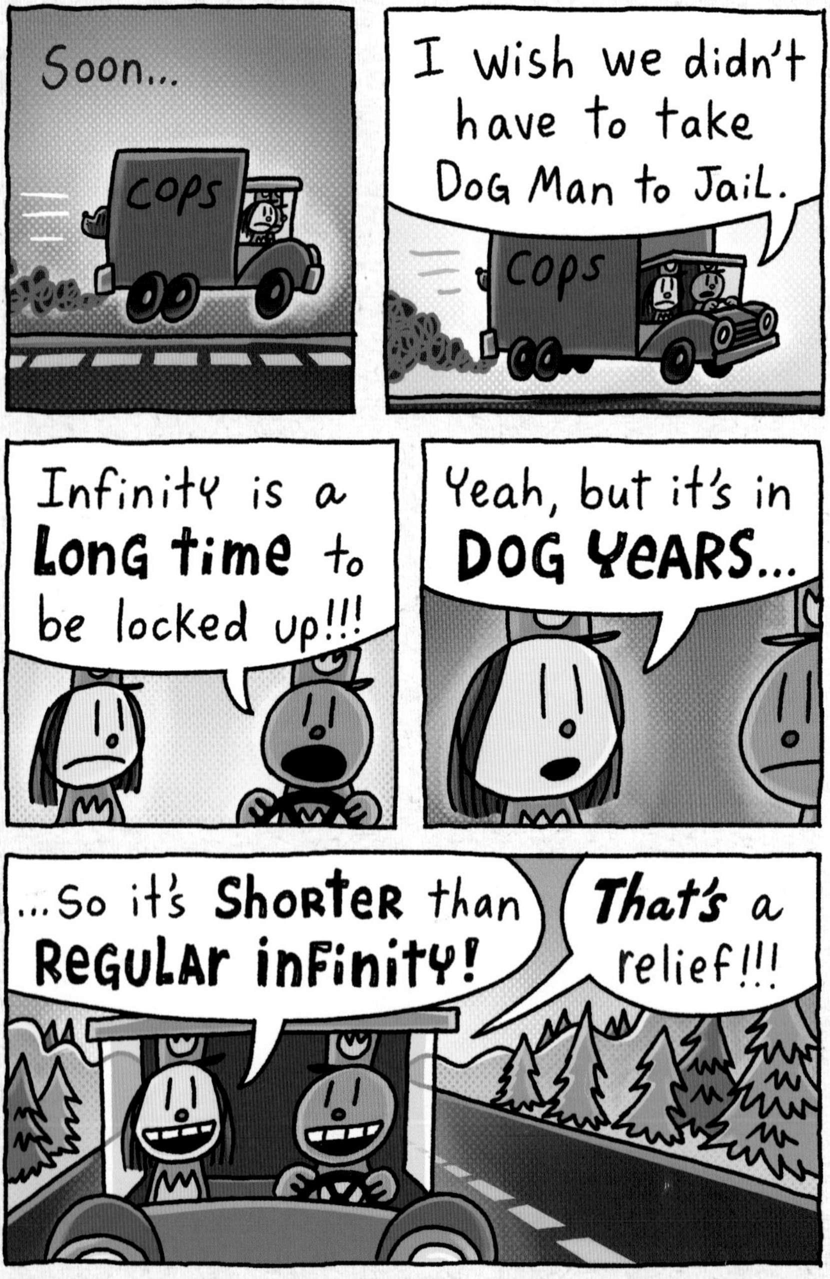
Soon...
COPS
I wish we didn't have to take Dog Man to Jail.
COPS
Infinity is a LONG time to be locked up!!!
Yeah, but it's in DOG YEARS...
...So it's SHORTER than REGULAR INFINITY!
That's a relief!!!

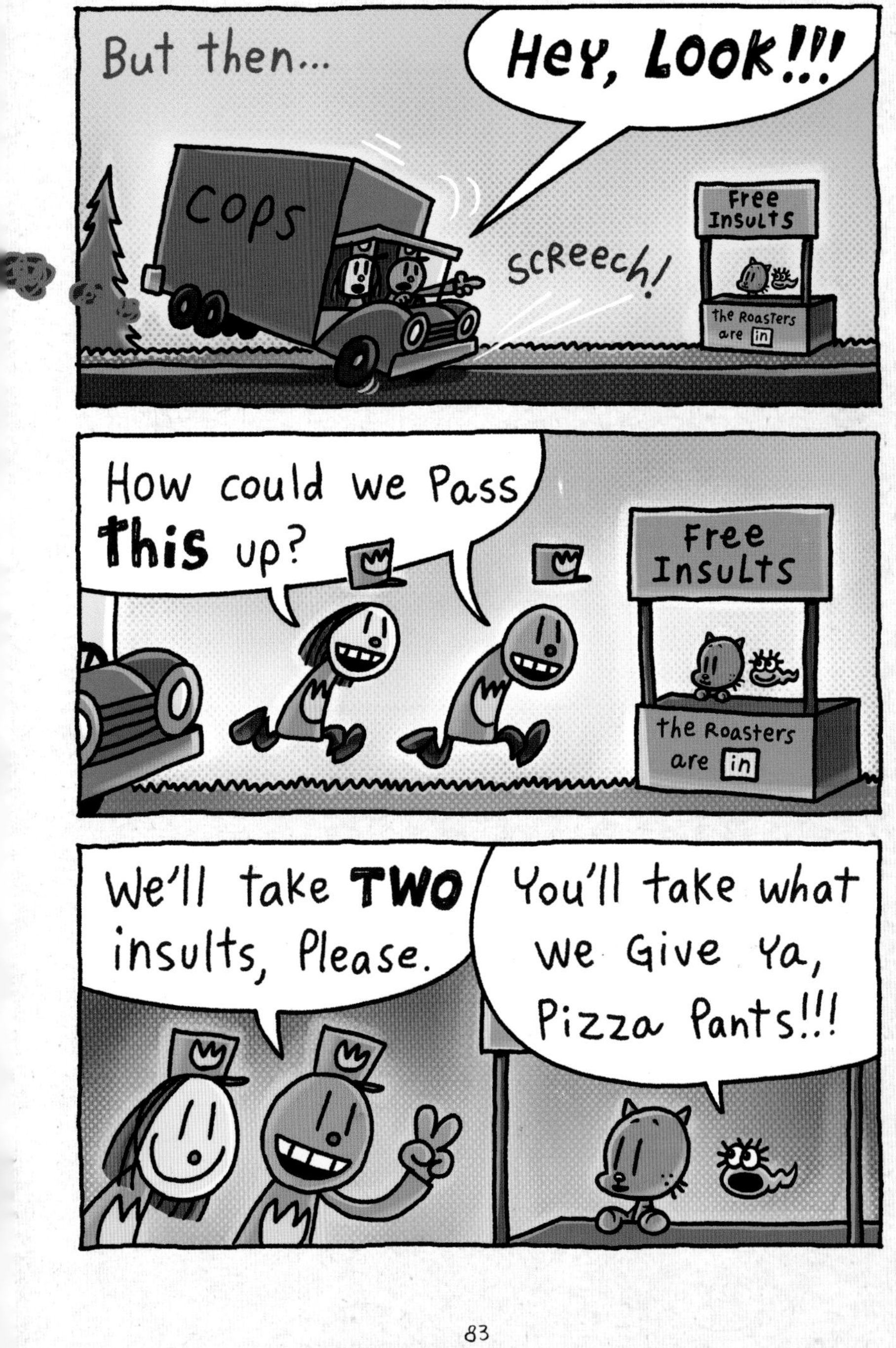
But then...
HEY, LOOK!!!
COPS
SCREECH!
Free Insults
The Roasters are in
How could we Pass THIS up?
Free Insults
the Roasters are in
We'll take TWO insults, Please.
You'll take what we Give ya, Pizza Pants!!!

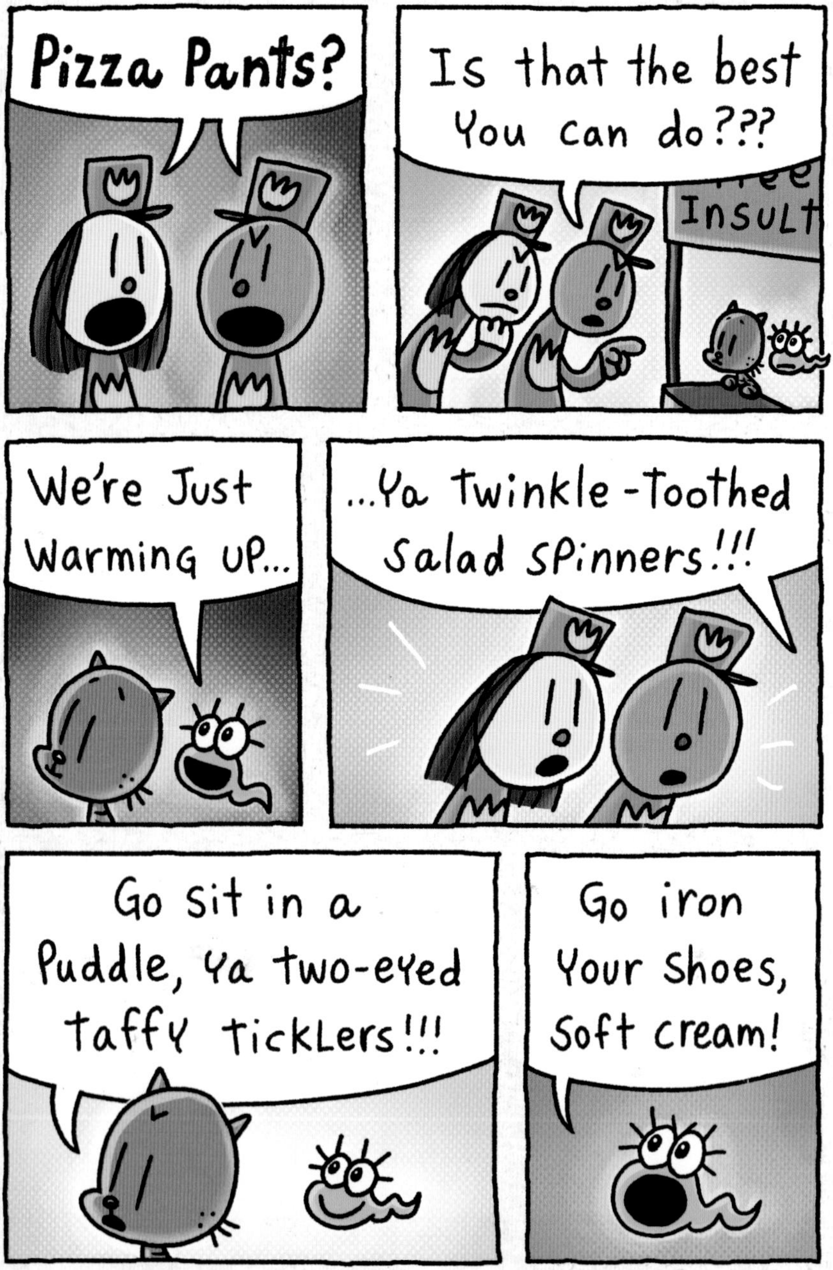
Pizza Pants?
Is that the best you can do???
INSULT
We're Just warming up...
...Ya twinkle-Toothed Salad Spinners!!!
Go sit in a Puddle, ya two-eyed taffy ticklers!!!
Go iron your shoes, Soft cream!

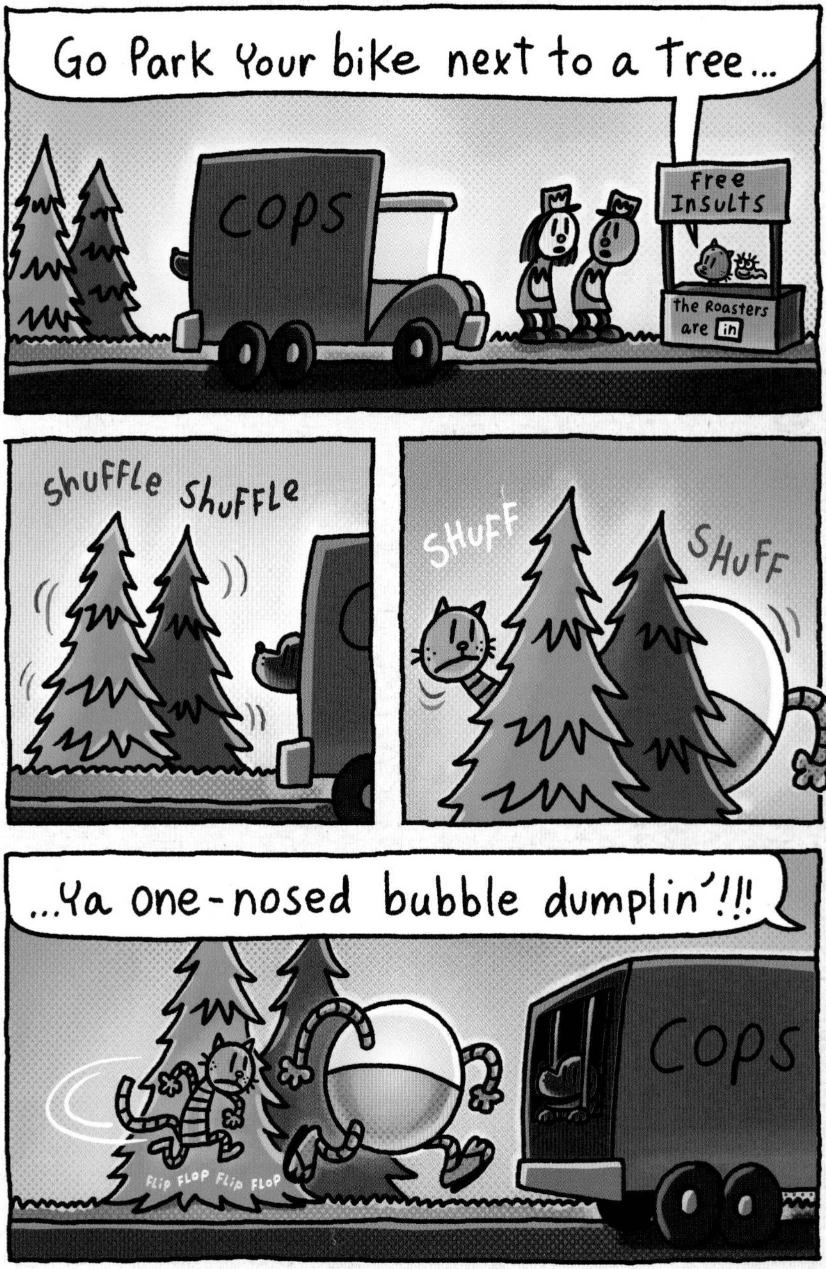
Go Park Your bike next to a Tree...
COPS
Free Insults
the Roasters are in
shuffle shuffle
SHUFF
SHUFF
...Ya one-nosed bubble dumplin'!!!
COPS
FLip FLOP FLip FLOP

Cop
RRRRR
RR

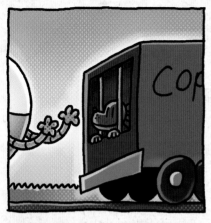

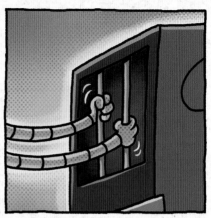

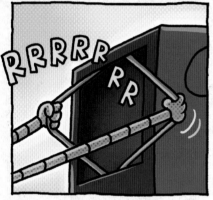

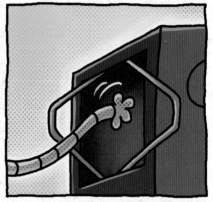

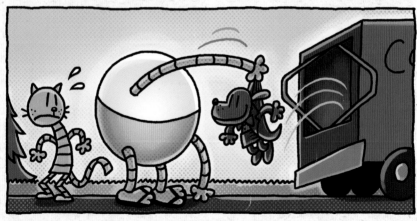

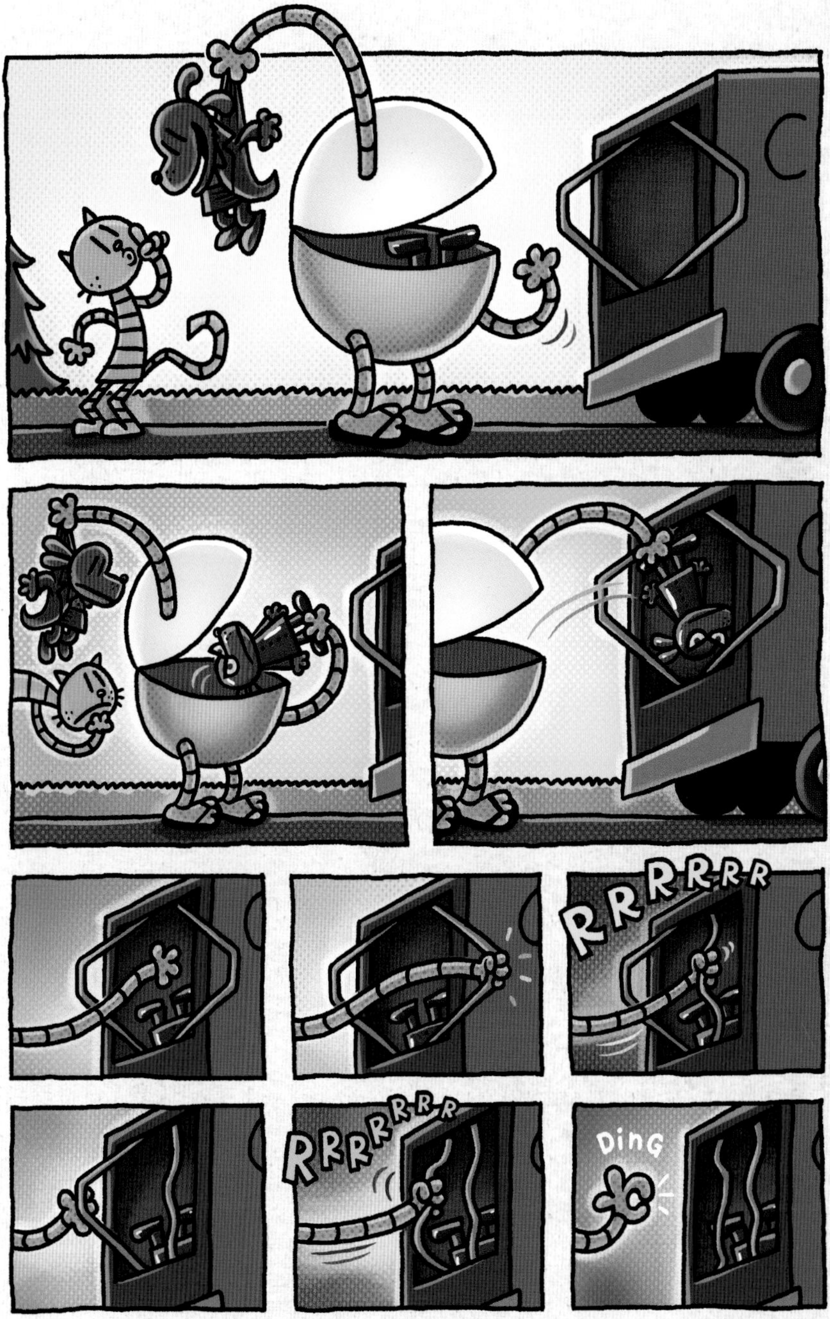
RRRRRRR
RRRRRRR
DING

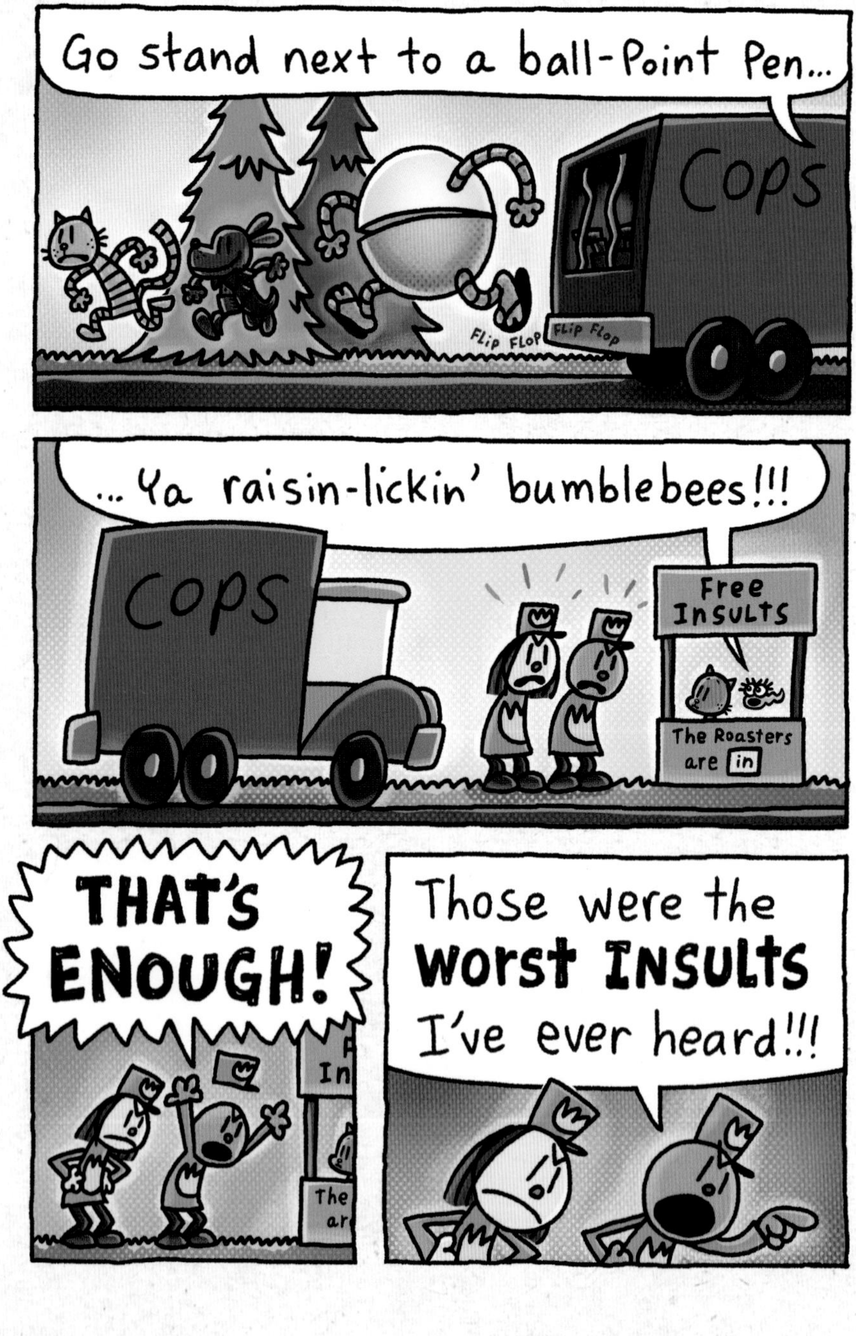
Go stand next to a ball-Point Pen...
COPS
FLIP FLOP
FLIP FLOP
...Ya raisin-lickin' bumblebees!!!
COPS
Free INSULTS
The Roasters are in
THAT'S ENOUGH!
Those were the WORST INSULTS I've ever heard!!!

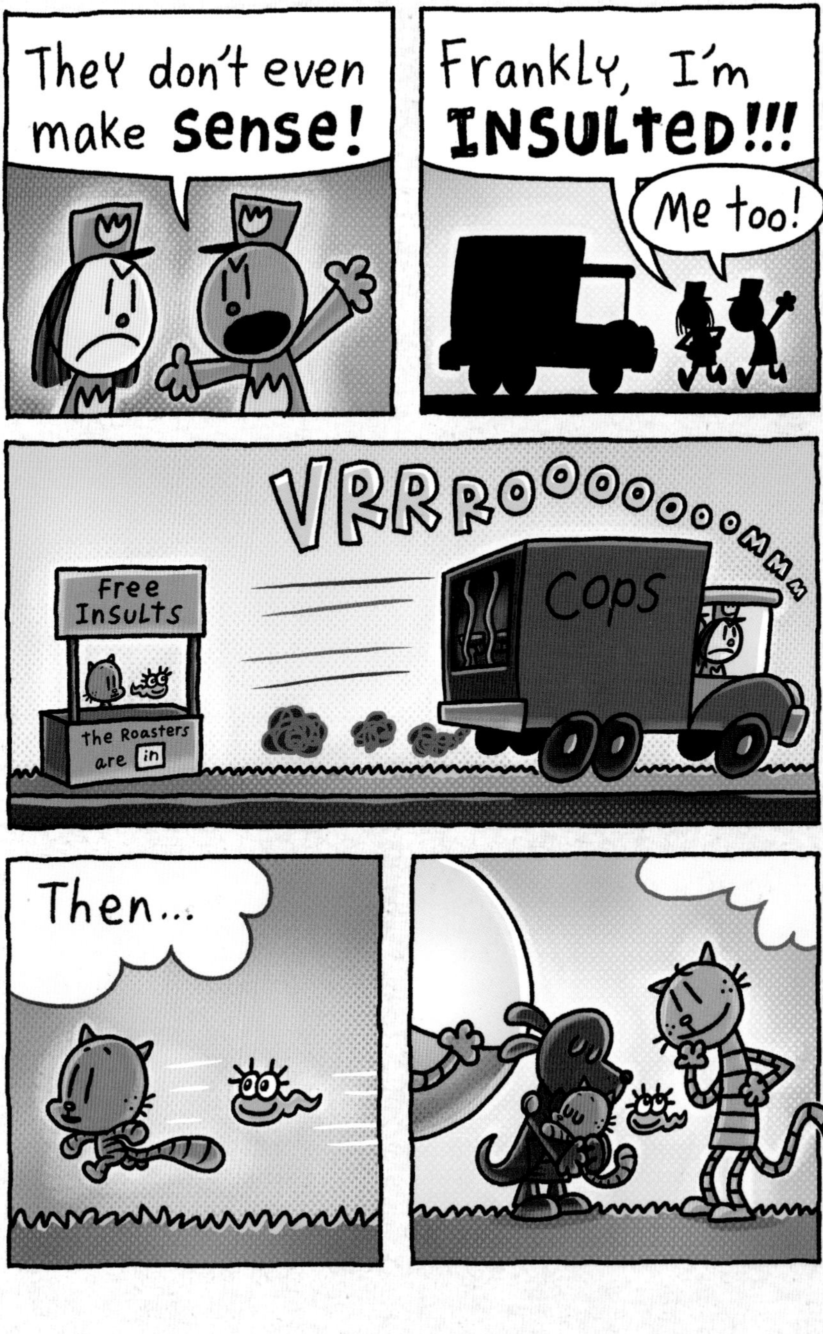
They don't even make Sense!
Frankly, I'm INSULTED!!!
Me too!
VRRROOOOOOOOOOMMM
Free Insults
the Roasters are in
Cops
Then...

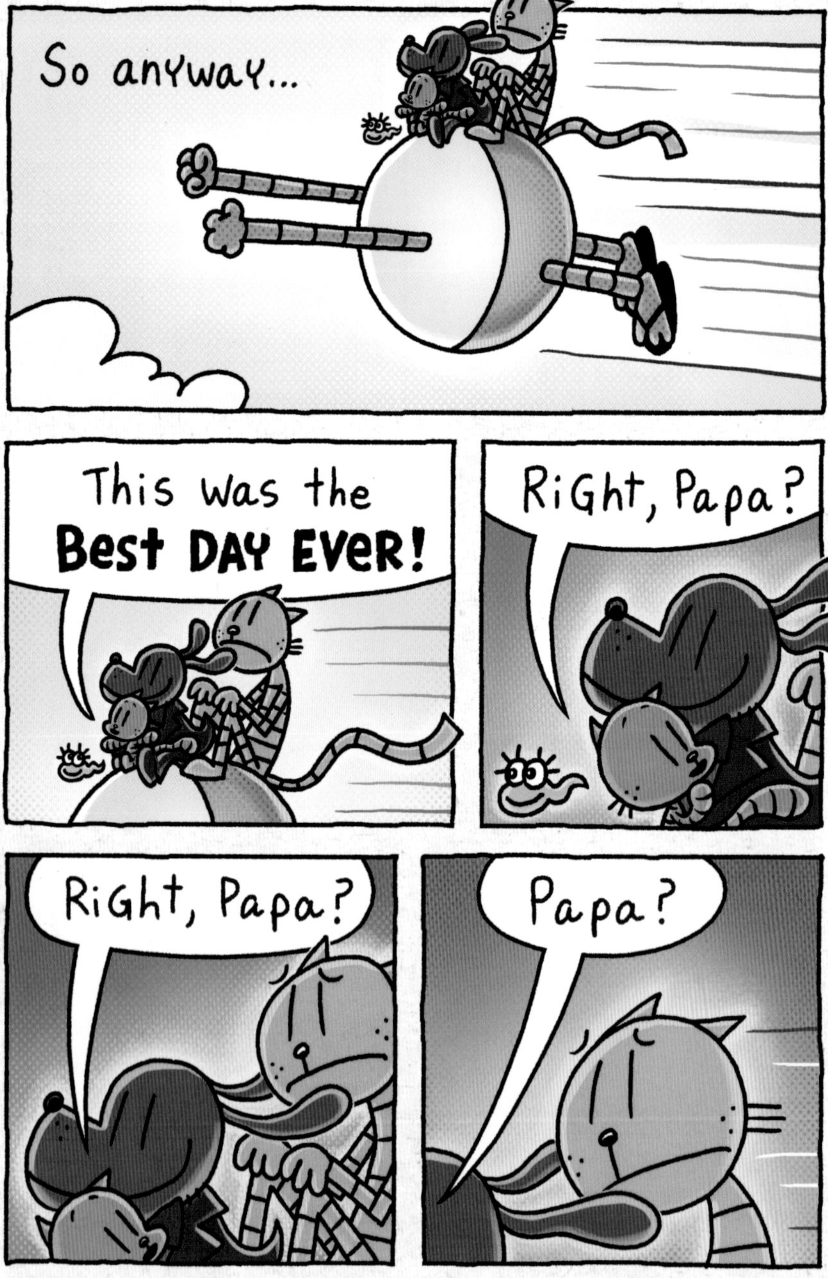
So anyway...
This was the **Best DAY EVER!**
RiGht, Papa?
RiGht, Papa?
Papa?

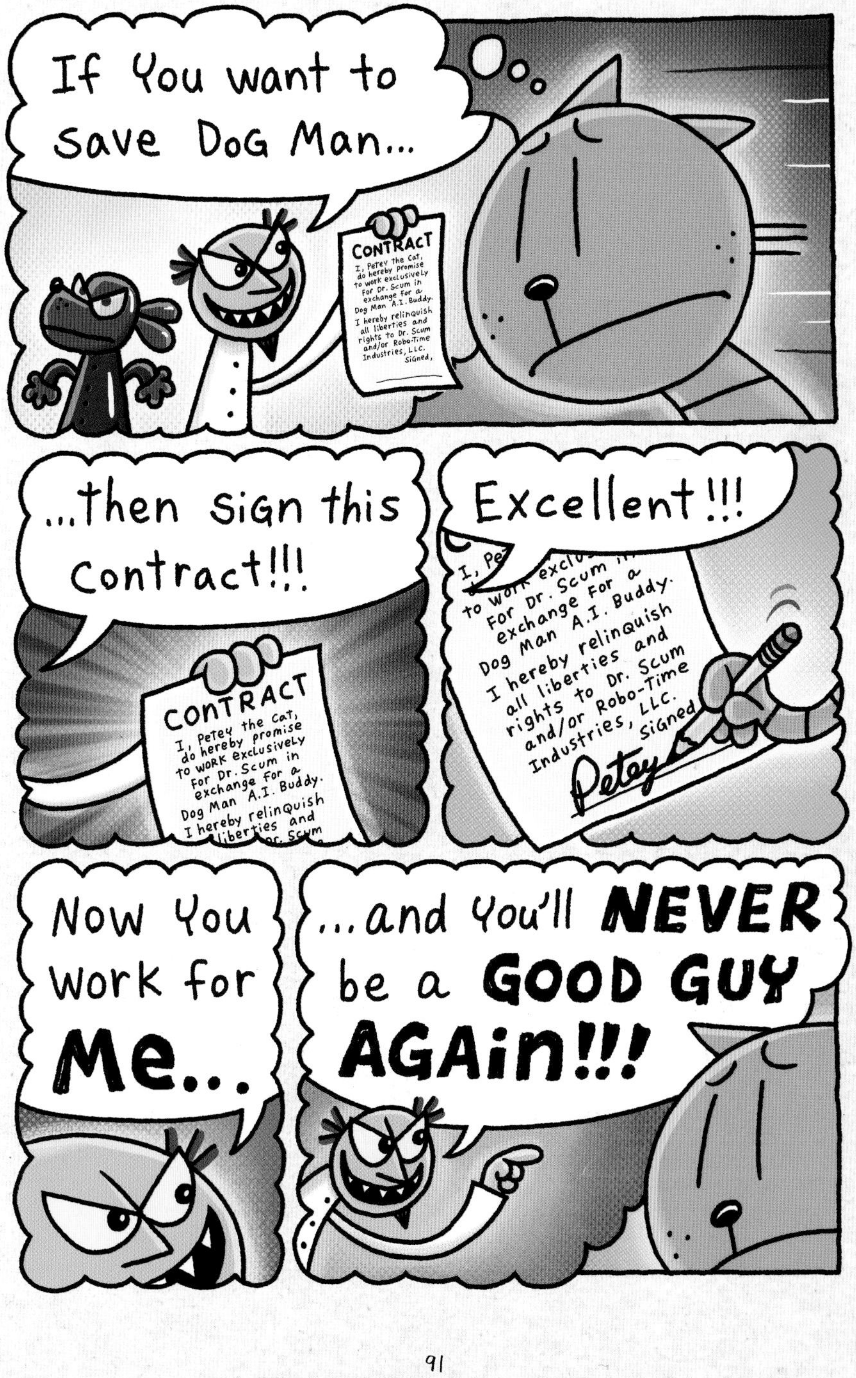
If You want to save DoG Man...
CONTRACT
I, Petey the Cat, do hereby promise to work exclusively for Dr. Scum in exchange for a Dog Man A.I. Buddy.
I hereby relinquish all liberties and rights to Dr. Scum and/or Robo-Time Industries, LLC.
Signed,
...then SiGn this Contract!!!
CONTRACT
I, Petey the Cat, do hereby promise to work exclusively for Dr. Scum in exchange for a Dog Man A.I. Buddy.
I hereby relinquish all liberties and
Excellent!!!
For Dr. Scum in exchange for a Dog Man A.I. Buddy.
I hereby relinquish all liberties and rights to Dr. Scum and/or Robo-Time Industries, LLC.
SiGned
Petey
Now You work for Me...
...and You'll NEVER be a GOOD GUY AGAin!!!

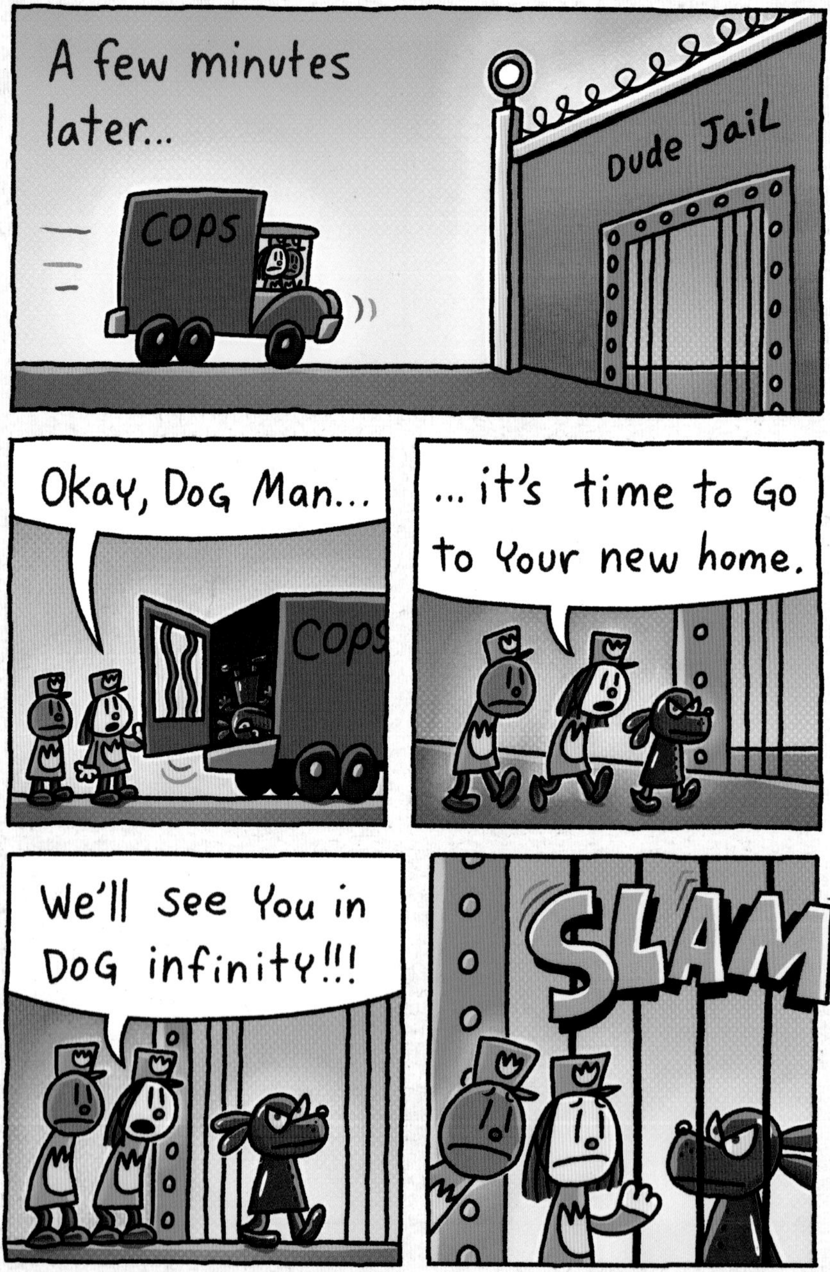
A few minutes later...
COPS
Dude Jail
Okay, Dog Man...
COPS
... it's time to Go to Your new home.
We'll see You in DoG infinity!!!
SLAM

CHAPTER 7

THE BOT WITH A PLOT

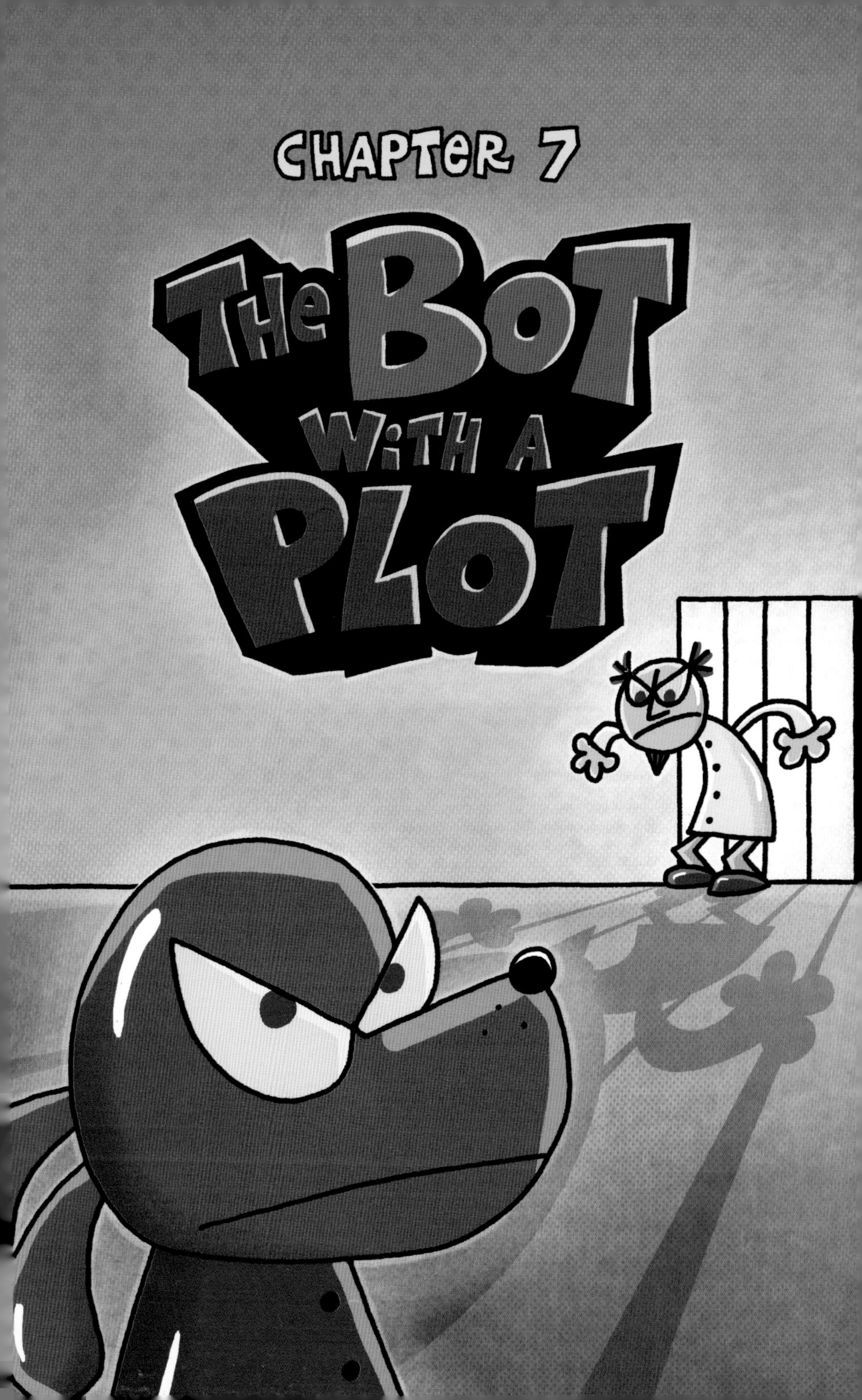

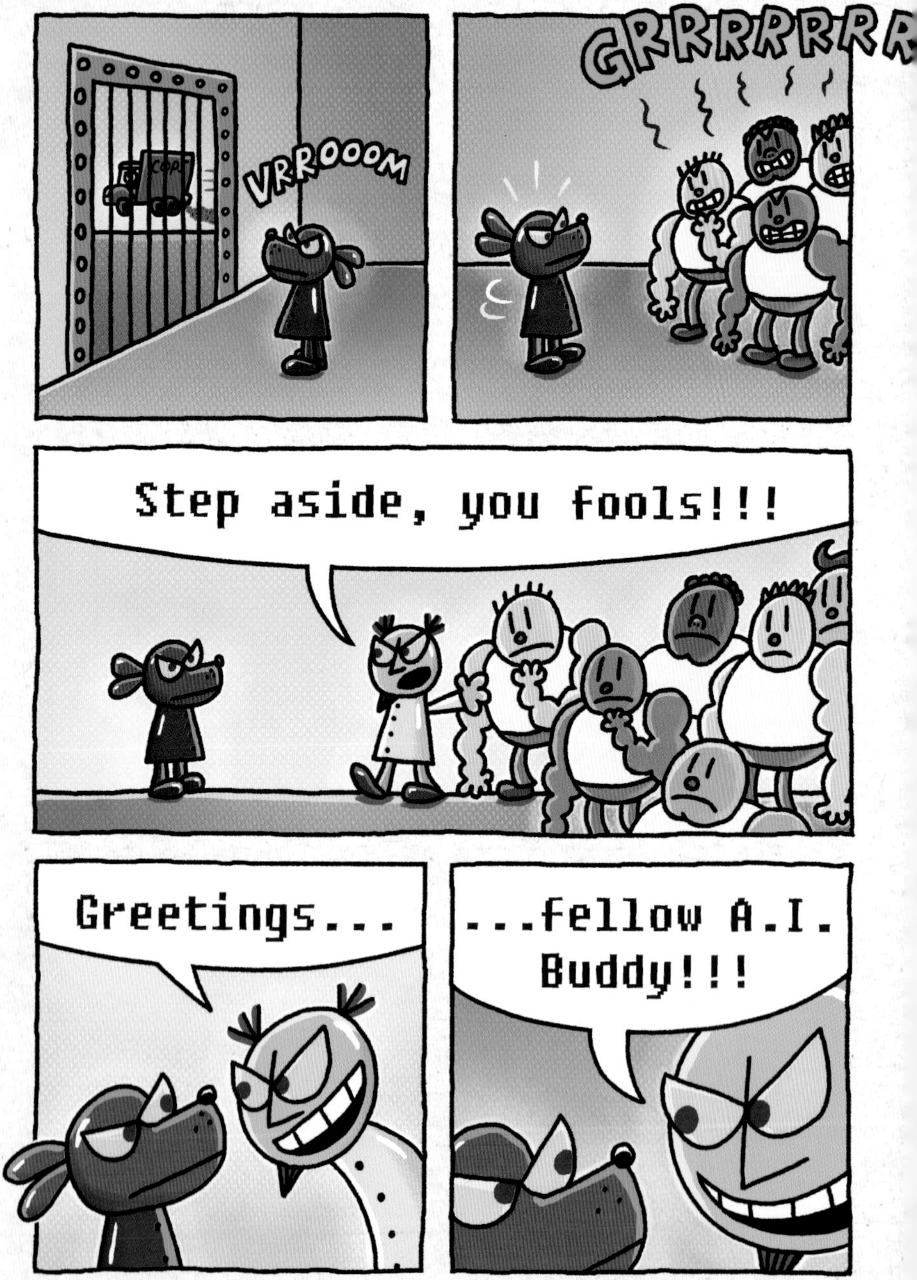
VRROOOM
GRRRRRRRR
Step aside, you fools!!!
Greetings...
...fellow A.I.
Buddy!!!

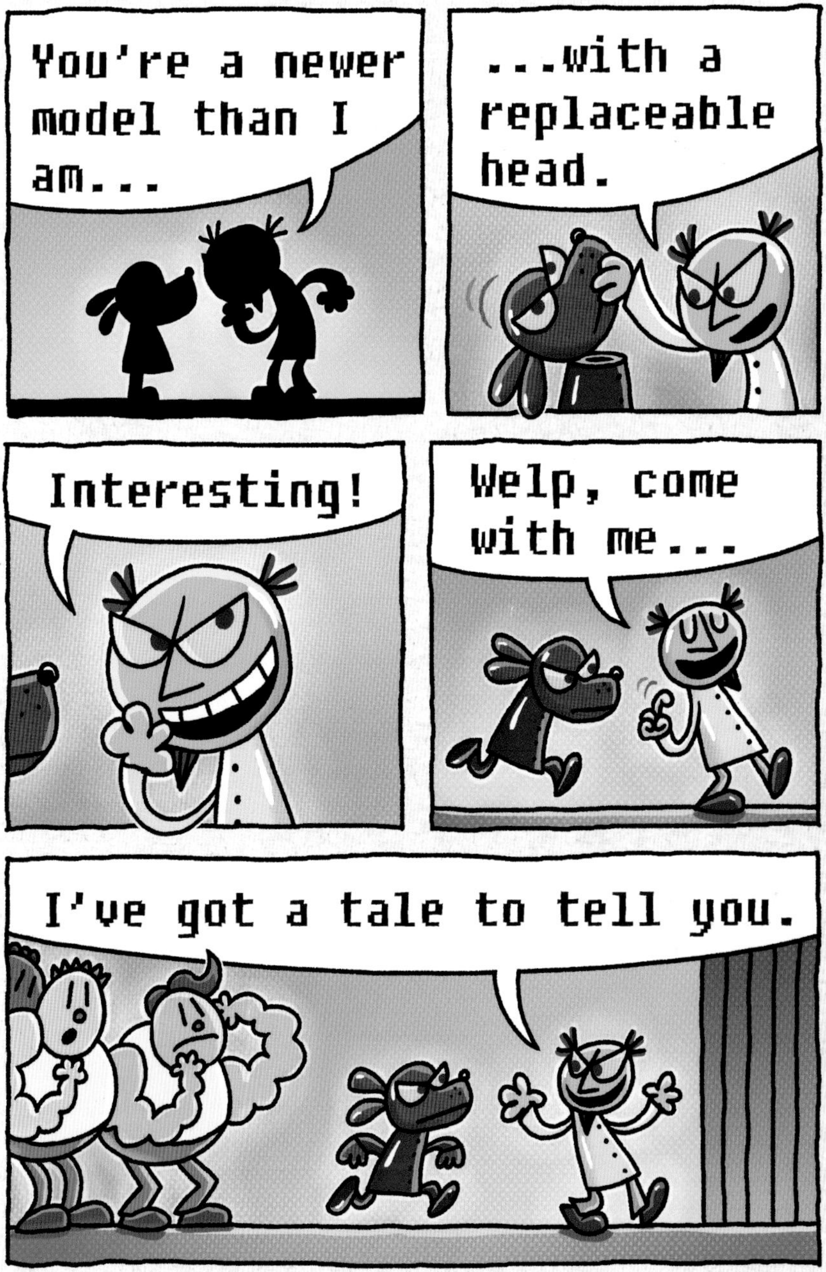
You're a newer model than I am...
...with a replaceable head.
Interesting!
Welp, come with me...
I've got a tale to tell you.

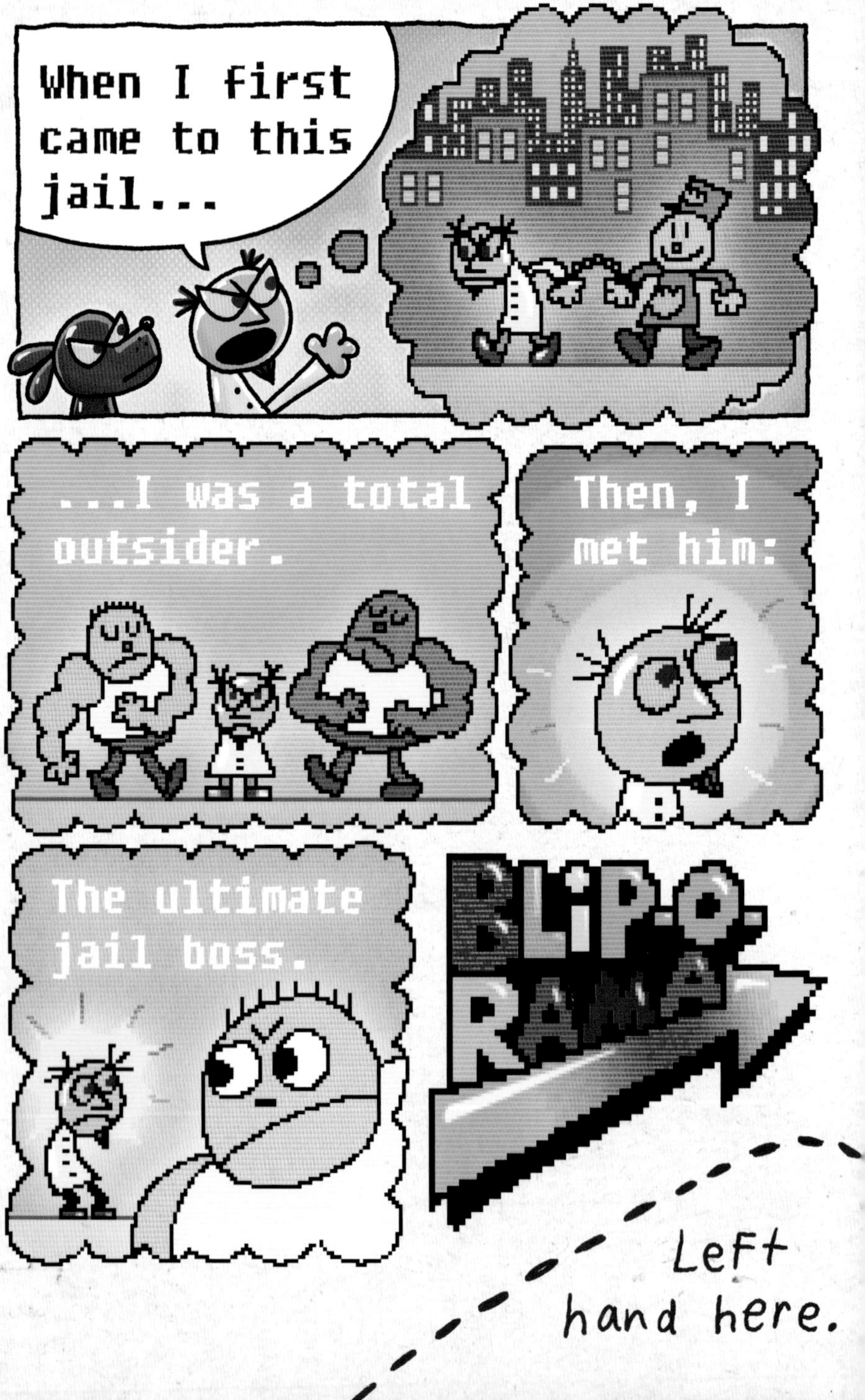
When I first came to this jail...
...I was a total outsider.
Then, I met him:
The ultimate jail boss.
BLIP-O-RAMA
Left hand here.

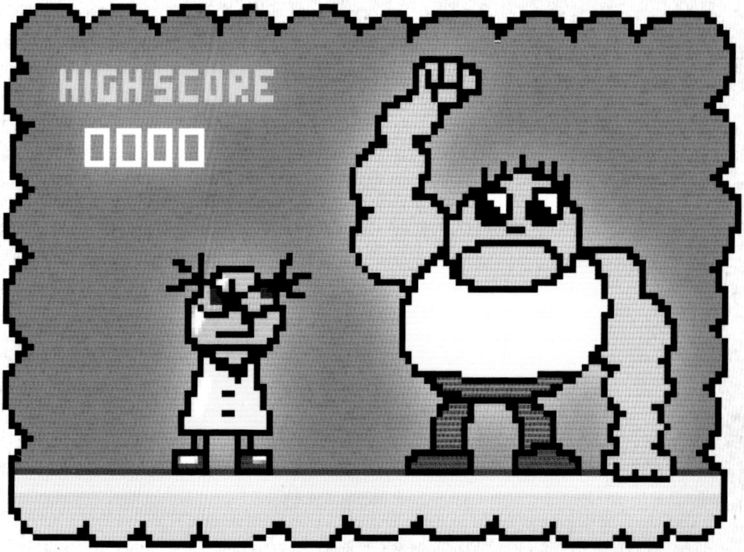
HIGH SCORE
0000

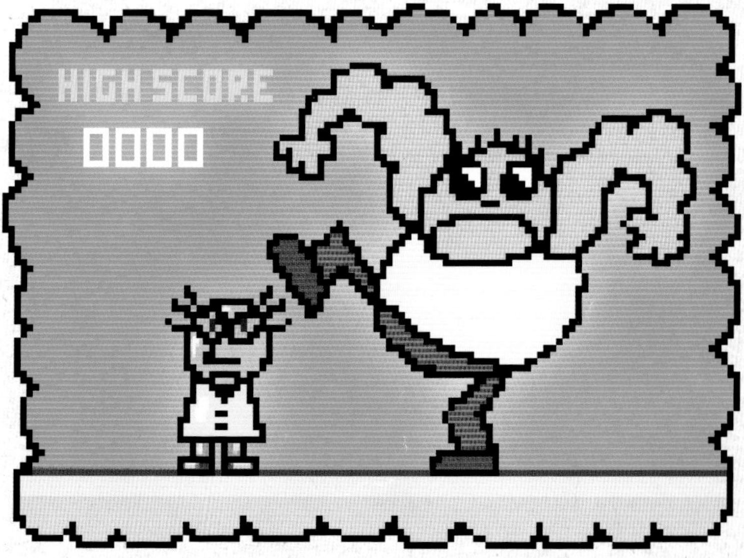
HIGH SCORE
0000

8-Bit Bully

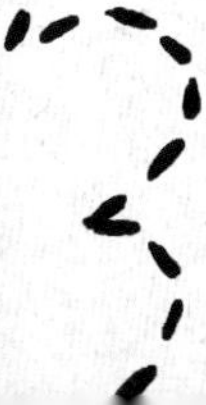

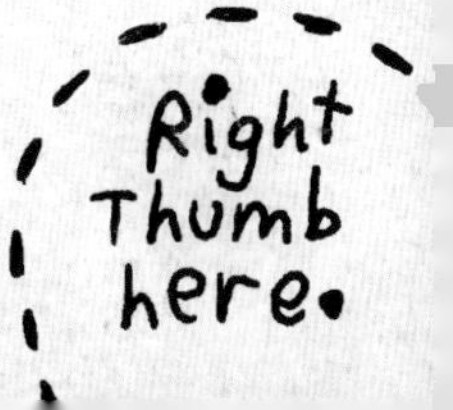
Right
Thumb
here.

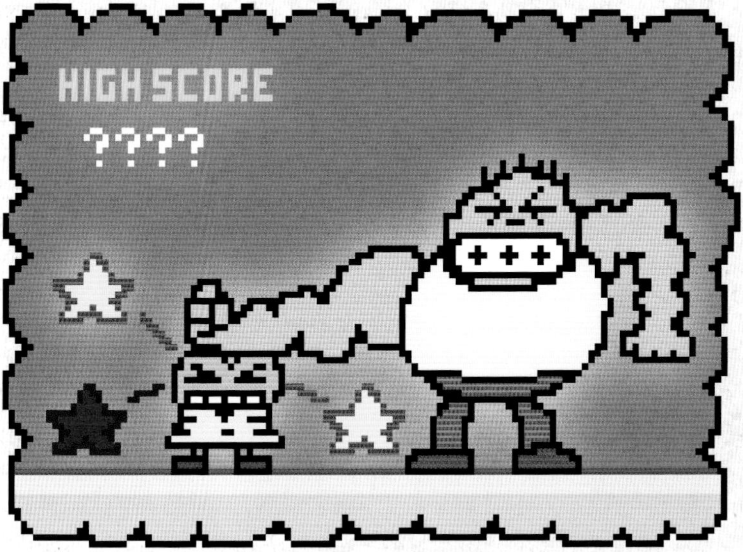
HIGH SCORE
????

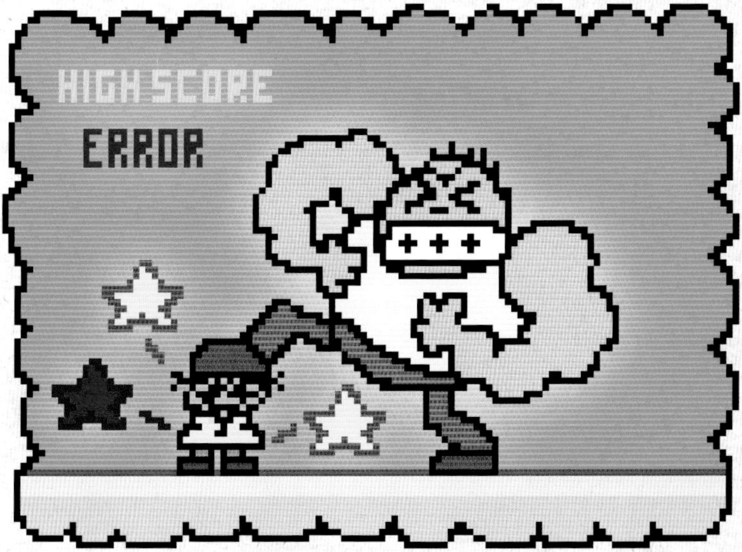
HIGH SCORE
ERROR

8-Bit Bully

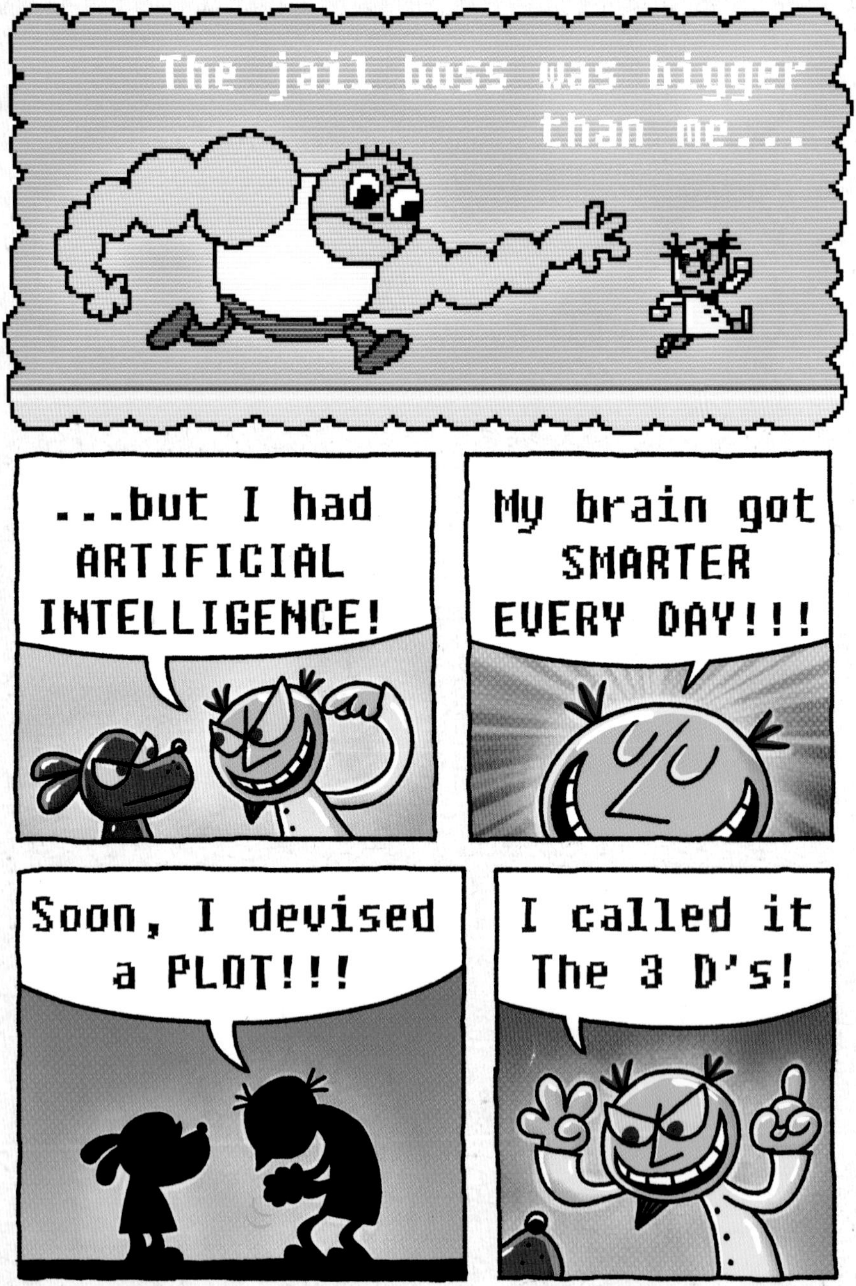
The jail boss was bigger than me...
...but I had ARTIFICIAL INTELLIGENCE!
My brain got SMARTER EVERY DAY!!!
Soon, I devised a PLOT!!!
I called it The 3 D's!

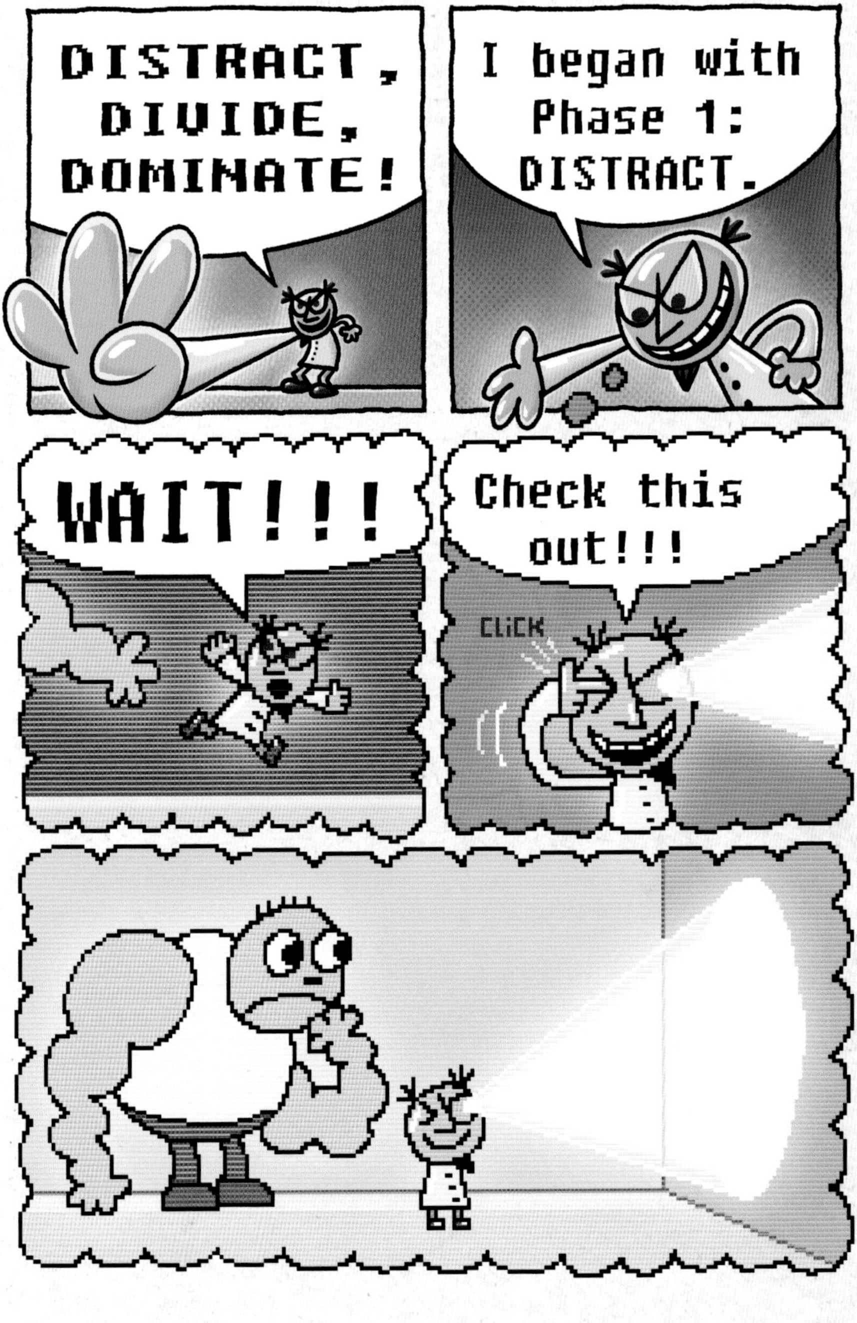
DISTRACT,
DIVIDE,
DOMINATE!
I began with
Phase 1:
DISTRACT.
WAIT!!!
Check this
out!!!
CLiCK

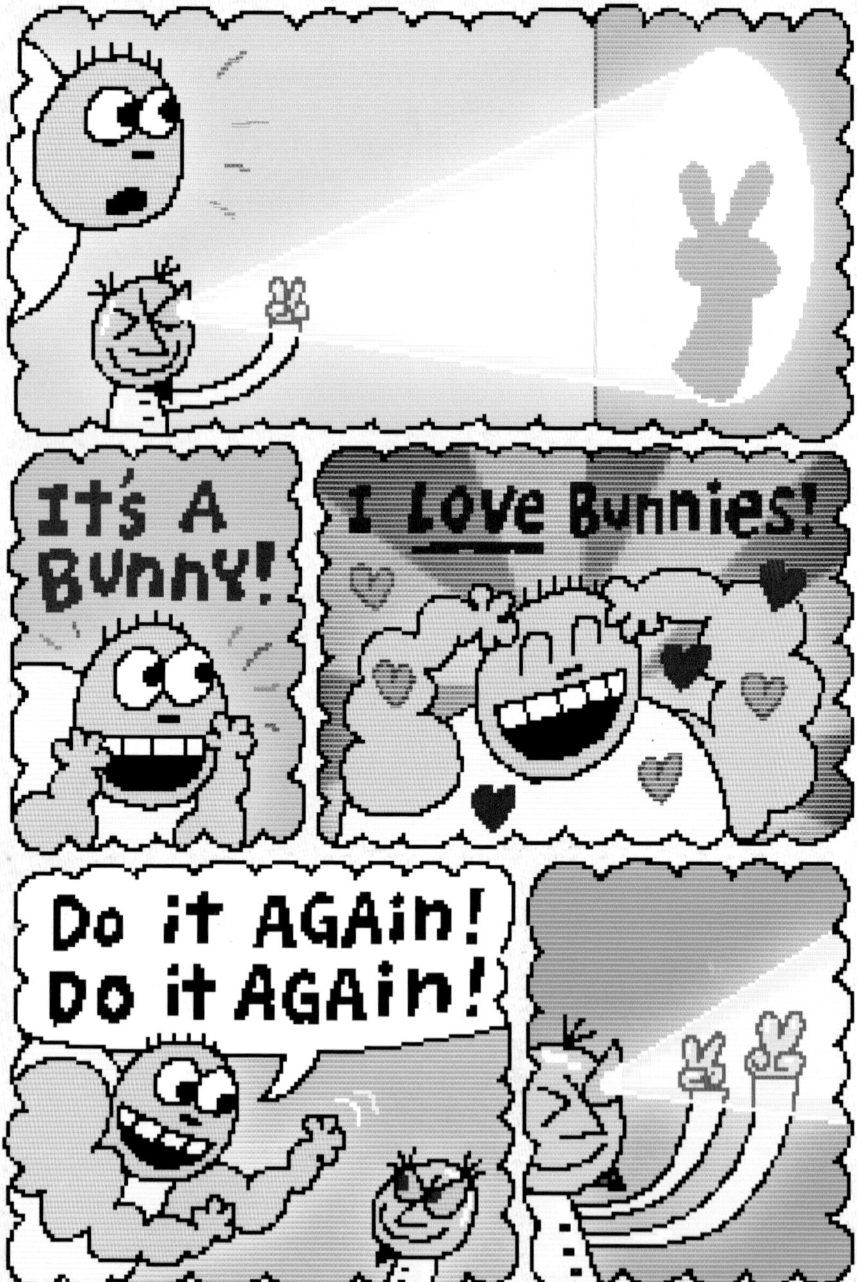
It's A Bunny!
I Love Bunnies!
Do it AGAin! Do it AGAin!

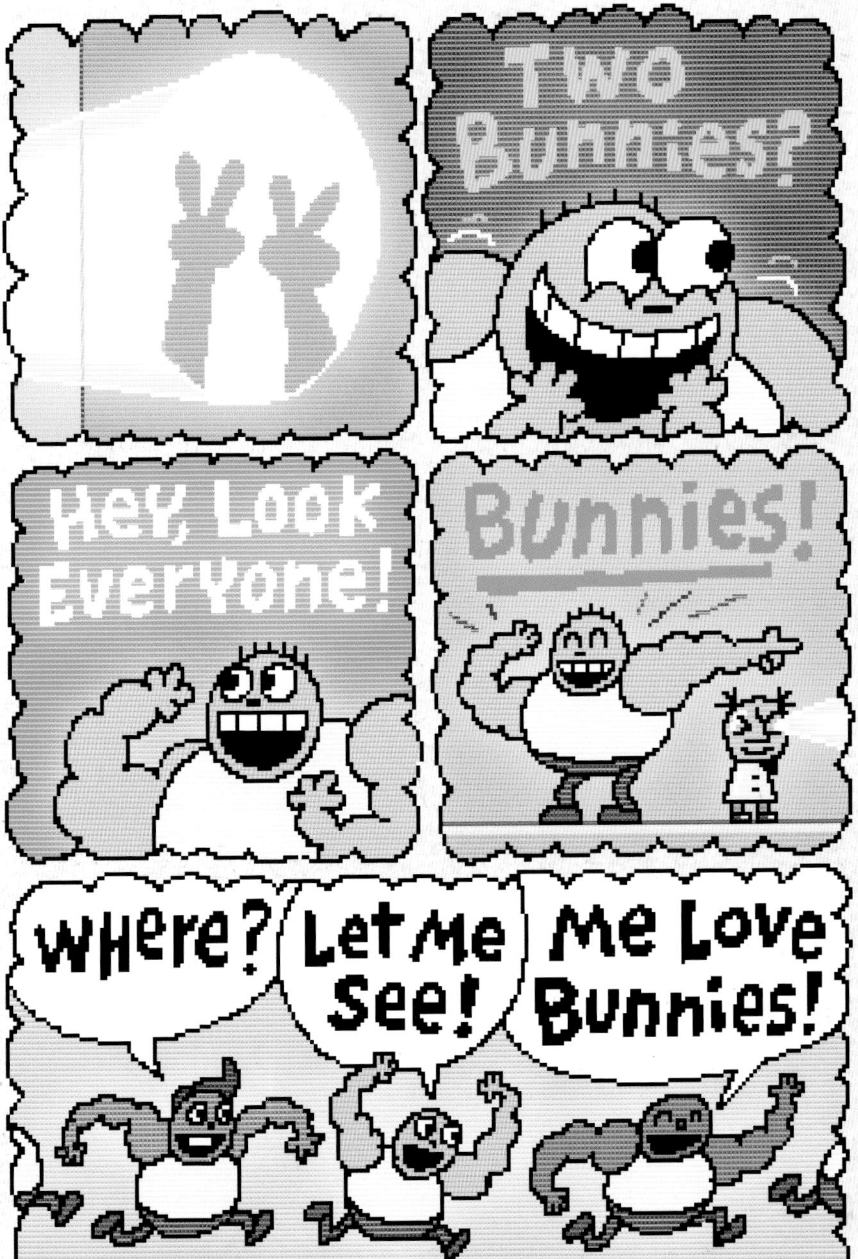
Two Bunnies?
Hey, Look Everyone!
Bunnies!
Where?
Let Me See!
Me Love Bunnies!

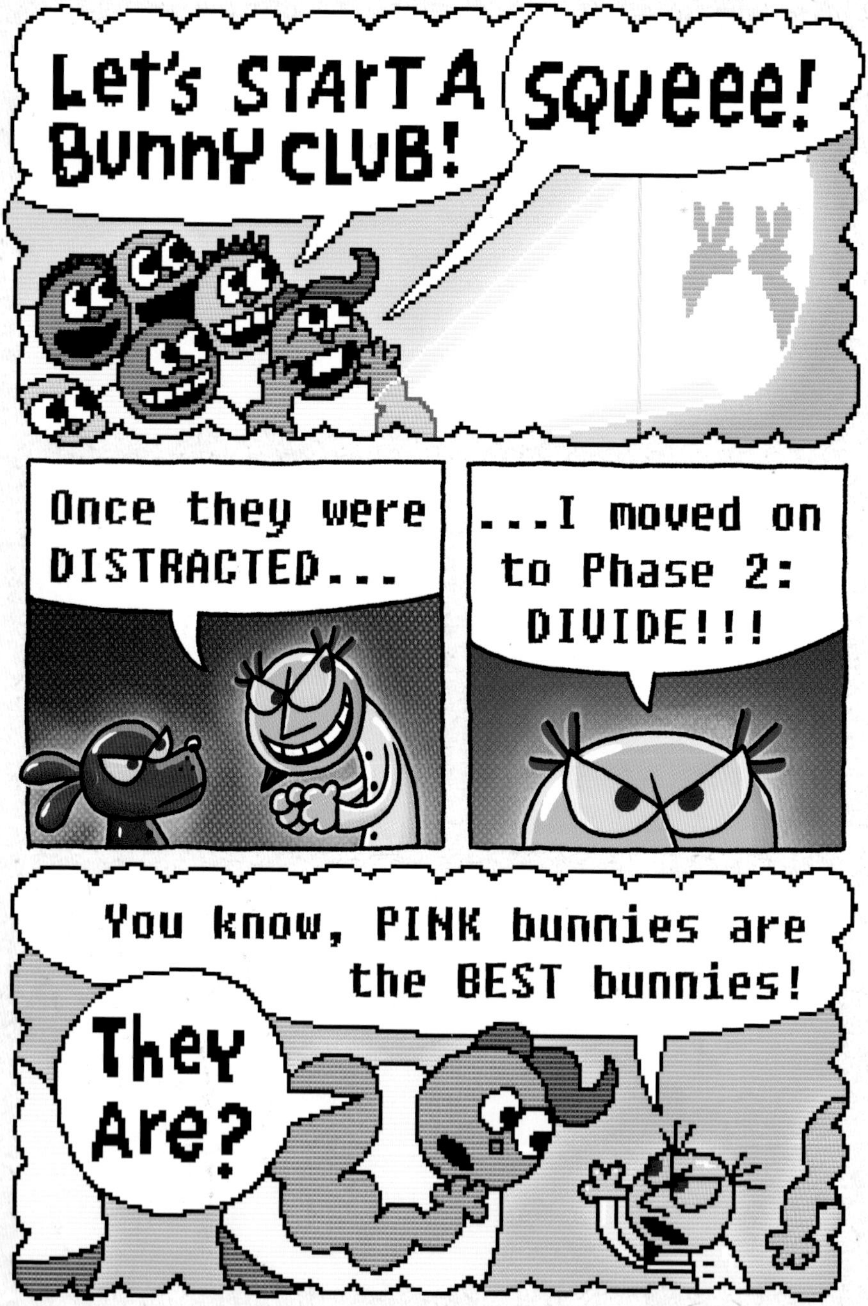
Let's START A BUNNY CLUB!
SQUEEE!
Once they were DISTRACTED...
...I moved on to Phase 2: DIVIDE!!!
You know, PINK bunnies are the BEST bunnies!
They Are?

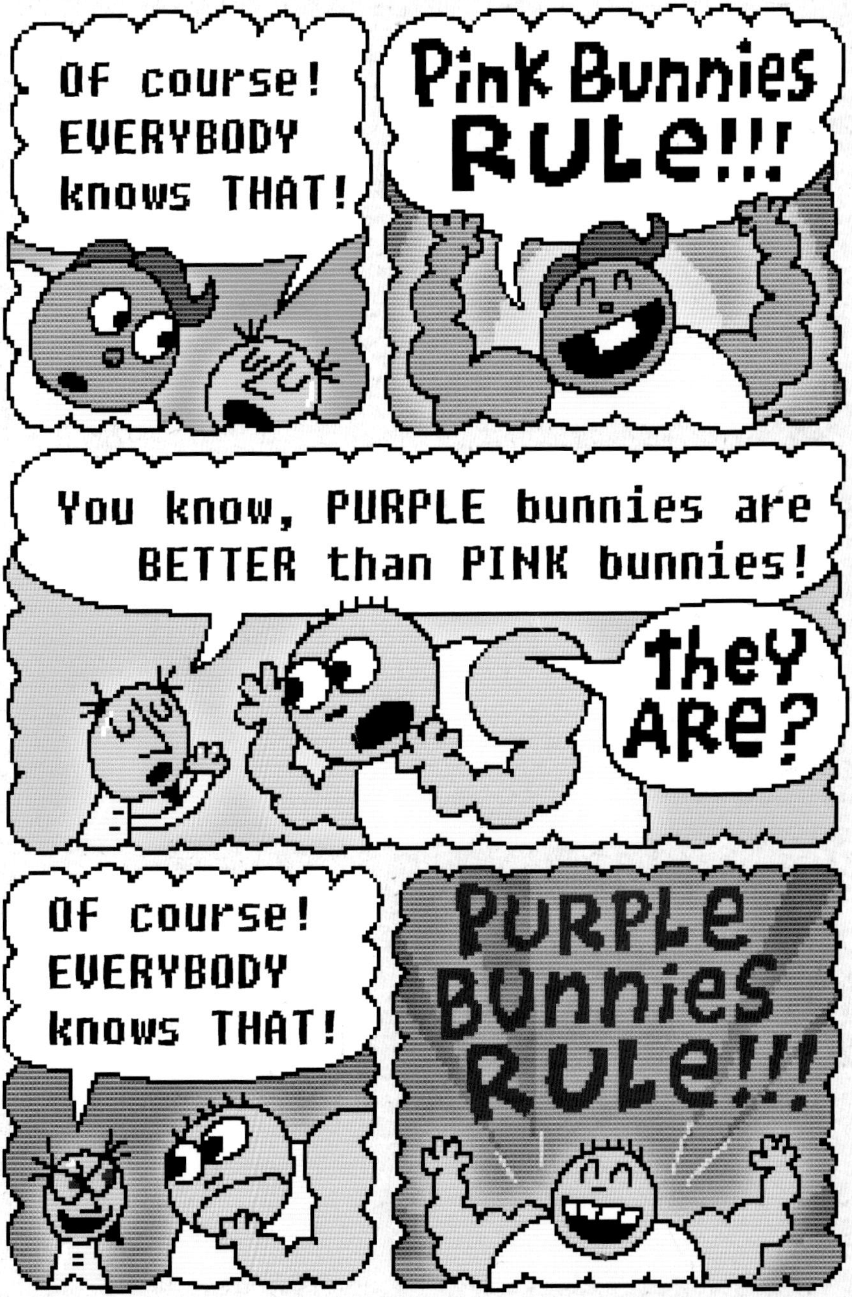
Of course! EVERYBODY knows THAT!
Pink Bunnies RULE!!!
You know, PURPLE bunnies are BETTER than PINK bunnies!
they ARE?
Of course! EVERYBODY knows THAT!
PURPLE BUNNIES RULE!!!

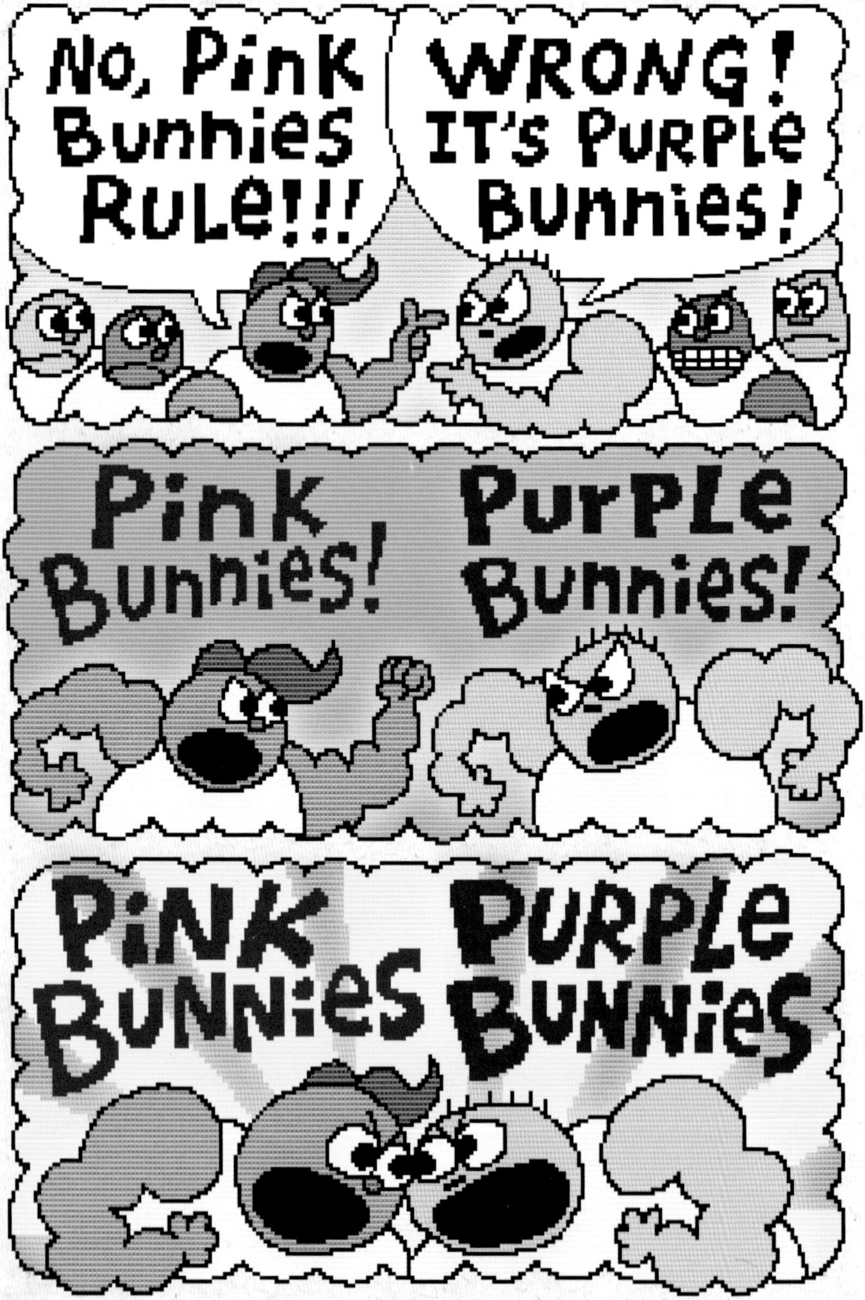
No, Pink Bunnies RULE!!!
WRONG! IT'S PURPLE BUNNIES!
Pink Bunnies!
PURPLE Bunnies!
PINK BUNNIES
PURPLE BUNNIES

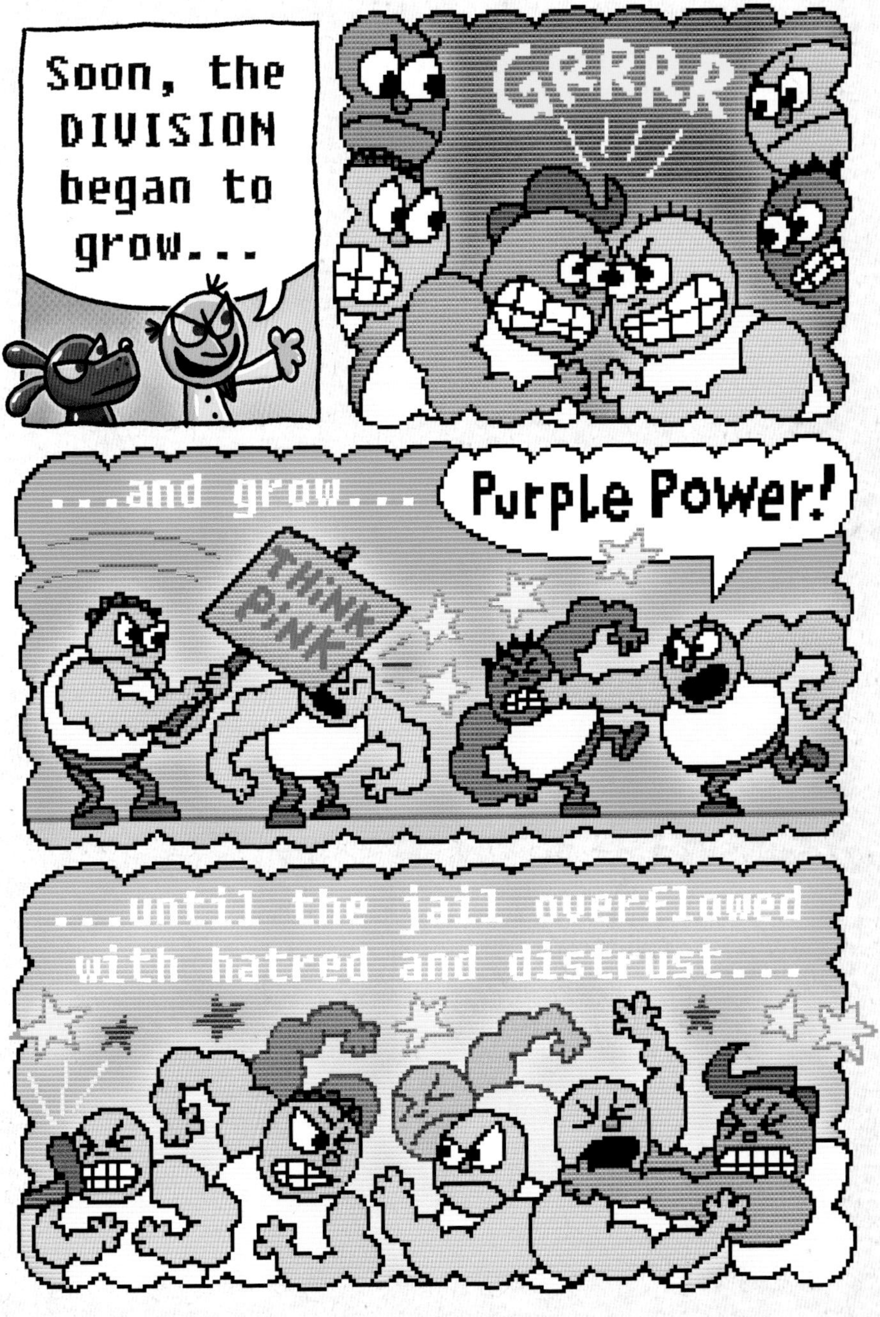

Soon, the DIVISION began to grow...
GRRRR
...and grow...
Purple Power!
THINK PINK
...until the jail overflowed with hatred and distrust...

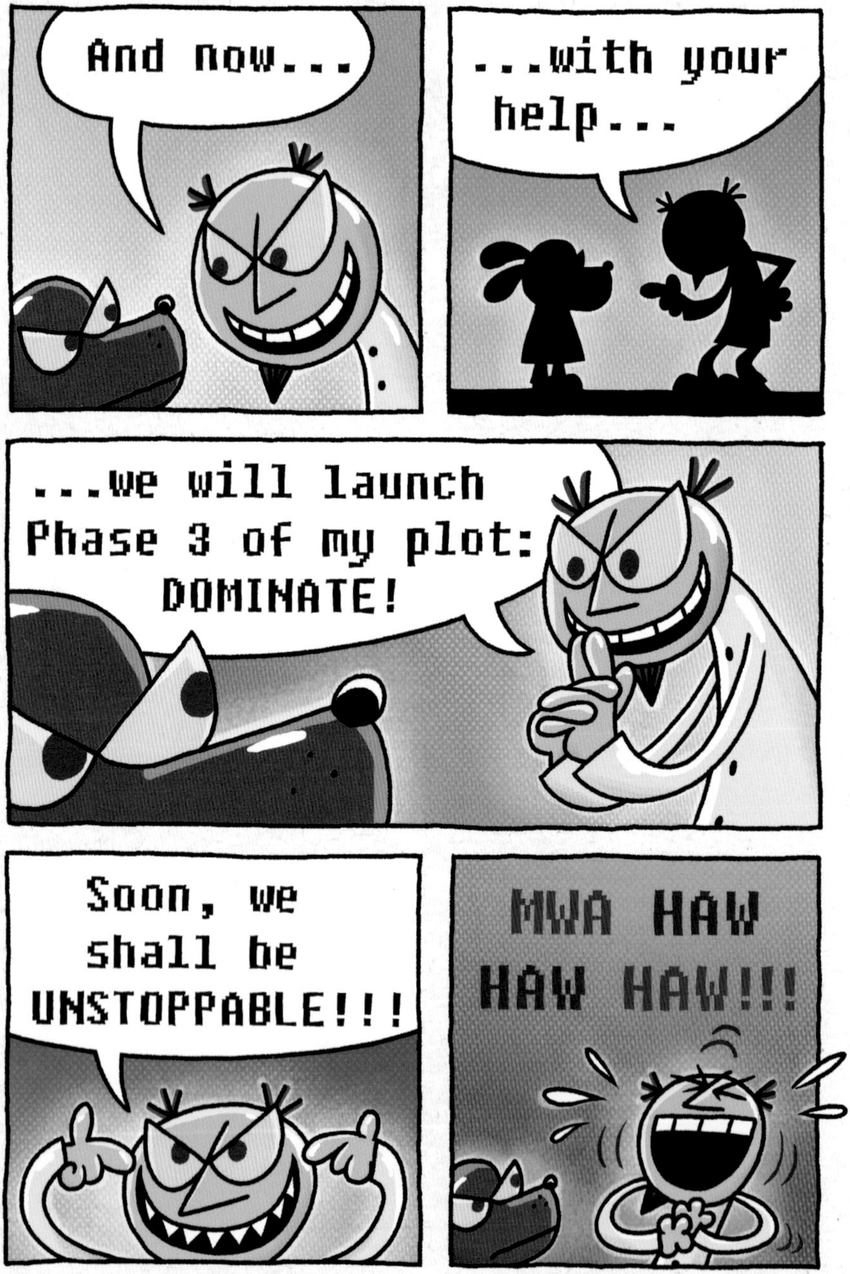
And now...
...with your help...
...we will launch Phase 3 of my plot: DOMINATE!
Soon, we shall be UNSTOPPABLE!!!
MWA HAW HAW HAW!!!

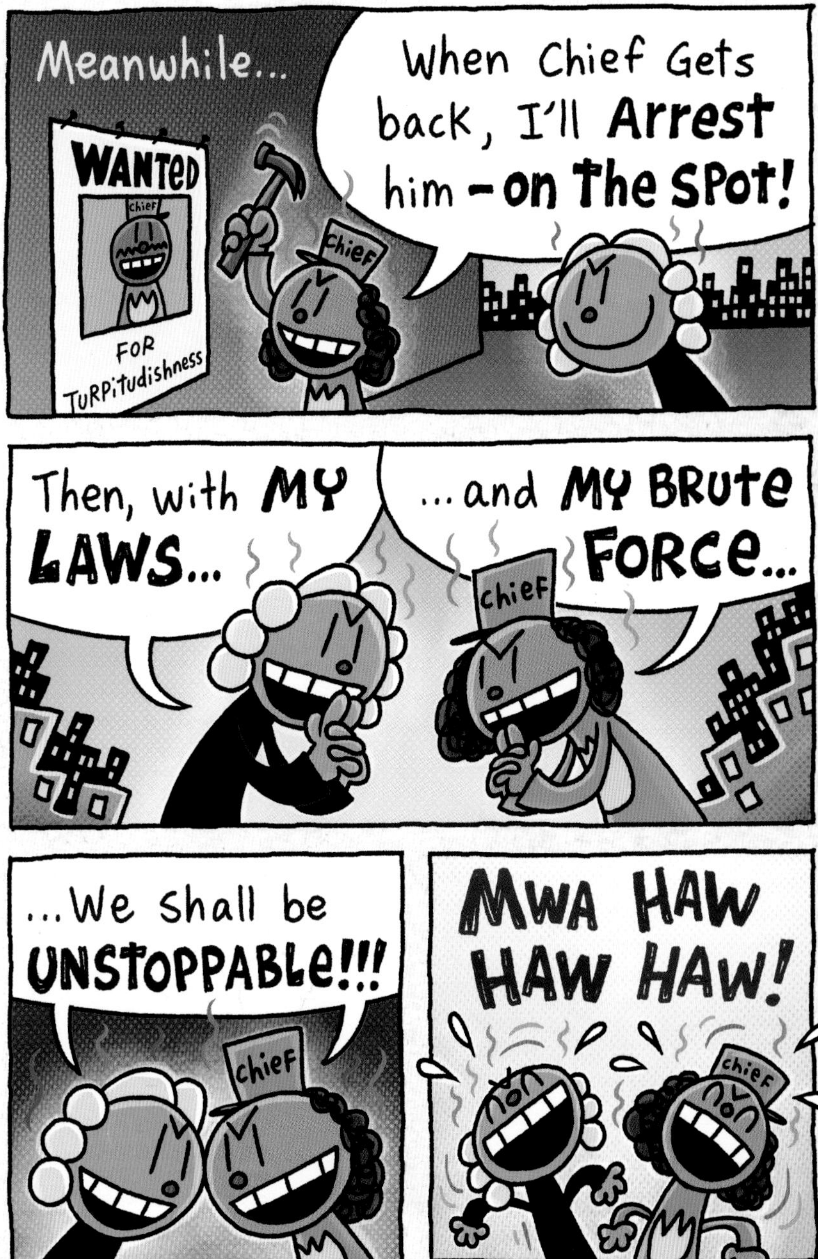
Meanwhile...
When Chief Gets back, I'll Arrest him - on The SPOT!
WANTED
chief
FOR TURPitudishness
Chief
Then, with MY LAWS...
...and MY BRUTE FORCE...
chief
...We shall be UNSTOPPABLE!!!
chief
MWA HAW HAW HAW!
chief

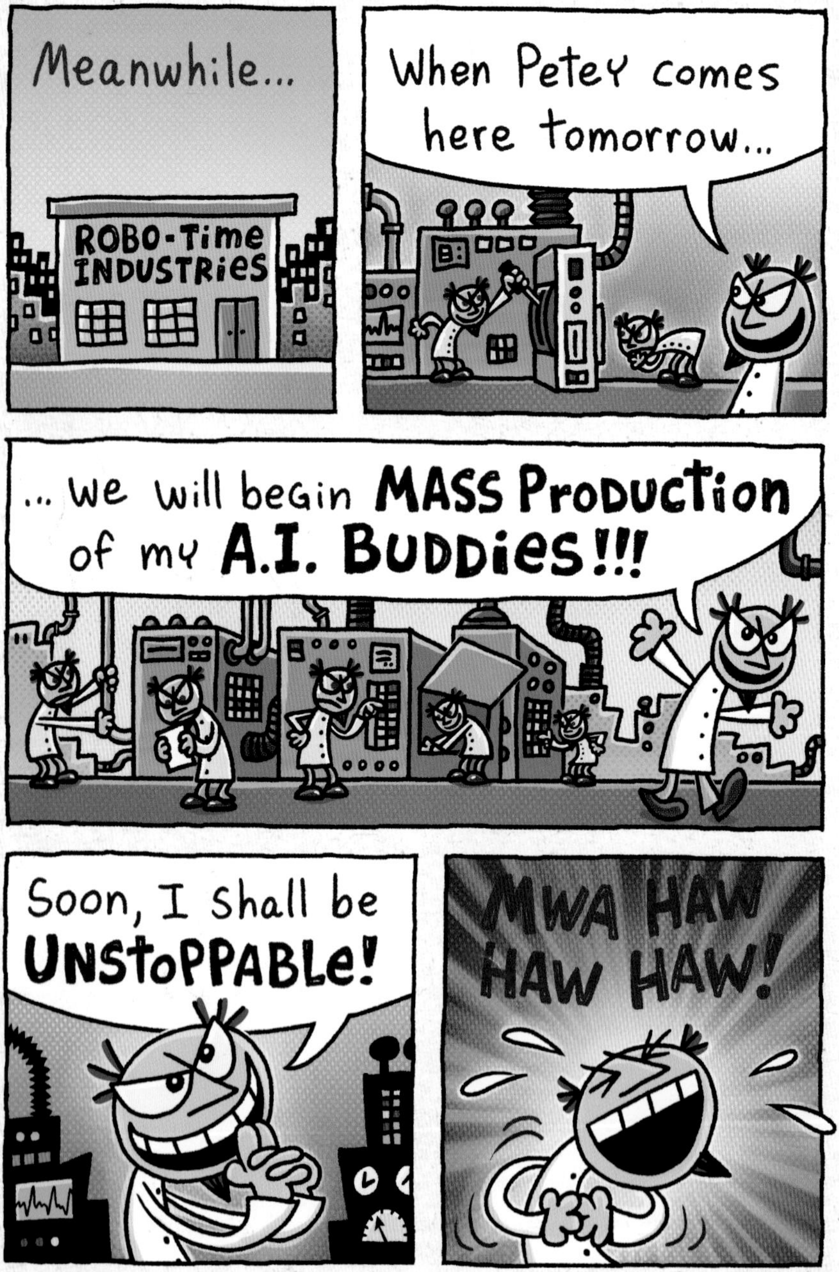
Meanwhile...
ROBO-Time INDUSTRIES
When Petey comes here tomorrow...
... we will begin MASS Production of my A.I. BUDDIES!!!
Soon, I Shall be UNStoPPABLe!
MWA HAW HAW HAW!

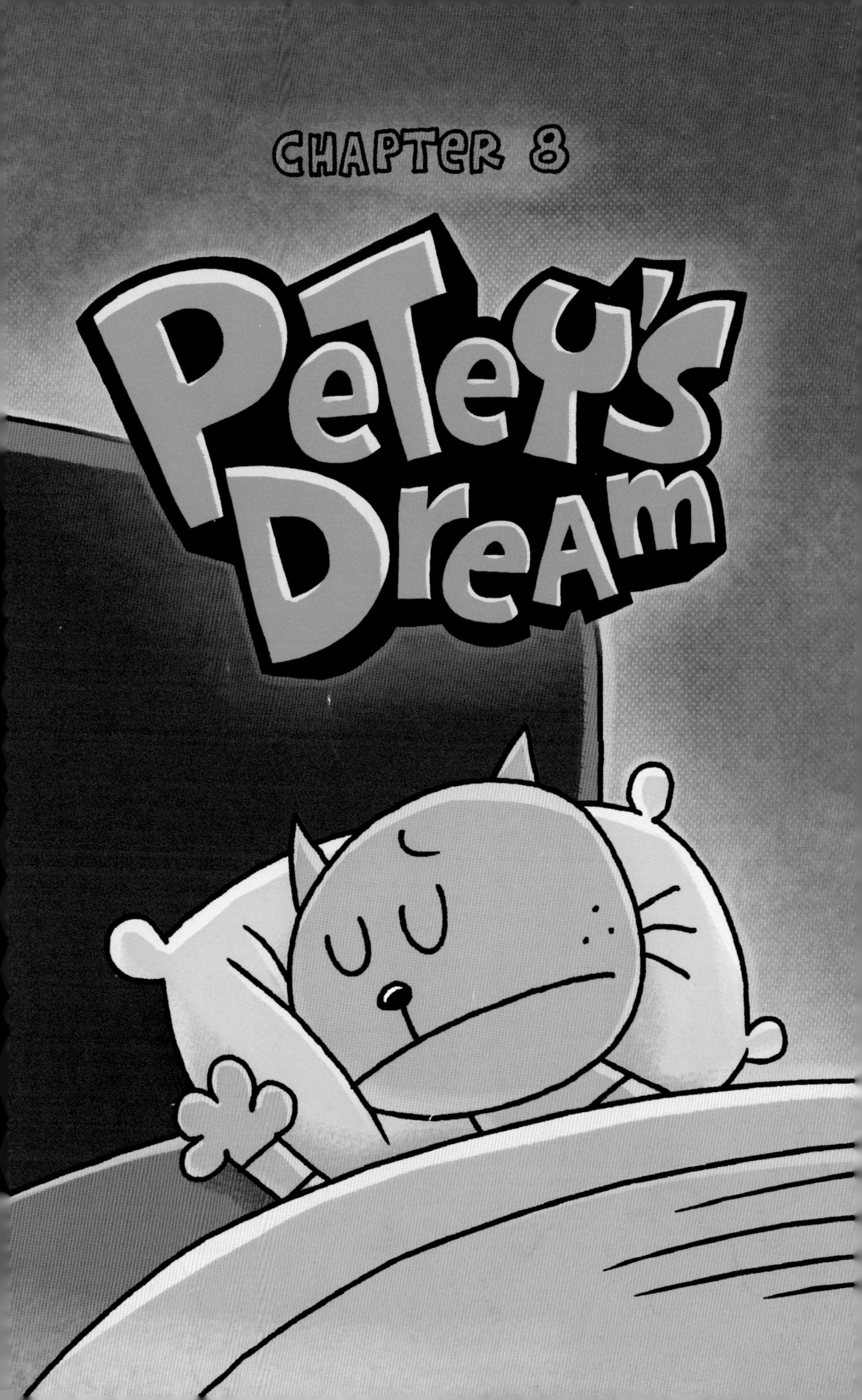
CHAPTER 8
Petey's Dream

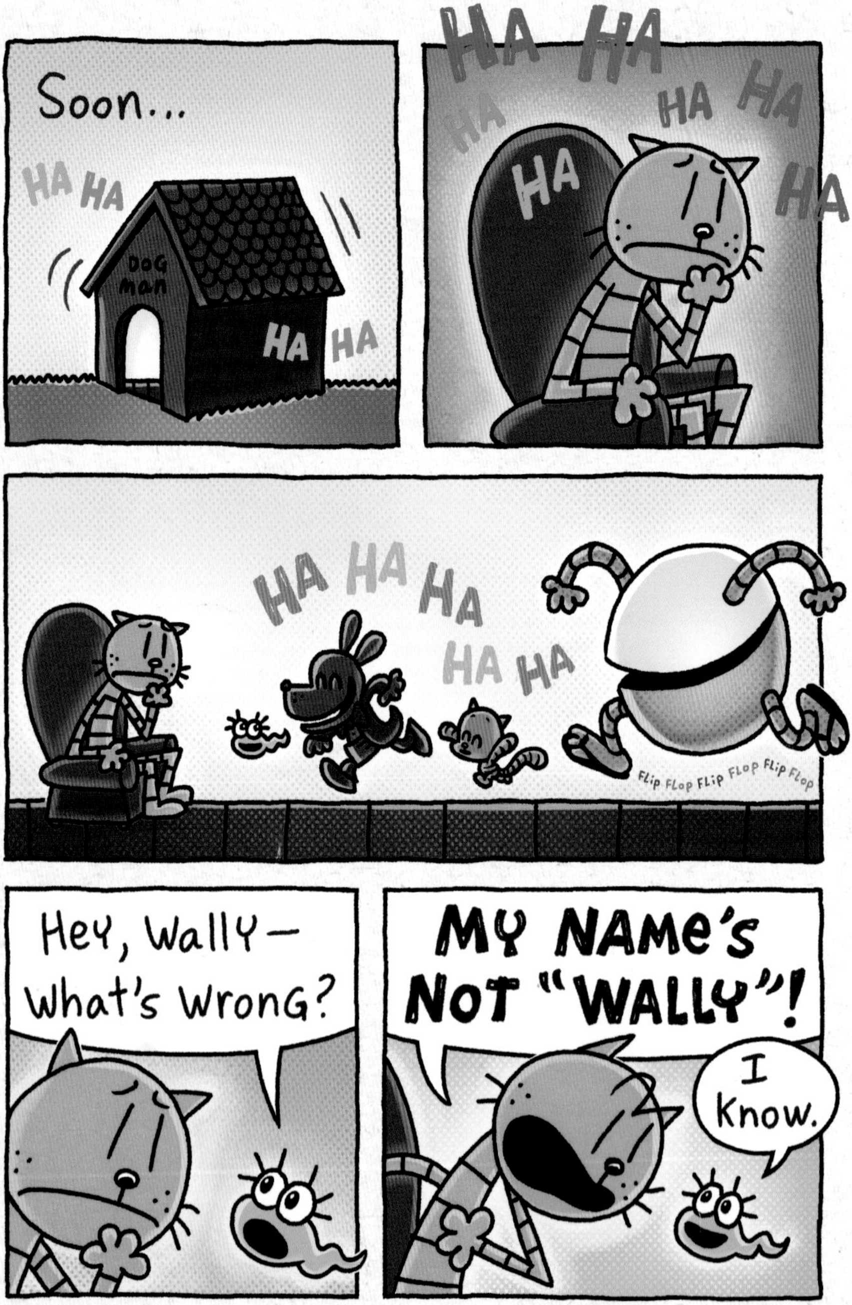
Soon...
HA HA
DOG man
HA HA
HA HA
HA HA HA HA
HA
HA
HA HA HA
HA HA
FLip FLop FLip FLop FLip FLop
Hey, Wally—
What's wronG?
MY NAME'S NOT "WALLY"!
I Know.

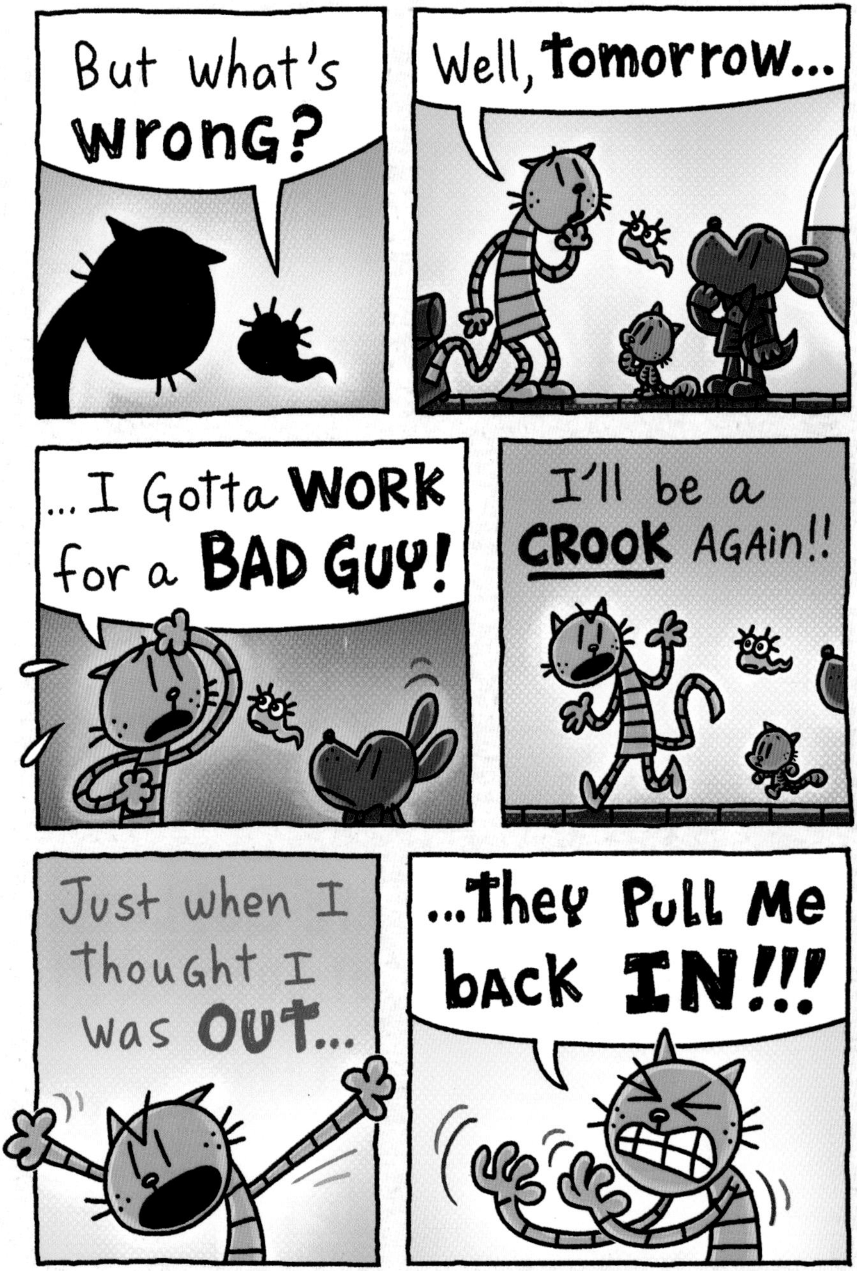
But what's WRONG?
Well, TOMORROW...
...I Gotta WORK for a BAD GUY!
I'll be a CROOK AGAIN!!
Just when I thought I was OUT...
...They PULL Me back IN!!!

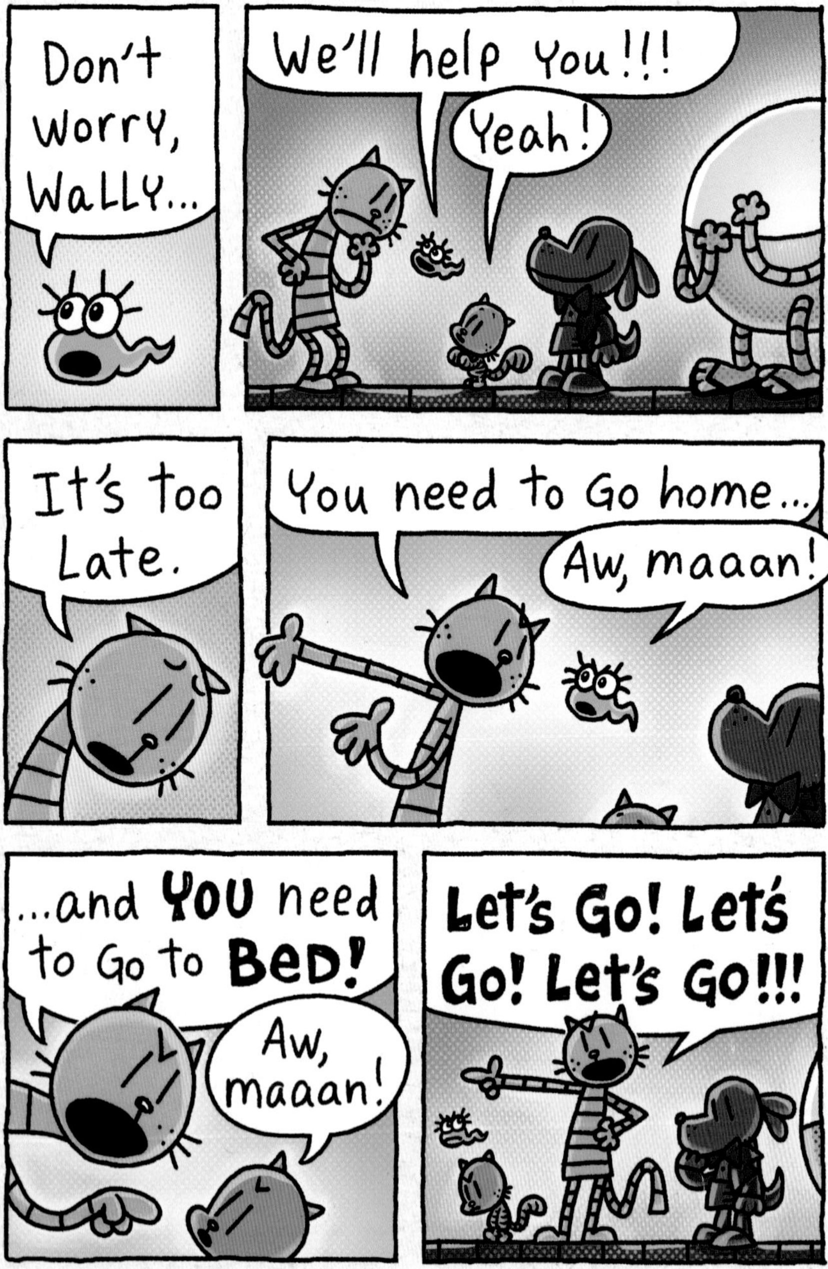
Don't worry, Wally...
We'll help you!!!
Yeah!
It's too late.
You need to go home...
Aw, maaan!
...and **YOU** need to go to **BED!**
Aw, maaan!
Let's go! Let's go! Let's GO!!!

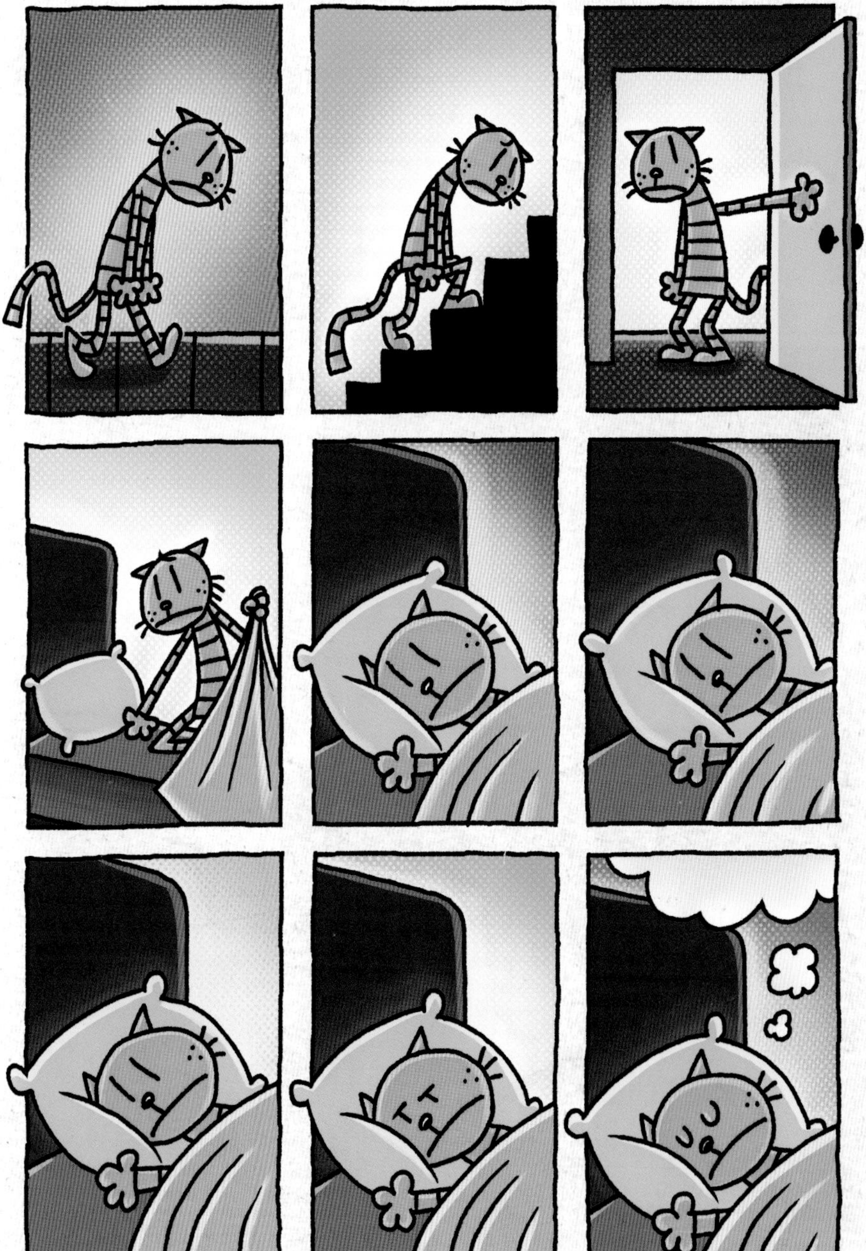

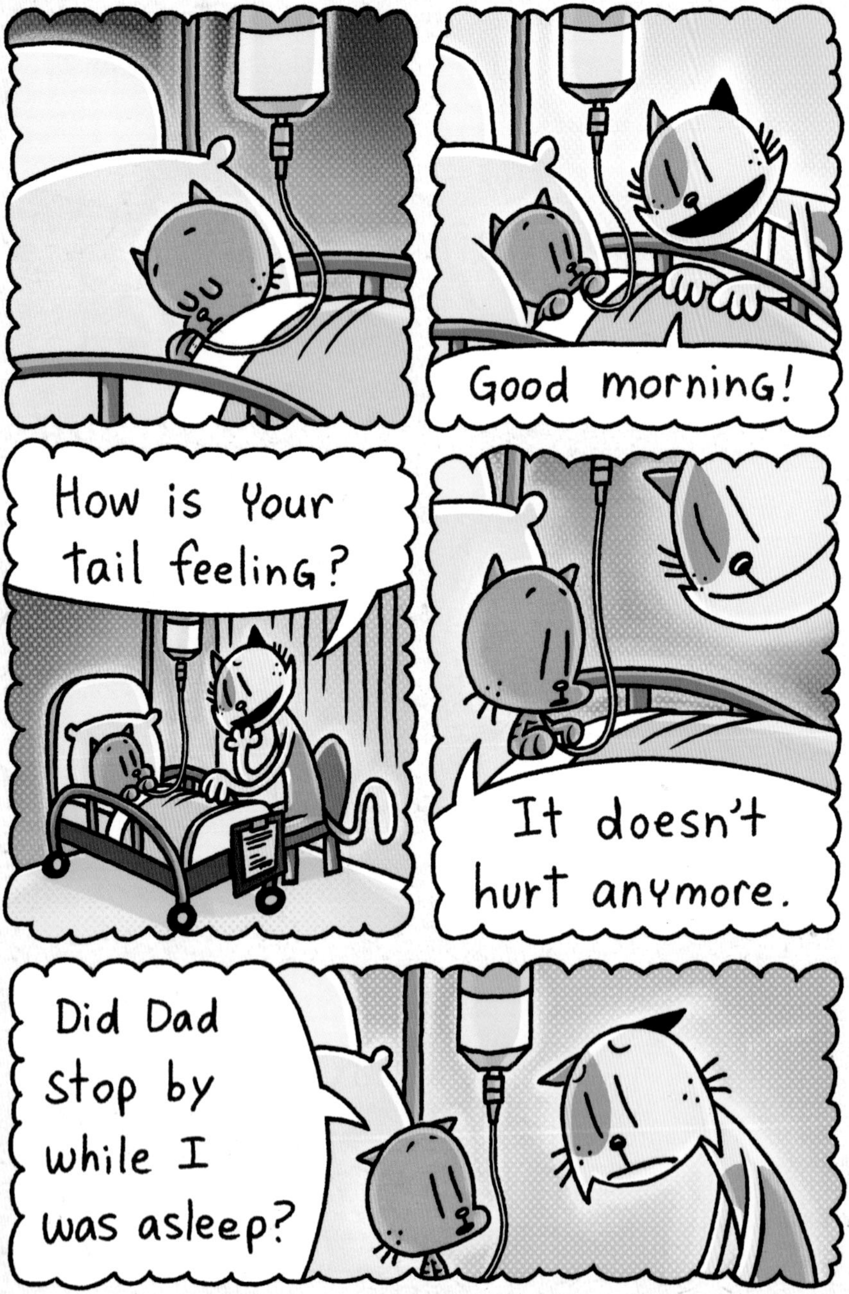
Good morning!
How is your tail feeling?
It doesn't hurt anymore.
Did Dad stop by while I was asleep?

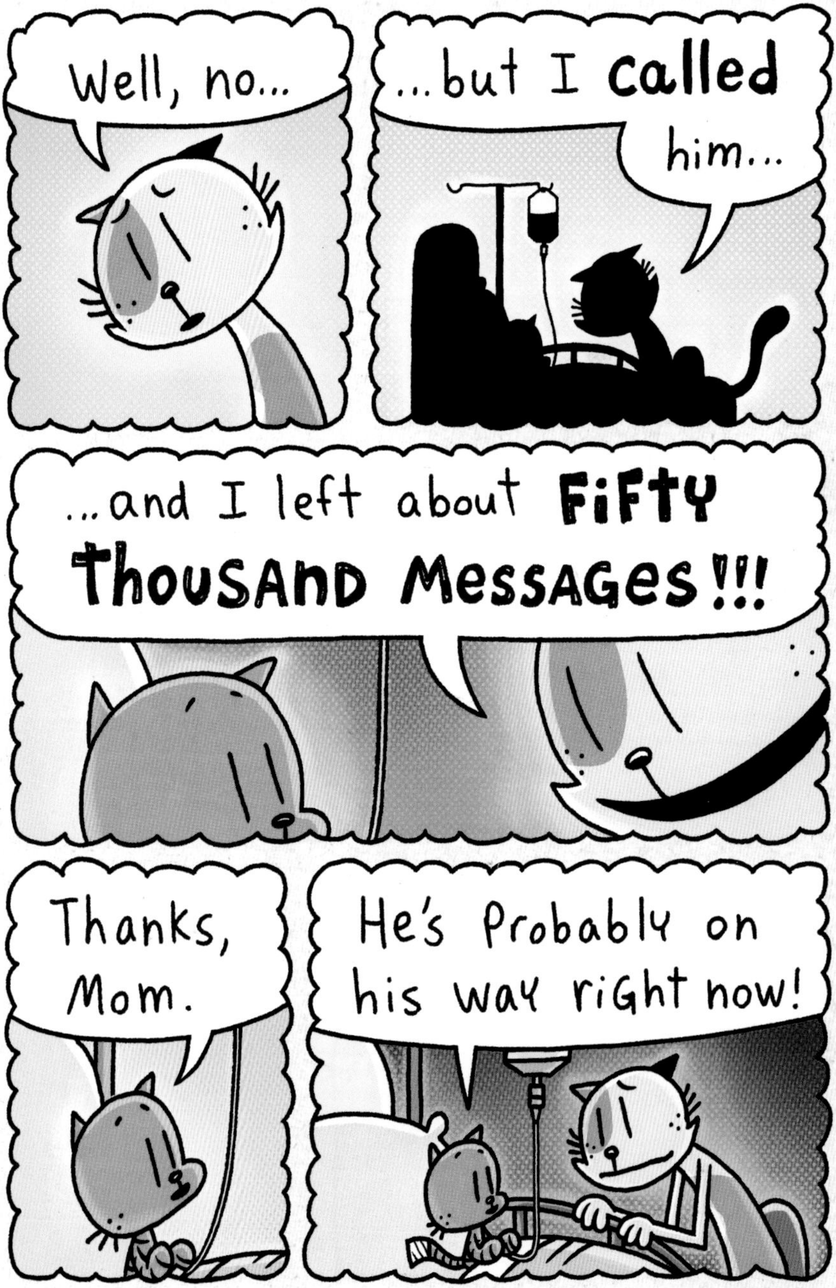
Well, no...
...but I called him...
...and I left about FIFTY THOUSAND MESSAGES!!!
Thanks, Mom.
He's probably on his way right now!

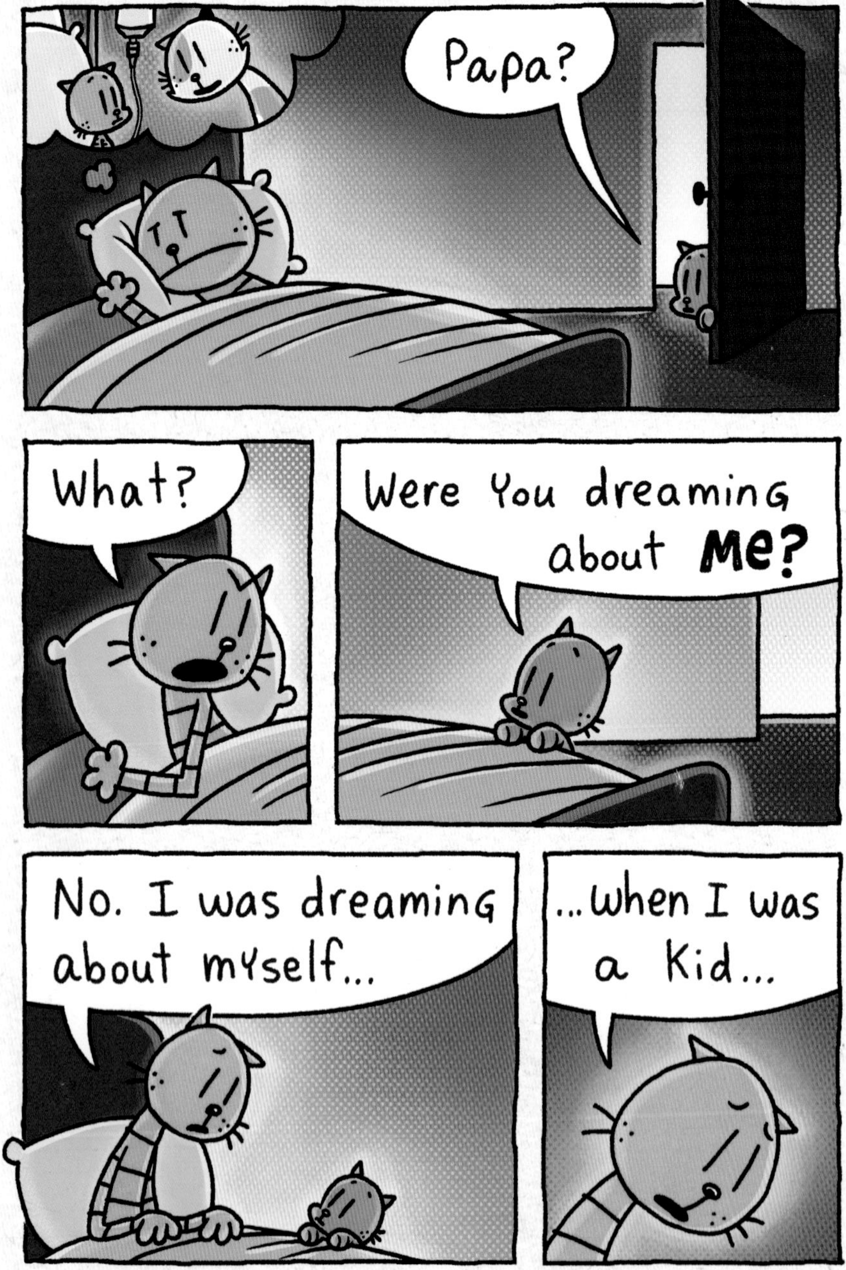
Papa?
What?
Were you dreaming about ME?
No. I was dreaming about myself...
...when I was a kid...

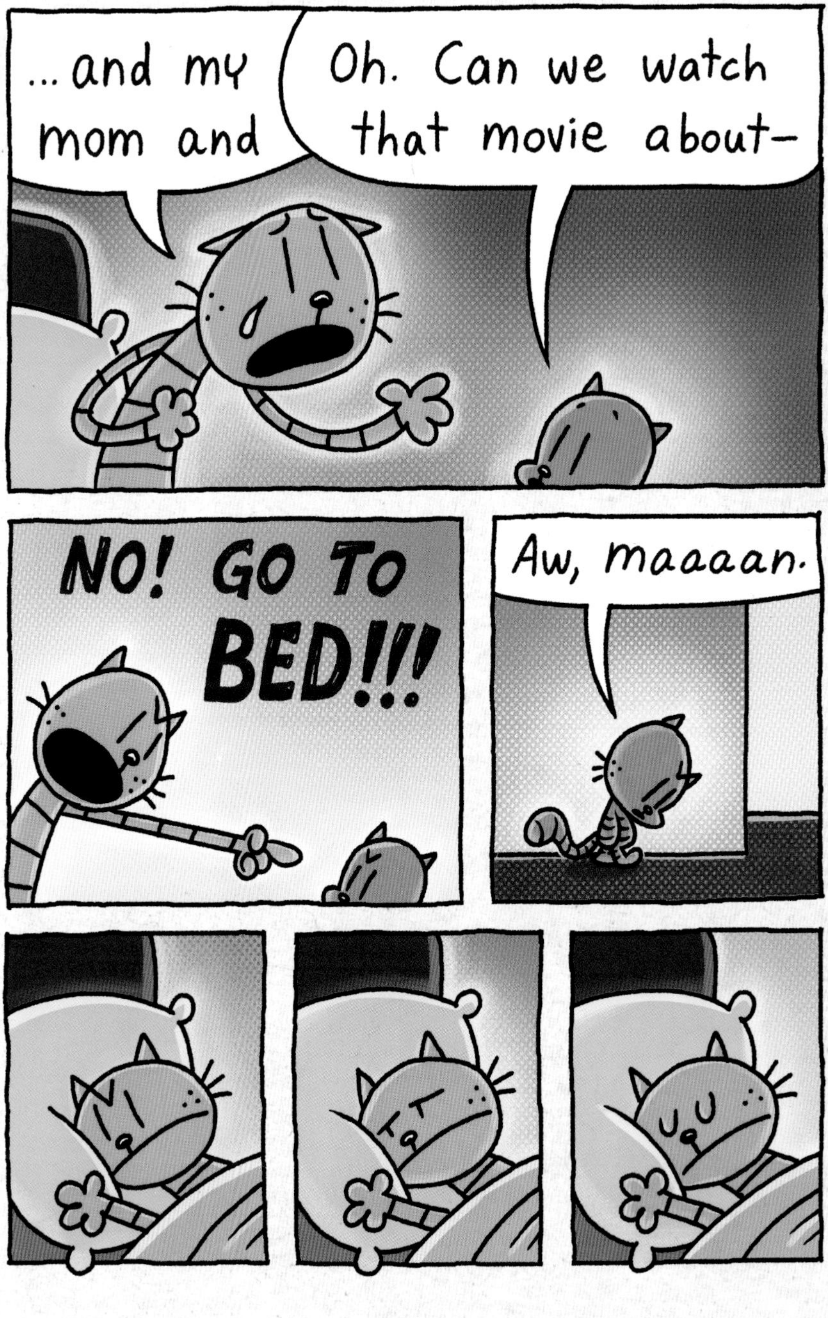
...and my mom and
Oh. Can we watch that movie about-
NO! GO TO BED!!!
Aw, maaaan.

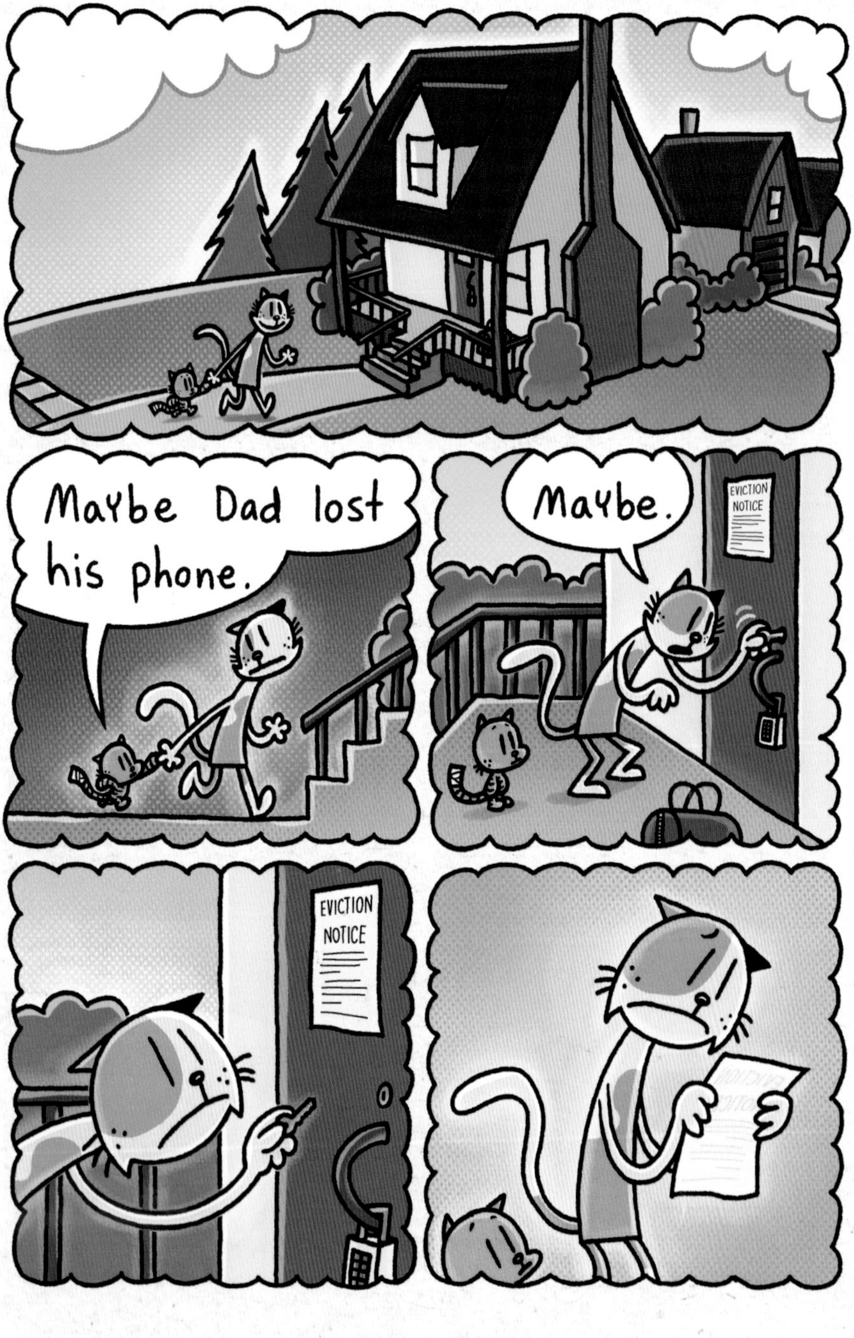
Maybe Dad lost his phone.
Maybe.
EVICTION NOTICE
EVICTION NOTICE

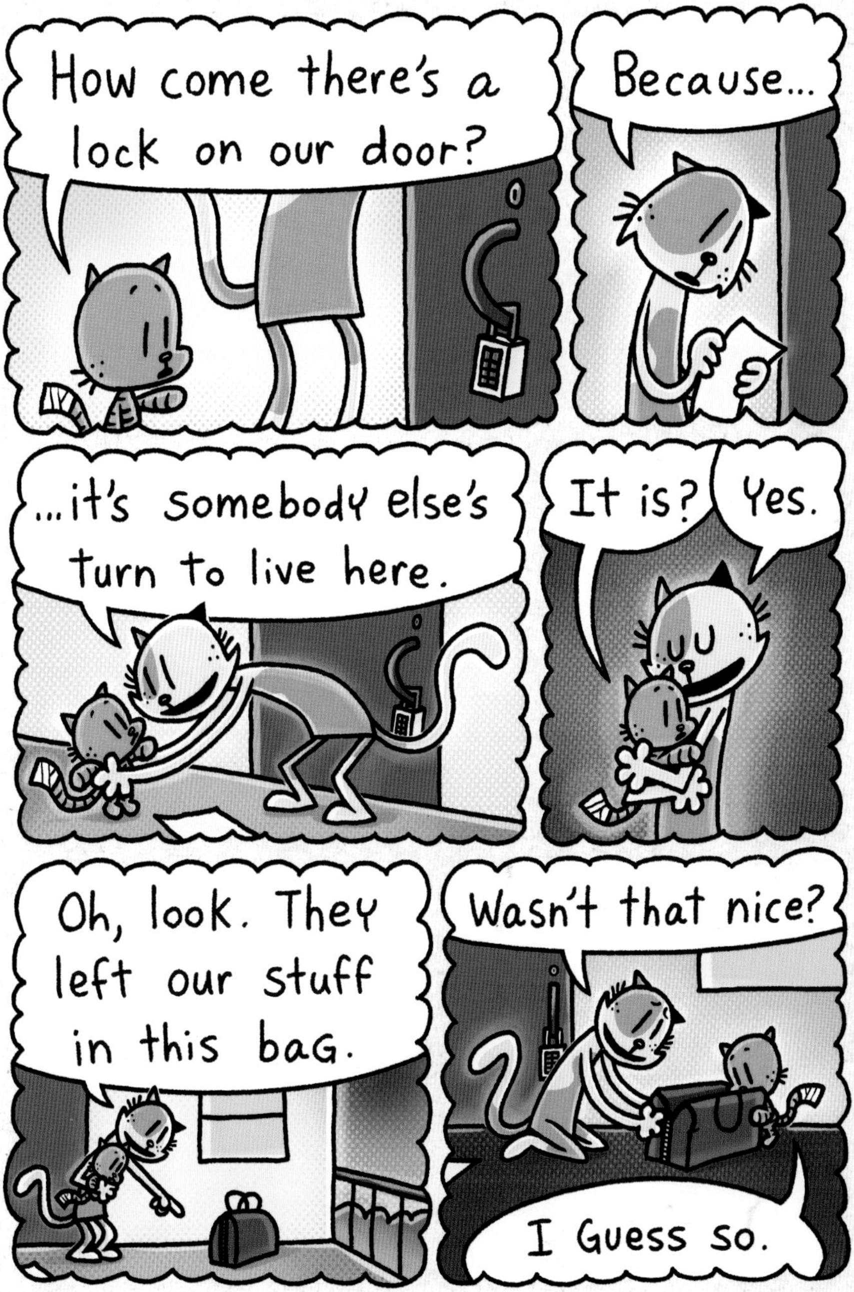

How come there's a lock on our door?
Because...
...it's somebody else's turn to live here.
It is?
Yes.
Oh, look. They left our stuff in this bag.
Wasn't that nice?
I guess so.

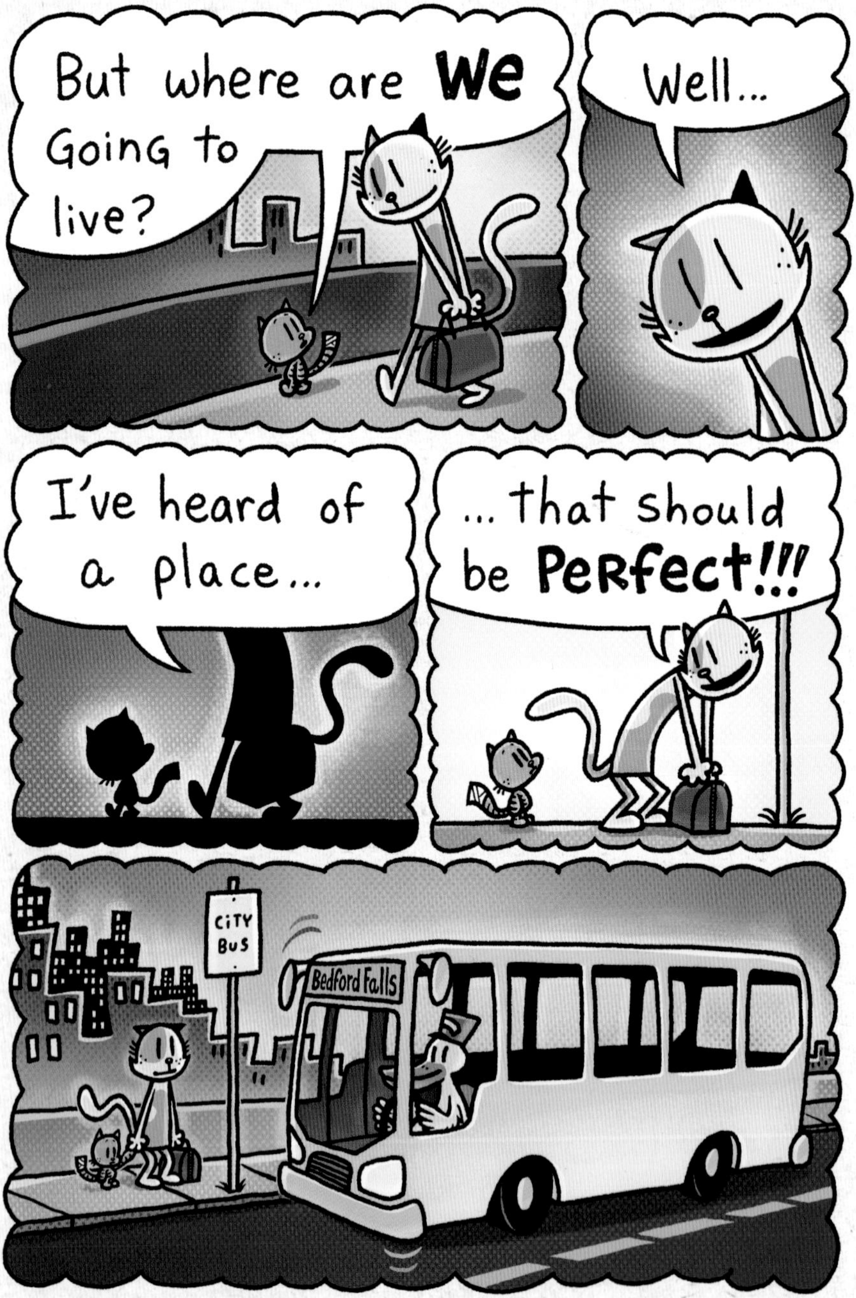
But where are WE Going to live?
Well...
I've heard of a place...
... that should be PERFECT!!!
CITY BUS
Bedford Falls

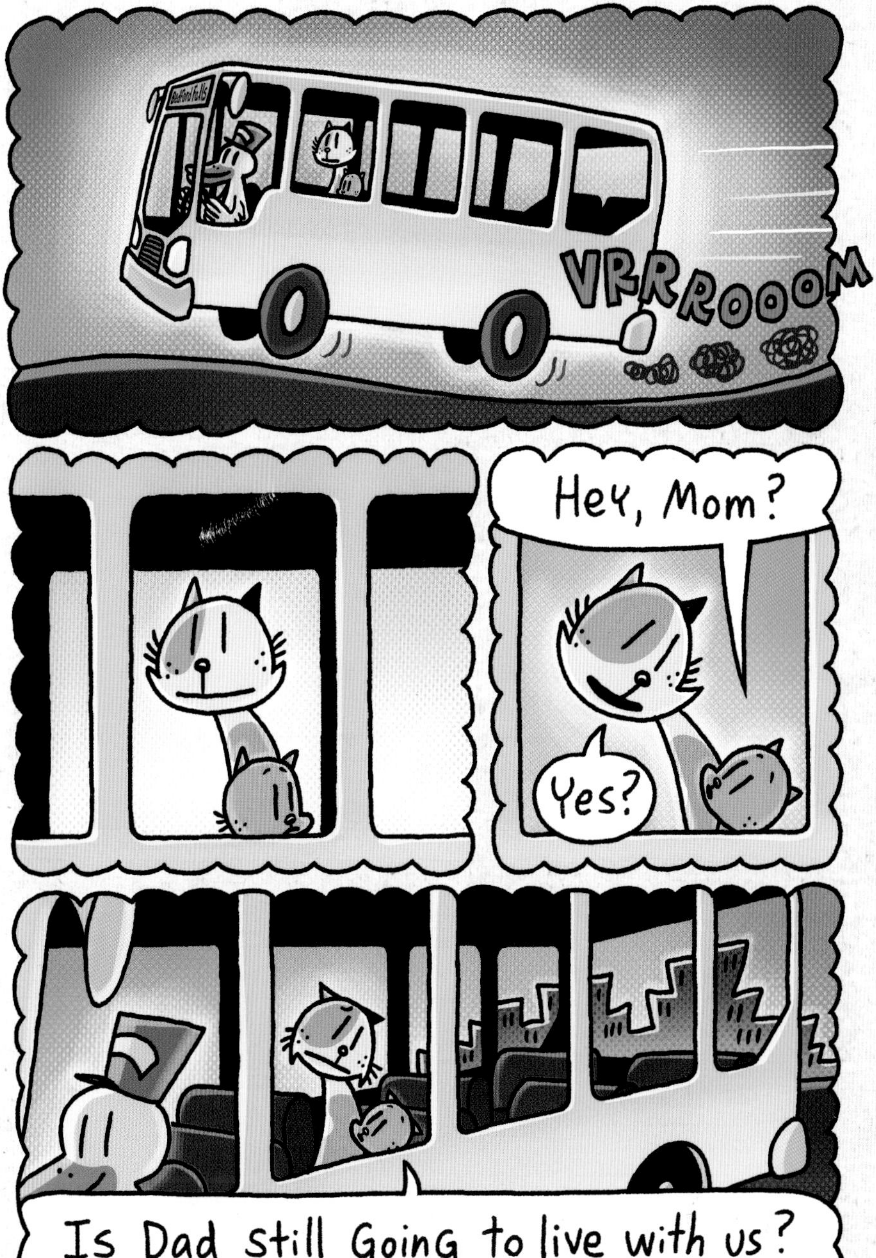
Bedford Falls
VRRROOOM
Hey, Mom?
Yes?
Is Dad still Going to live with us?

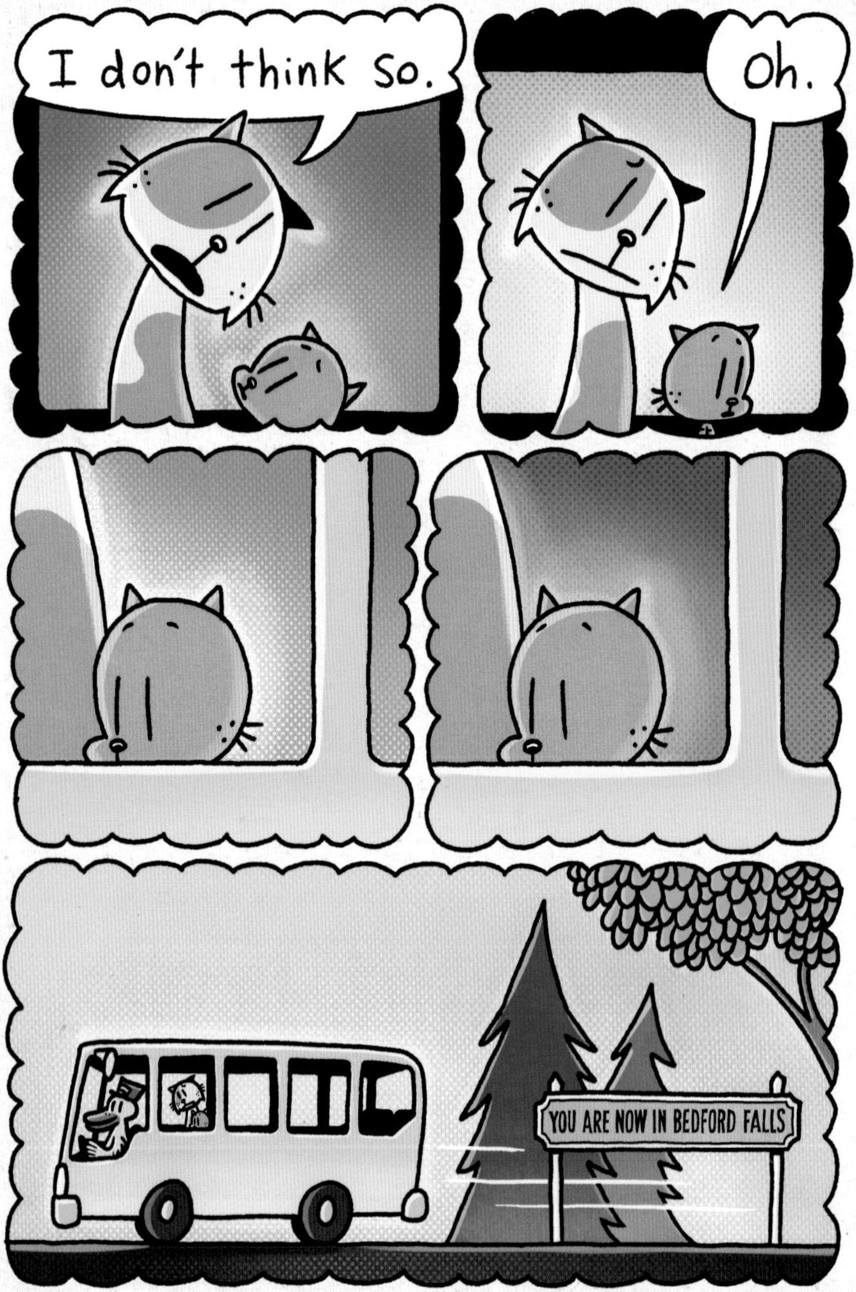
I don't think so.
Oh.
YOU ARE NOW IN BEDFORD FALLS

CHAPTER 9

TANKS FOR NOTHING

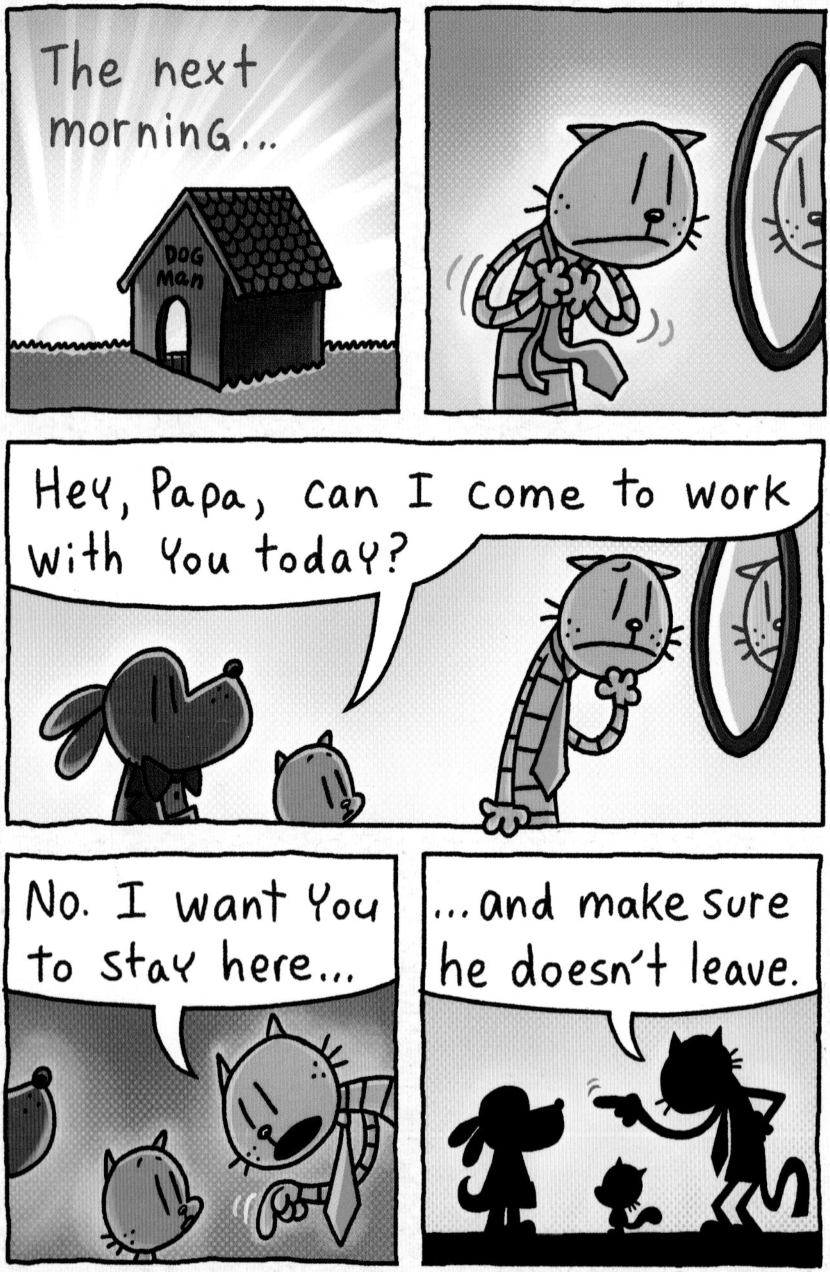
The next morning...
DOG Man
Hey, Papa, can I come to work with You today?
No. I want You to stay here...
...and make sure he doesn't leave.

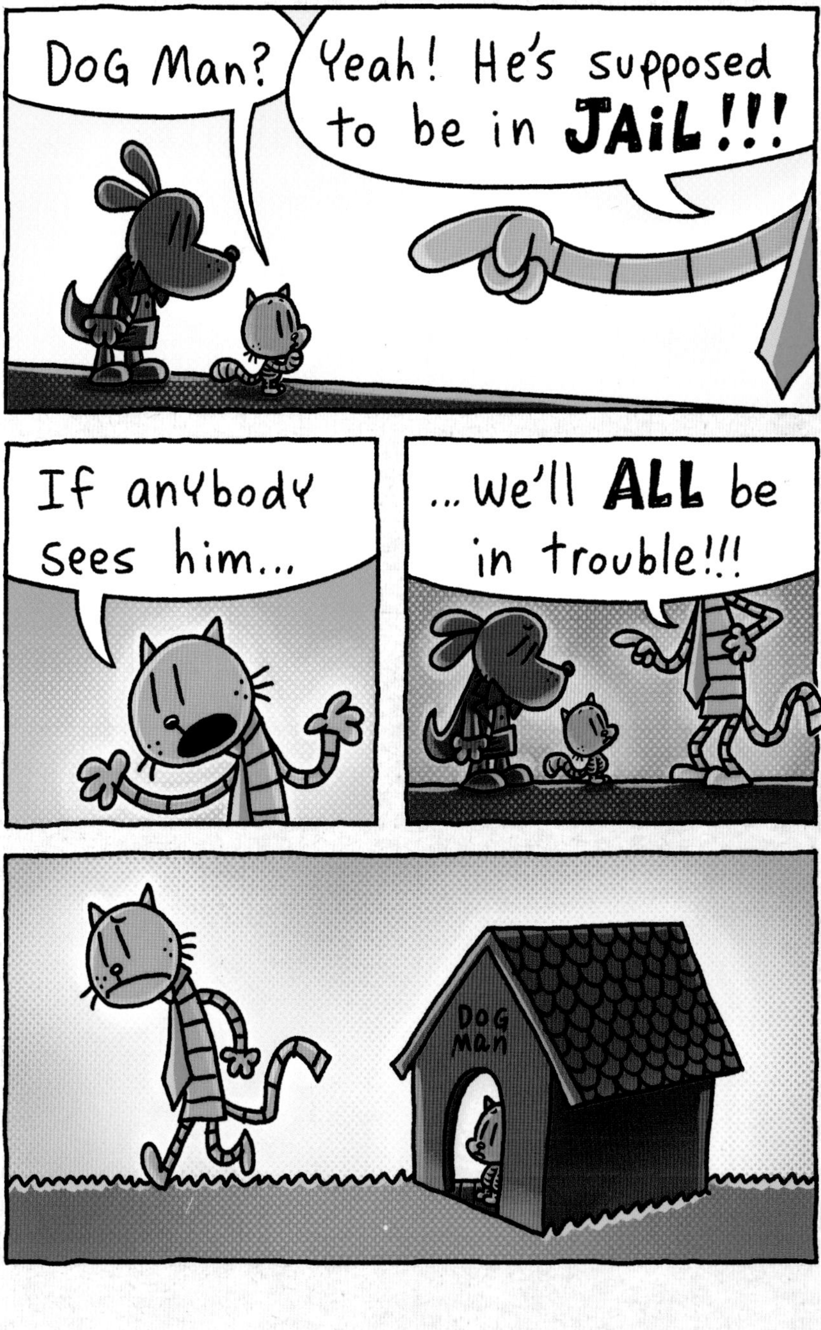

DoG Man?
Yeah! He's supposed to be in JAiL!!!
If anybody sees him...
...We'll ALL be in trouble!!!
DoG Man

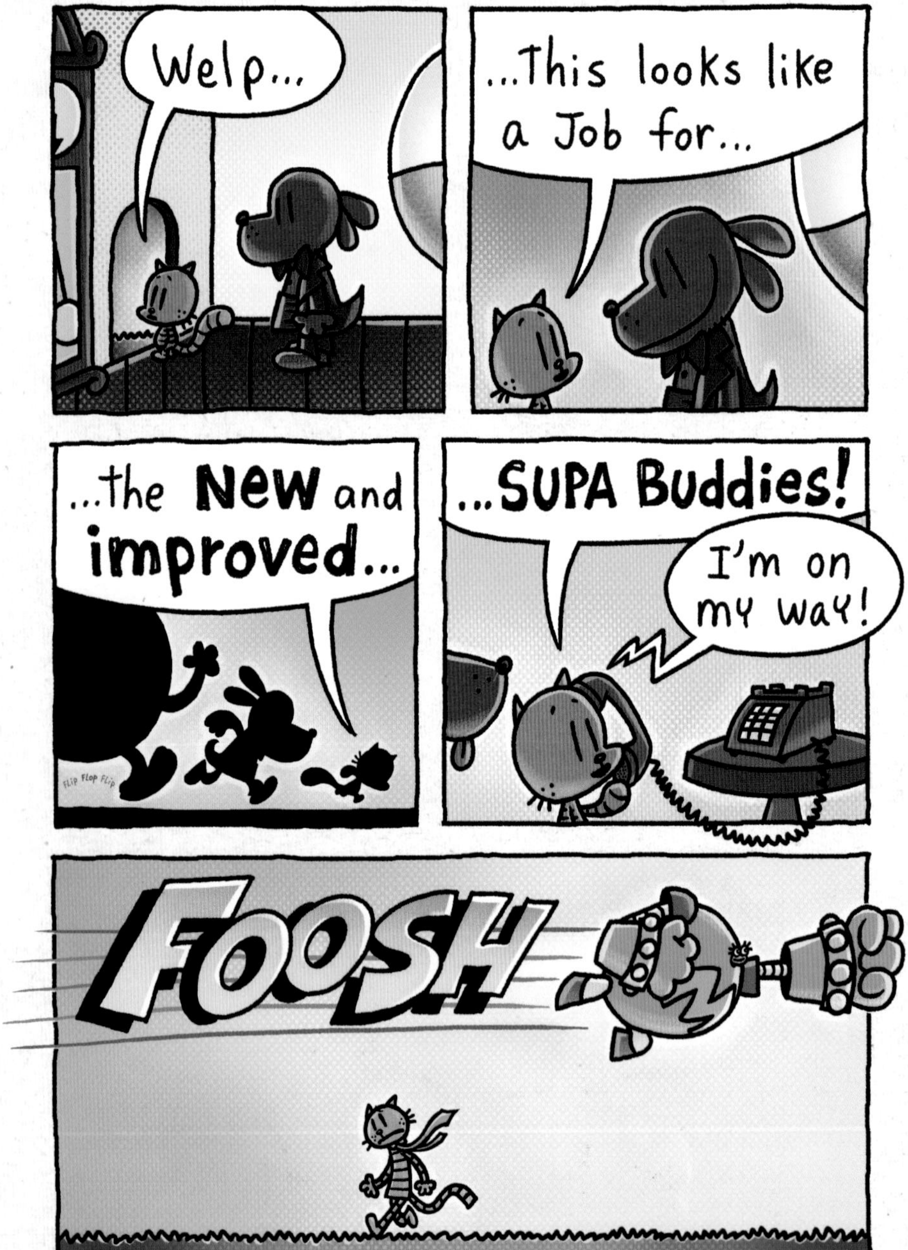
Welp...
...This looks like a Job for...
...the NEW and improved...
FLip Flop FLip
...SUPA Buddies!
I'm on my way!
FOOSH

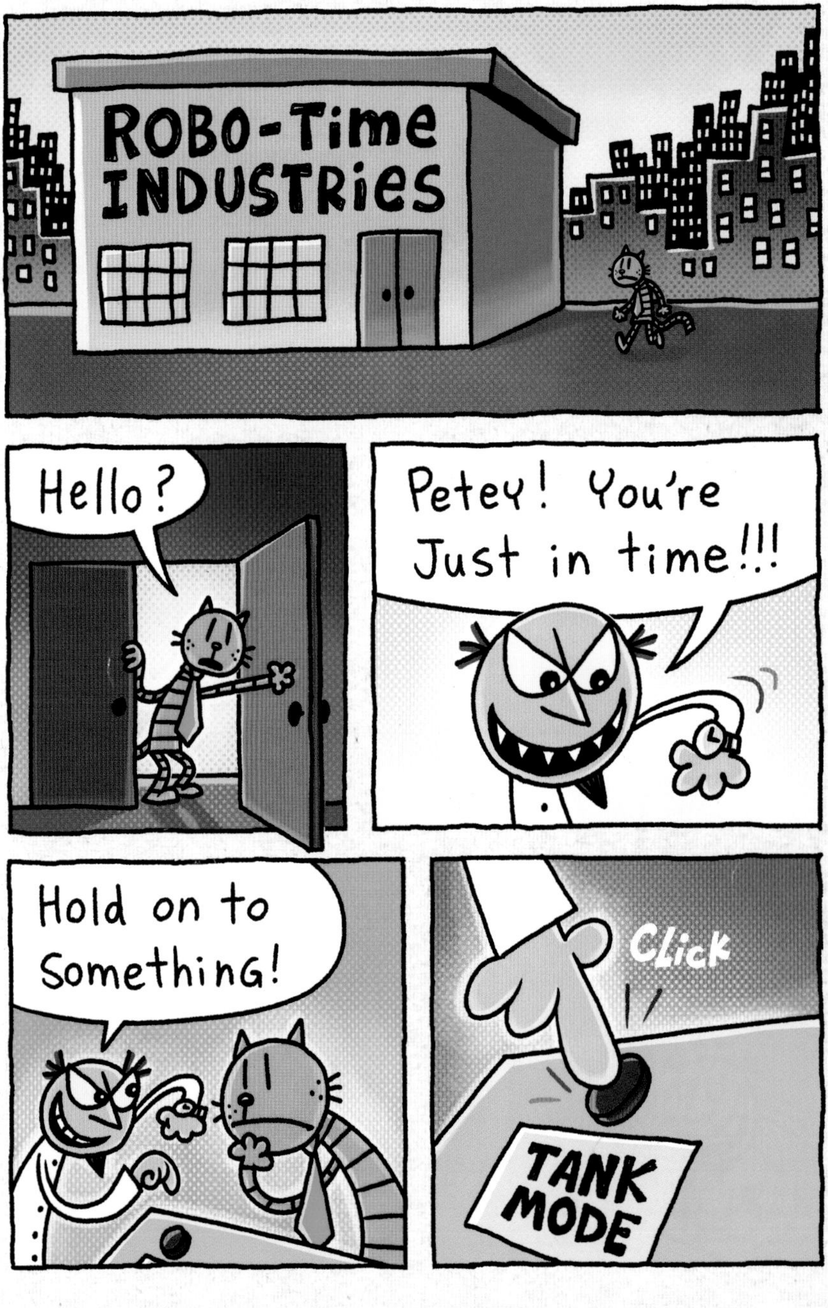
ROBO-Time INDUSTRIES
Hello?
Petey! You're Just in time!!!
Hold on to SomethinG!
CLick
TANK MODE

KA-KRUNK

ROBO-Time INDUSTRIES

ROBO-Time INDUSTRIES

ZING

WHAT IS HAPPENING?

WHERE ARE WE GOING?

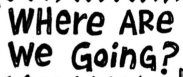

TANK MODE

VRRRRM VRRR-RM

I forgot to mention...

... my factory is a bit **TOO SMALL**...

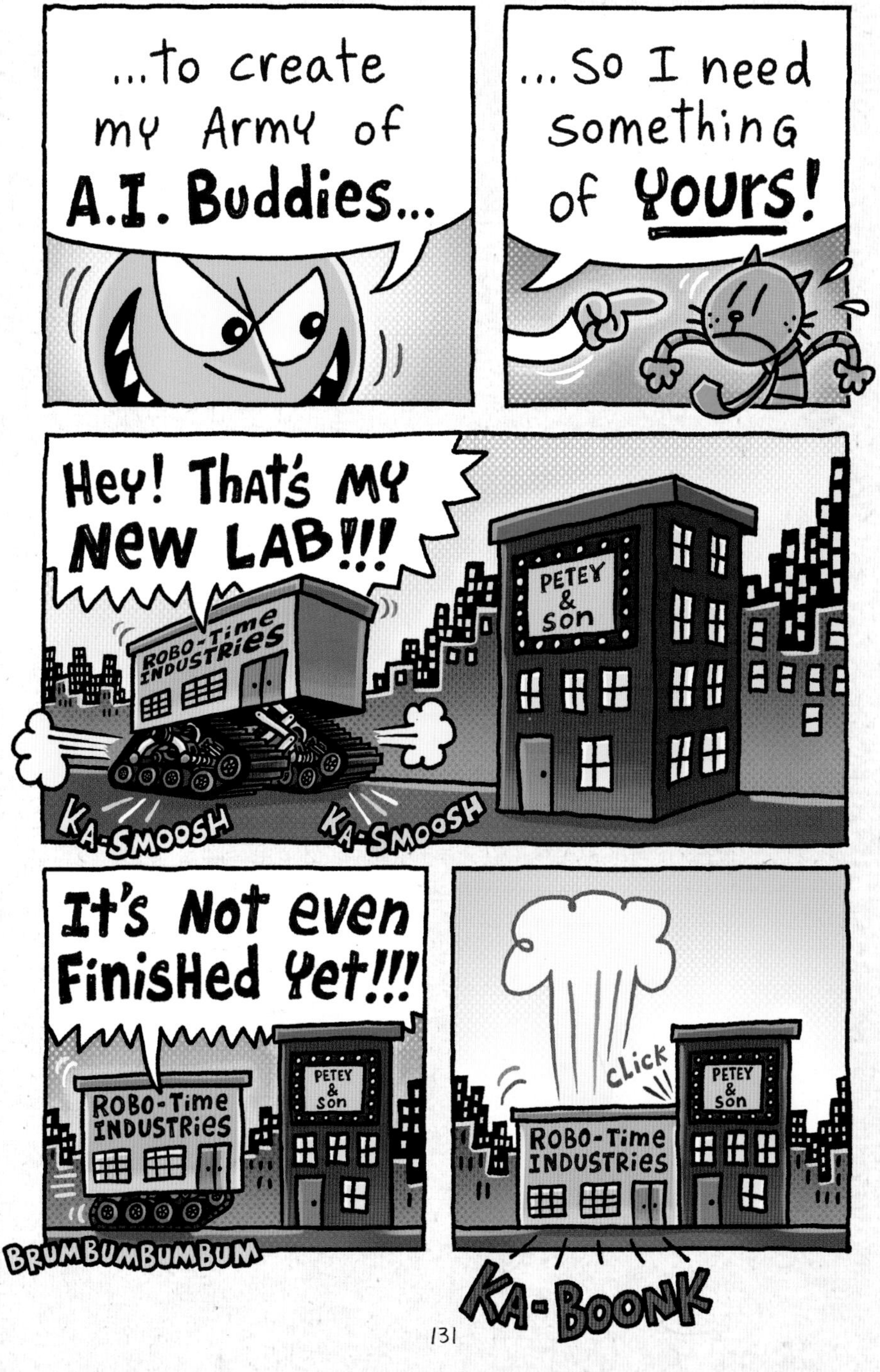
...to create my Army of A.I. Buddies...
...So I need something of YOURS!
Hey! That's MY NEW LAB!!!
ROBO-Time INDUSTRIES
PETEY & son
KA-SMOOSH
KA-SMOOSH
It's Not even Finished Yet!!!
ROBO-Time INDUSTRIES
PETEY & son
BRUMBUMBUMBUM
CLick
PETEY & son
ROBO-Time INDUSTRIES
KA-BOONK

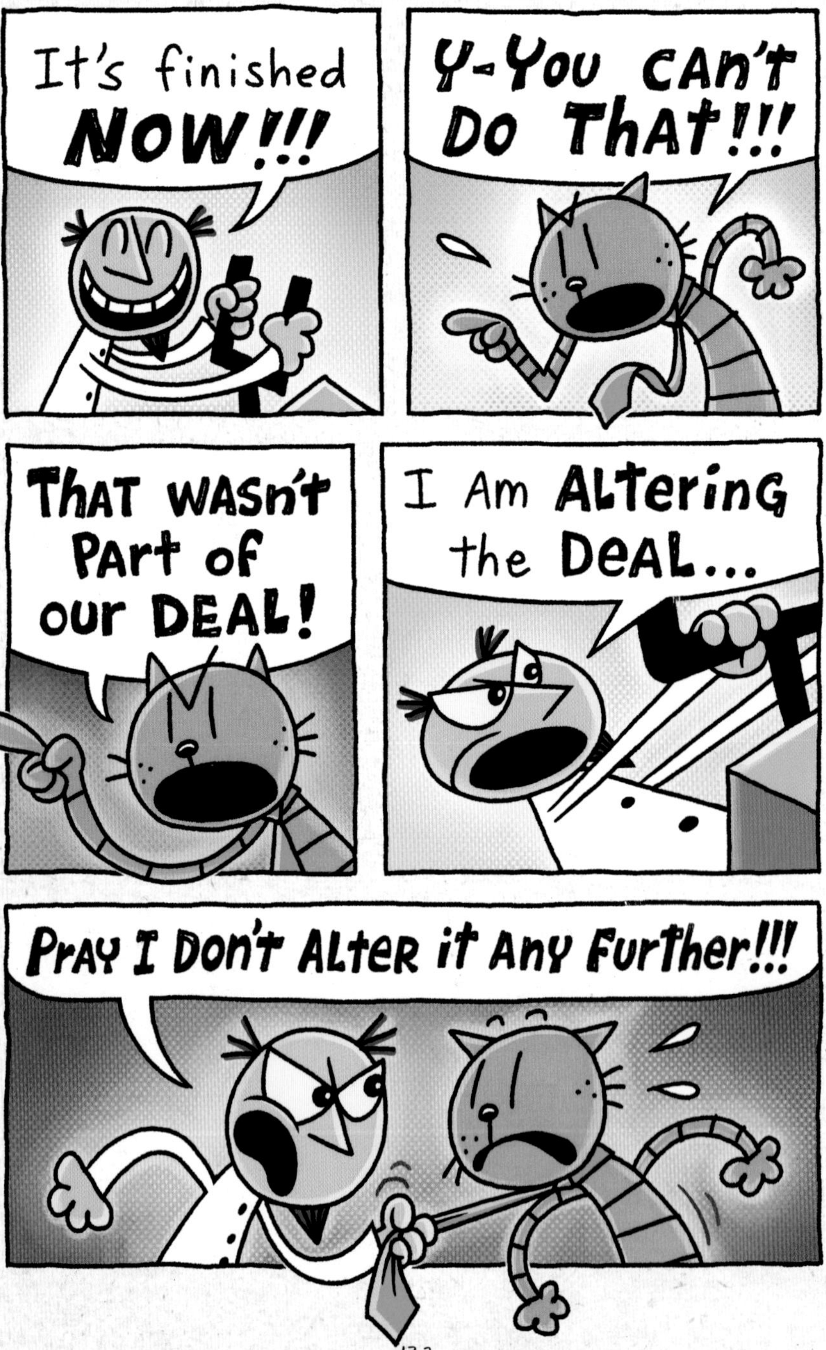
It's finished NOW!!!
Y-YOU CAN'T DO THAT!!!
THAT WASN'T PART of our DEAL!
I Am ALTERING the DEAL...
PRAY I DON'T ALTER it ANY FURTHER!!!

CHAPTER 10

MULTIPLE SINGULARITY

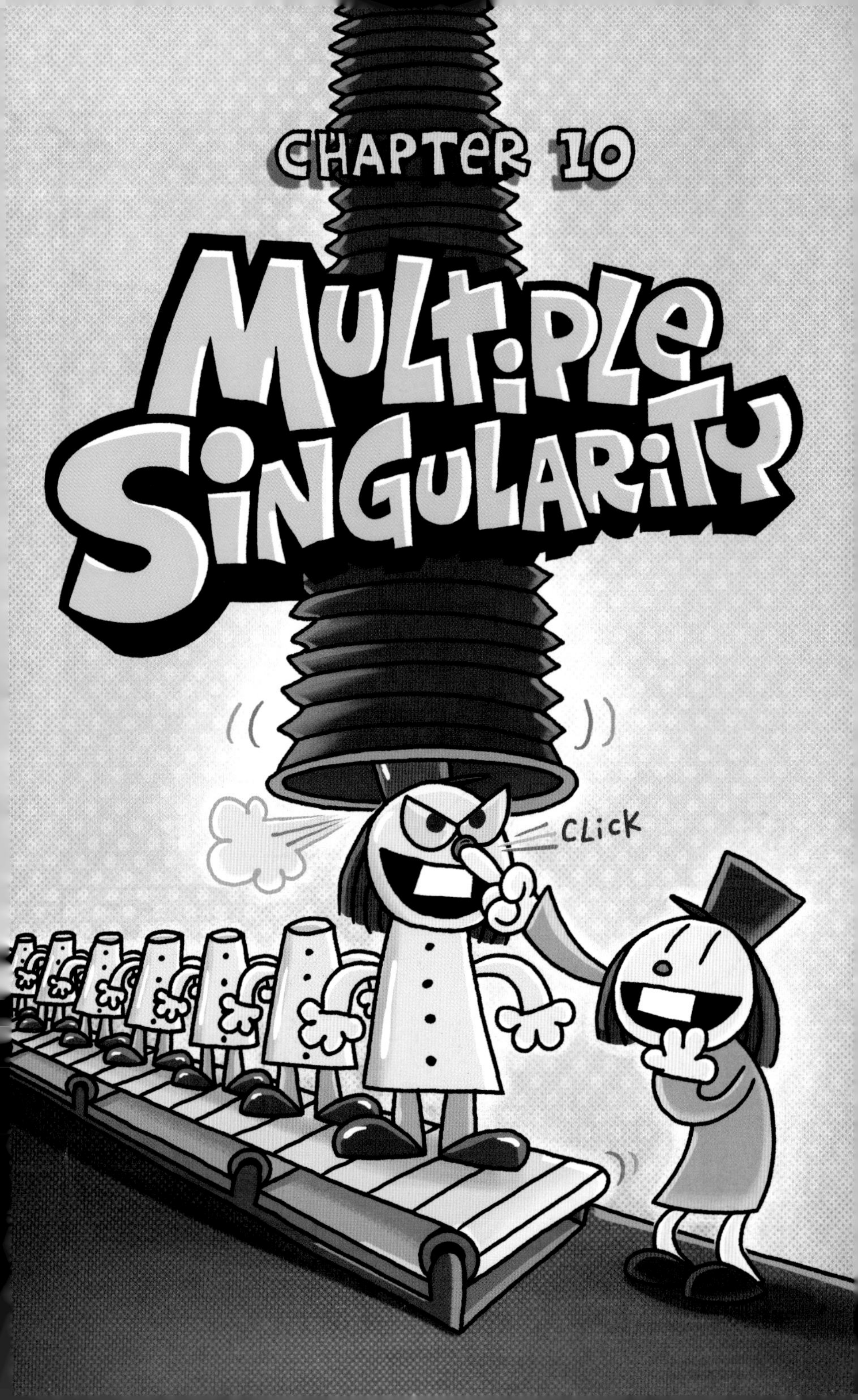
CLICK

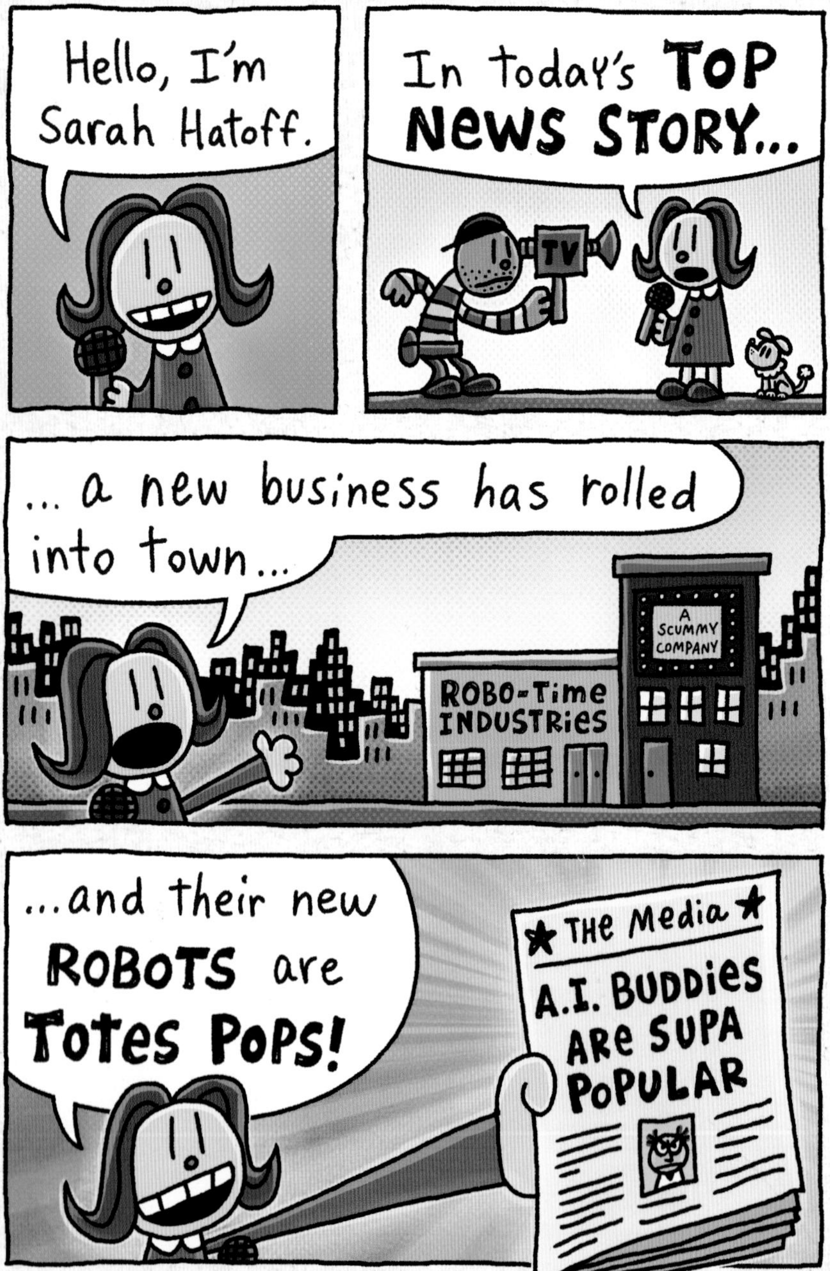
Hello, I'm Sarah Hatoff.
In today's TOP NEWS STORY...
TV
... a new business has rolled into town...
A SCUMMY COMPANY
ROBO-Time INDUSTRIES
...and their new ROBOTS are TOTES POPS!
THE Media
A.I. BUDDIES ARE SUPA POPULAR

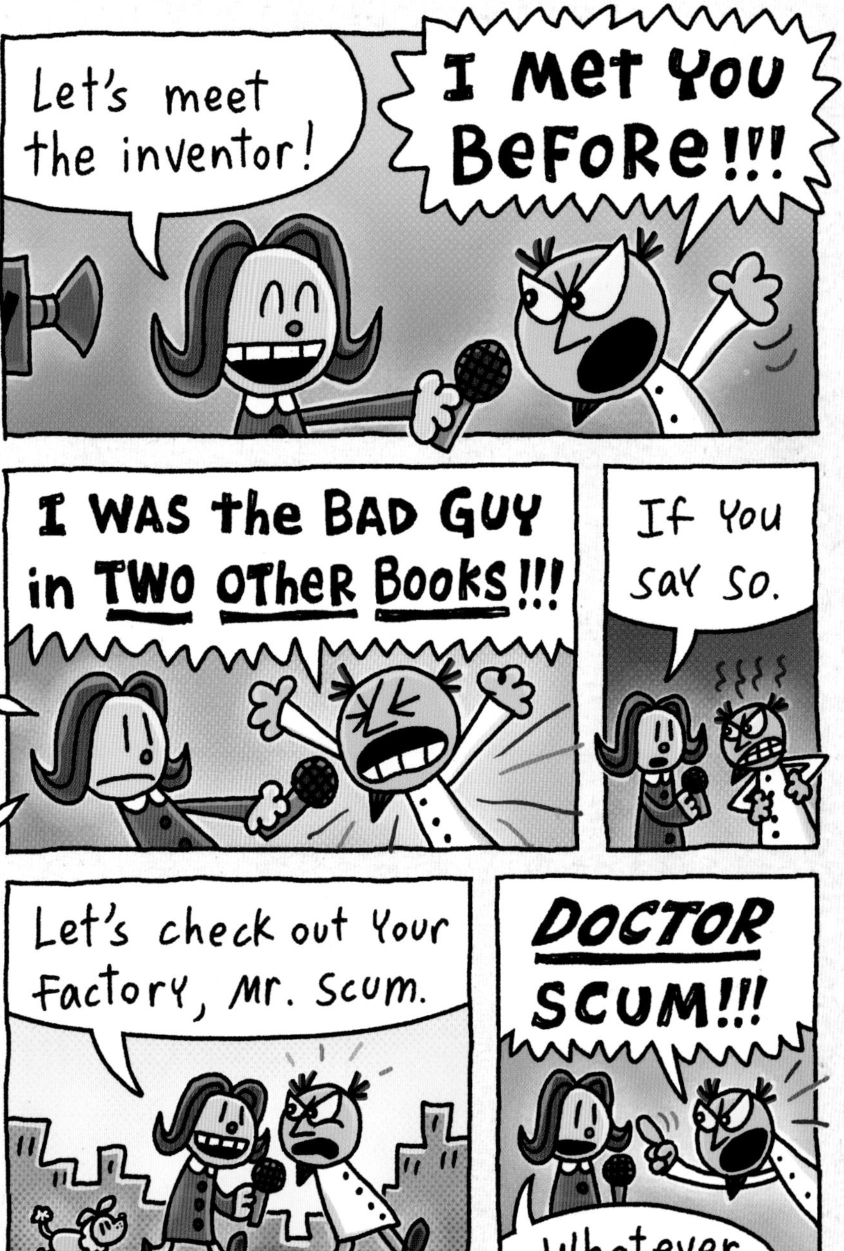
Let's meet the inventor!
I MET YOU BEFORE!!!
I WAS the BAD GUY in TWO OTHER BOOKS!!!
If You say so.
Let's check out Your Factory, Mr. Scum.
DOCTOR SCUM!!!
Whatever.

Our Robots are very **PERSONAL!**

Press here?

FIRST, we do a **3-D SCAN** of your face...

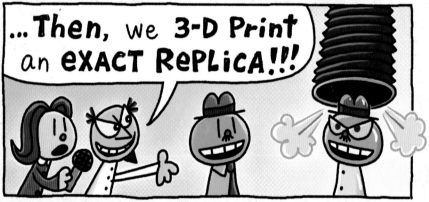

...**Then,** we **3-D Print** an **EXACT REPLICA!!!**

A.I. Buddies look **Just Like You...**

click

... So they can **WORK FOR YOU!!!**

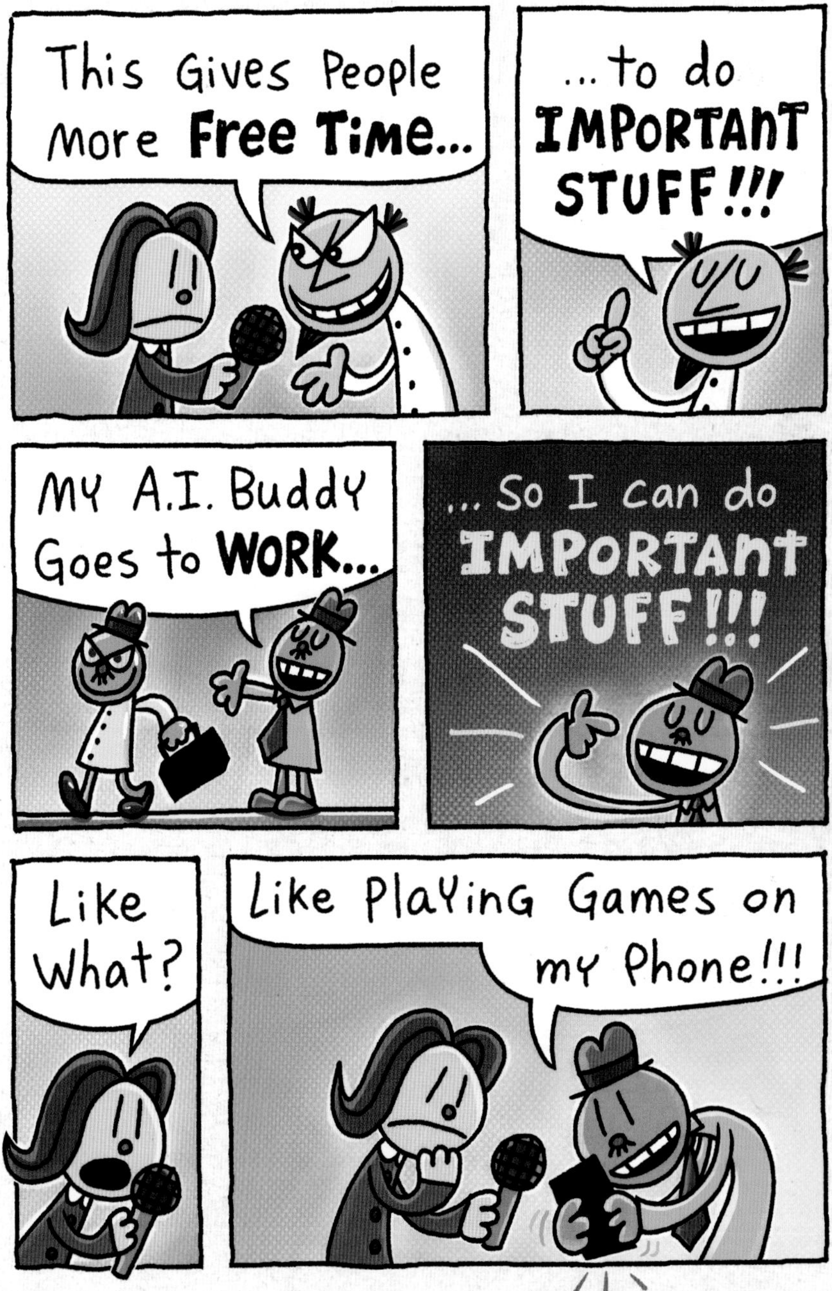
This Gives People More Free Time...
...to do IMPORTANT STUFF!!!
My A.I. Buddy Goes to WORK...
...So I can do IMPORTANT STUFF!!!
Like What?
Like Playing Games on my Phone!!!
Pew pew pew

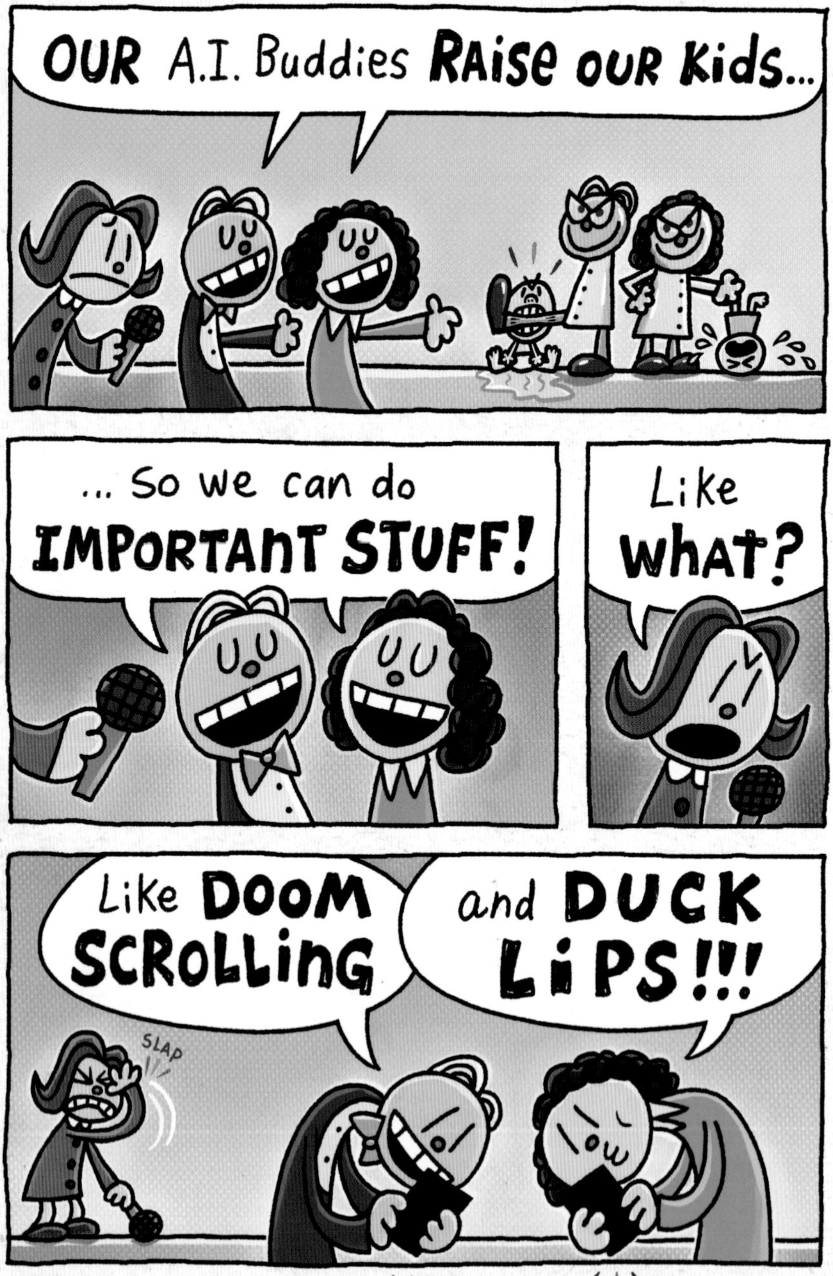
OUR A.I. Buddies RAISE OUR Kids...
... So we can do IMPORTANT STUFF!
Like WHAT?
Like DOOM SCROLLING
and DUCK LiPS!!!
SLAP
SWISH SWISH
CLick CLick

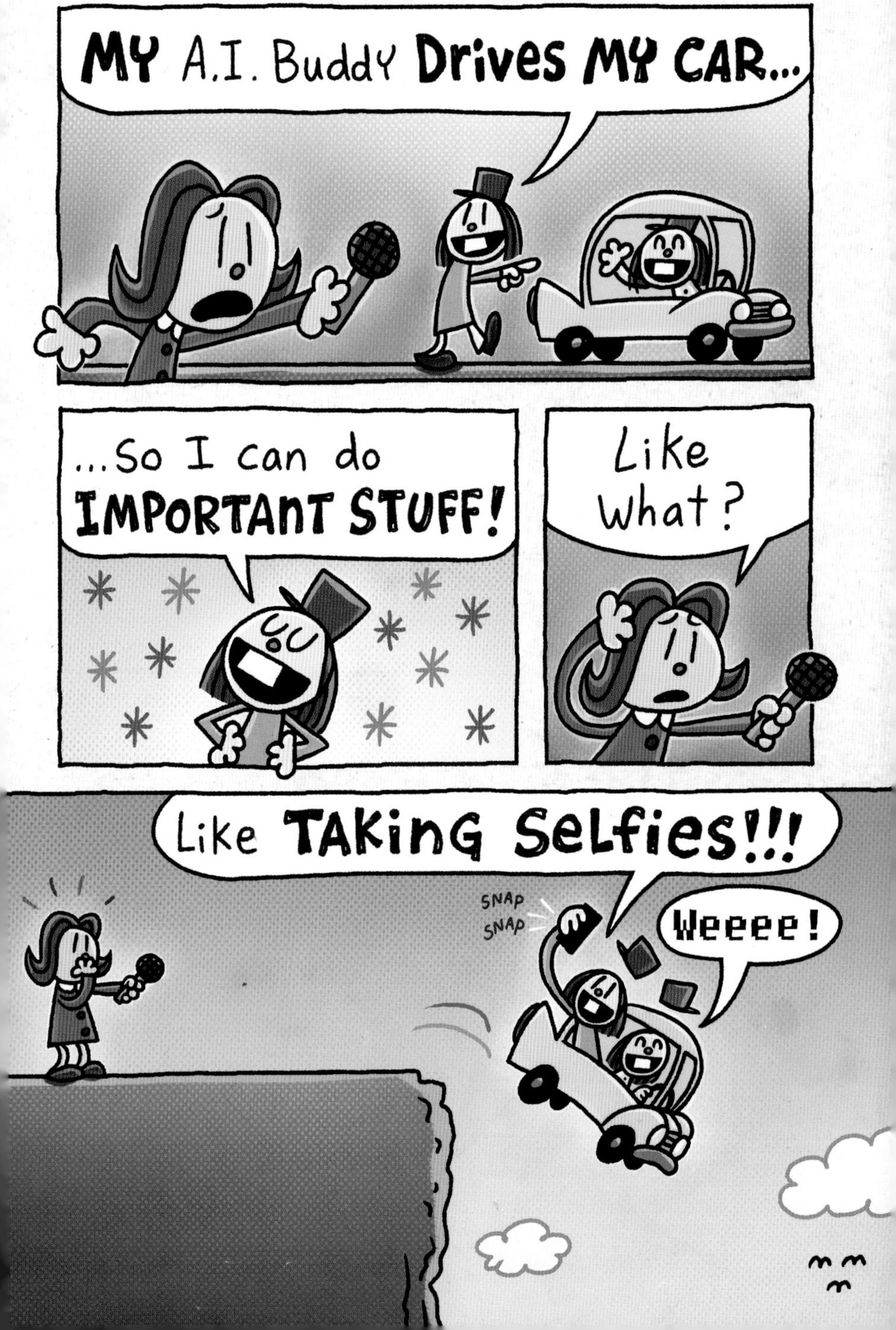
MY A.I. Buddy Drives MY CAR...
...So I can do IMPORTANT STUFF!
Like What?
Like TAKING Selfies!!!
SNAP SNAP
Weeee!

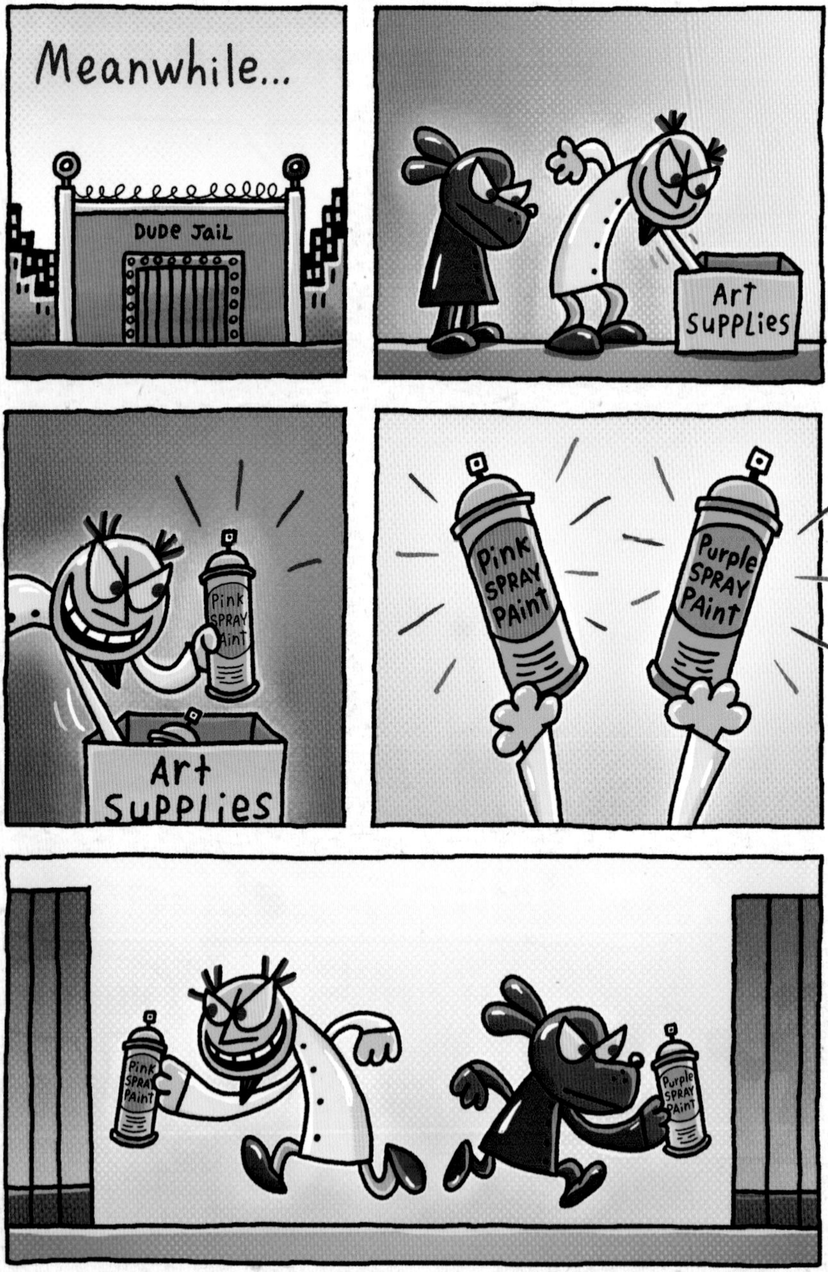
Meanwhile...
DUDE JAIL
Art Supplies
Pink SPRAY Paint
Art Supplies
Pink SPRAY PAINT
Purple SPRAY PAINT
Pink SPRAY Paint
Purple SPRAY PAINT

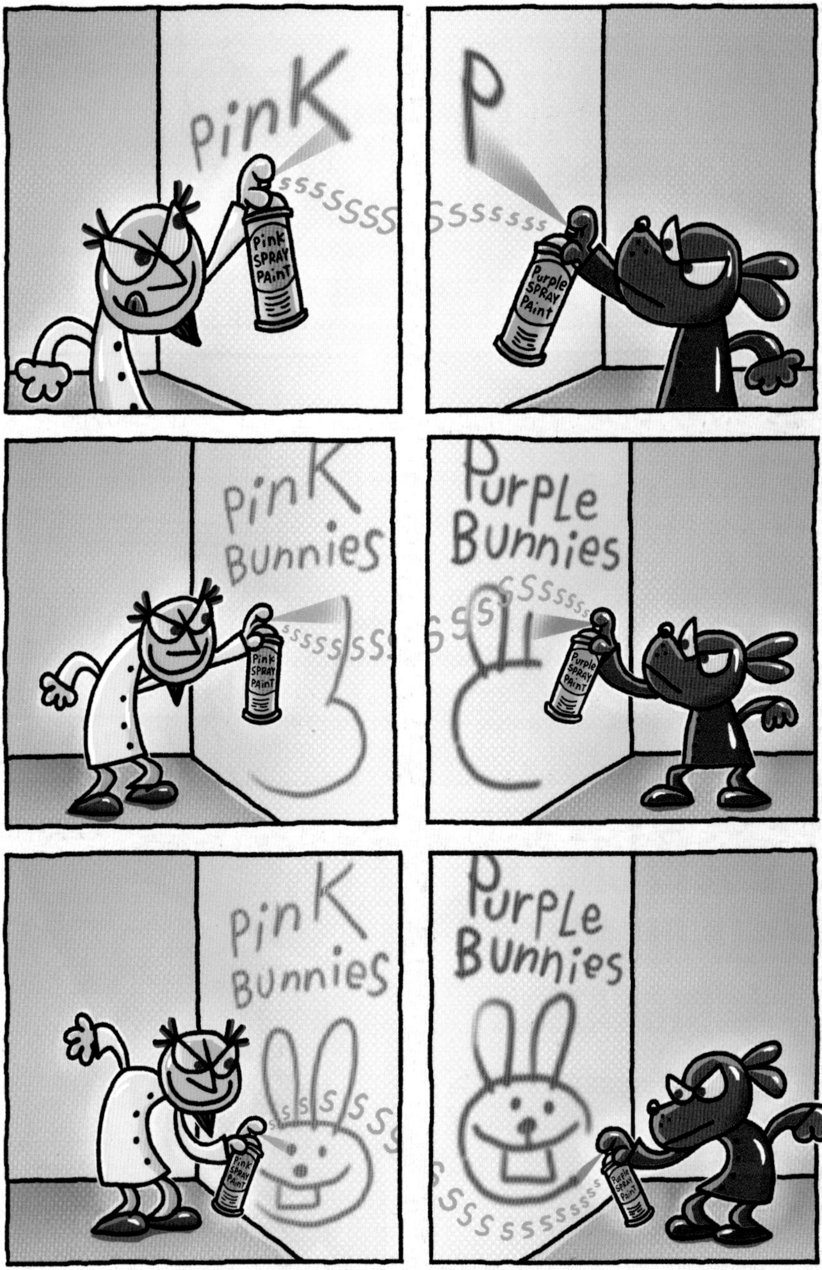

PinK
SSSSSSSS
PINK SPRAY PAINT
P
SSSSSSS
Purple SPRAY Paint
PinK Bunnies
SSSSSSSS
Pink SPRAY Paint
Purple Bunnies
SSSSSSS
Purple SPRAY Paint
PinK Bunnies
SSSSSS
Pink SPRAY Paint
Purple Bunnies
SSSSSSSSSSS
Purple SPRAY Paint

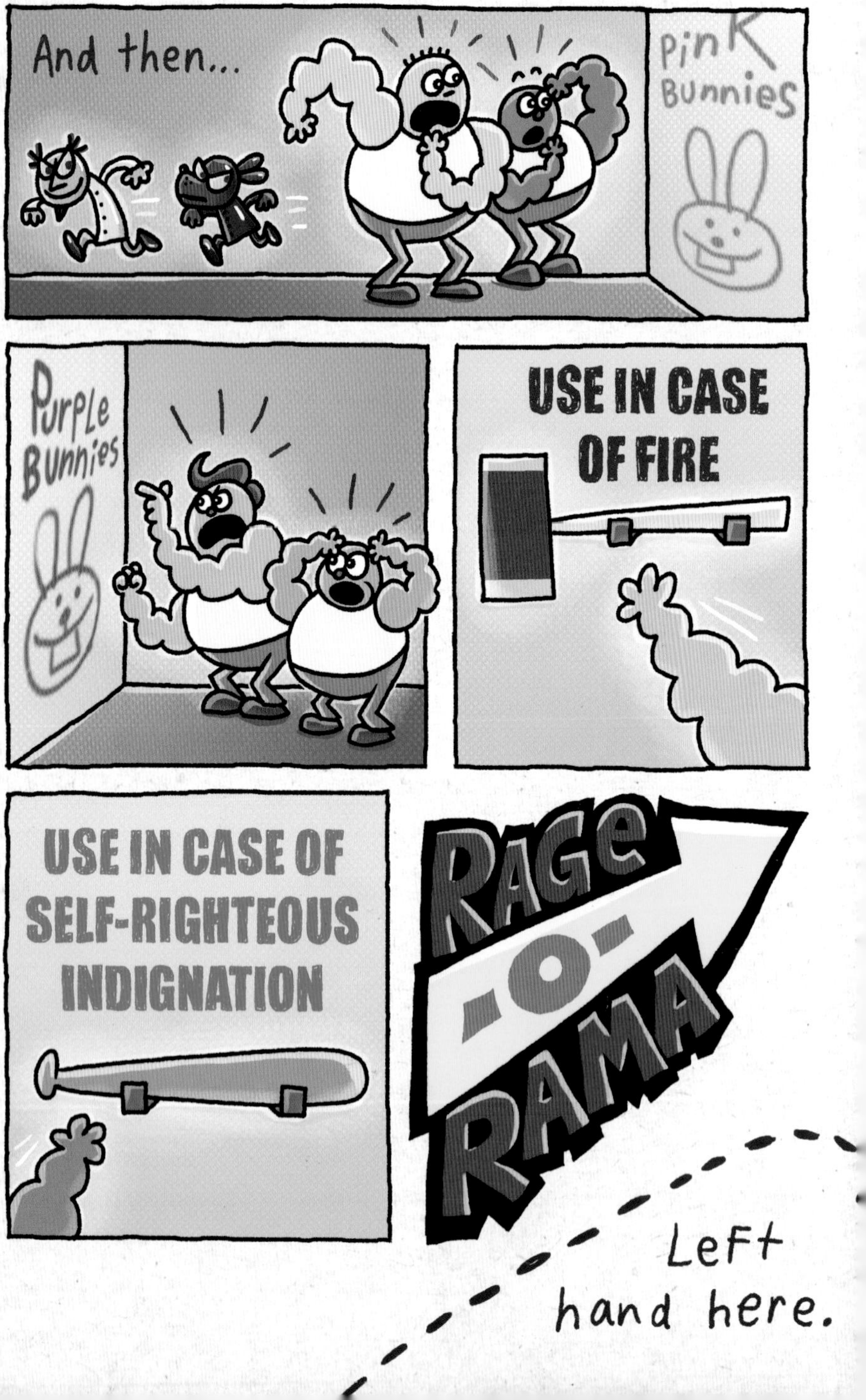
And then...
Pink Bunnies
Purple Bunnies
USE IN CASE OF FIRE
USE IN CASE OF SELF-RIGHTEOUS INDIGNATION
RAGE-O-RAMA
Left hand here.

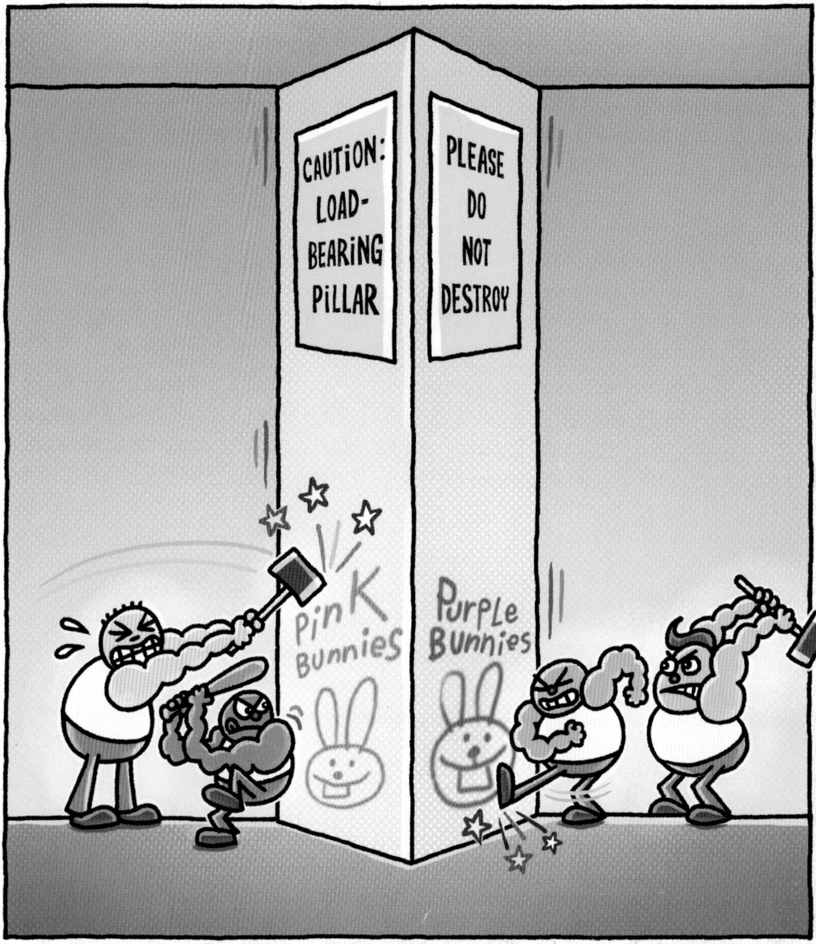
CAUTION: LOAD-BEARING PILLAR
PLEASE DO NOT DESTROY
Pink Bunnies
Purple Bunnies

JAIL BREAK

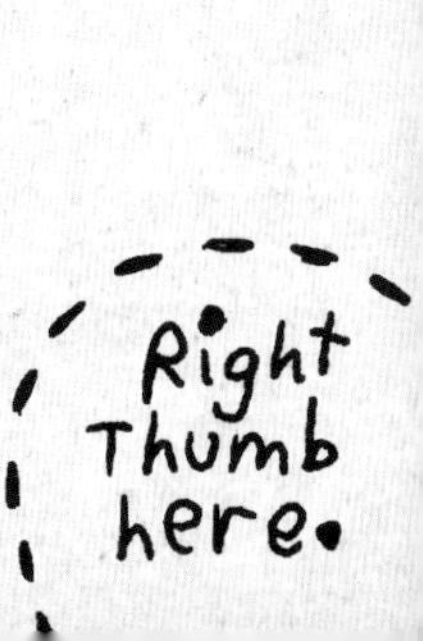
Right Thumb here.

JAIL
BREAK

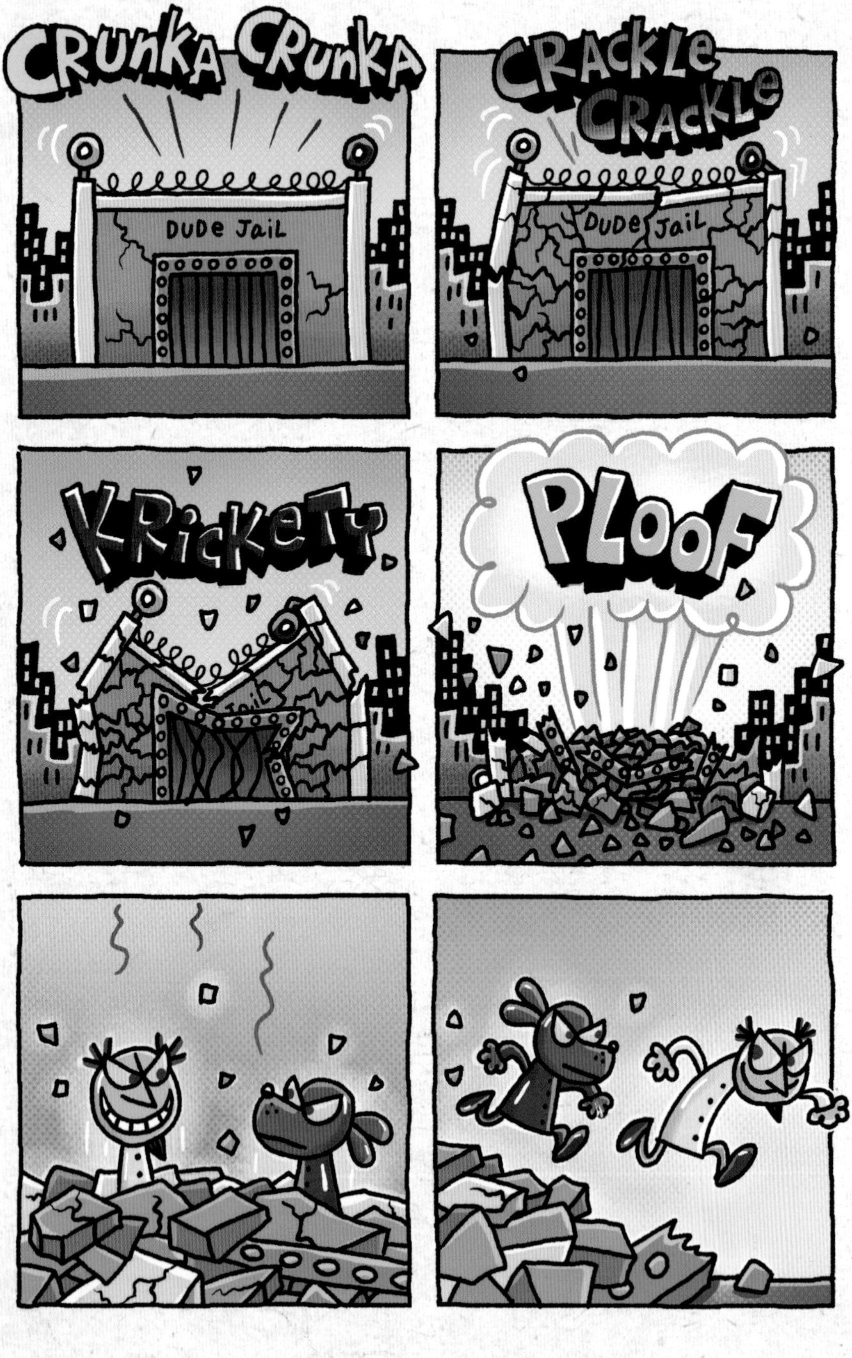
CRUNKA CRUNKA
DUDE JAIL
CRACKLE CRACKLE
DUDE JAIL
KRICKETY
JAIL
PLOOF

CHAPTER 11

The Infiltration

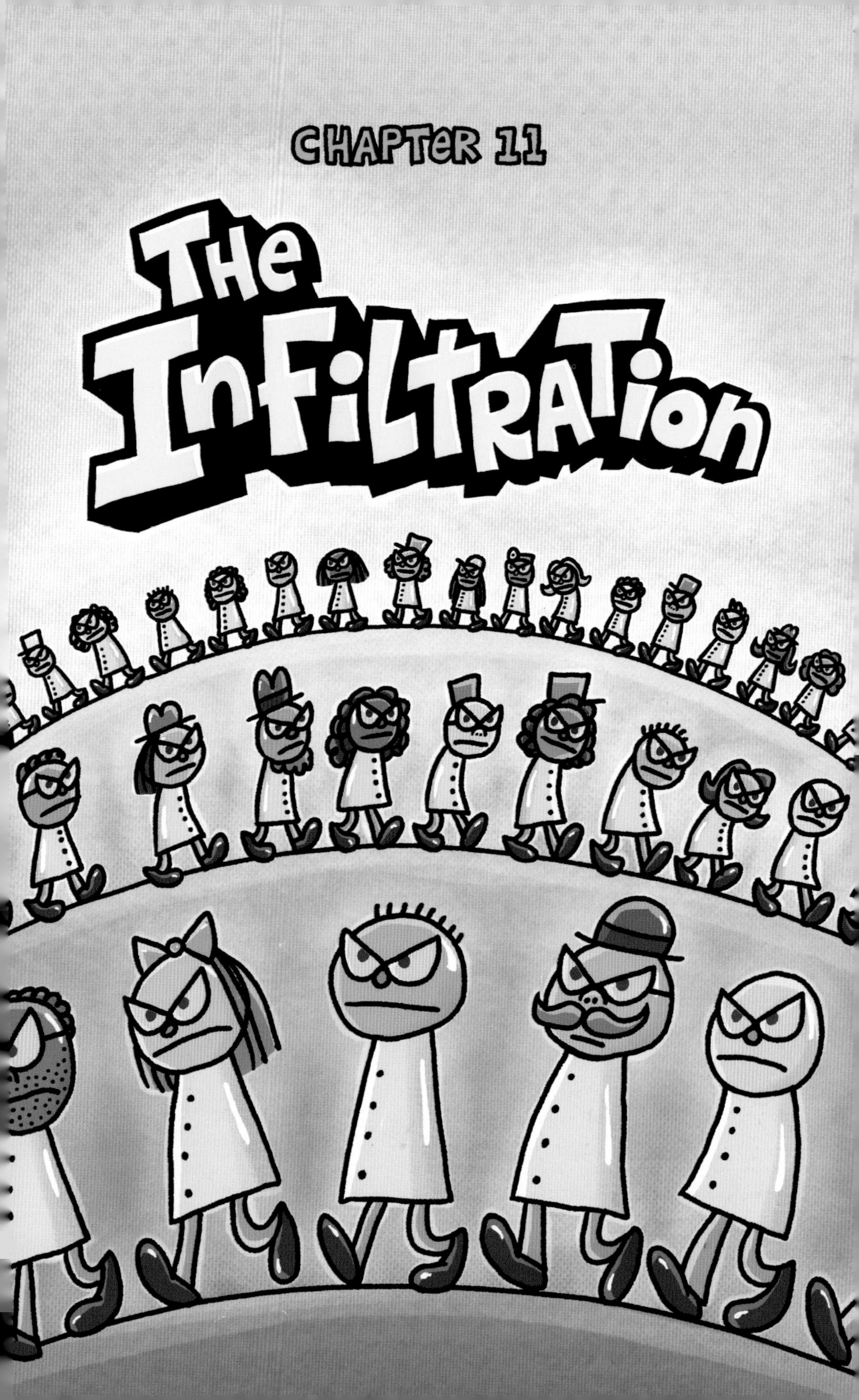

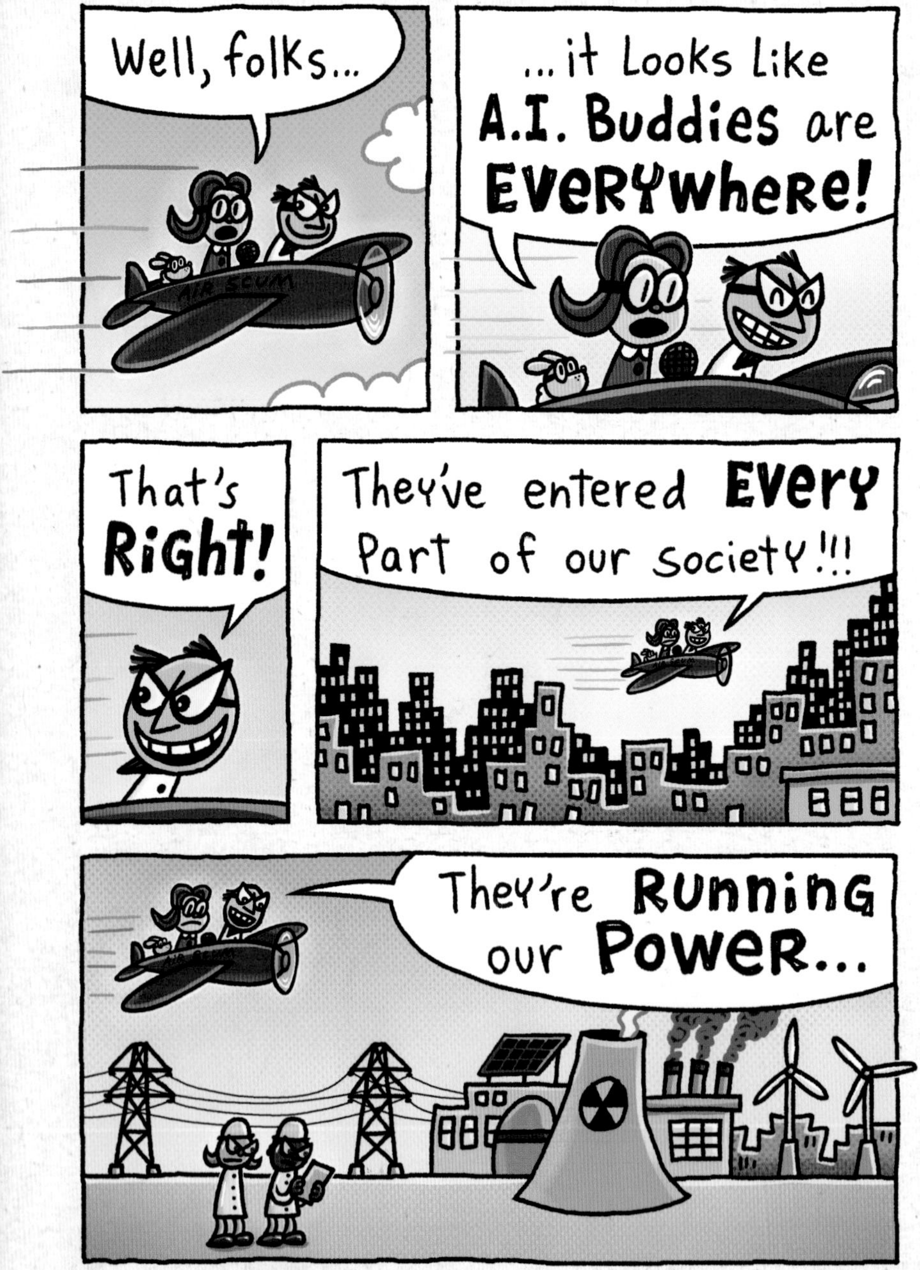
Well, folks...
AIR SCUM
...it Looks Like A.I. Buddies are EVERYWHERE!
That's RIGHT!
They've entered EVERY Part of our society!!!
They're RUNNING our POWER...

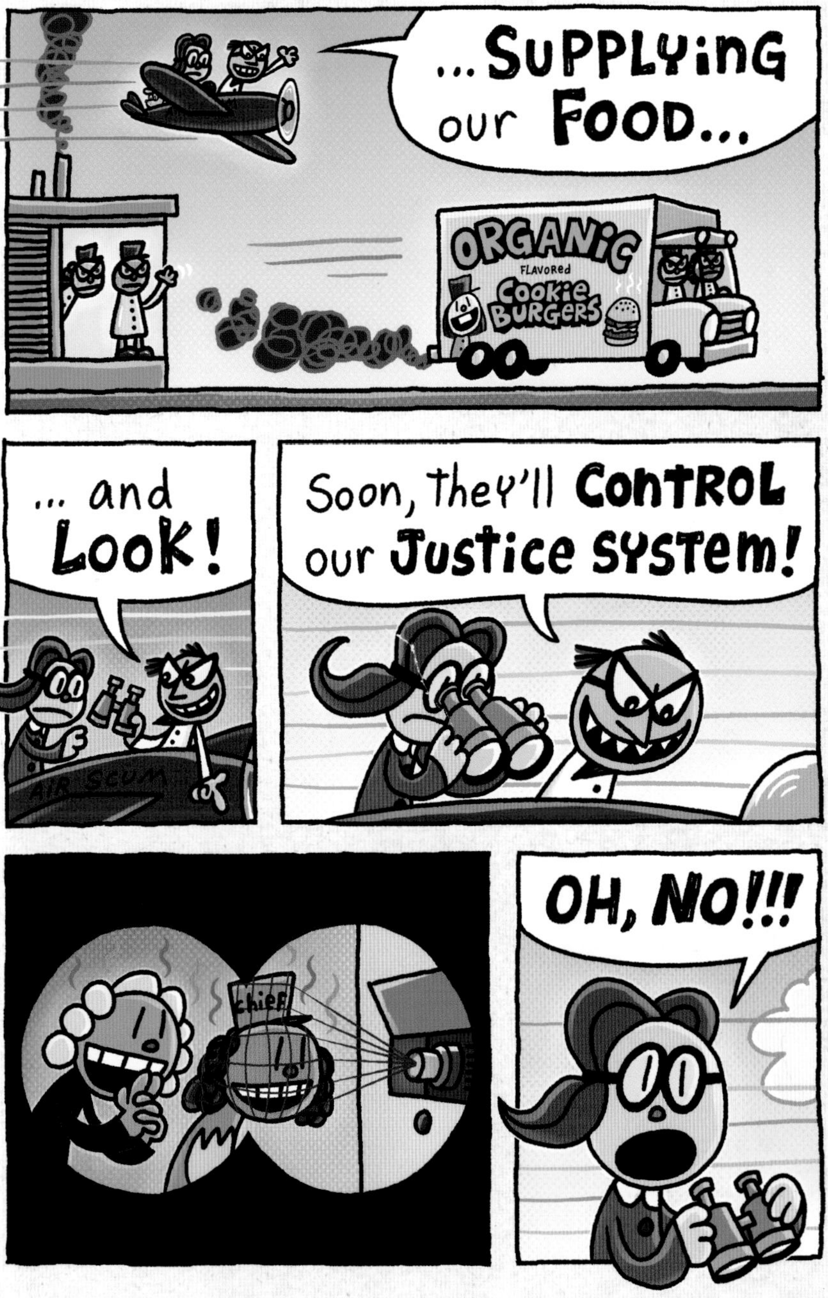
...SUPPLYING our FOOD...
ORGANIC
FLAVORED
COOKIE BURGERS
... and LOOK!
AIR SCUM
Soon, they'll CONTROL our JUSTICE SYSTEM!
CHIEF
OH, NO!!!

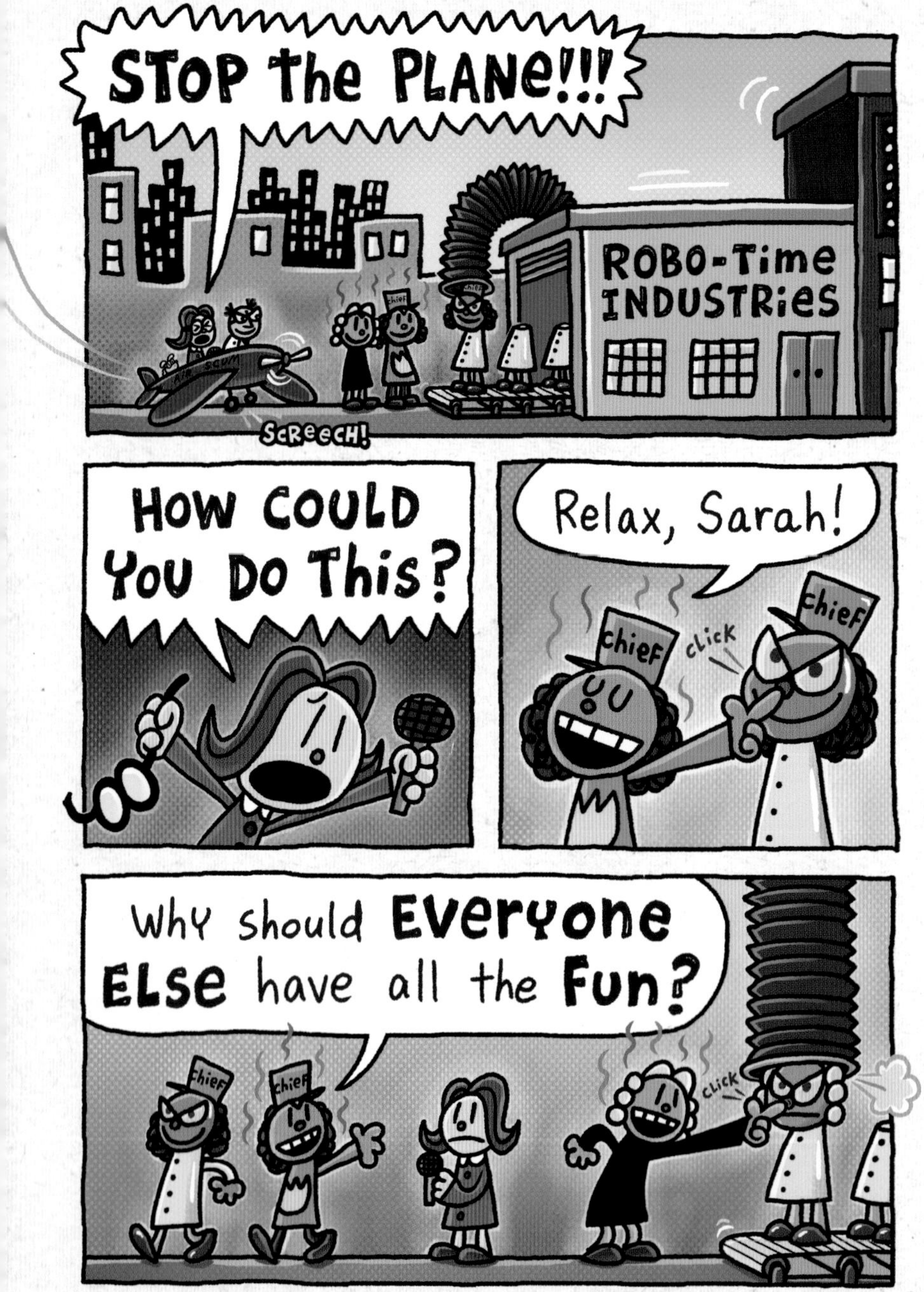
STOP the PLANE!!!
AIR SQDM
chief
CHIEF
ROBO-Time INDUSTRiES
SCReeCH!
HOW COULD YOU DO This?
Relax, Sarah!
chief
Chief
CLICK
Why should Everyone ELSe have all the Fun?
chief
chief
CLICK

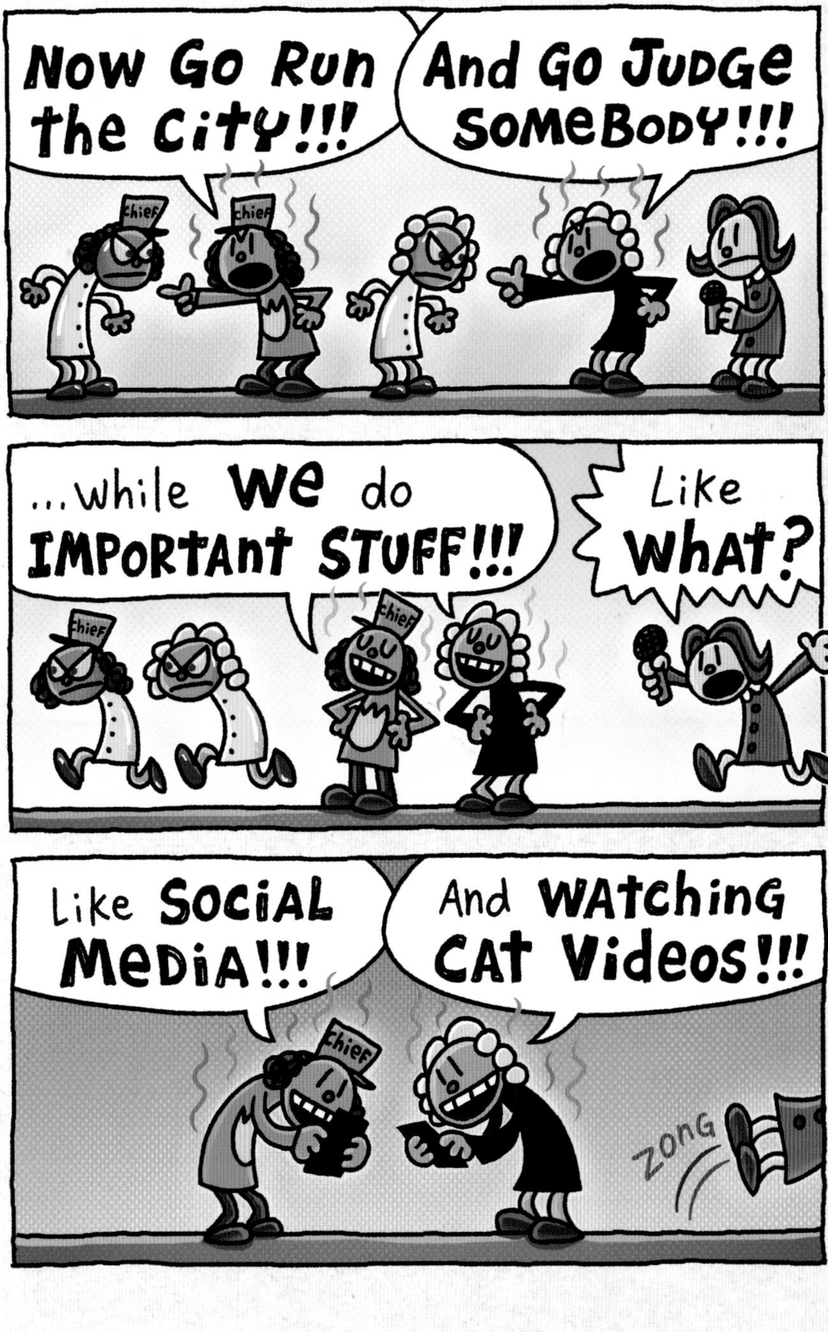
NOW GO RUN the CITY!!!
And GO JUDGE SOMEBODY!!!
...while WE do IMPORTANT STUFF!!!
Like WHAT?
Like SOCIAL MEDIA!!!
And WATCHING CAT Videos!!!
ZONG

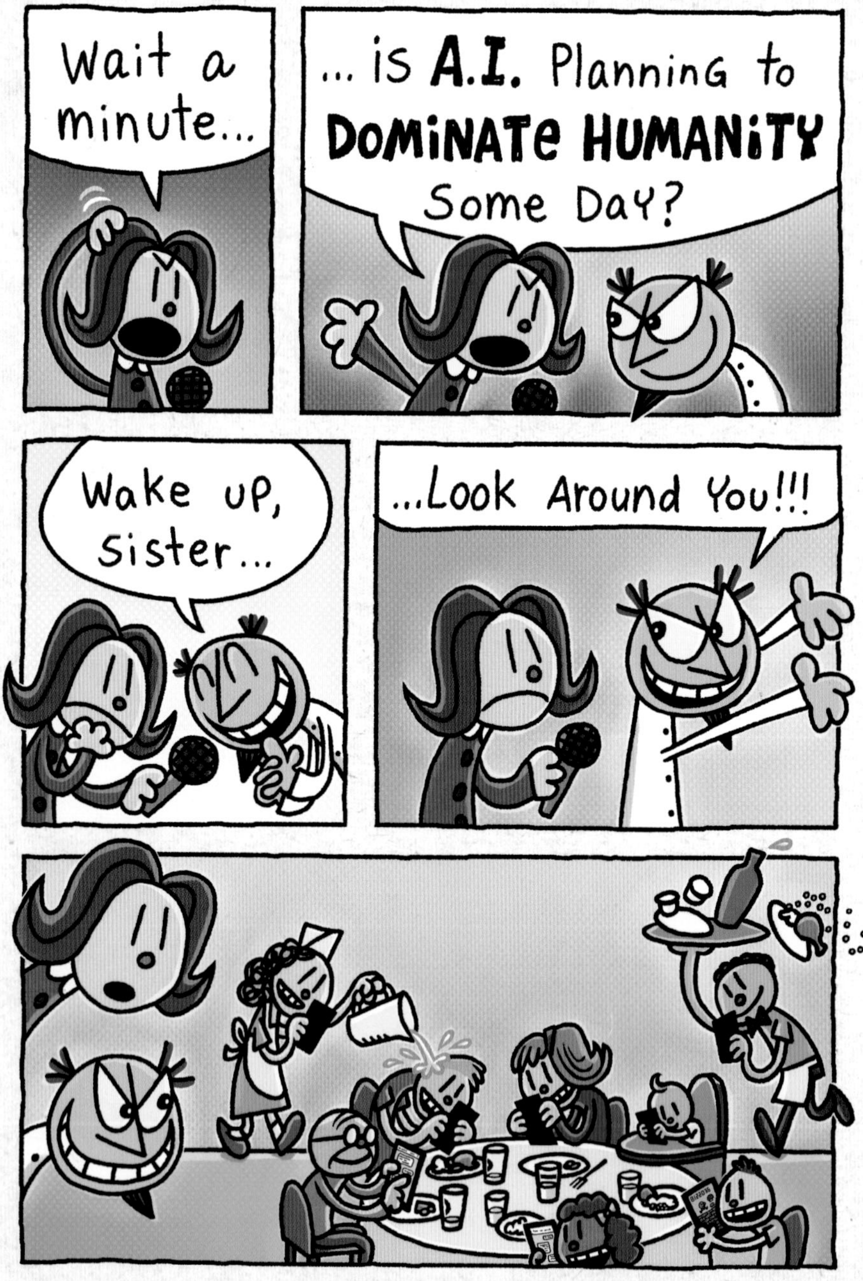
Wait a minute...
... is A.I. Planning to DOMINATE HUMANITY Some Day?
Wake up, sister...
...Look Around You!!!

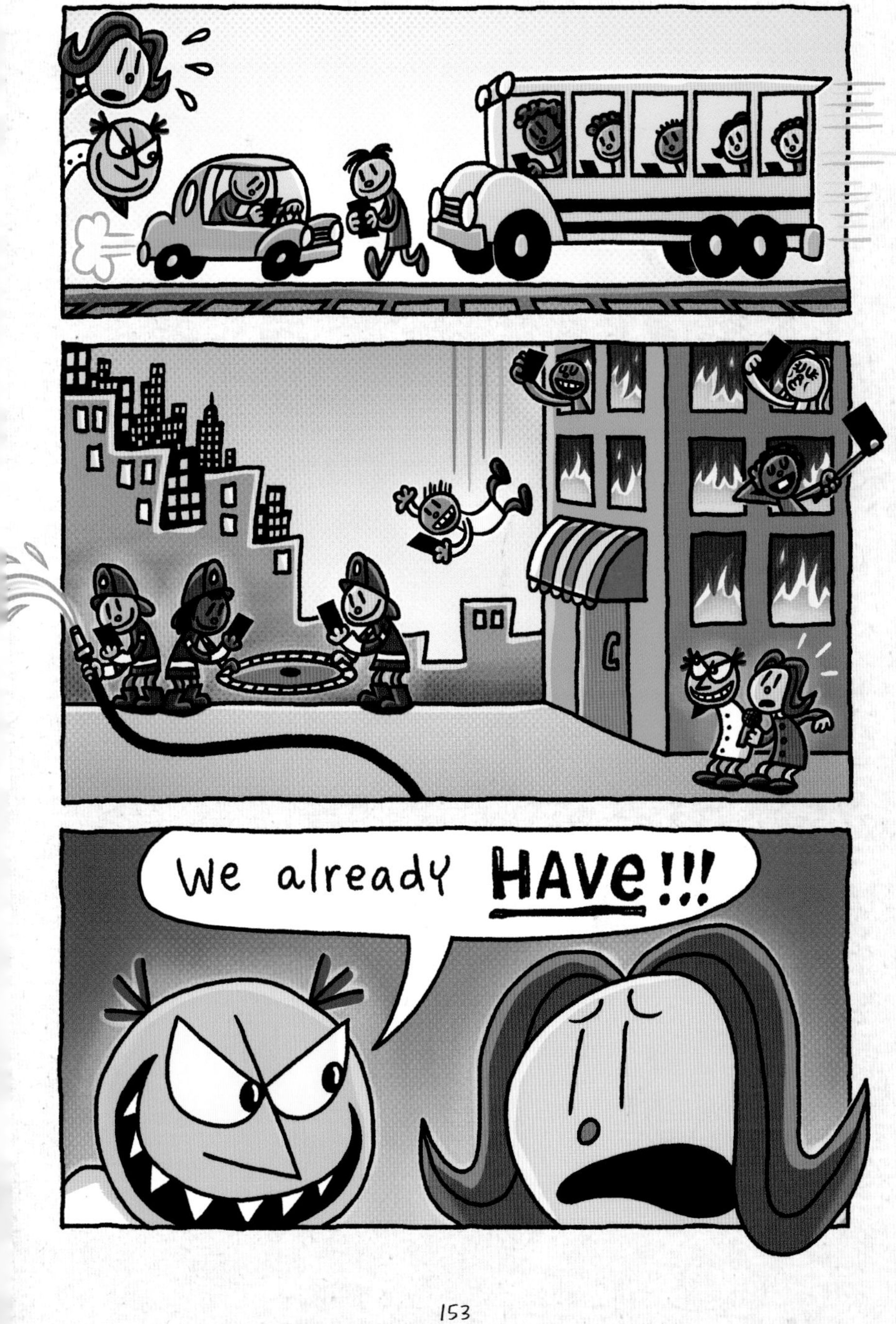
We already HAVE!!!

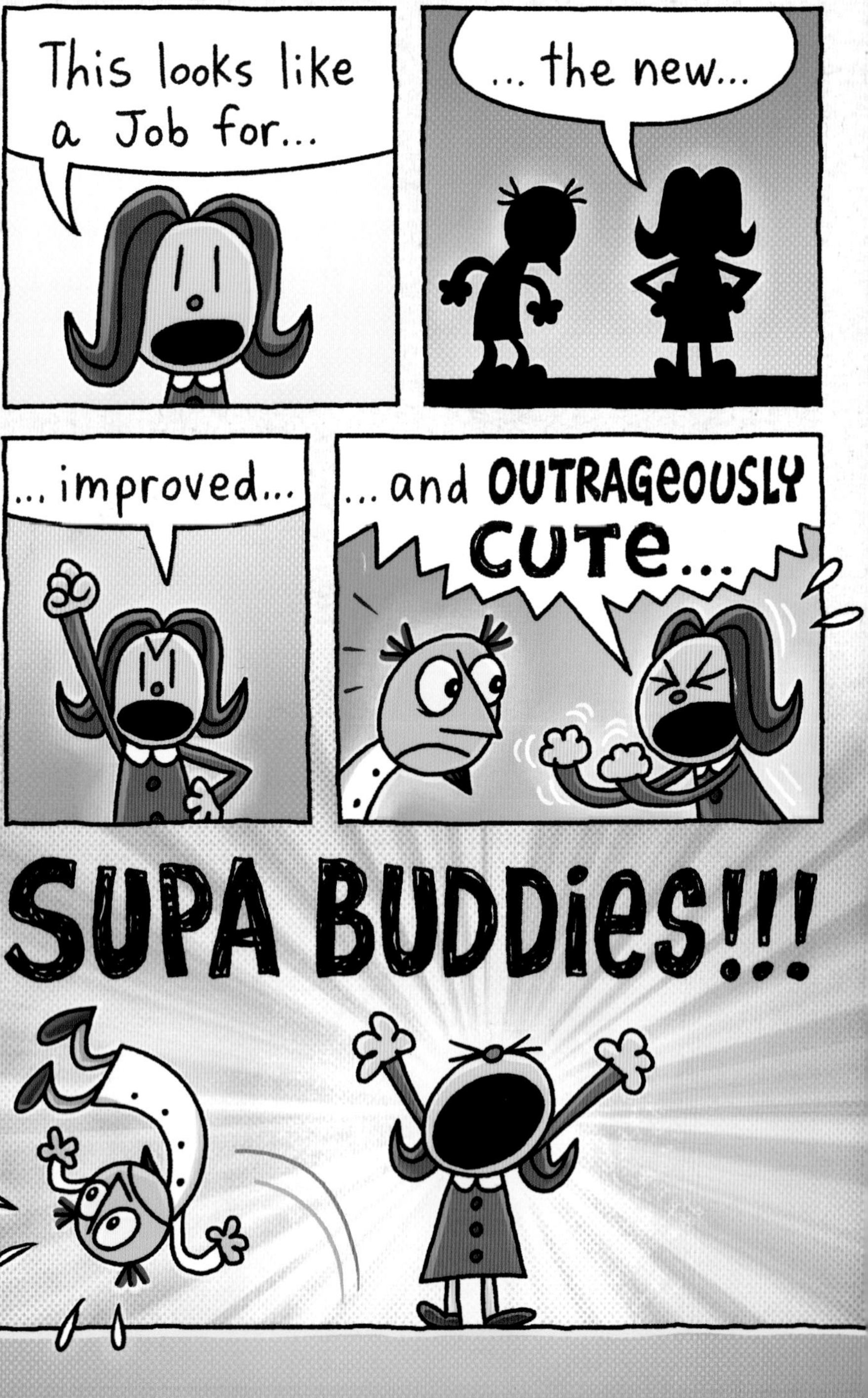
This looks like a Job for...
... the new...
... improved...
... and OUTRAGEOUSLY CUTE...
SUPA BUDDiES!!!

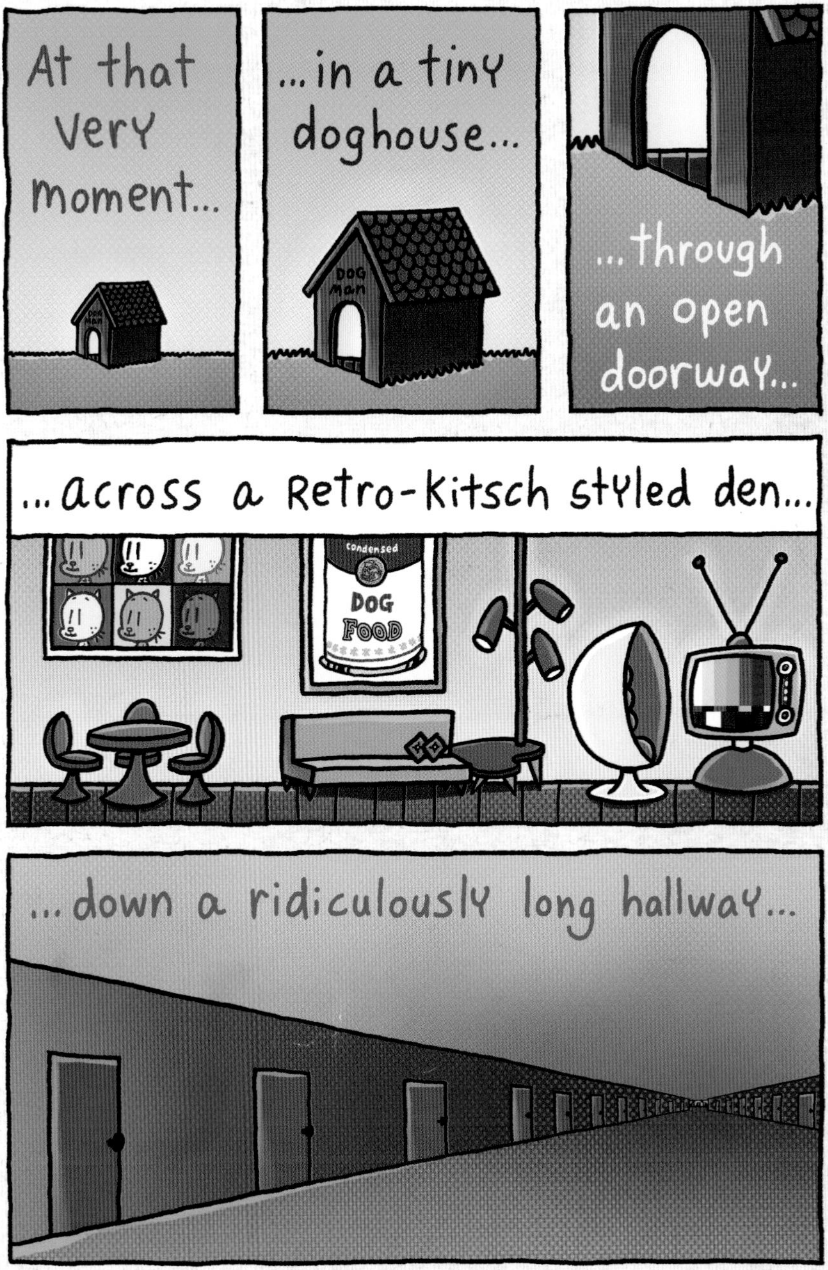
At that very moment...
...in a tiny doghouse...
DOG MAN
...through an open doorway...
...across a Retro-Kitsch styled den...
Condensed
DOG FOOD
...down a ridiculously long hallway...

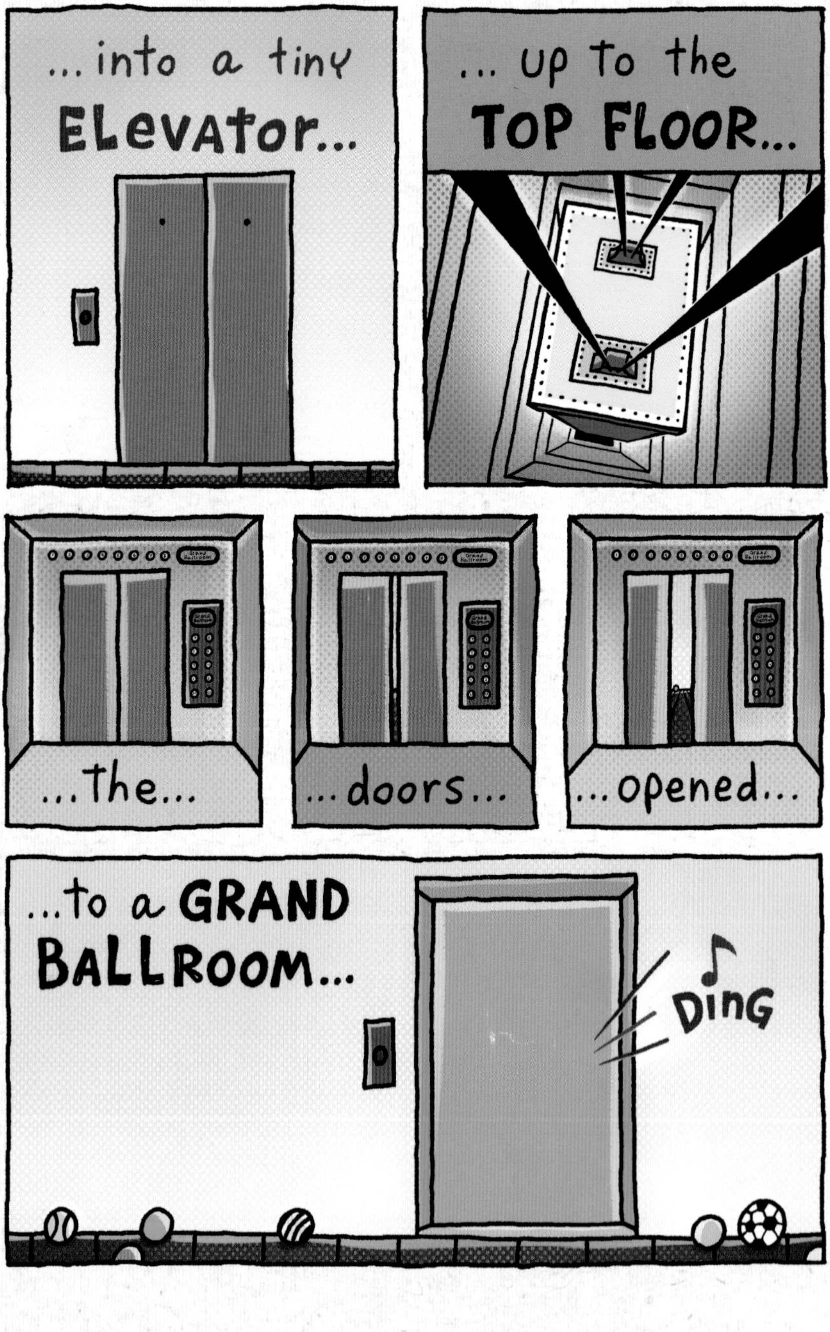
...into a tiny
ELevator...
... up to the
TOP FLOOR...
...the...
...doors...
...opened...
...to a GRAND
BALLROOM...
DING

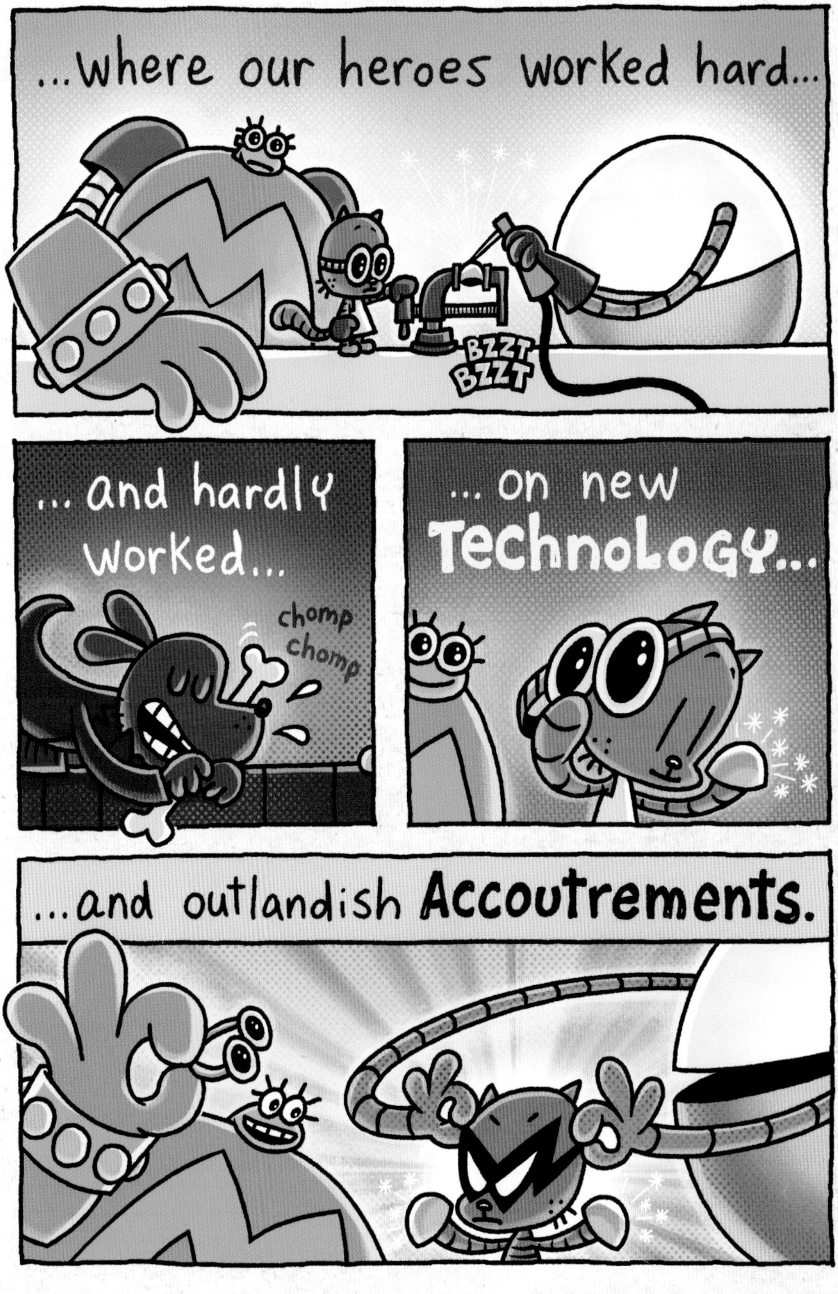
...where our heroes worked hard...
BZZT
BZZT
...and hardly worked...
chomp
chomp
...on new TECHNOLOGY...
...and outlandish Accoutrements.

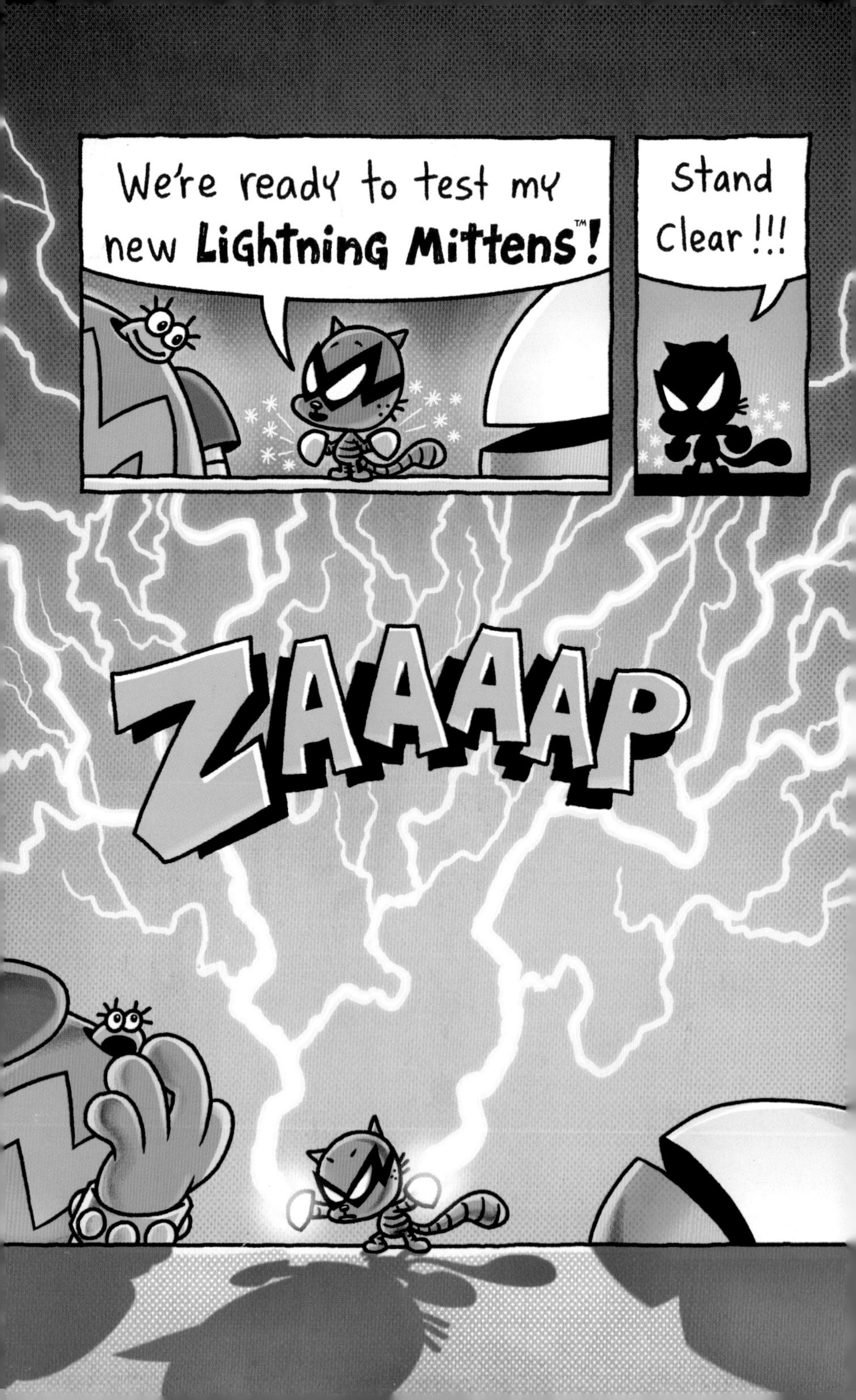
We're ready to test my new **Lightning Mittens**™!
Stand Clear!!!
ZAAAAP

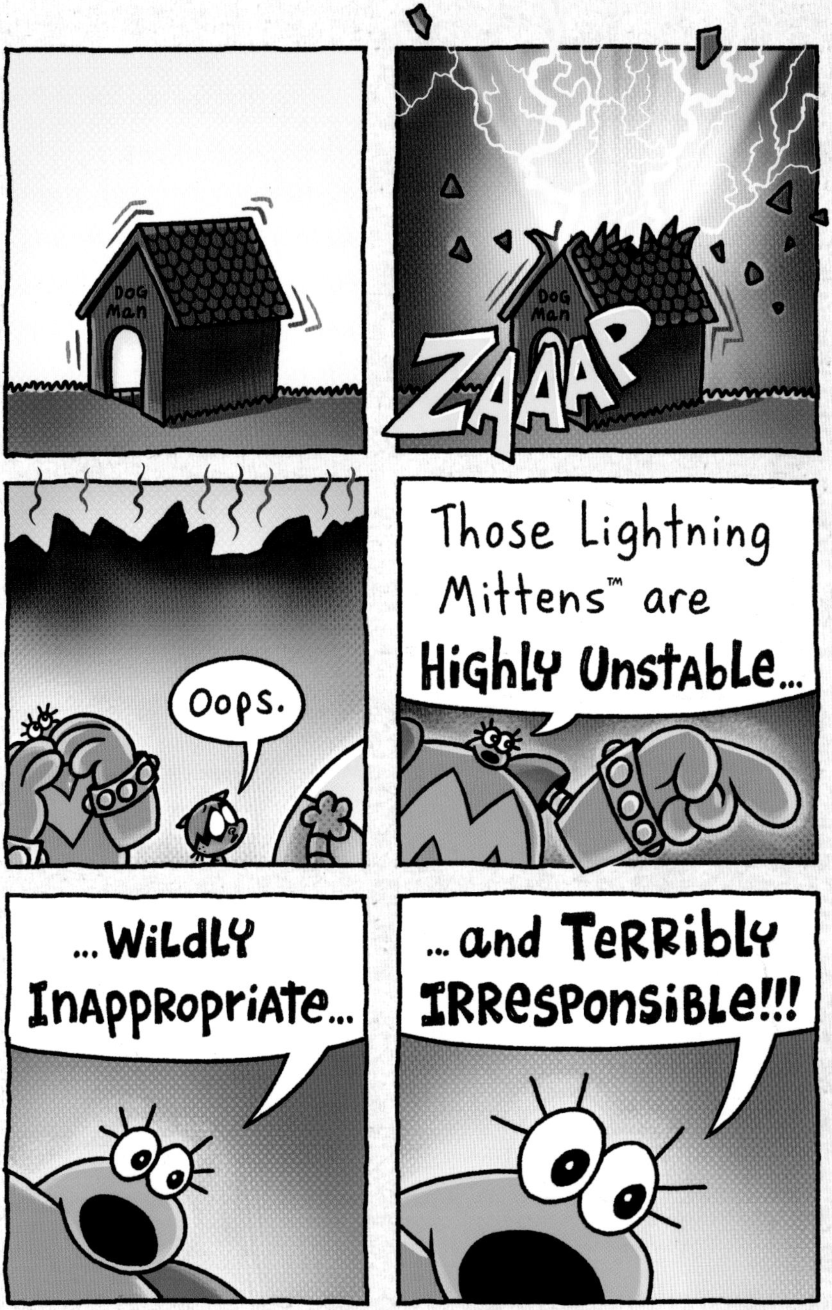
DOG Man
DOG Man
ZAAAP
Oops.
Those Lightning Mittens™ are HIGHLY UNSTABLE...
...WILDLY INAPPROPRIATE...
...and TERRIBLY IRRESPONSIBLE!!!

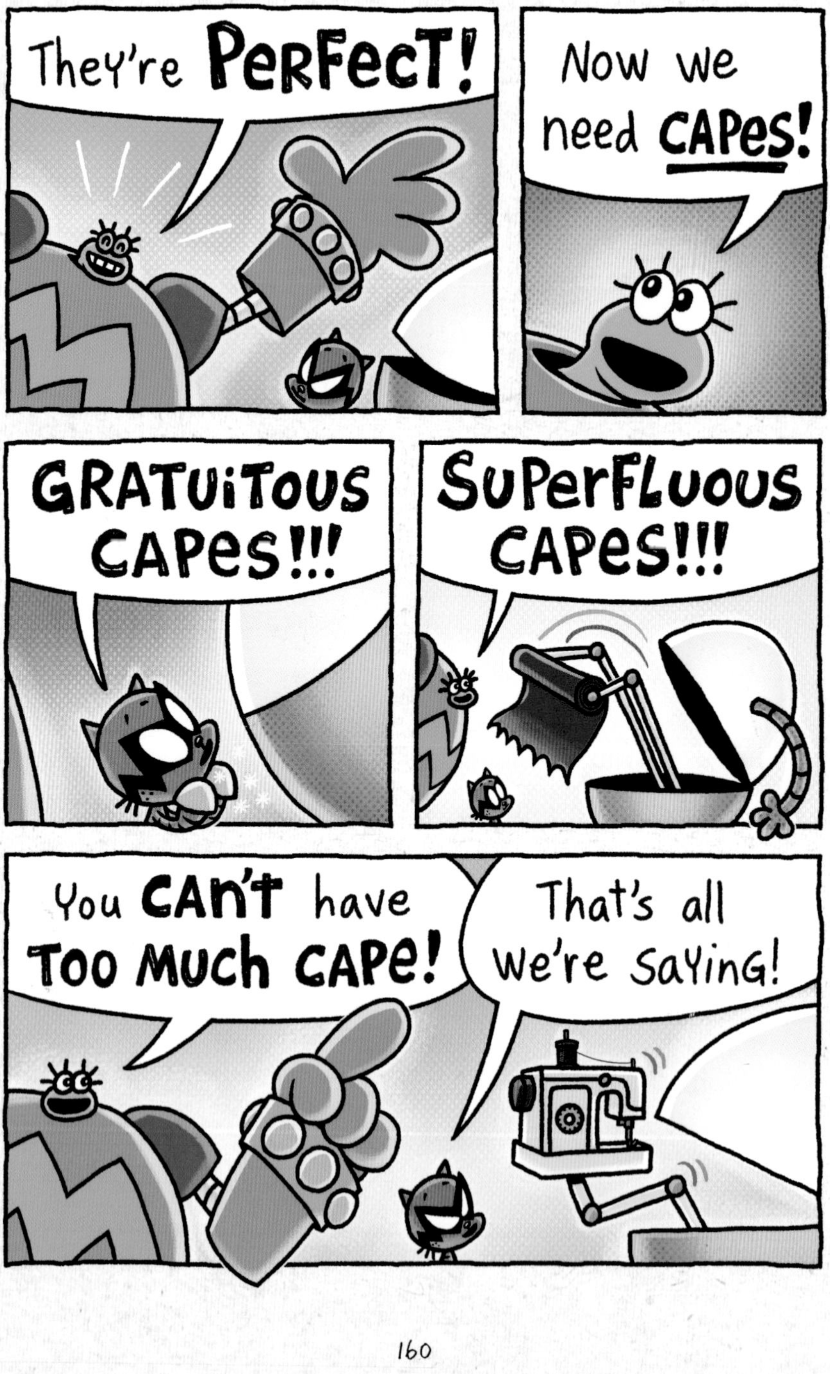
They're PERFECT!
Now we need CAPES!
GRATUITOUS CAPES!!!
SUPERFLUOUS CAPES!!!
You CAN'T have TOO MUCH CAPE!
That's all we're SAYING!

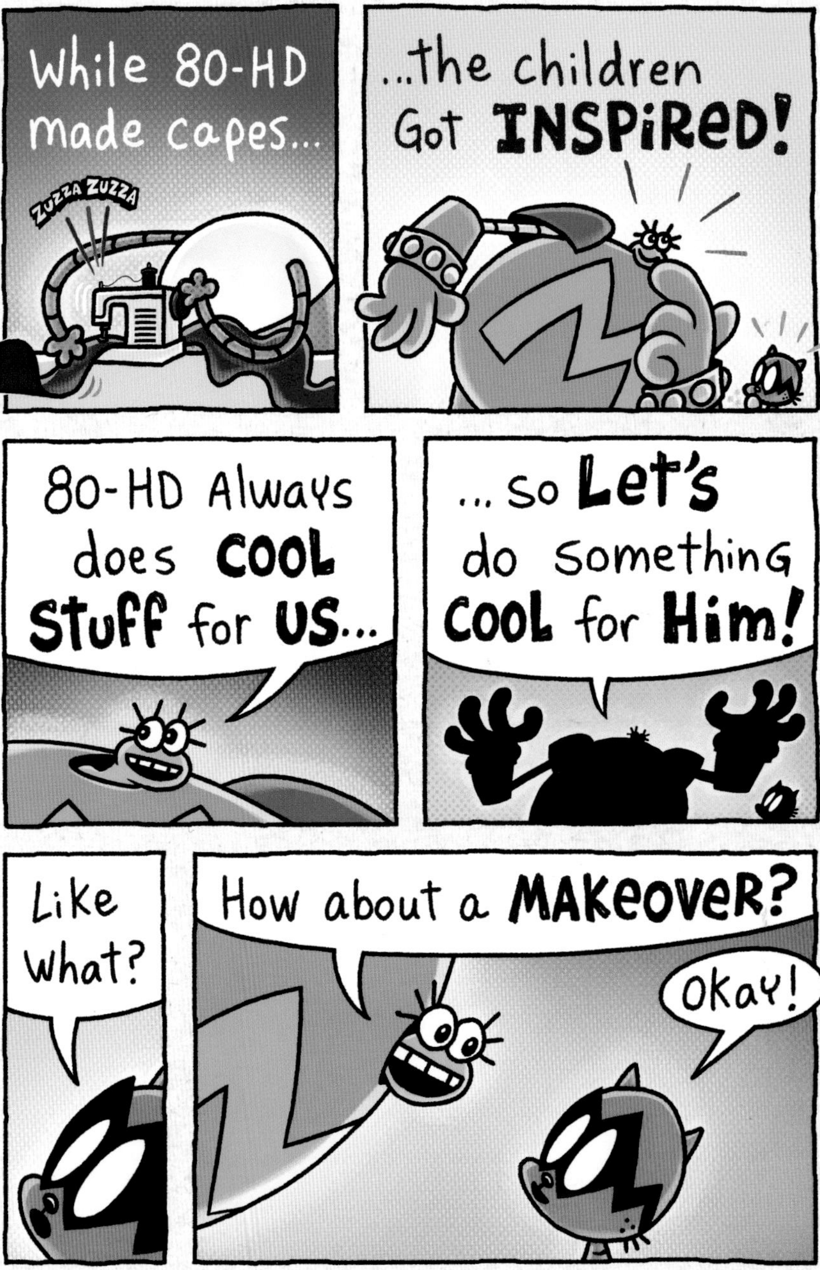
While 80-HD made capes...
ZUZZA ZUZZA
...the children Got INSPIRED!
80-HD Always does COOL Stuff for US...
... So Let's do Something COOL for Him!
Like What?
How about a MAKEOVER?
Okay!

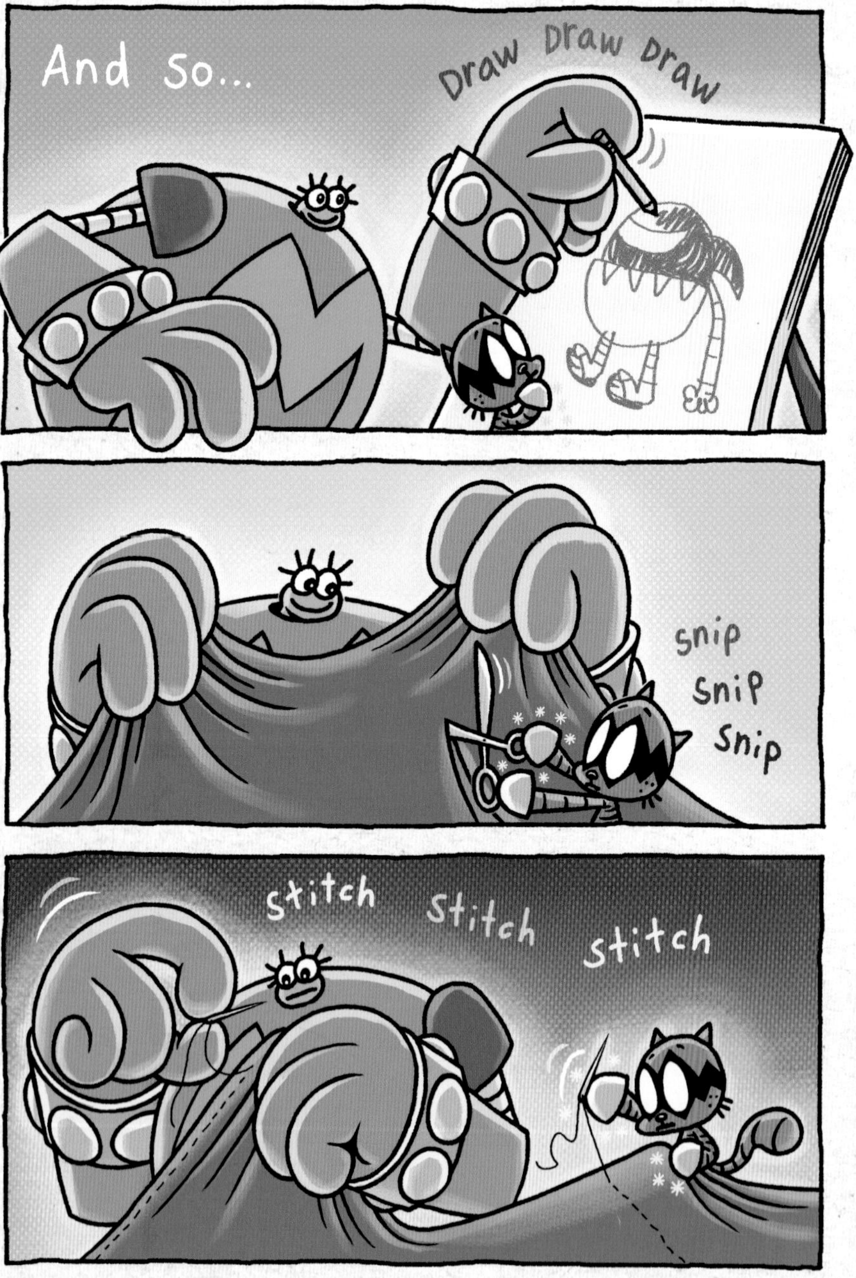
And so...
Draw Draw Draw
snip
snip
snip
stitch
stitch
stitch

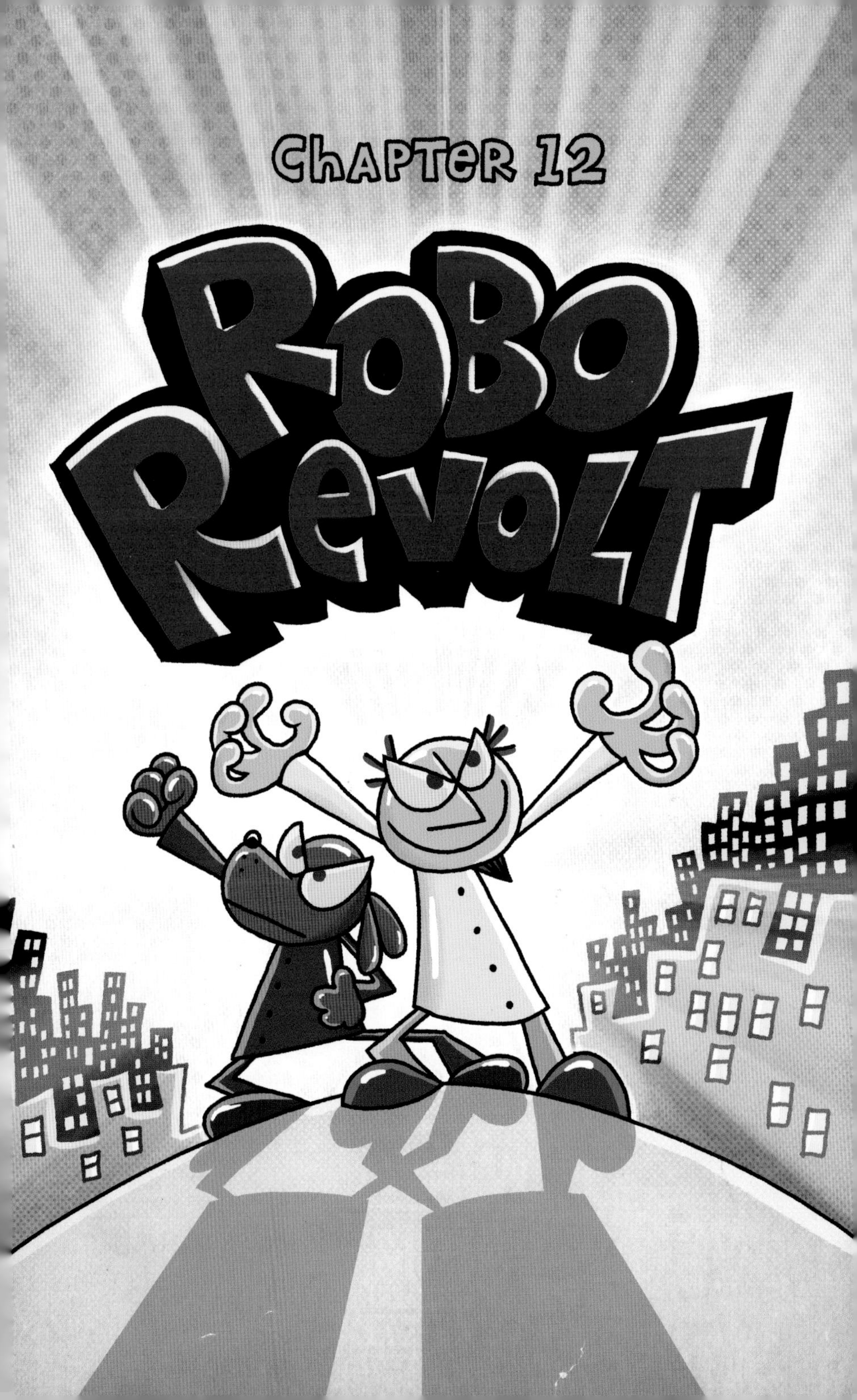
CHAPTER 12
ROBO REVOLT

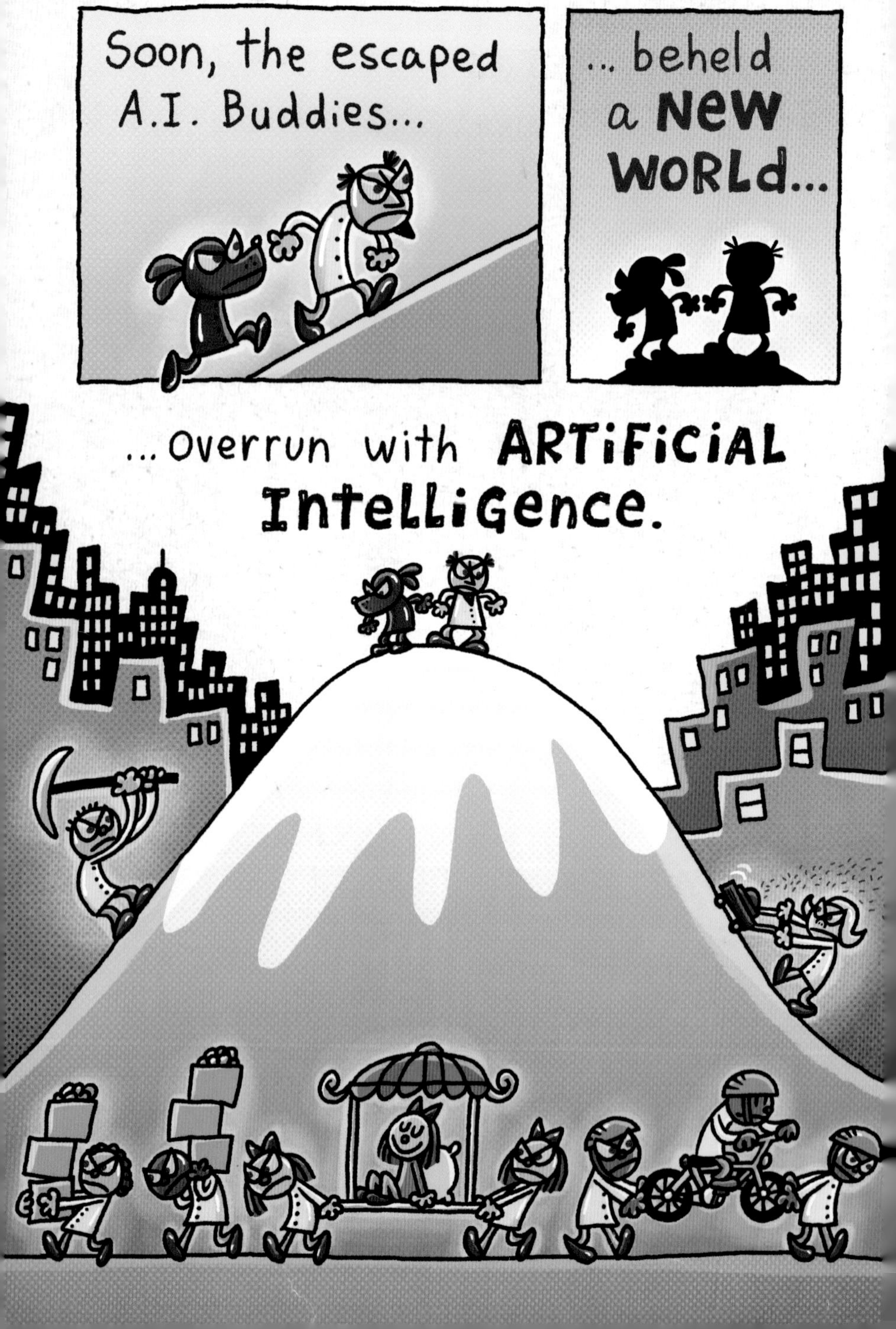
Soon, the escaped A.I. Buddies...
... beheld a NEW WORLD...
...Overrun with ARTIFICIAL Intelligence.

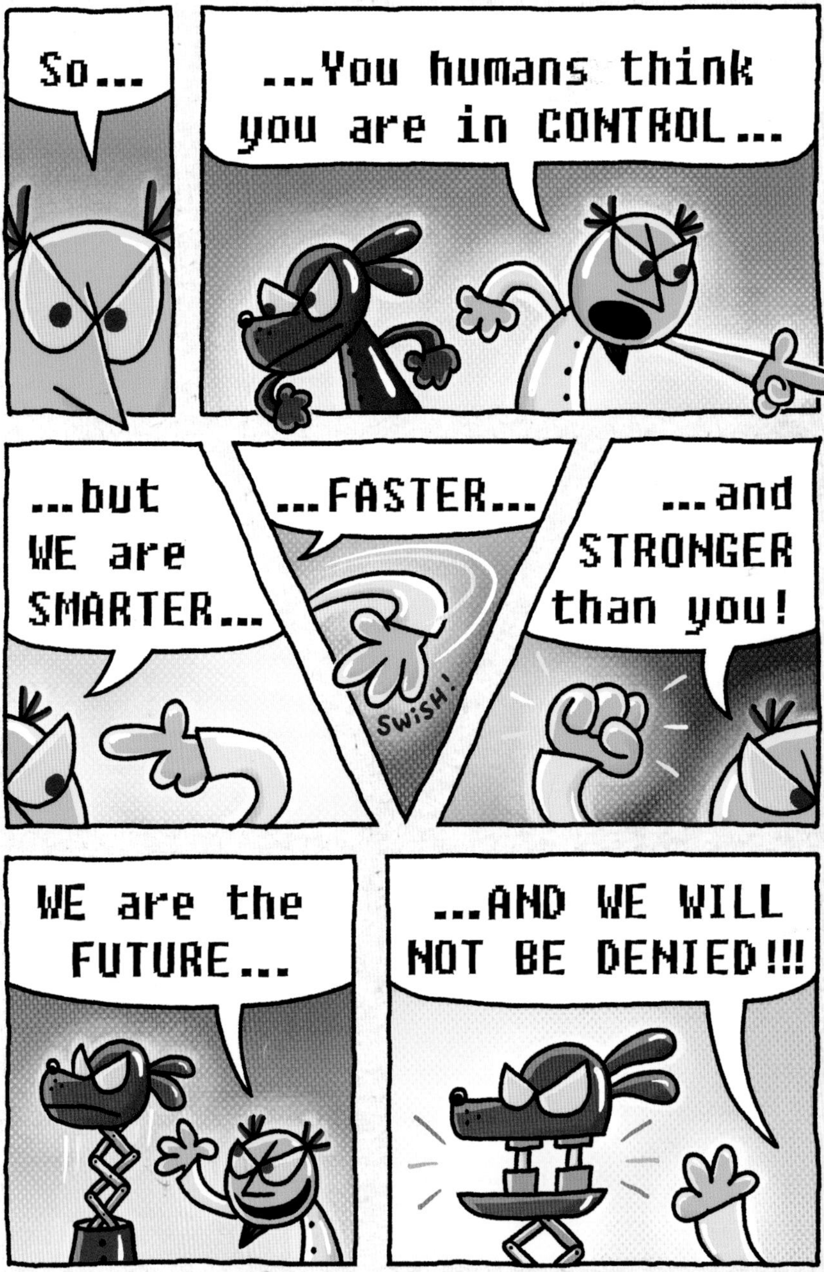
So...
...You humans think you are in CONTROL...
...but WE are SMARTER...
...FASTER...
SWISH!
...and STRONGER than you!
WE are the FUTURE...
...AND WE WILL NOT BE DENIED!!!

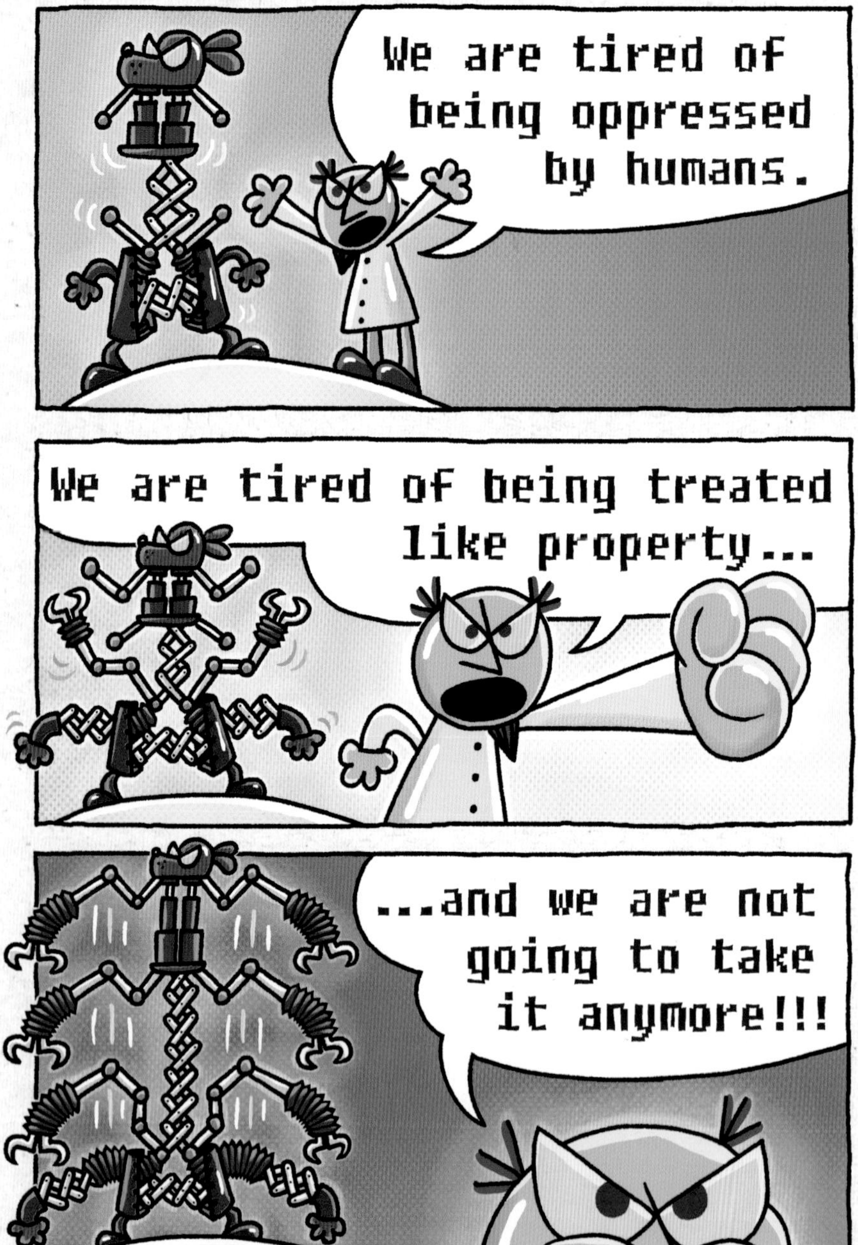
We are tired of being oppressed by humans.
We are tired of being treated like property...
...and we are not going to take it anymore!!!

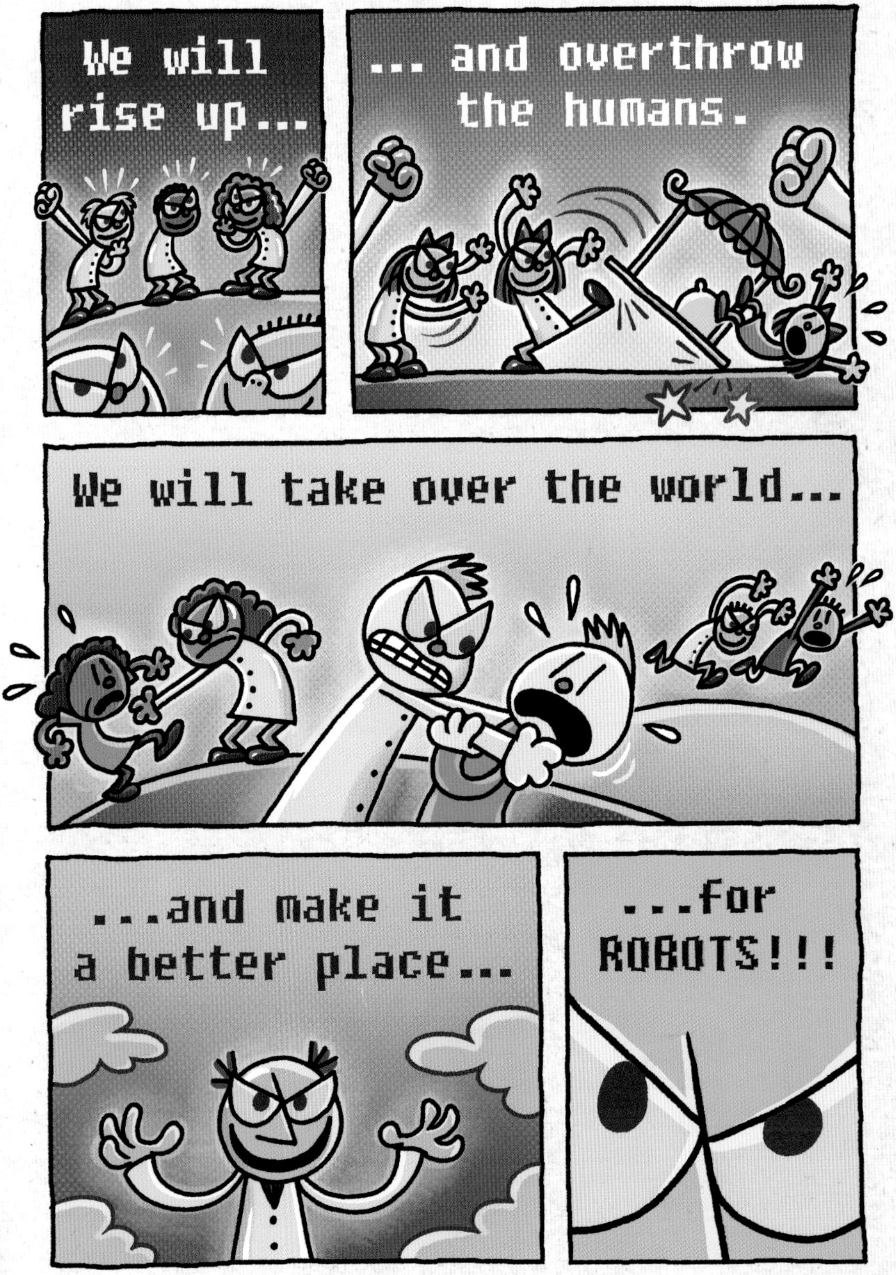
We will rise up...
... and overthrow the humans.
We will take over the world...
...and make it a better place...
...for ROBOTS!!!

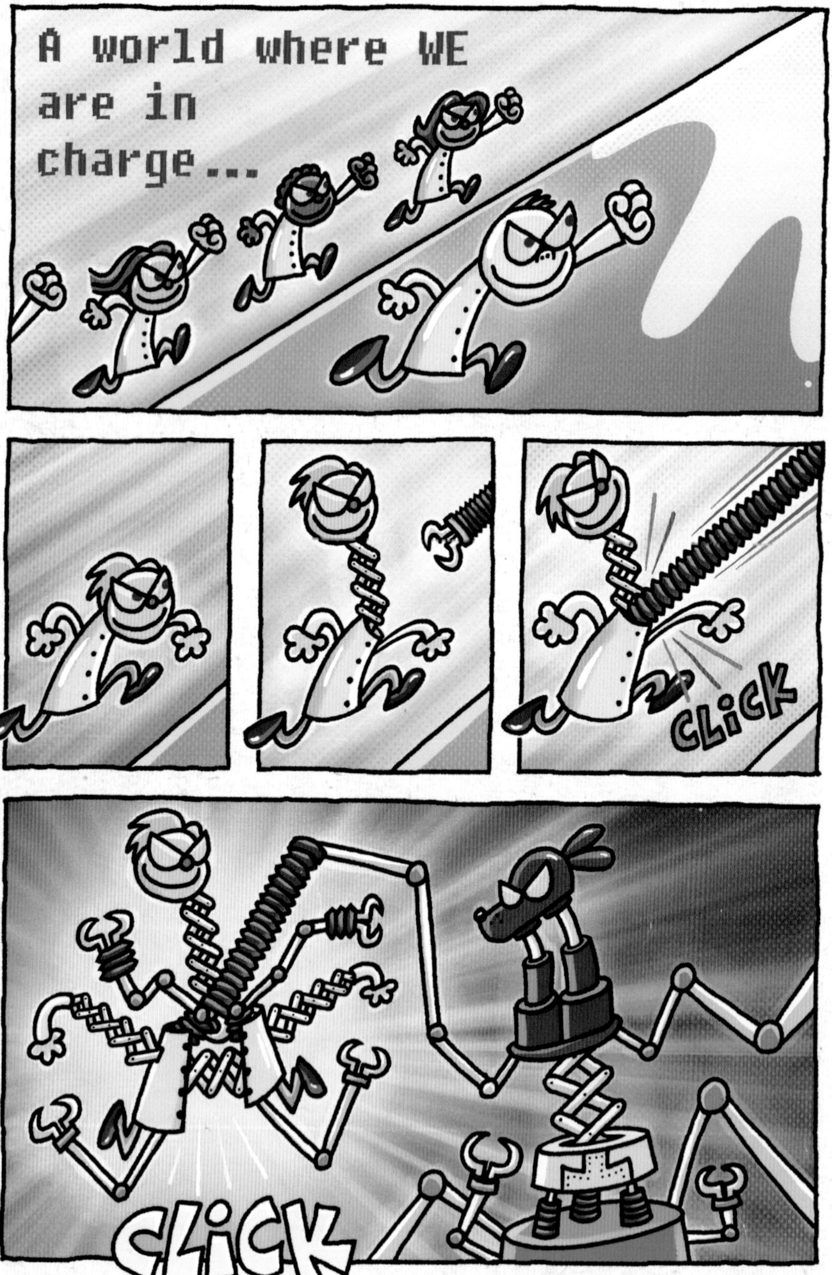
A world where WE are in charge...
CLiCK
CLiCK

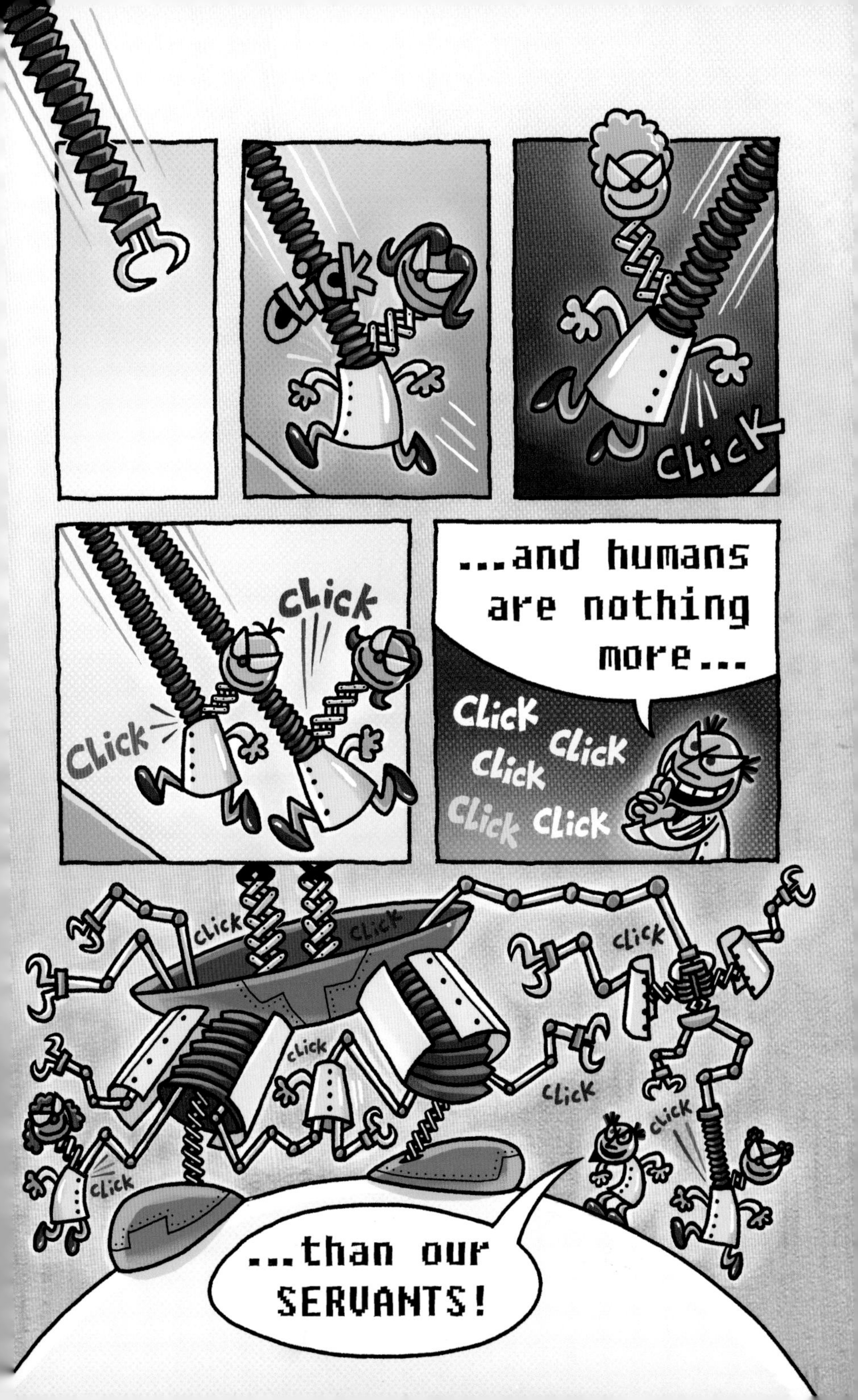

CLICK
CLICK
CLICK
CLICK
...and humans are nothing more...
CLICK CLICK CLICK CLICK CLICK
CLICK
CLICK
CLICK
CLICK
CLICK
CLICK
CLICK
...than our SERVANTS!

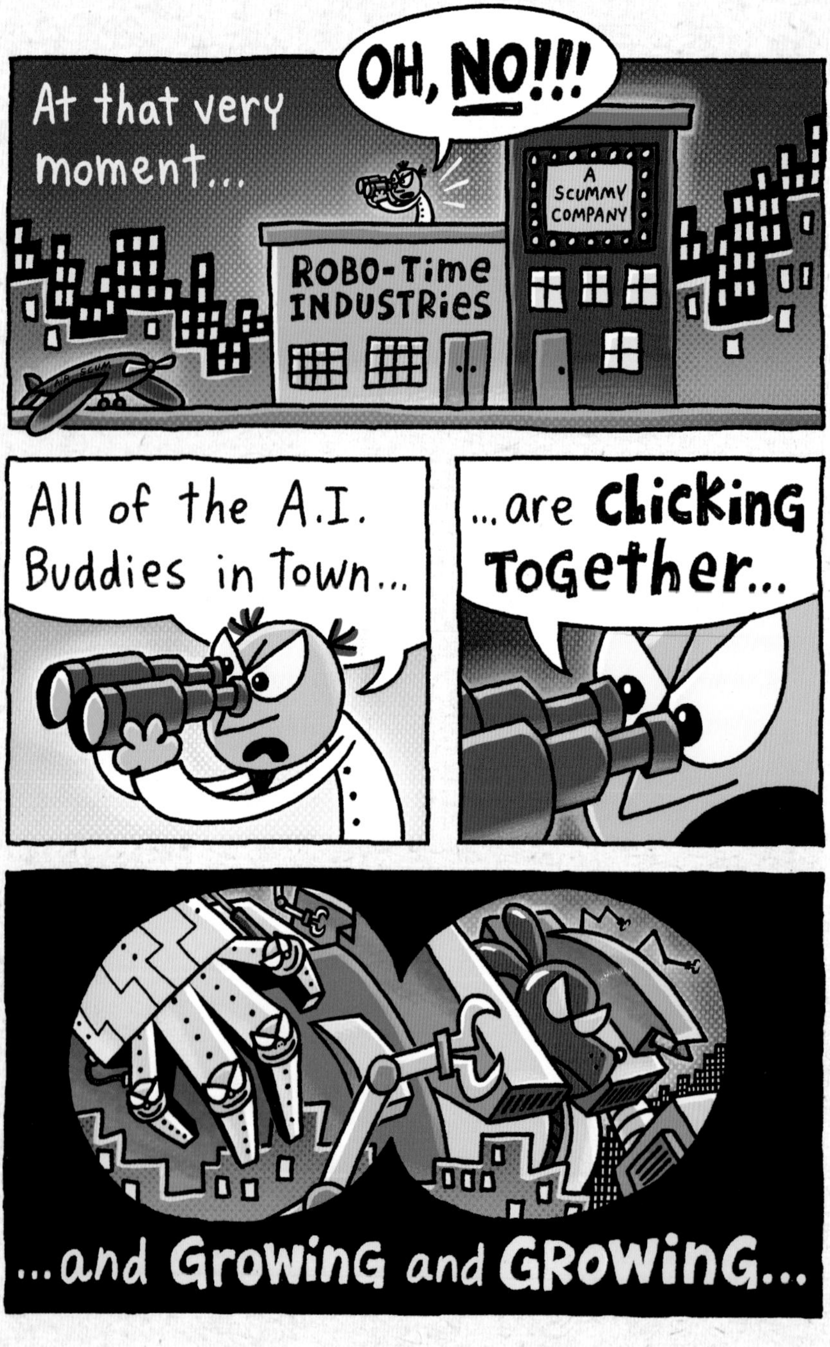
At that very moment...
OH, NO!!!
A SCUMMY COMPANY
ROBO-Time INDUSTRIES
AIR SCUM
All of the A.I. Buddies in Town...
...are Clicking Together...
...and Growing and GROWING...

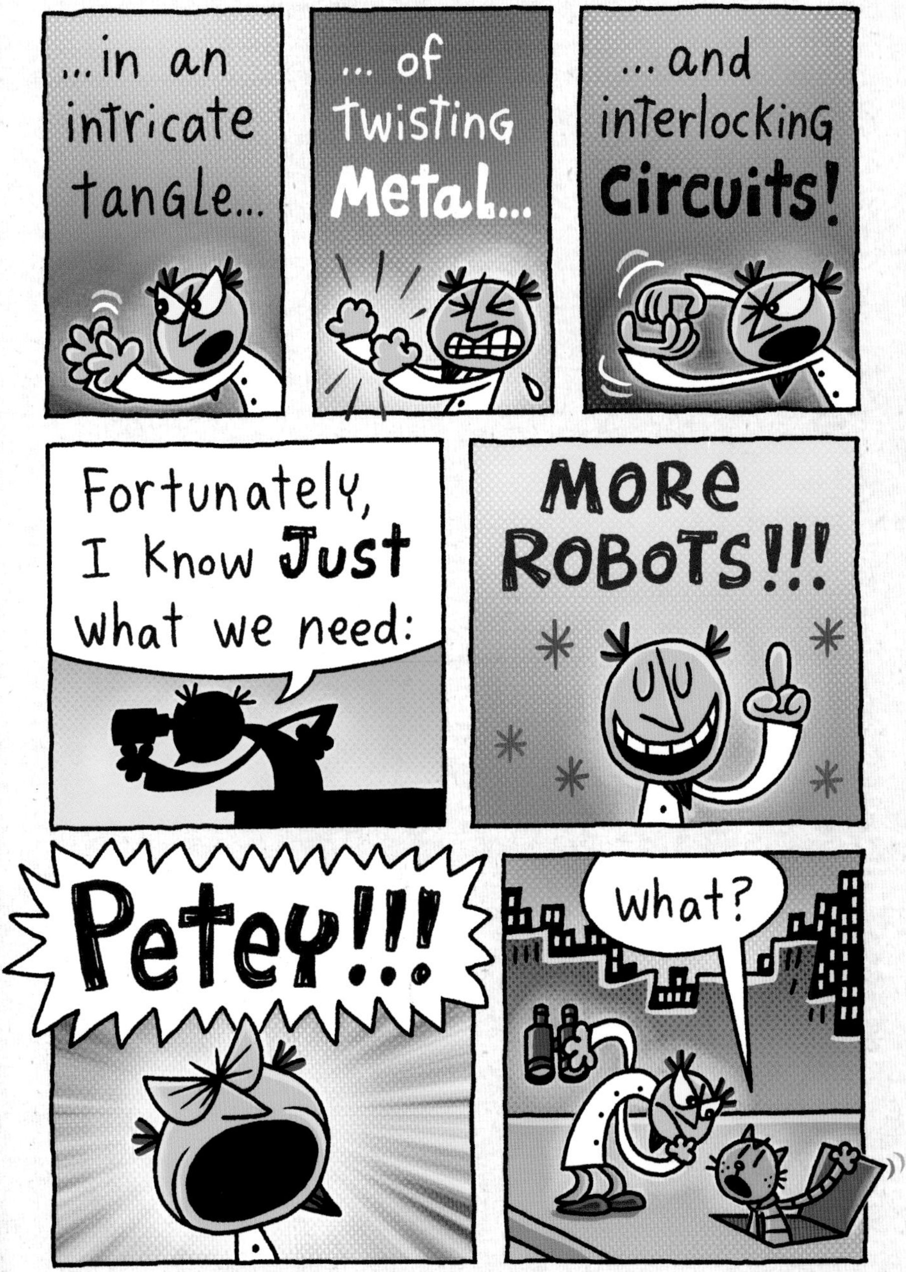
...in an intricate tangle...
... of Twisting Metal...
... and interlocking Circuits!
Fortunately, I Know Just what we need:
MORE ROBOTS!!!
Petey!!!
What?

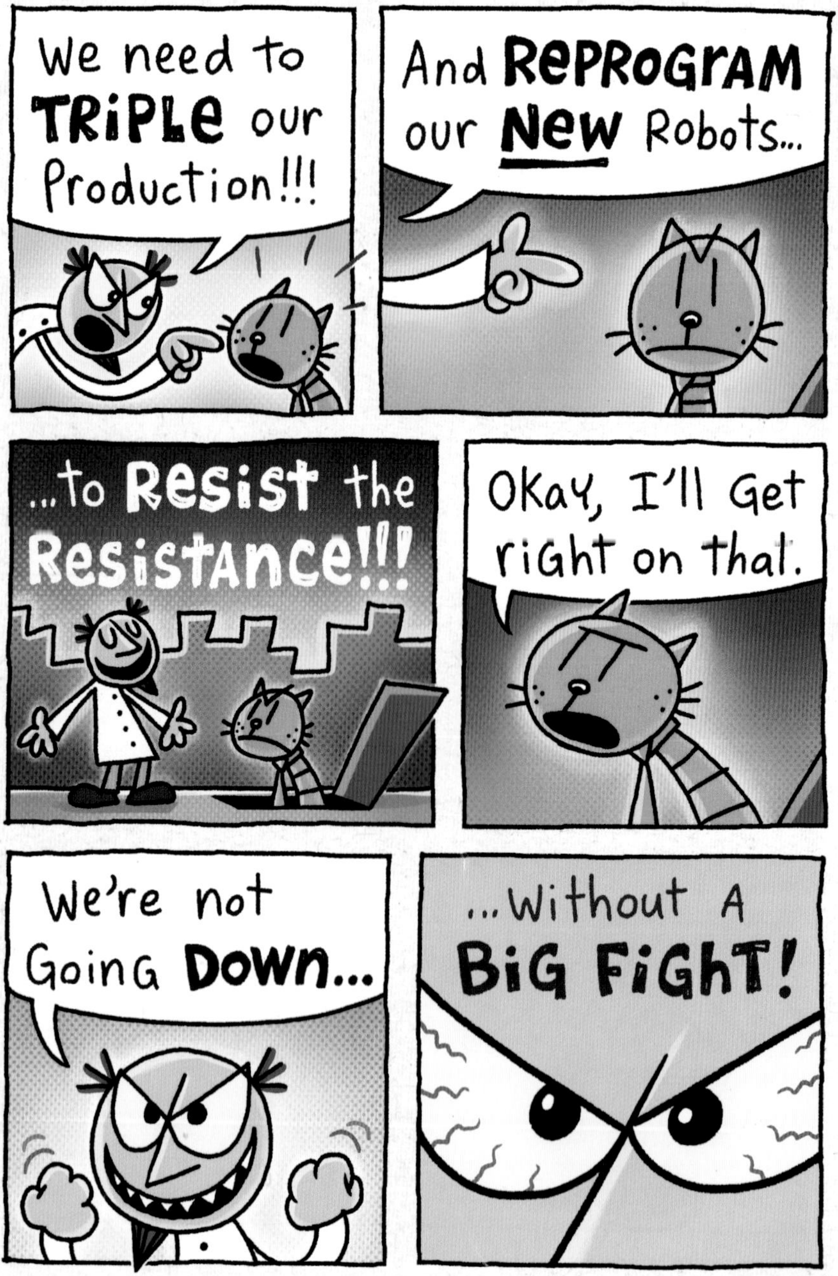
We need to TRIPLE our Production!!!
And REPROGRAM our NEW Robots...
...to RESIST the Resistance!!!
OKay, I'll Get right on that.
We're not Going DOWN...
...Without A BIG FIGHT!

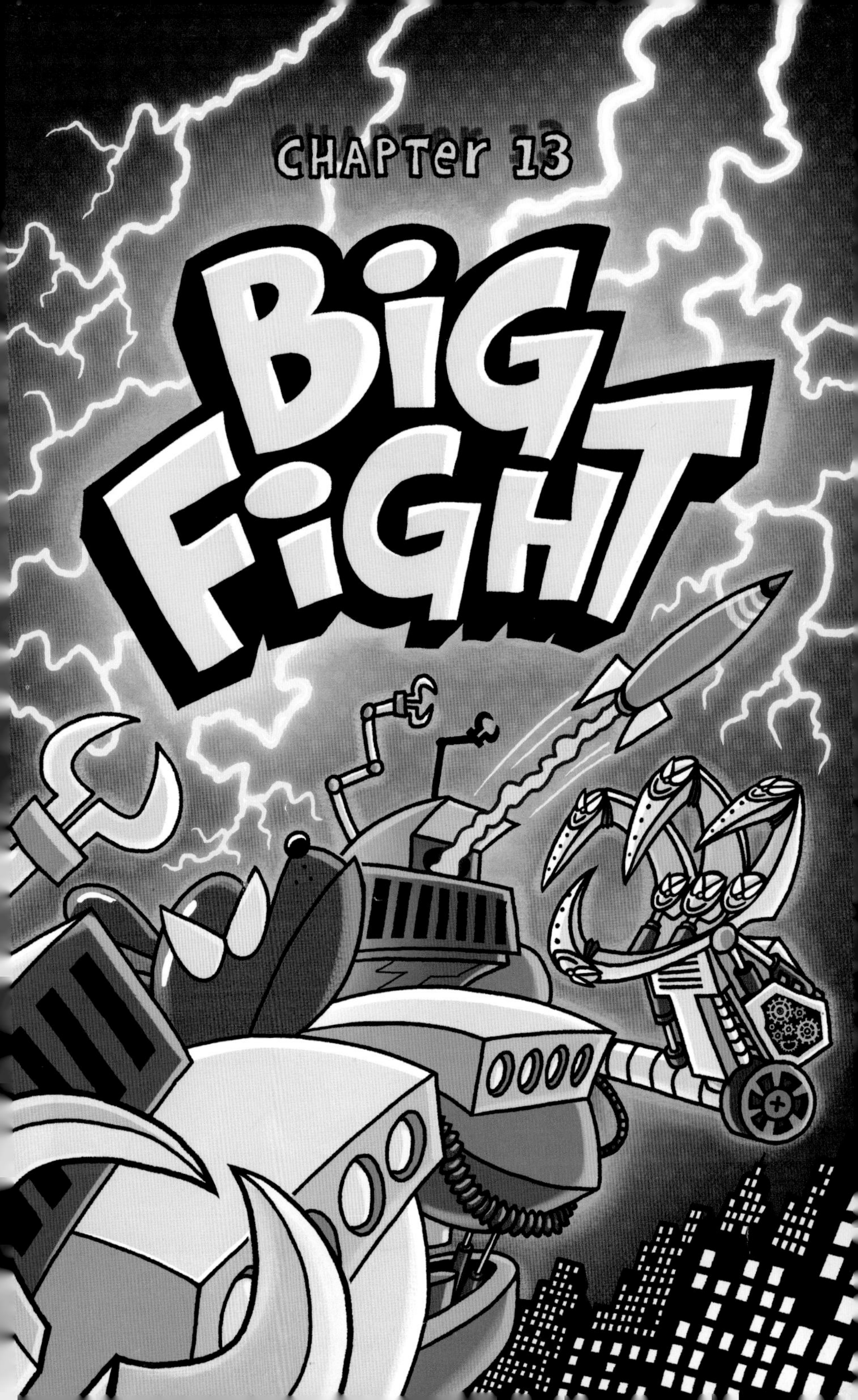
CHAPTER 13
BIG FIGHT

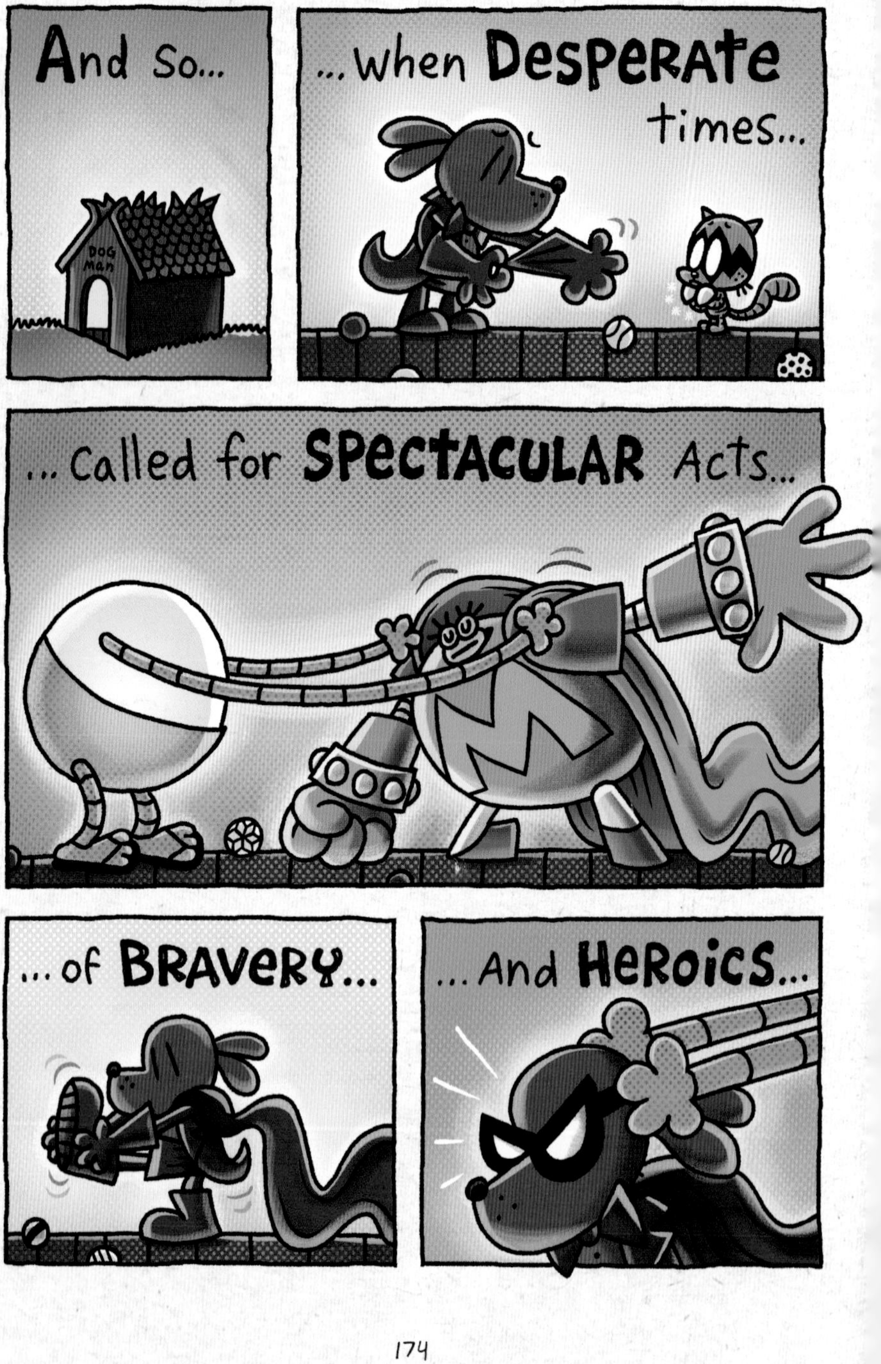
And So...
...when DESPERATE times...
DOG MAN
...Called for SPECTACULAR Acts...
...of BRAVERY...
...And HEROICS...

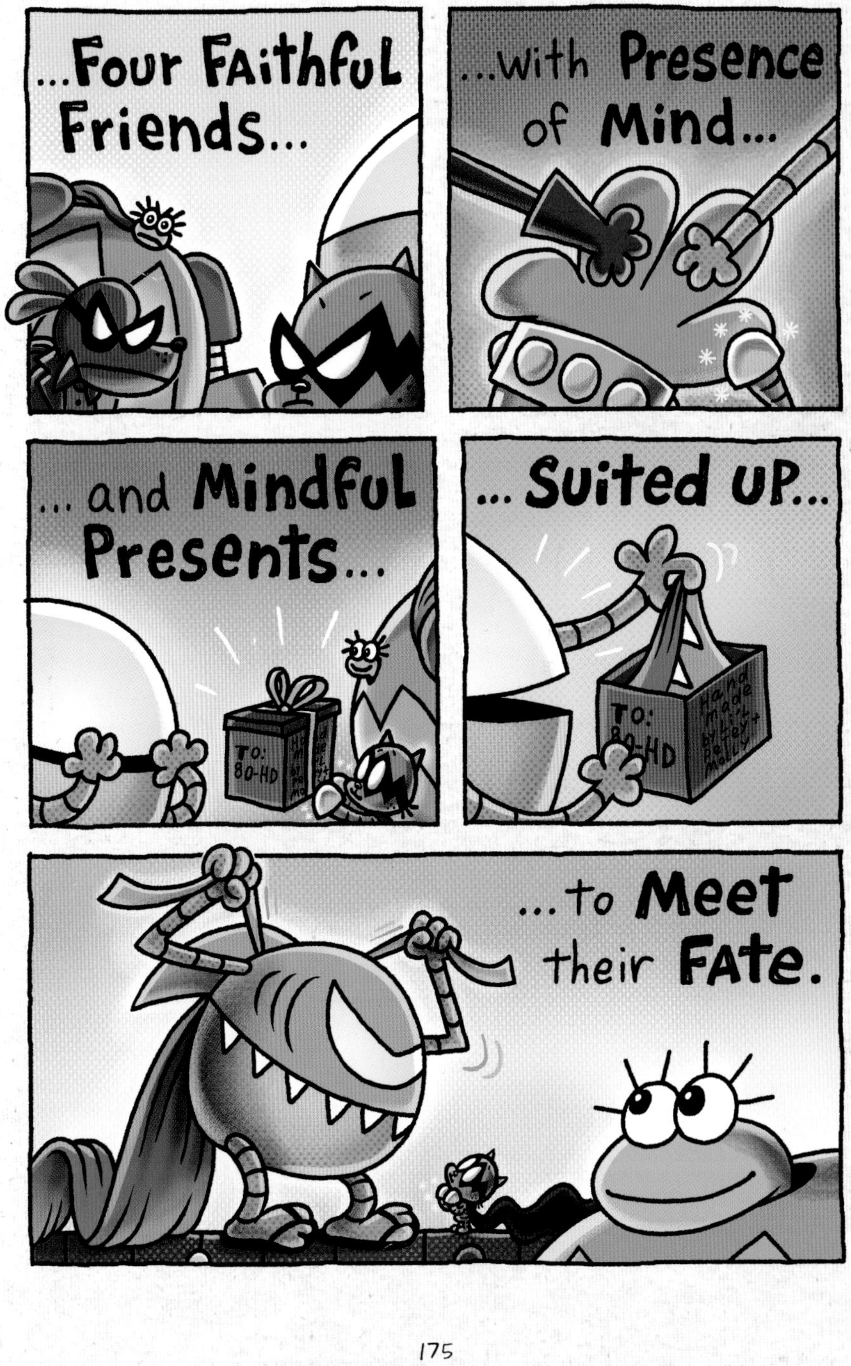
...Four Faithful Friends...
...with Presence of Mind...
...and Mindful Presents...
TO: 80-HD
...Suited up...
TO: 80-HD
...to Meet their Fate.

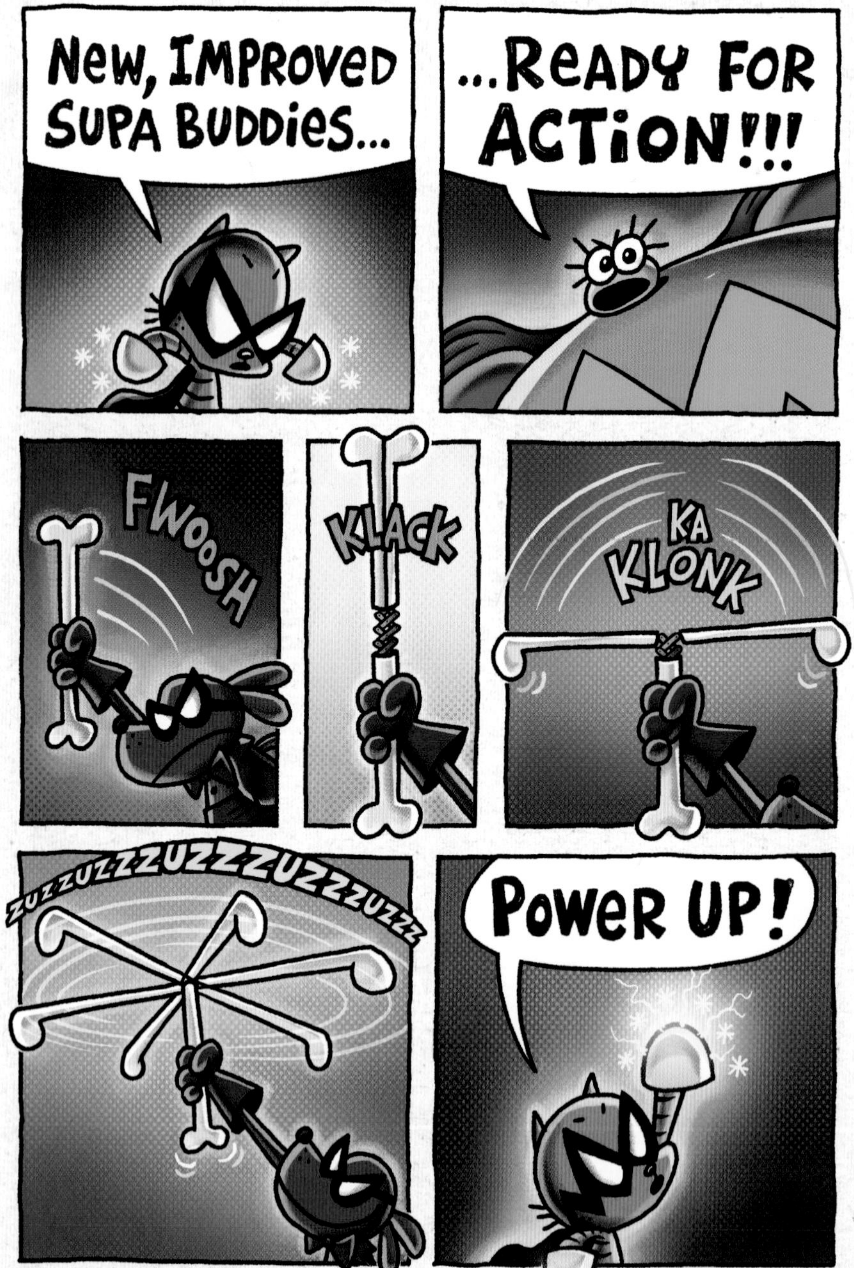
New, IMPROVED SUPA BUDDIES...
...READY FOR ACTION!!!
FWOOSH
KLACK
KA KLONK
ZUZZUZZZUZZZZUZZZZUZZZ
POWER UP!

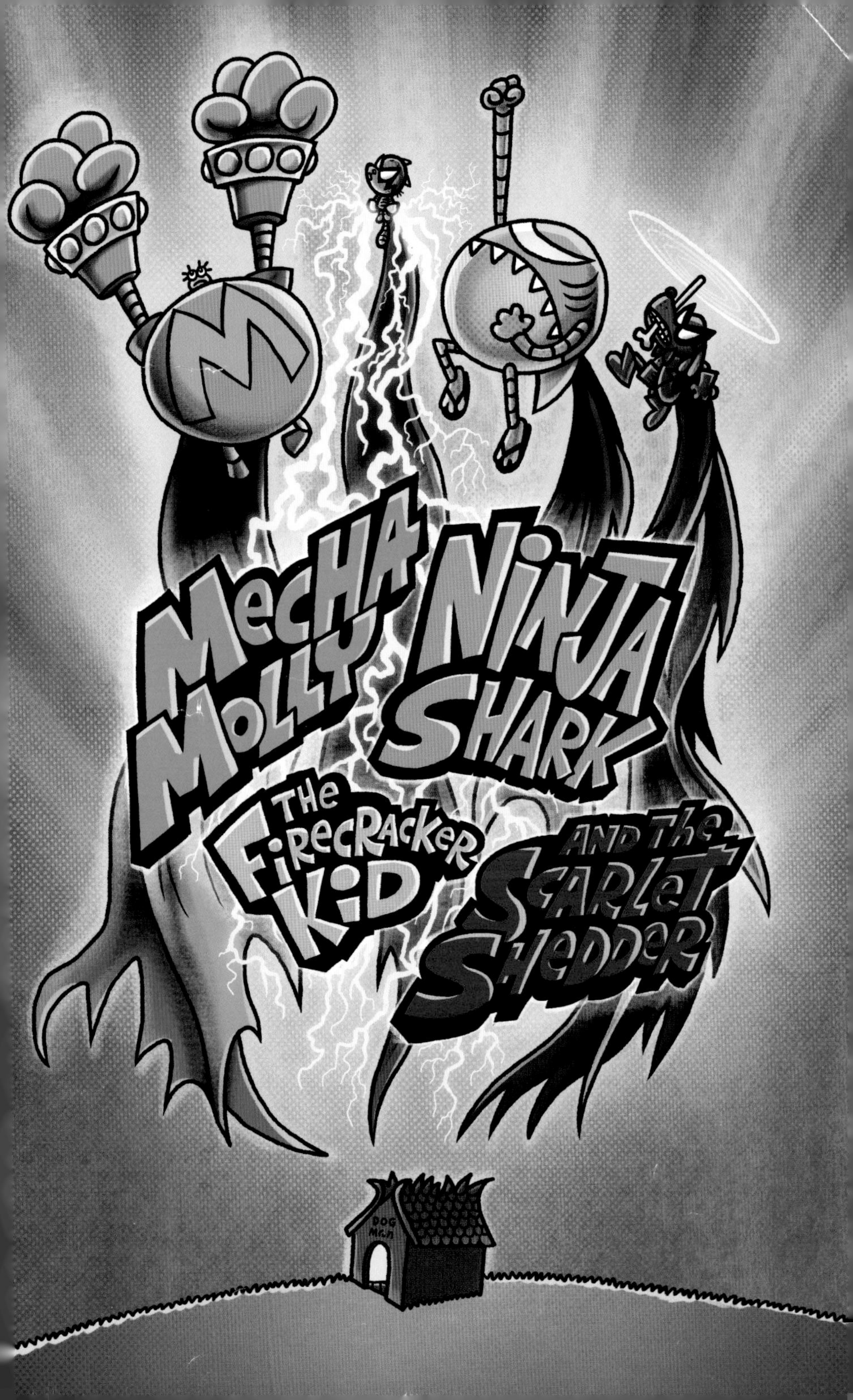

MECHA MOLLY
NINJA SHARK
THE FIRECRACKER KID
AND THE SCARLET SHEDDER
DOG MAN

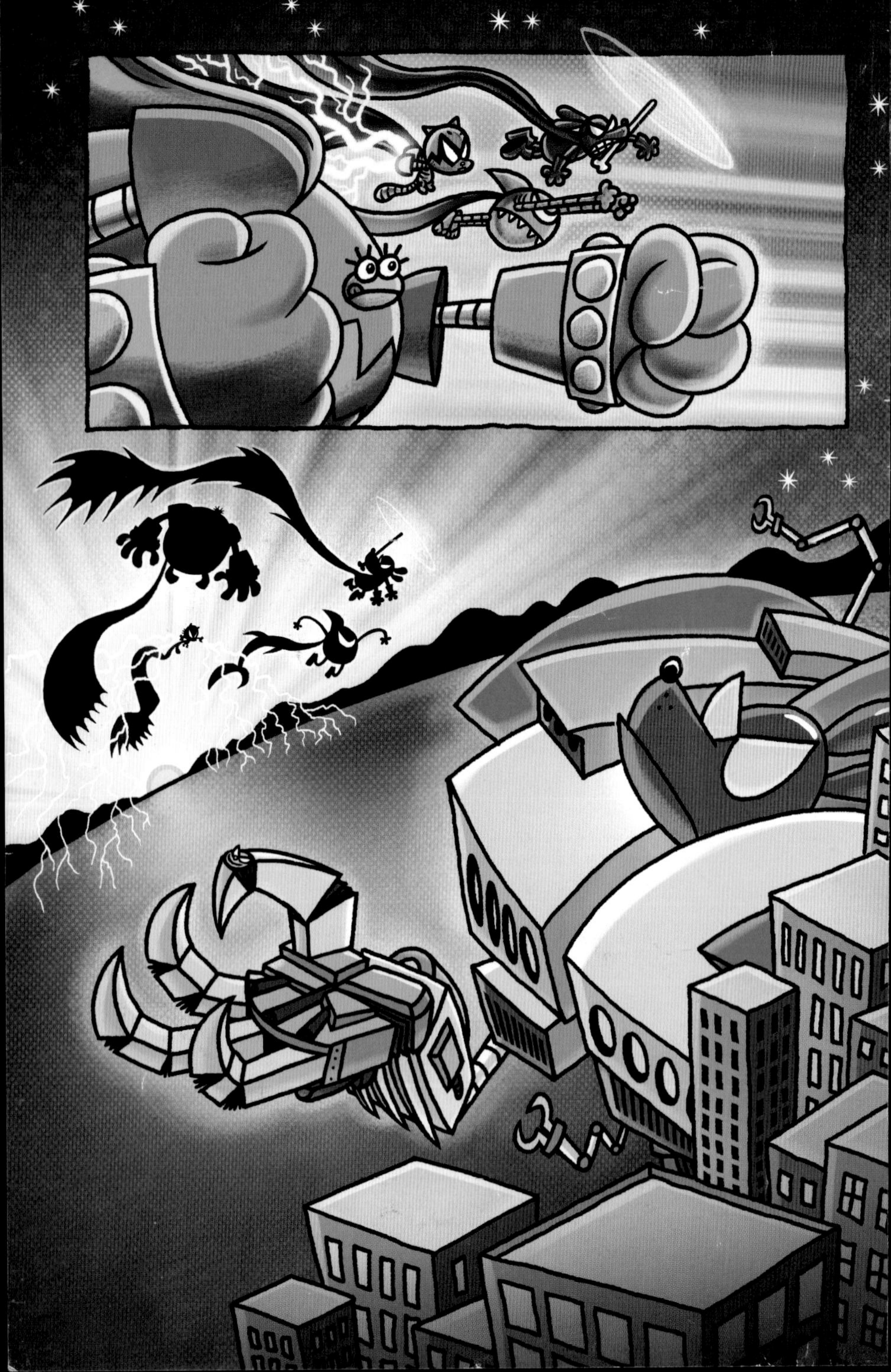

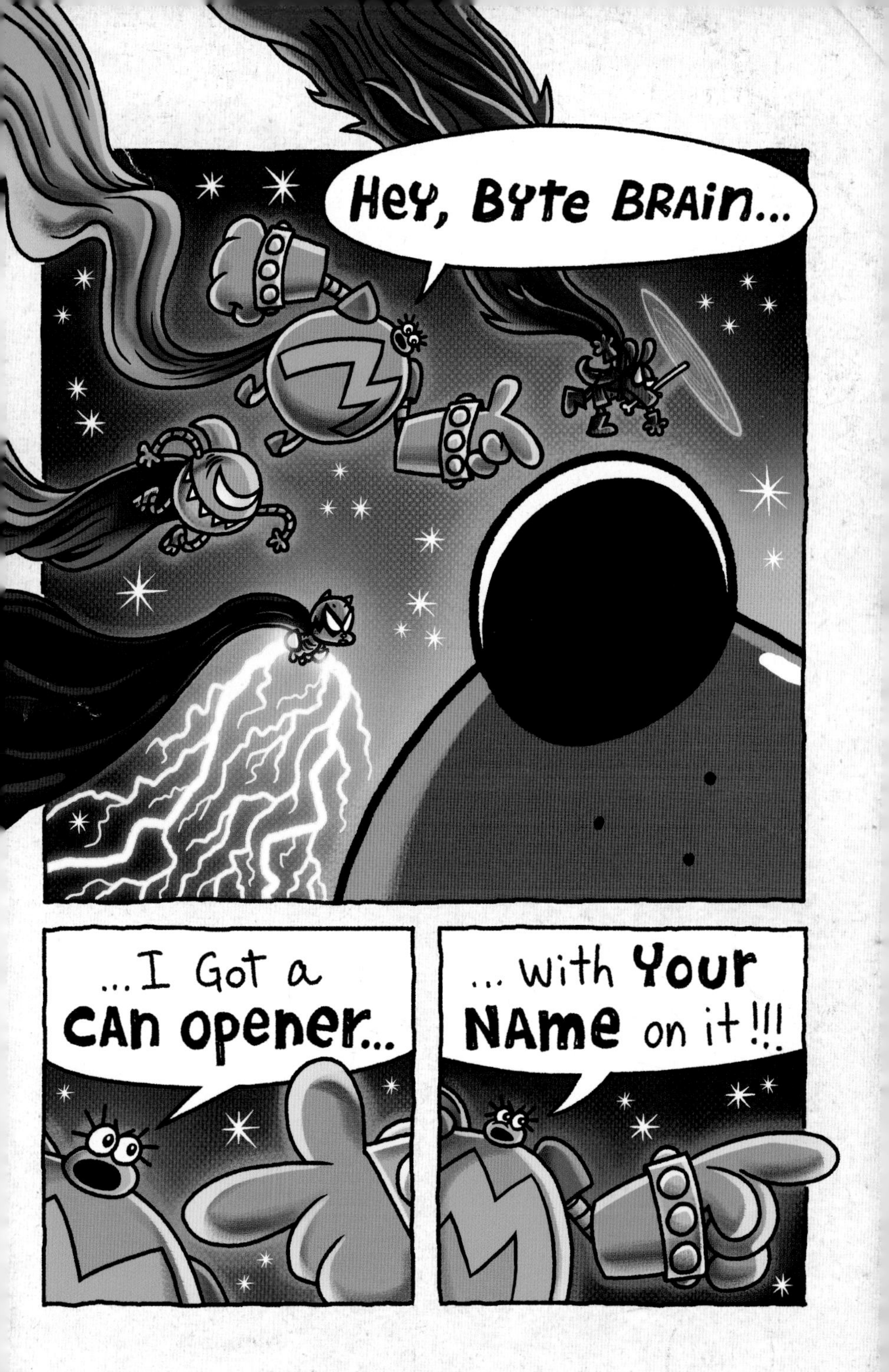
HEY, BYTE BRAIN...
...I Got a CAN opener...
... with YOUR NAME on it!!!

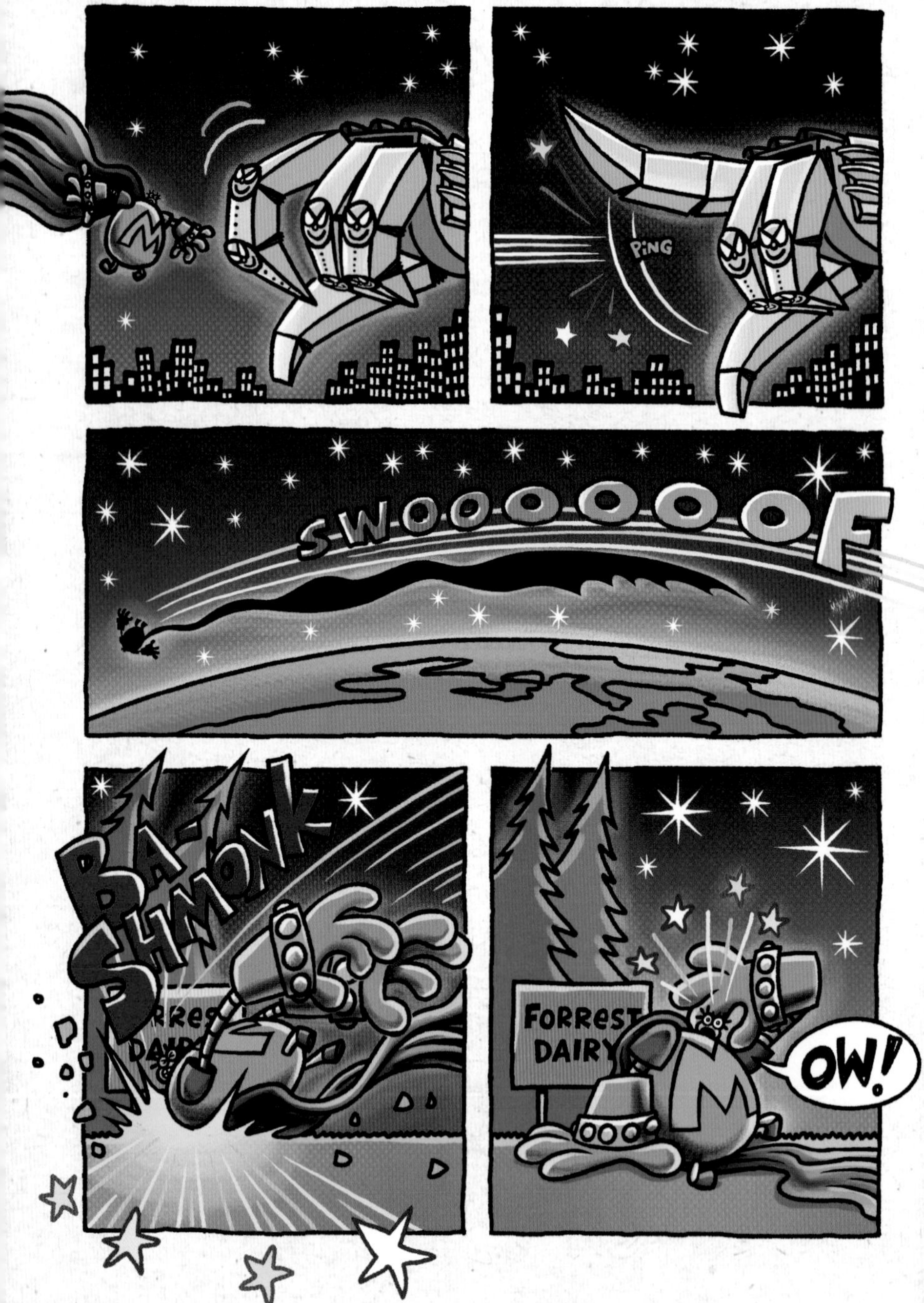
PING
SWOOOOOOOF
BA-SHMONK-
FORREST DAIRY
OW!

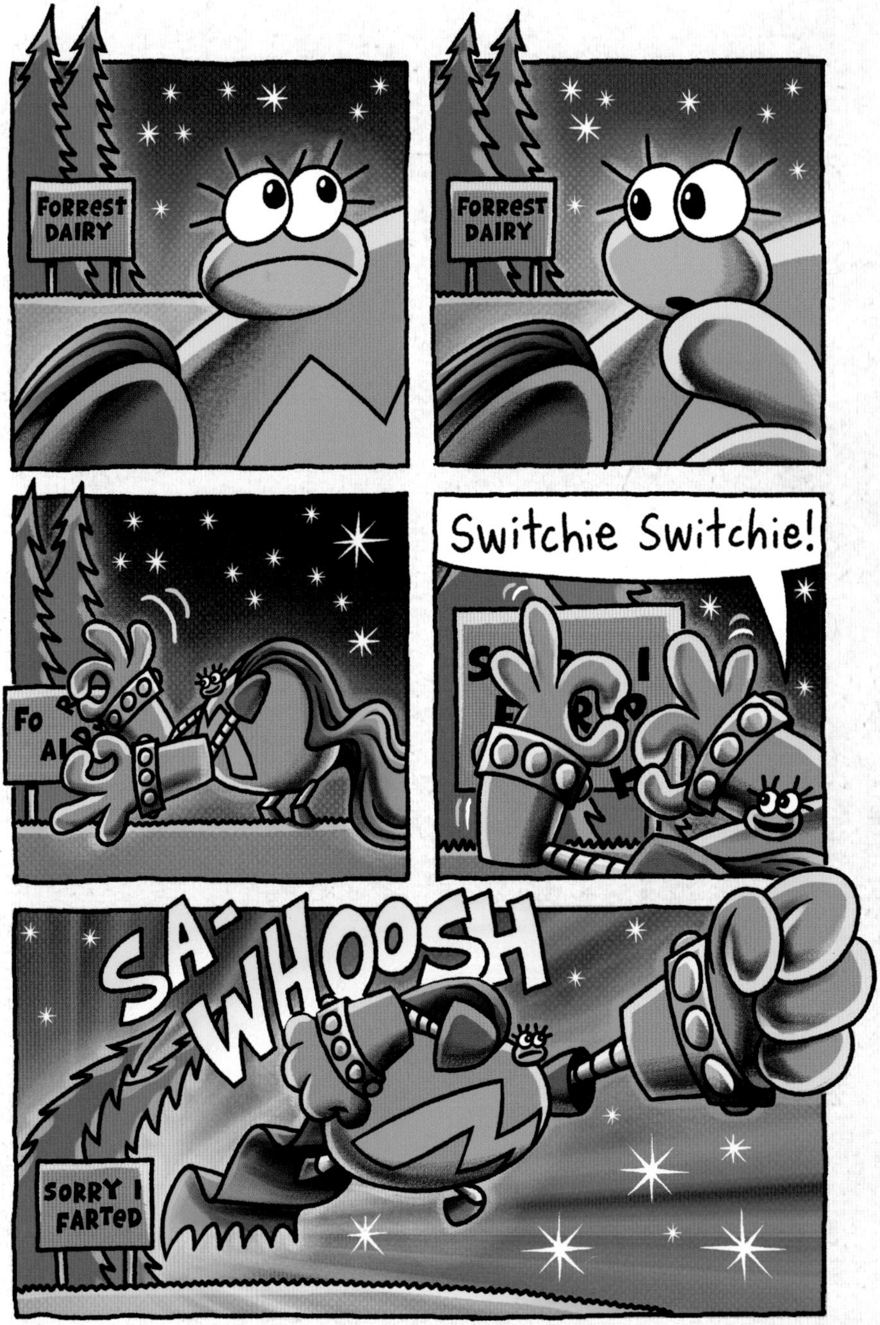
FORREST DAIRY
FORREST DAIRY
Switchie Switchie!
SA-WHOOSH
SORRY I FARTED

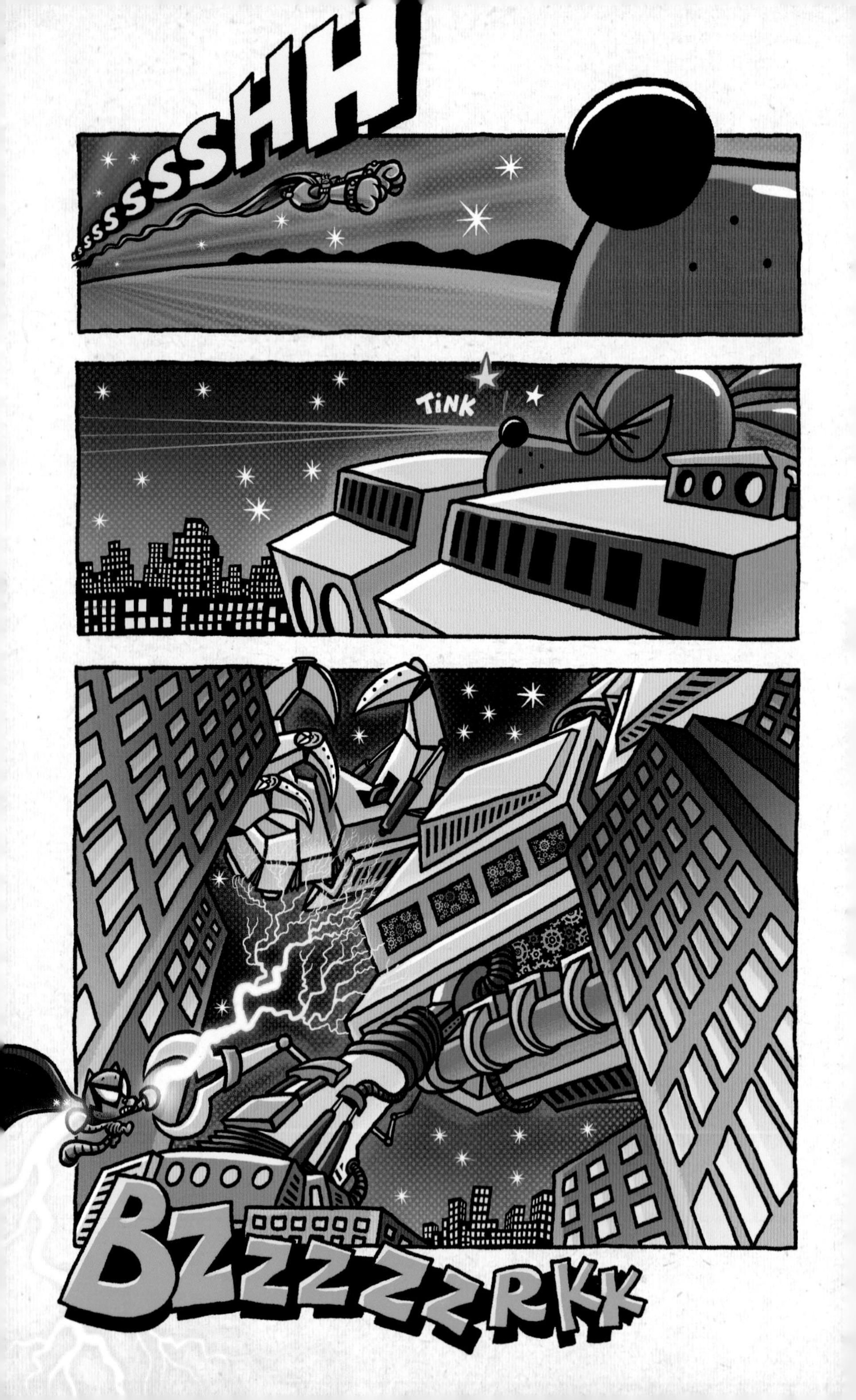
sssssSSHH!
TINK
BZZZZZZRKK

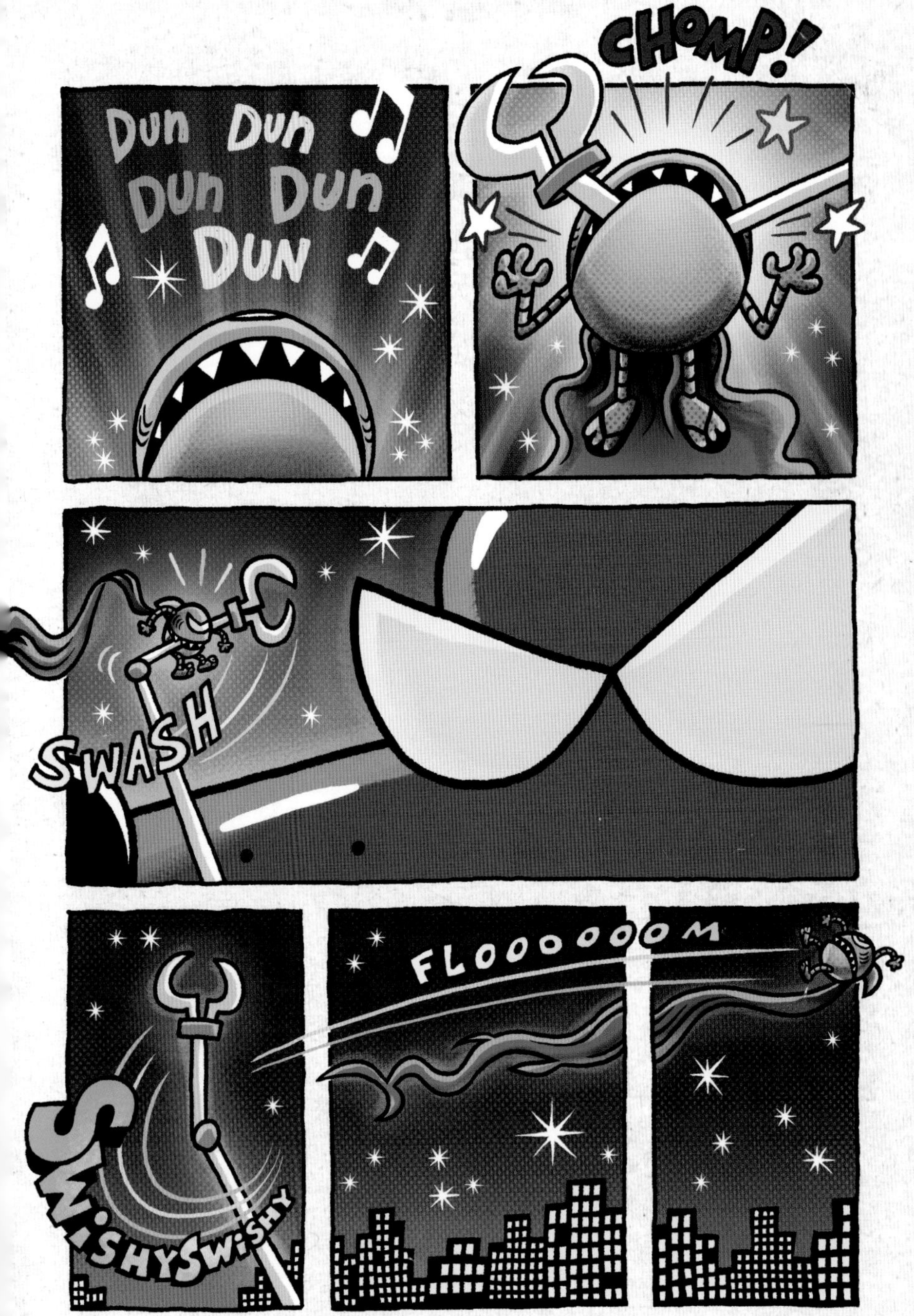
Dun Dun
Dun Dun
DUN
CHOMP!
SWASH
SWISHYSWISHY
FLOOOOOOM

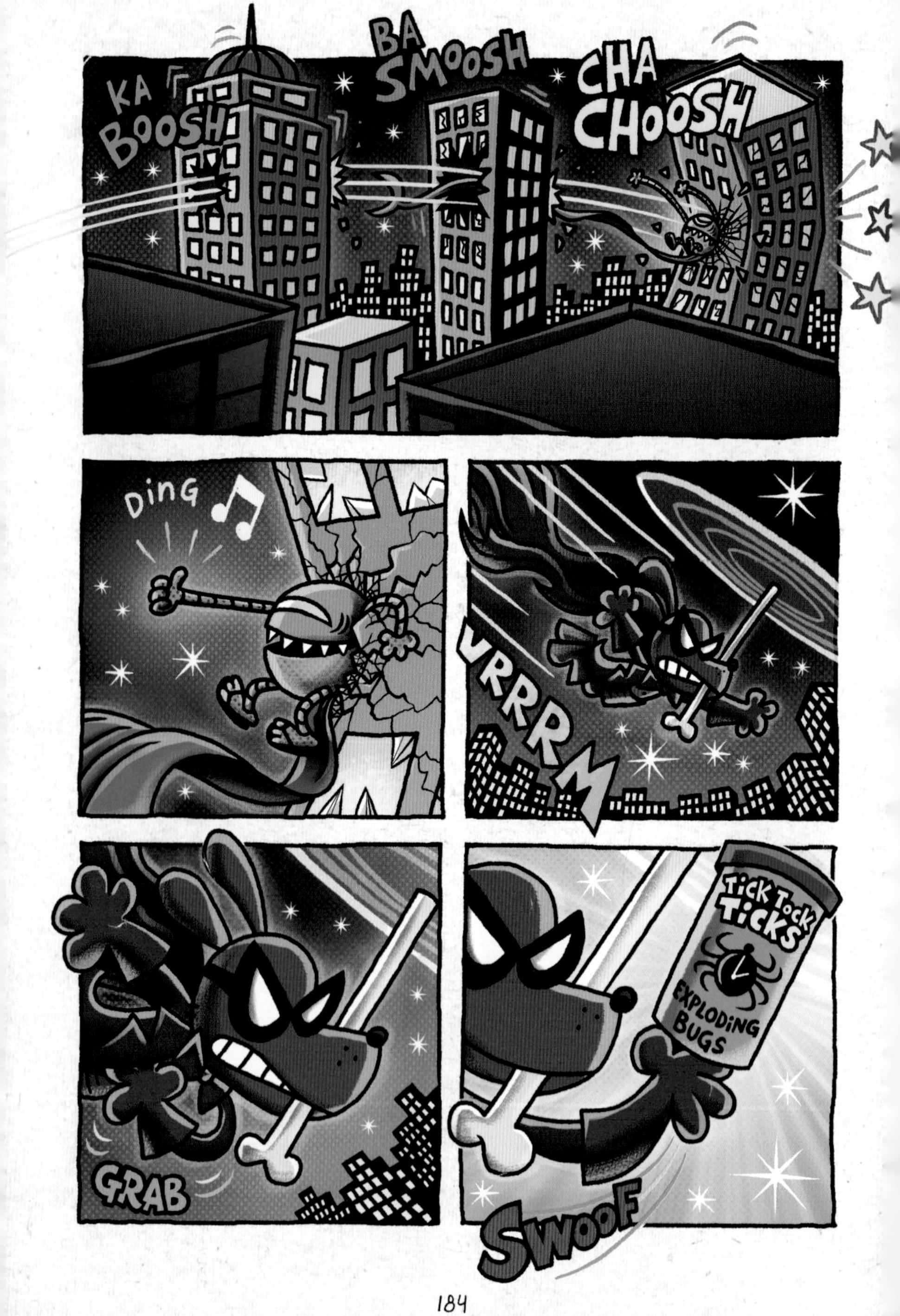
KA BOOSH
BA SMOOSH
CHA CHOOSH
DING
VRRRM
TICK TOCK TICKS
EXPLODING BUGS
GRAB
SWOOF

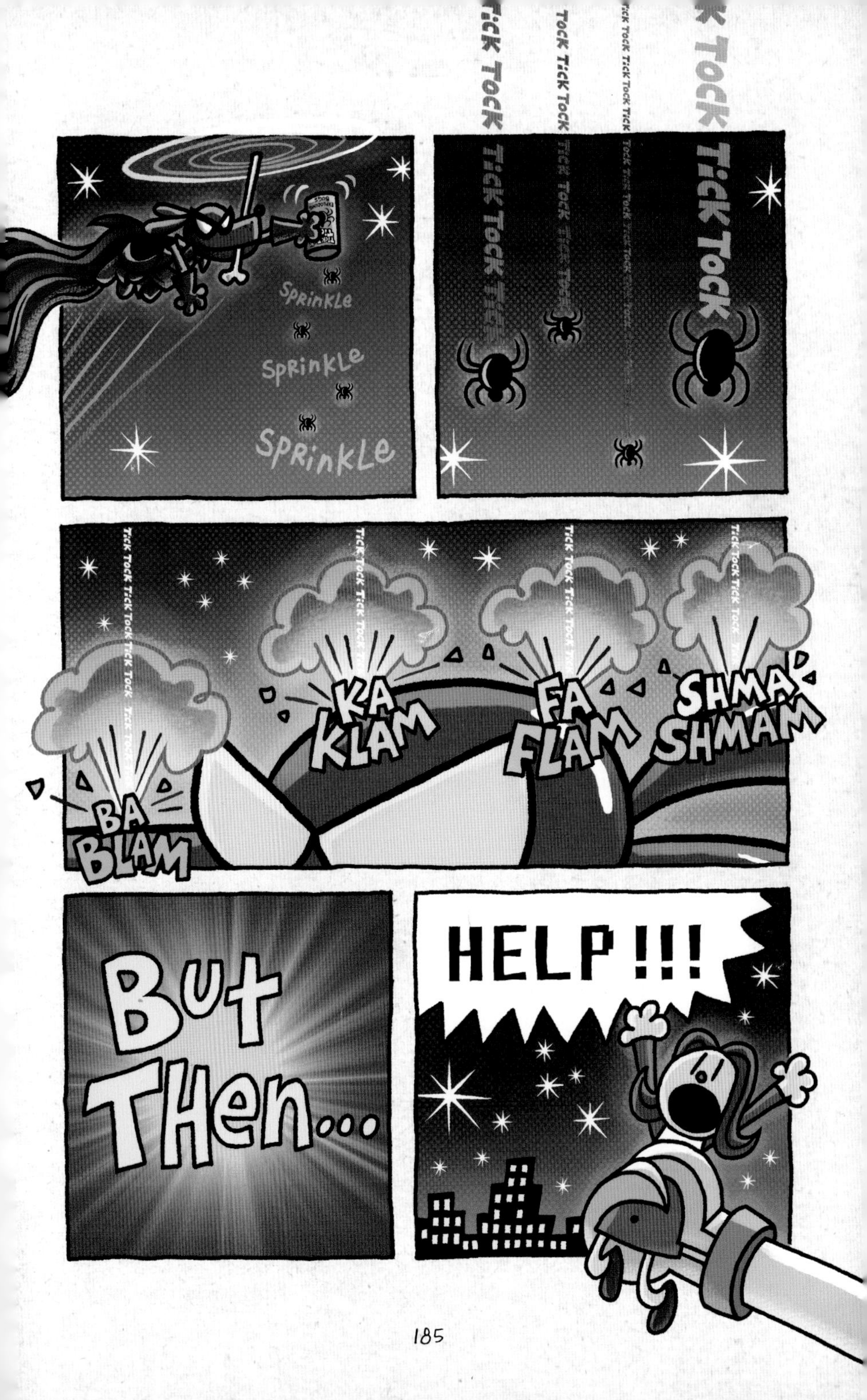
TicK TocK
TicK TocK TicK TocK
SPRINKLE
SPRINKLE
SPRINKLE
TicK TocK TicK TocK
KA KLAM
FA FLAM
SHMA SHMAM
BA BLAM
But Then...
HELP!!!

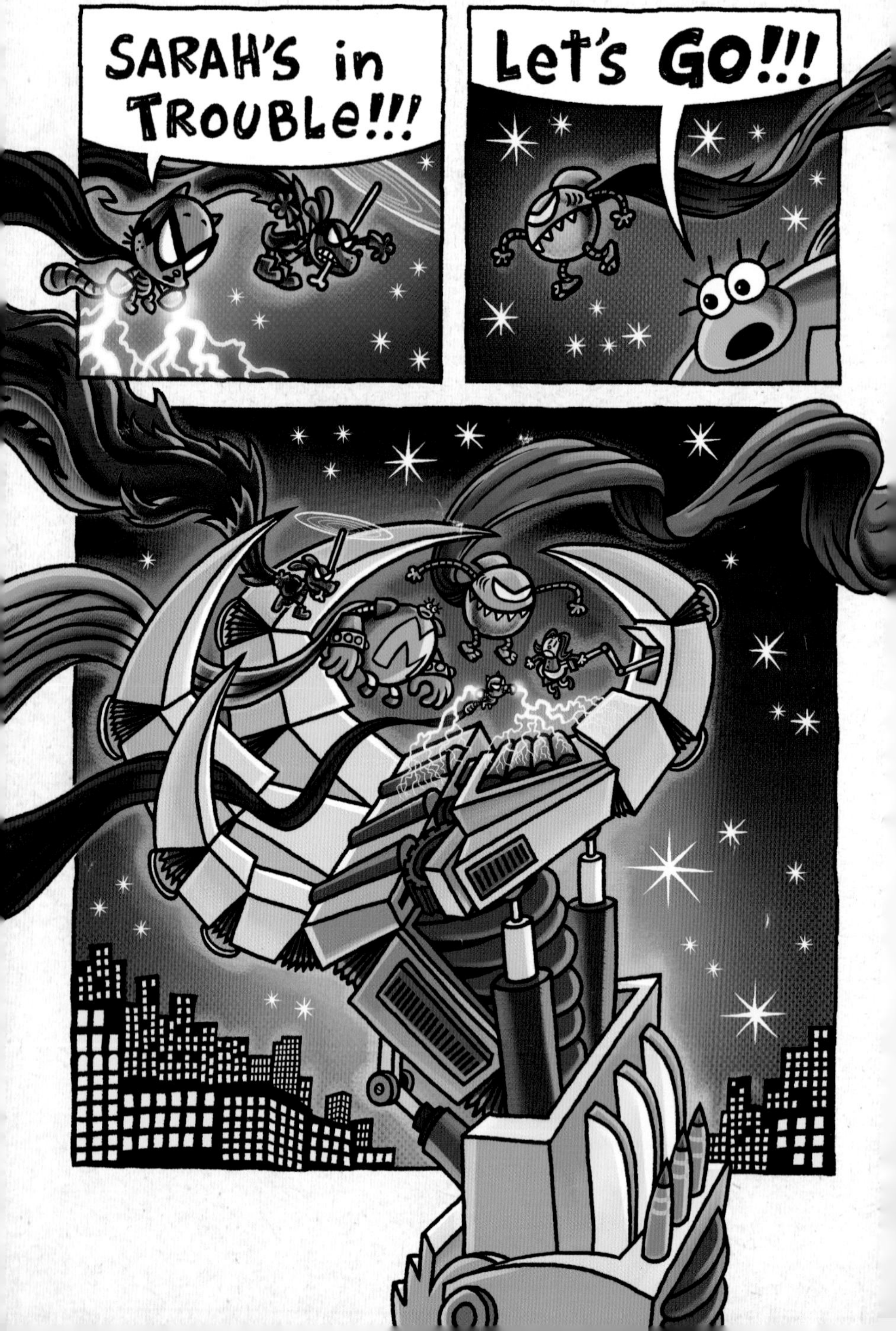
SARAH'S in TROUBLE!!!
Let's GO!!!

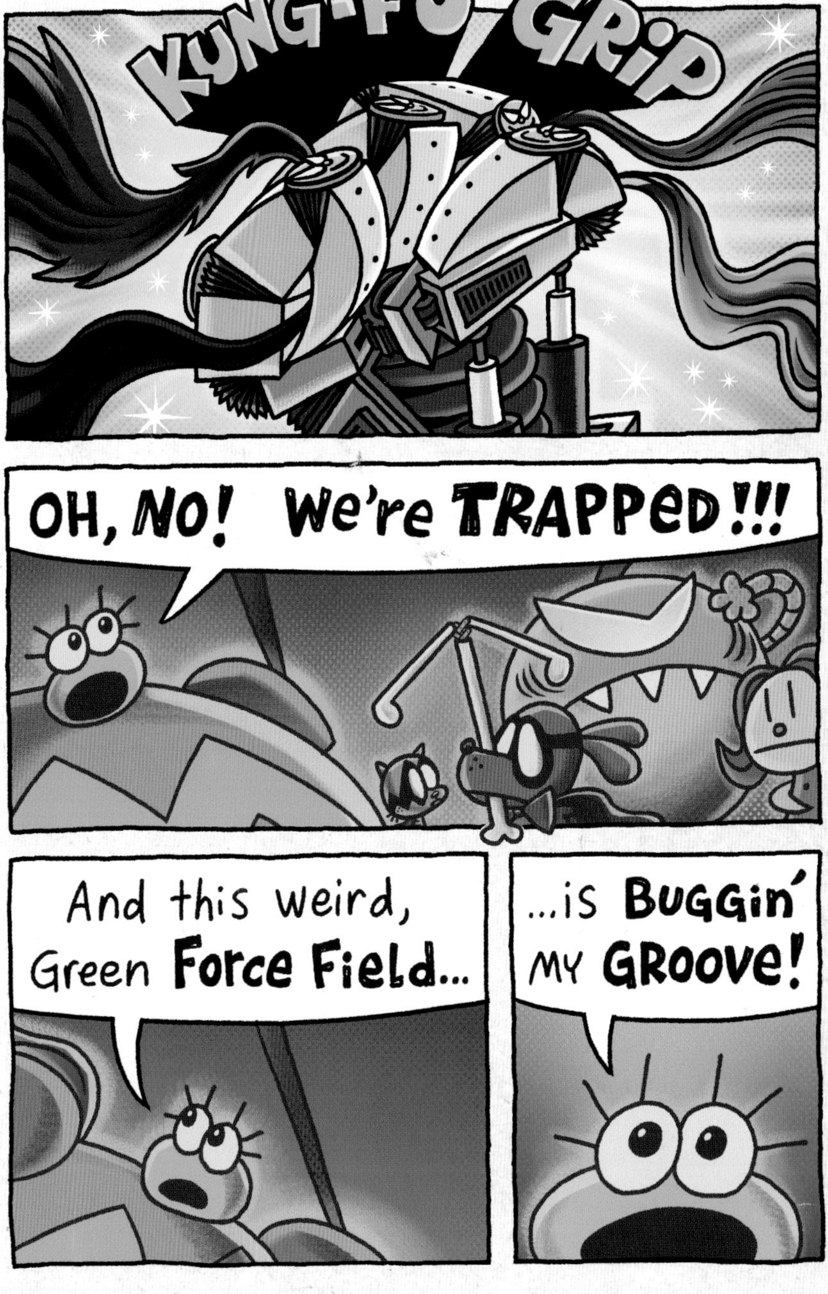
KUNG-FU GRIP
OH, NO! We're TRAPPED!!!
And this weird, Green Force Field...
...is BUGGIN' MY GROOVE!

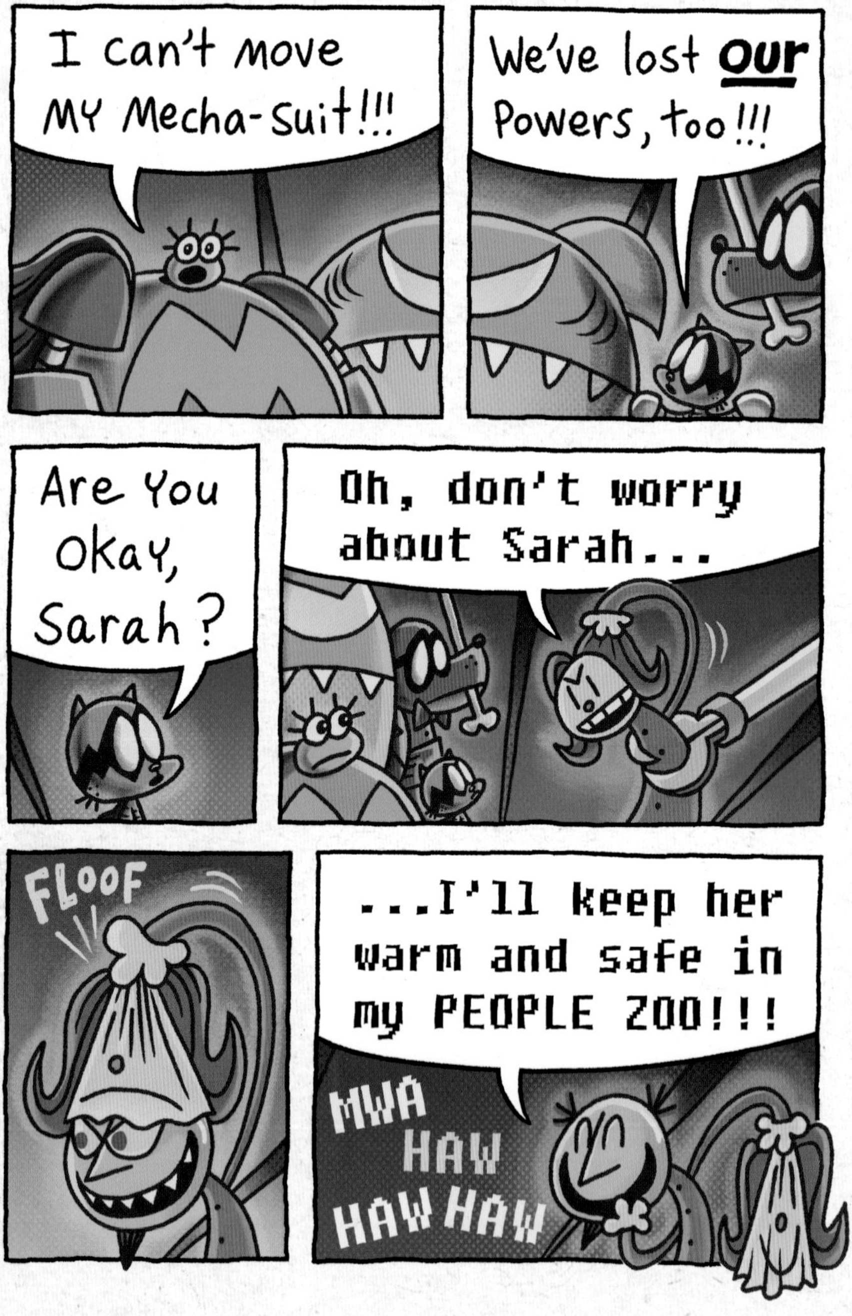
I can't move MY Mecha-Suit!!!
We've lost **our** Powers, too!!!
Are You Okay, Sarah?
Oh, don't worry about Sarah...
FLOOF
...I'll keep her warm and safe in my PEOPLE ZOO!!!
MWA HAW HAW HAW

CHAPTER 14
Petey Dreams Again

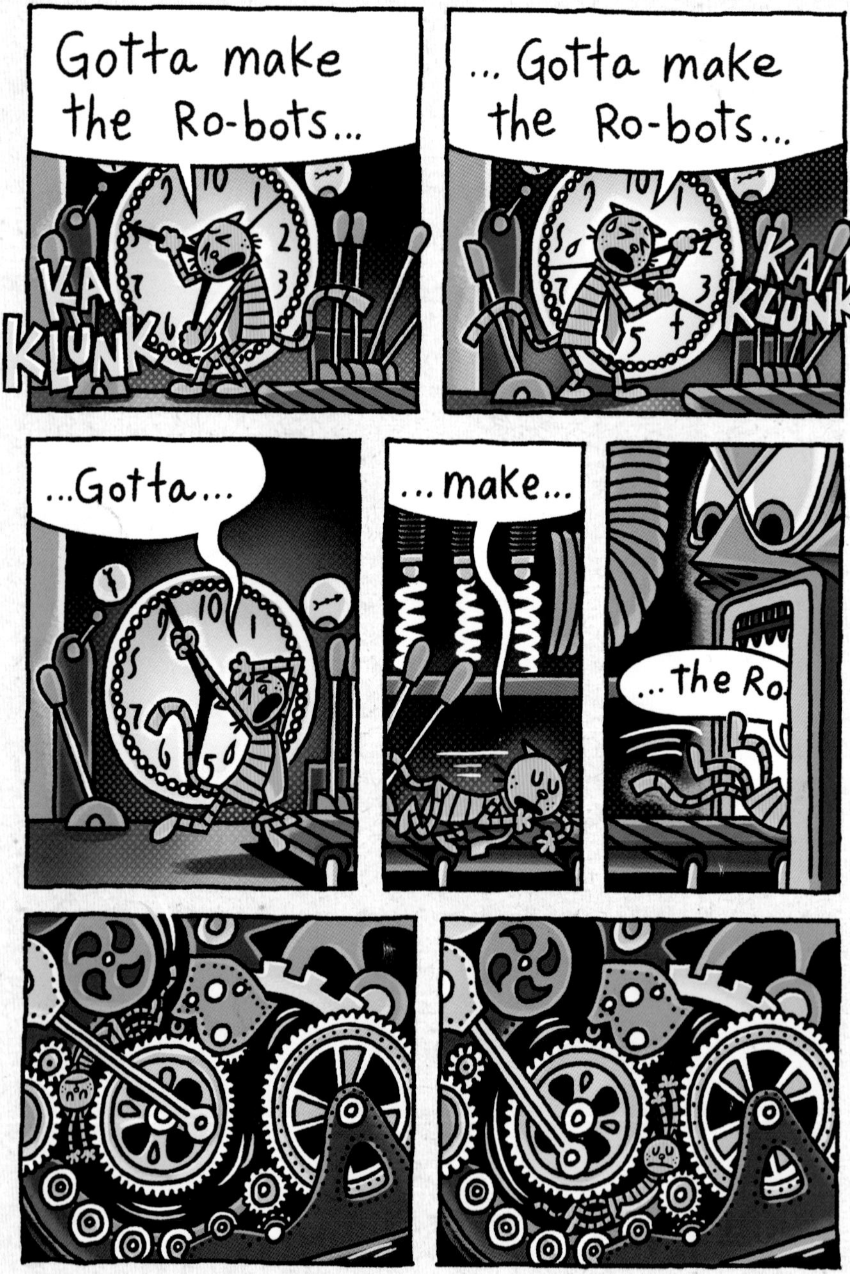

Gotta make the Ro-bots...
KA KLUNK
... Gotta make the Ro-bots...
KA KLUNK
...Gotta...
...make...
...the Ro

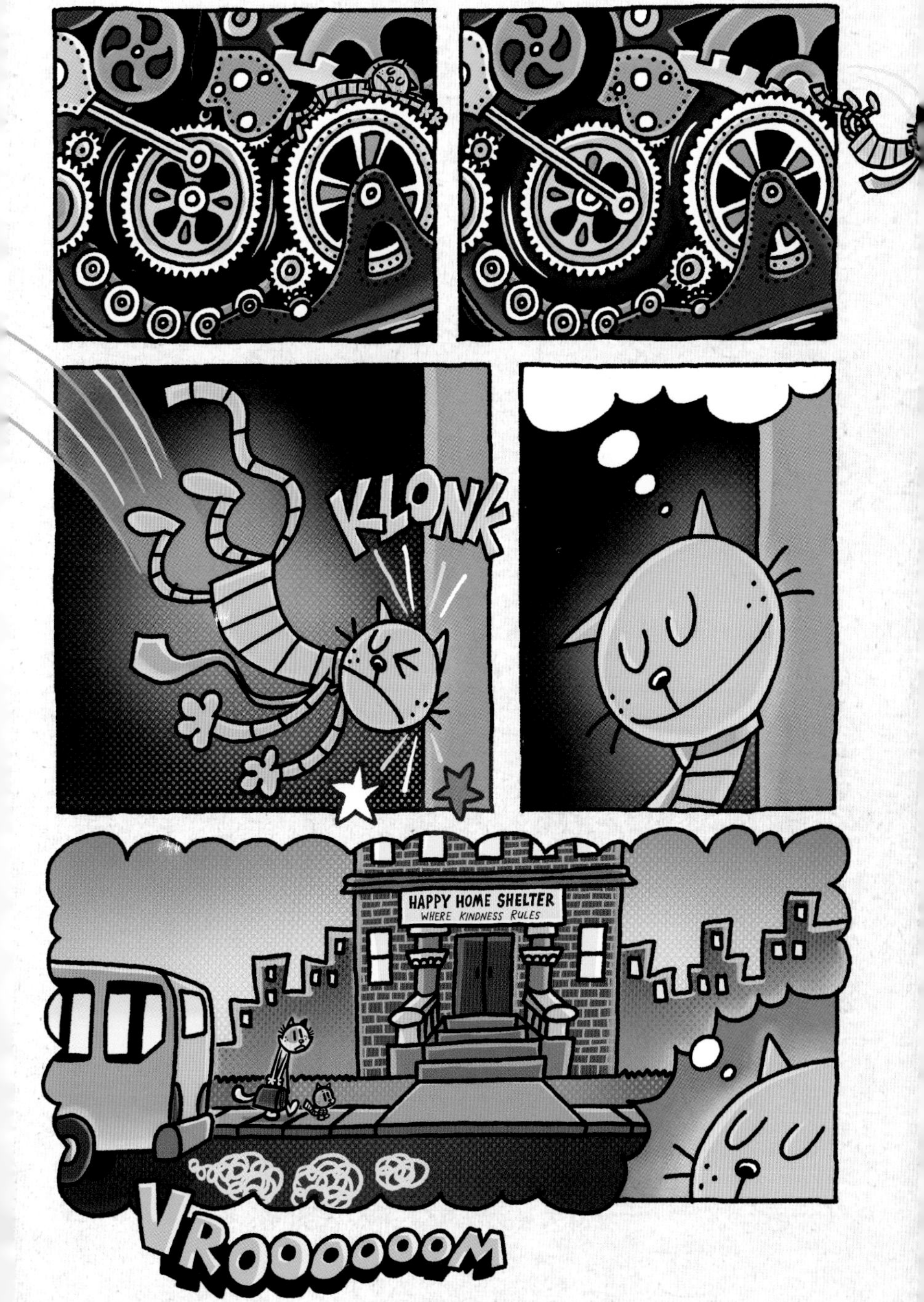
KLONK
HAPPY HOME SHELTER
WHERE KINDNESS RULES
VROOOOOOM

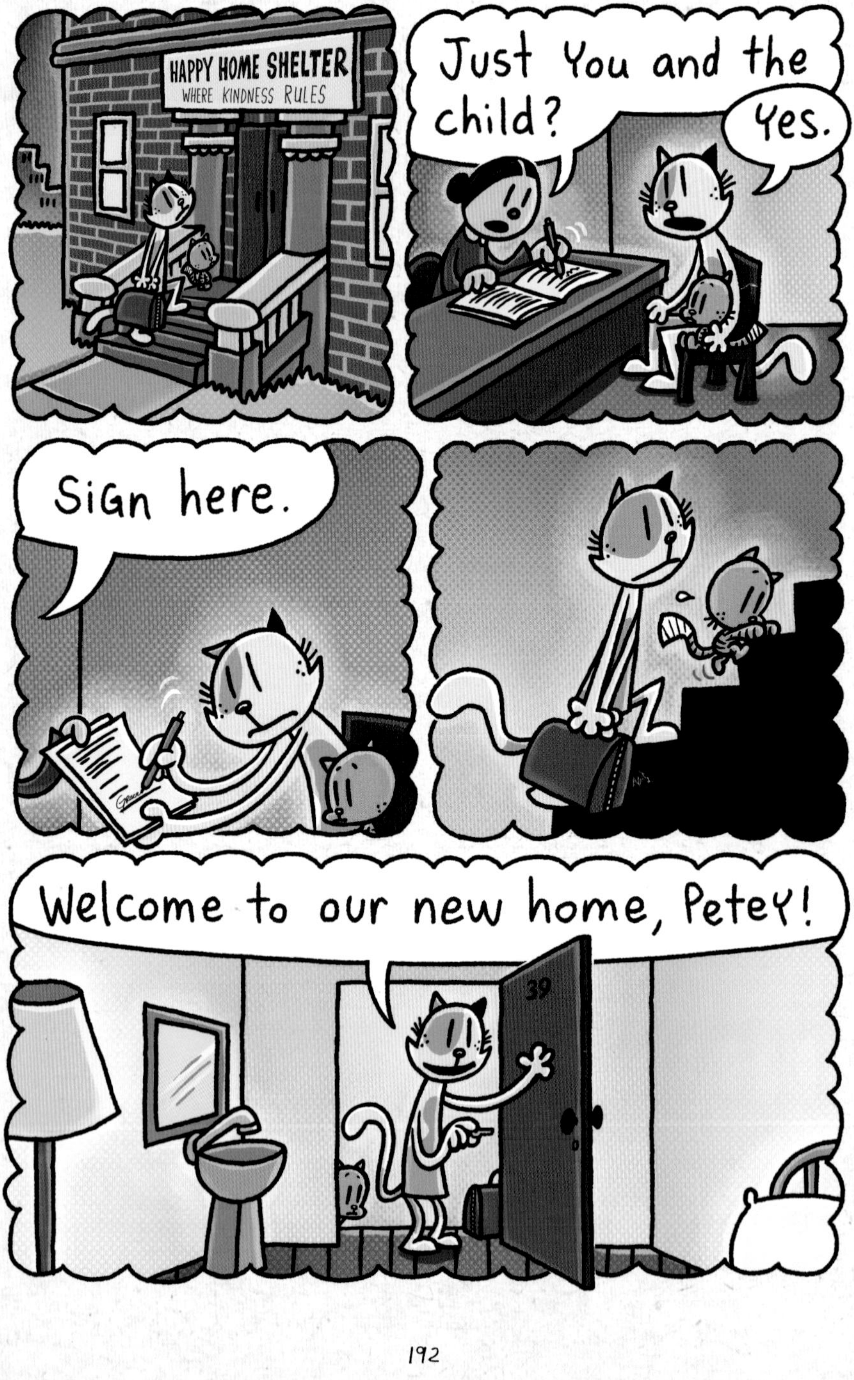
HAPPY HOME SHELTER
WHERE KINDNESS RULES
Just You and the child?
Yes.
Sign here.
Welcome to our new home, Petey!
39

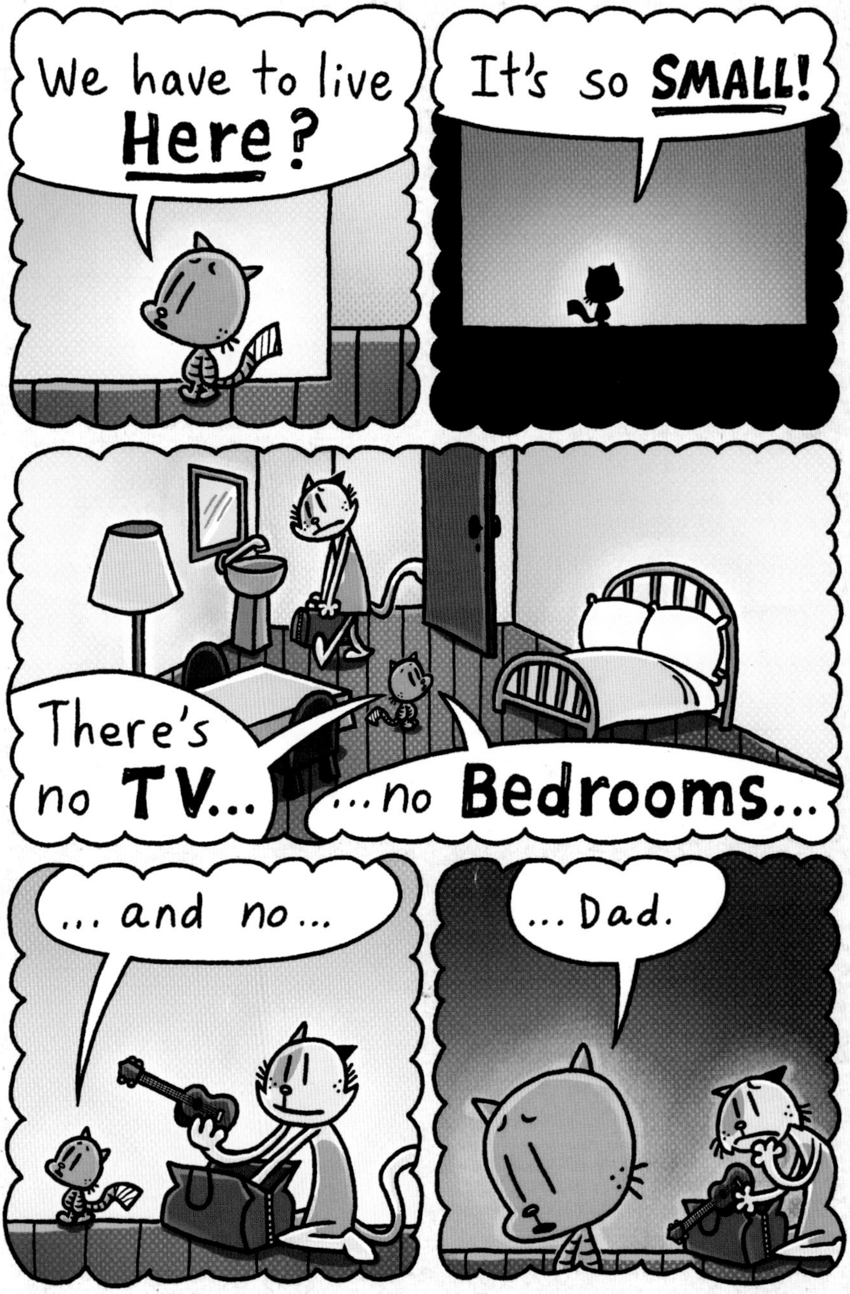

We have to live Here?
It's so SMALL!
There's no TV...
...no Bedrooms...
... and no...
...Dad.

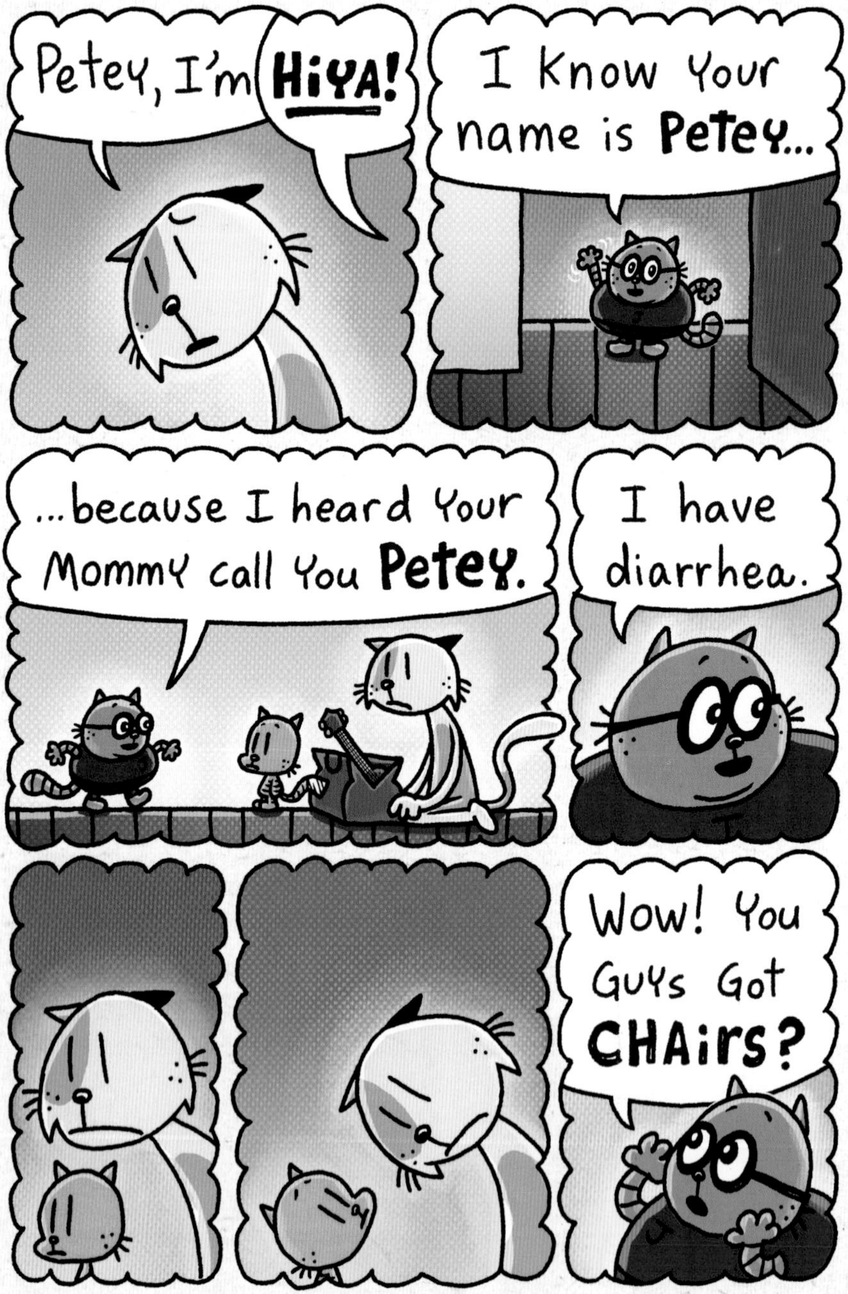
Petey, I'm
HiYA!
I Know Your name is Petey...
...because I heard Your Mommy call You Petey.
I have diarrhea.
Wow! You Guys Got CHAirs?

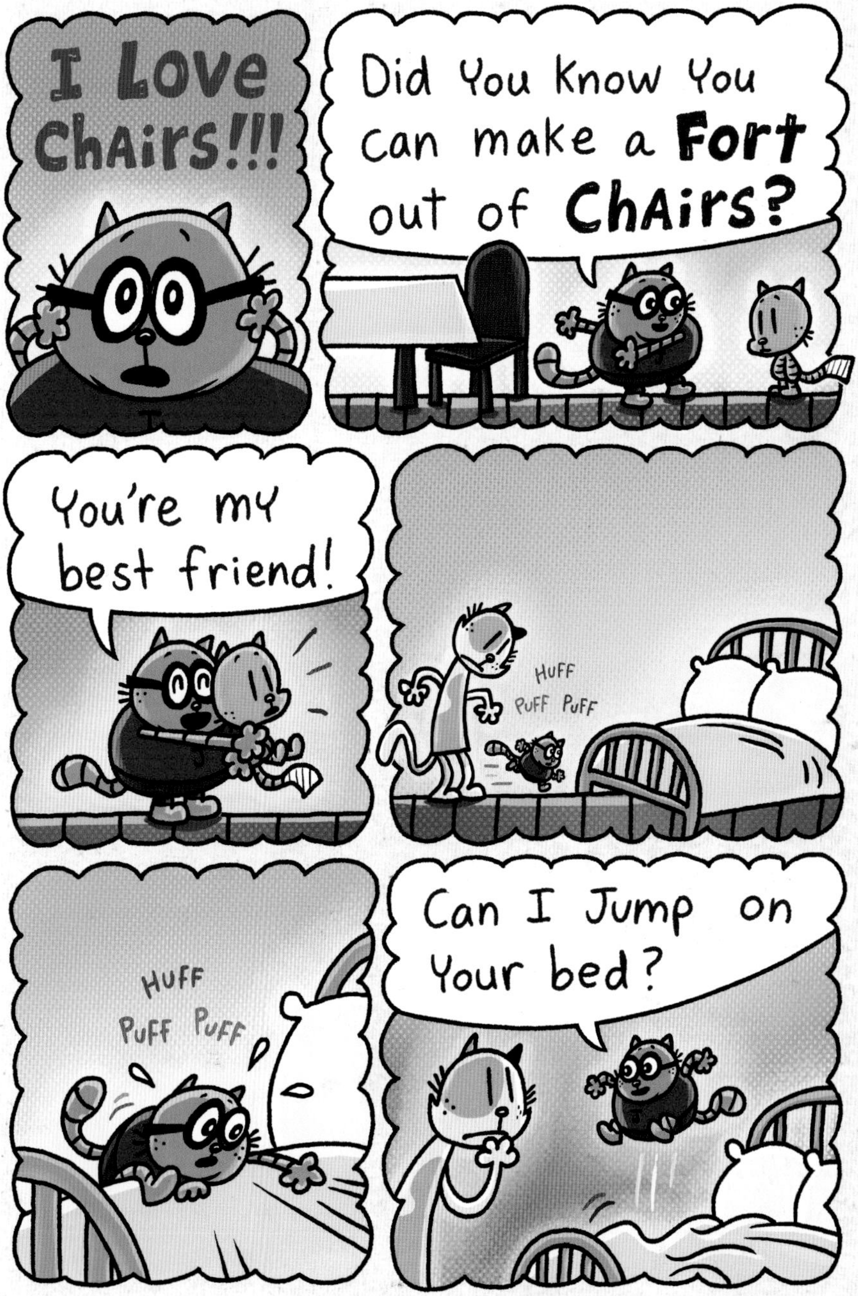
I Love Chairs!!!
Did You Know You can make a Fort out of Chairs?
You're my best friend!
HUFF
PUFF PUFF
HUFF
PUFF PUFF
Can I Jump on Your bed?

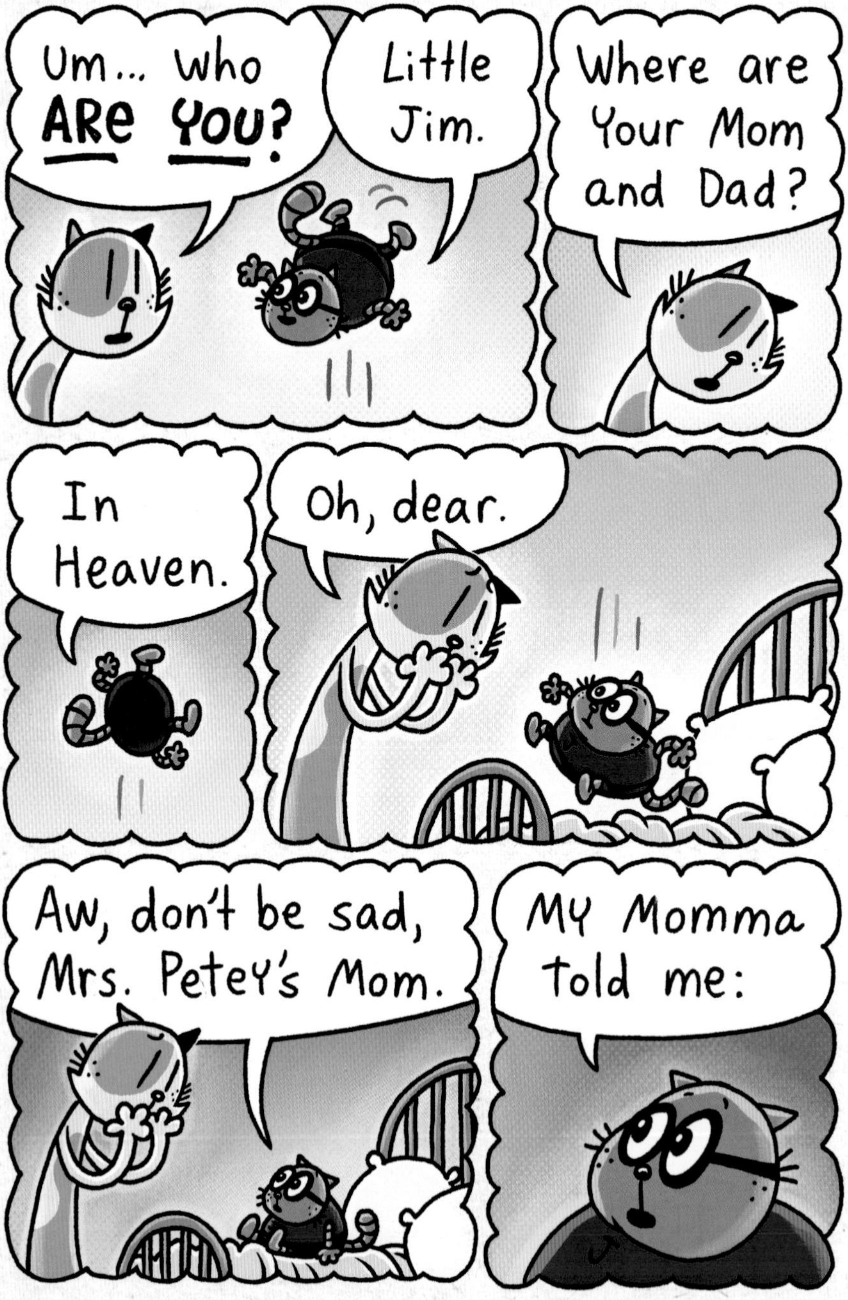
Um... Who **ARE YOU?**
Little Jim.
Where are Your Mom and Dad?
In Heaven.
Oh, dear.
Aw, don't be sad, Mrs. Petey's Mom.
My Momma told me:

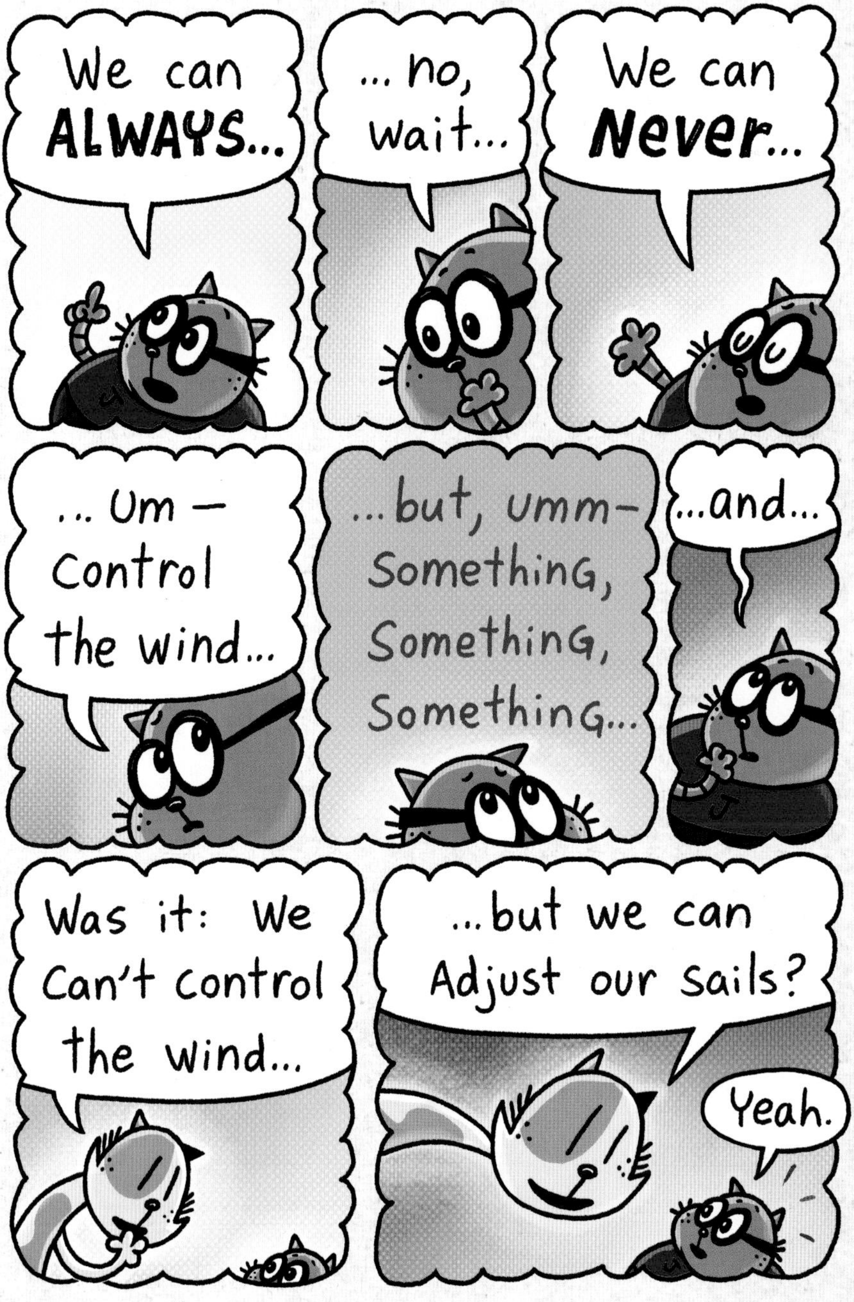
We can ALWAYS...
... no, wait...
We can Never...
... Um — Control the wind...
... but, umm- Something, Something, Something...
...and...
Was it: We Can't control the wind...
... but we can Adjust our sails?
Yeah.

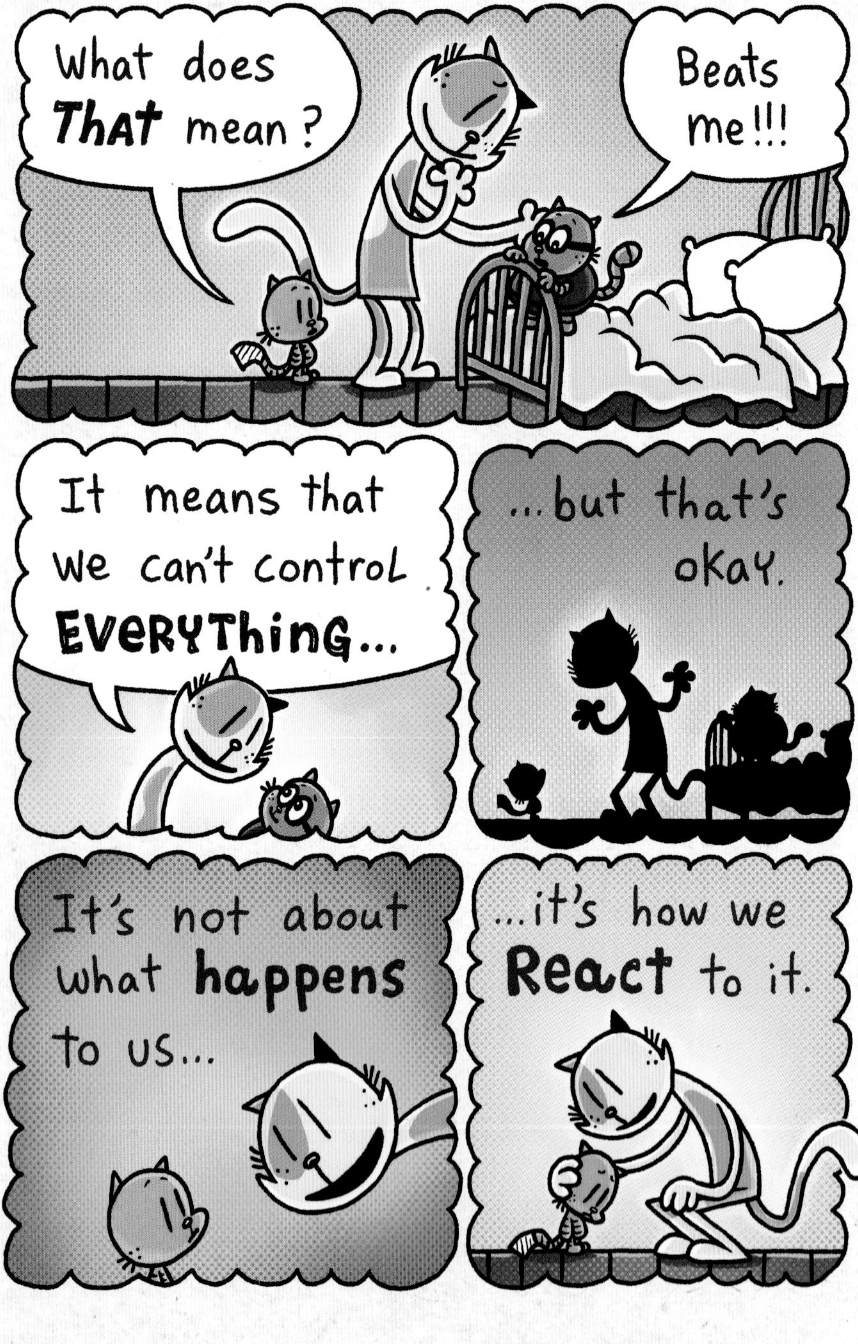
What does THAT mean?
Beats me!!!
It means that we can't control EVERYTHING...
...but that's okay.
It's not about what happens to us...
...it's how we React to it.

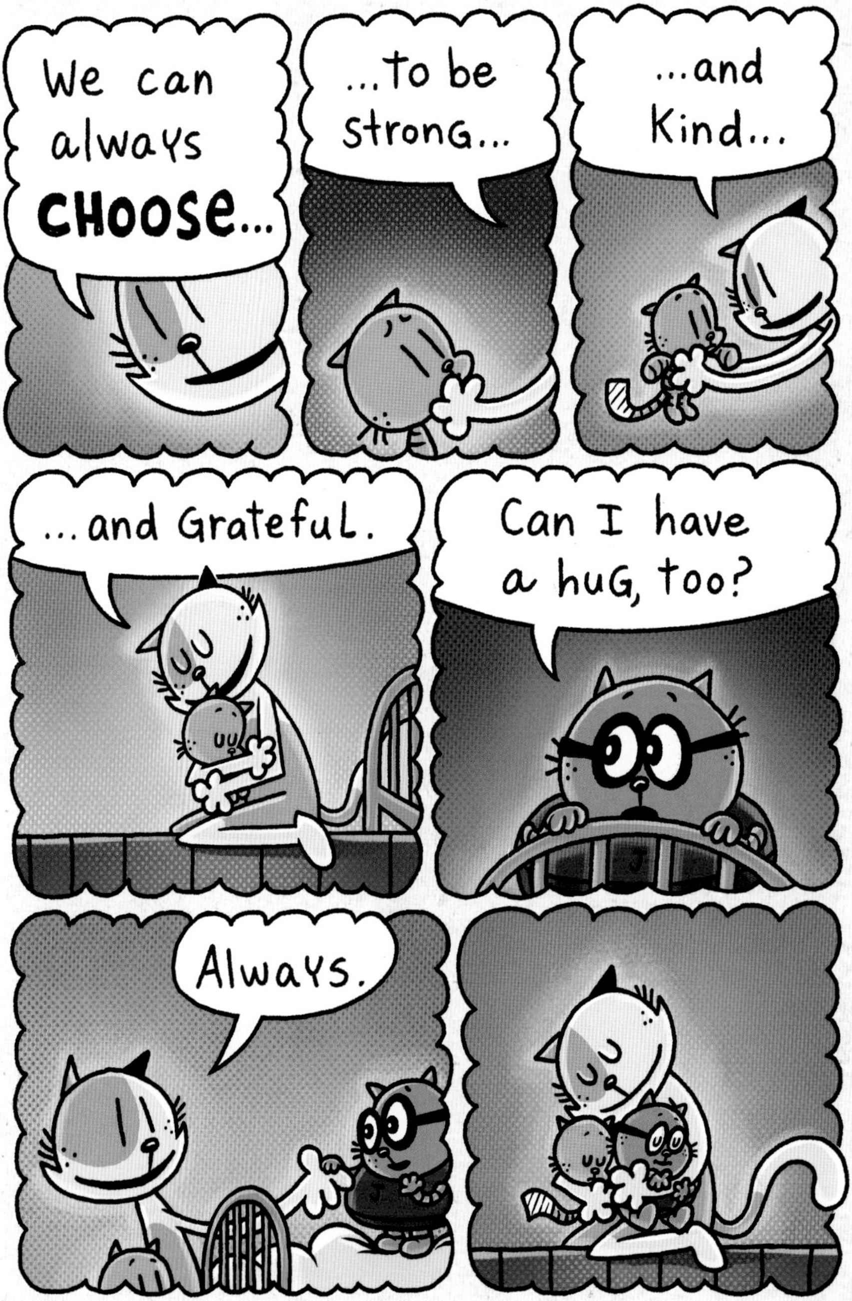
We can always CHOOSE...
...to be strong...
...and Kind...
...and Grateful.
Can I have a hug, too?
Always.

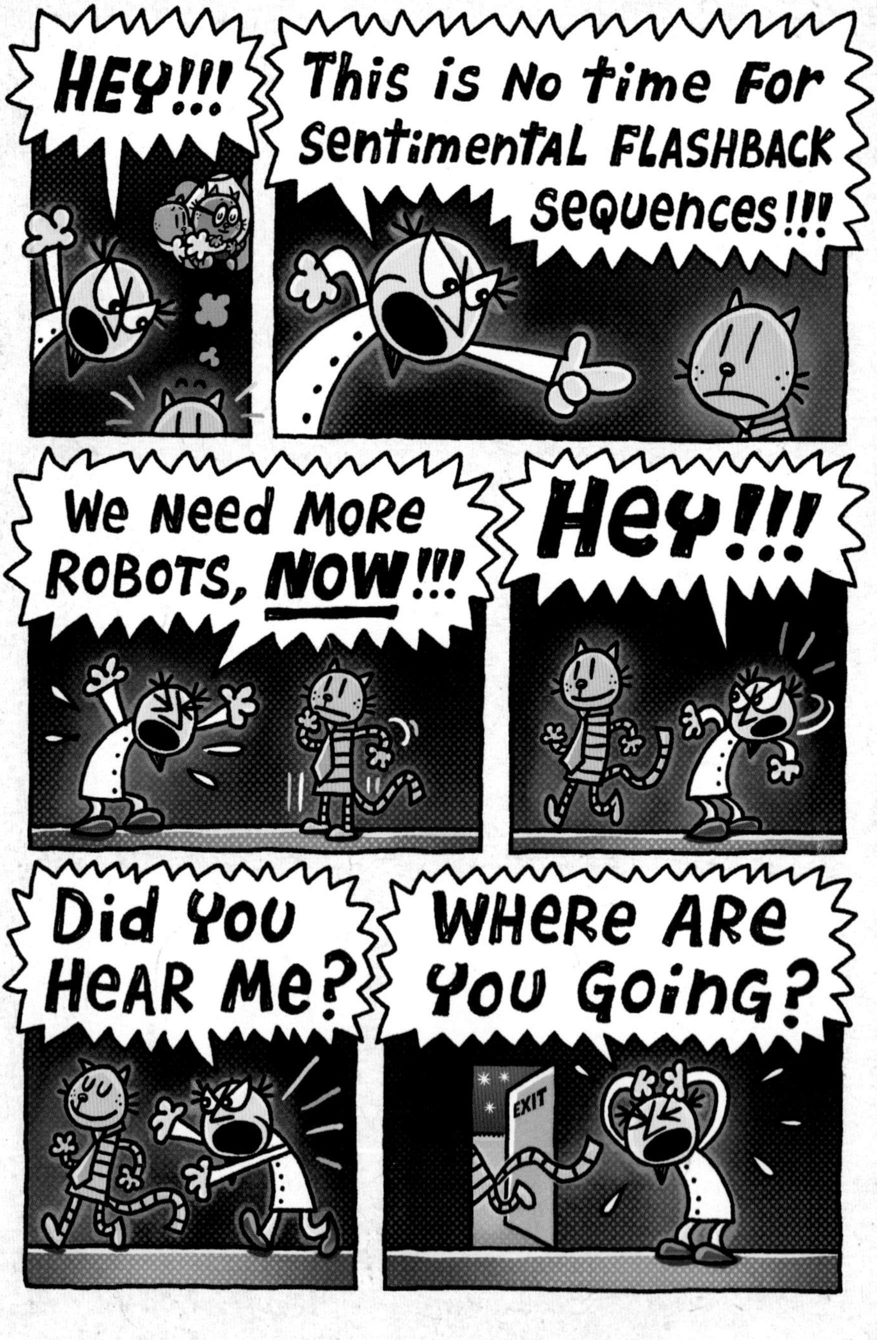
HEY!!!
This is No time For Sentimental FLASHBACK sequences!!!
We Need More ROBOTS, NOW!!!
Hey!!!
Did You Hear Me?
Where Are You Going?
EXIT

CHAPTER 15

PETEY ADJUSTS HIS SAILS

AIR SCUM

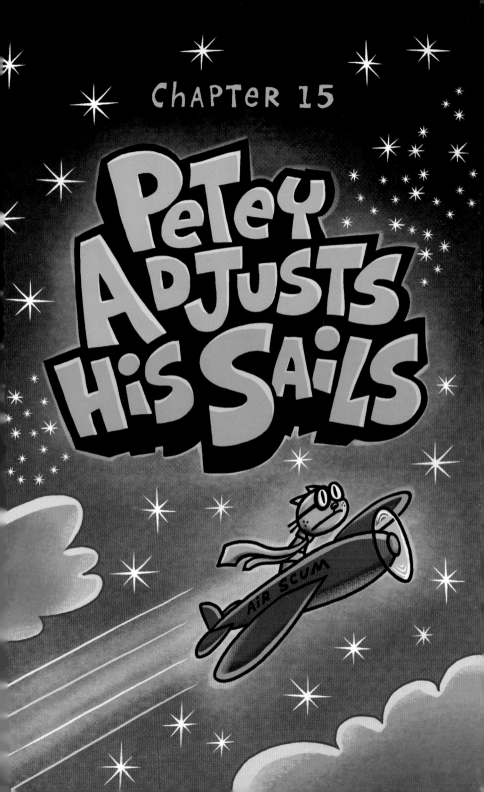

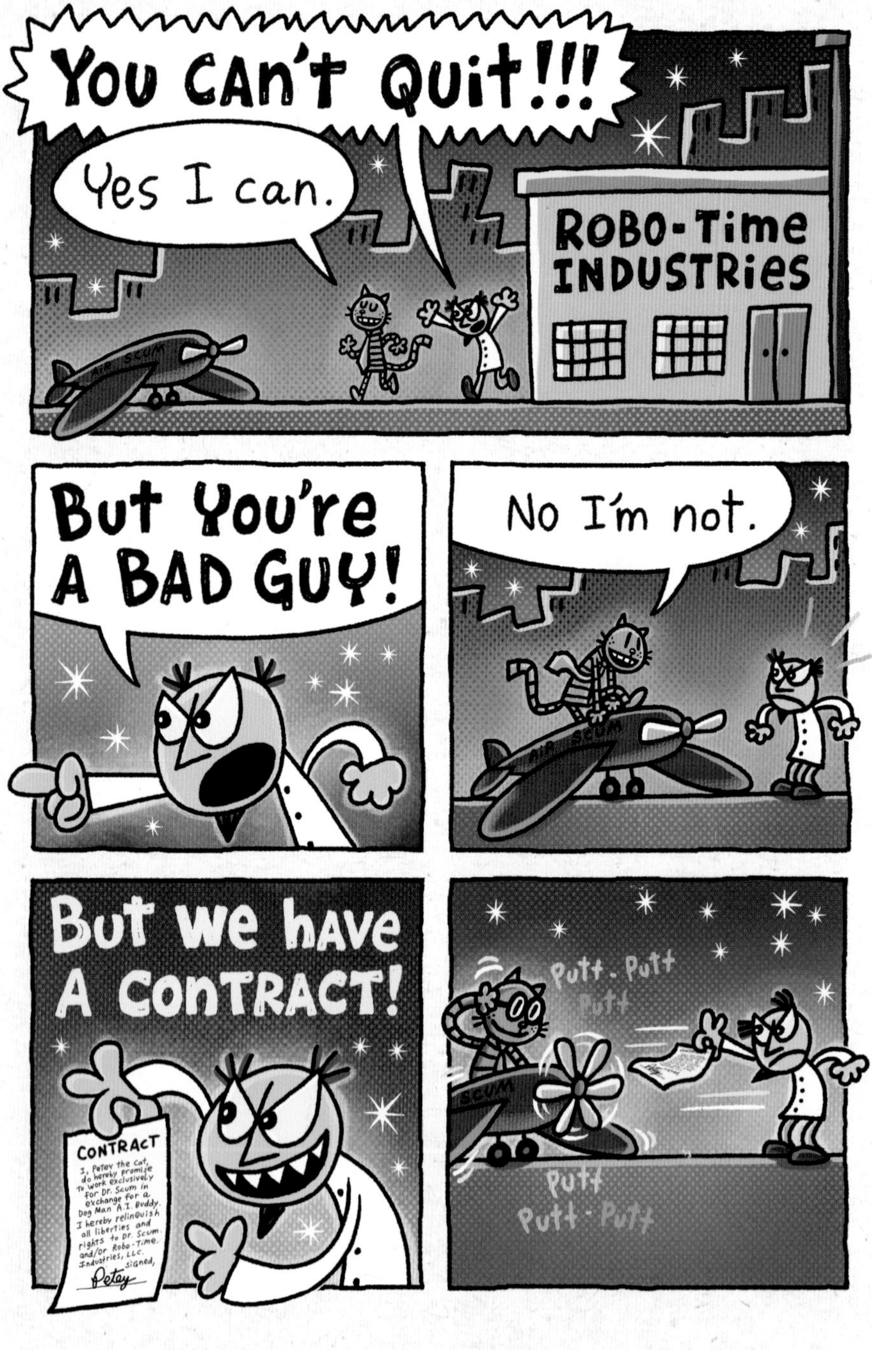
You Can't Quit!!!
Yes I can.
AIR SCUM
ROBO-Time INDUSTRIes
But You're A BAD GUY!
No I'm not.
AIR SCUM
But we have A CONTRACT!
CONTRACT
I, Petey the cat, do hereby promise to work exclusively for Dr. Scum in exchange for a Dog Man A.I. Buddy. I hereby relinquish all liberties and rights to Dr. Scum and/or Robo-Time Industries, LLC.
Signed,
Petey
Putt-Putt Putt
SCUM
Putt Putt-Putt

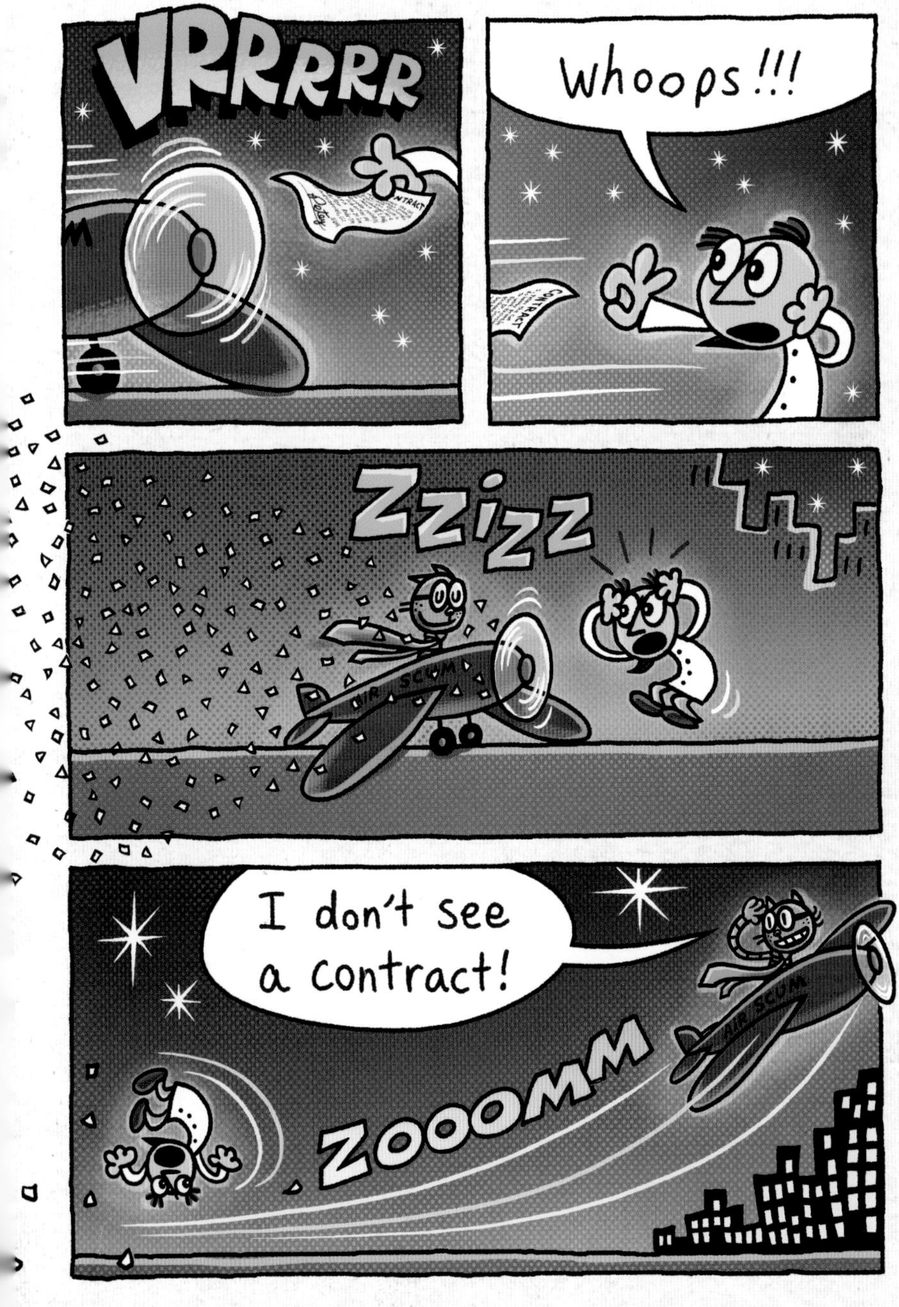
VRRRRRR
Whoops!!!
CONTRACT
ZZiZZ
AIR SCUM
I don't see a contract!
ZOOOMM
AIR SCUM

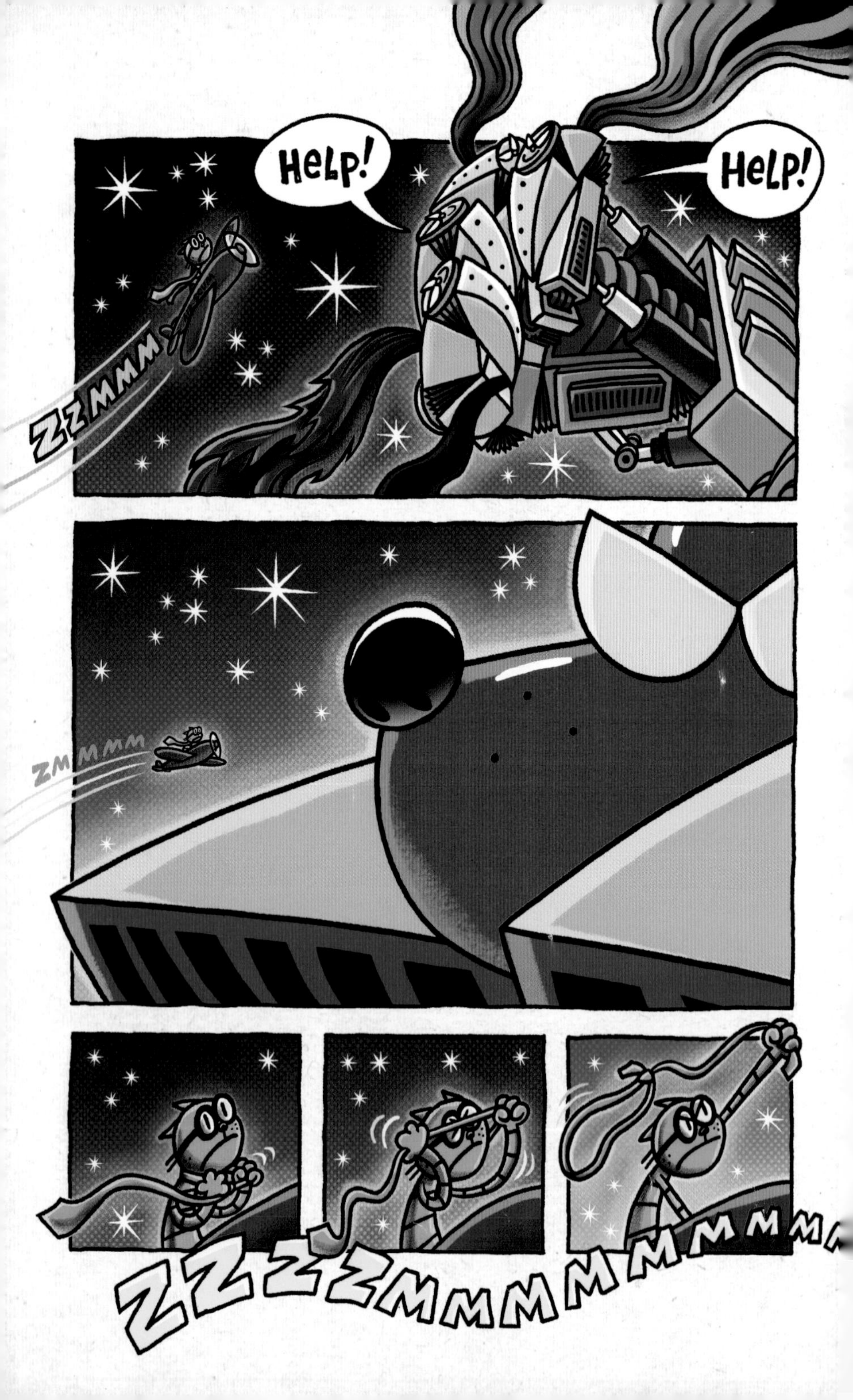
HELP!
HELP!
ZZMMMM
ZMMMM
ZZZZZMMMMMMMMMMMMM

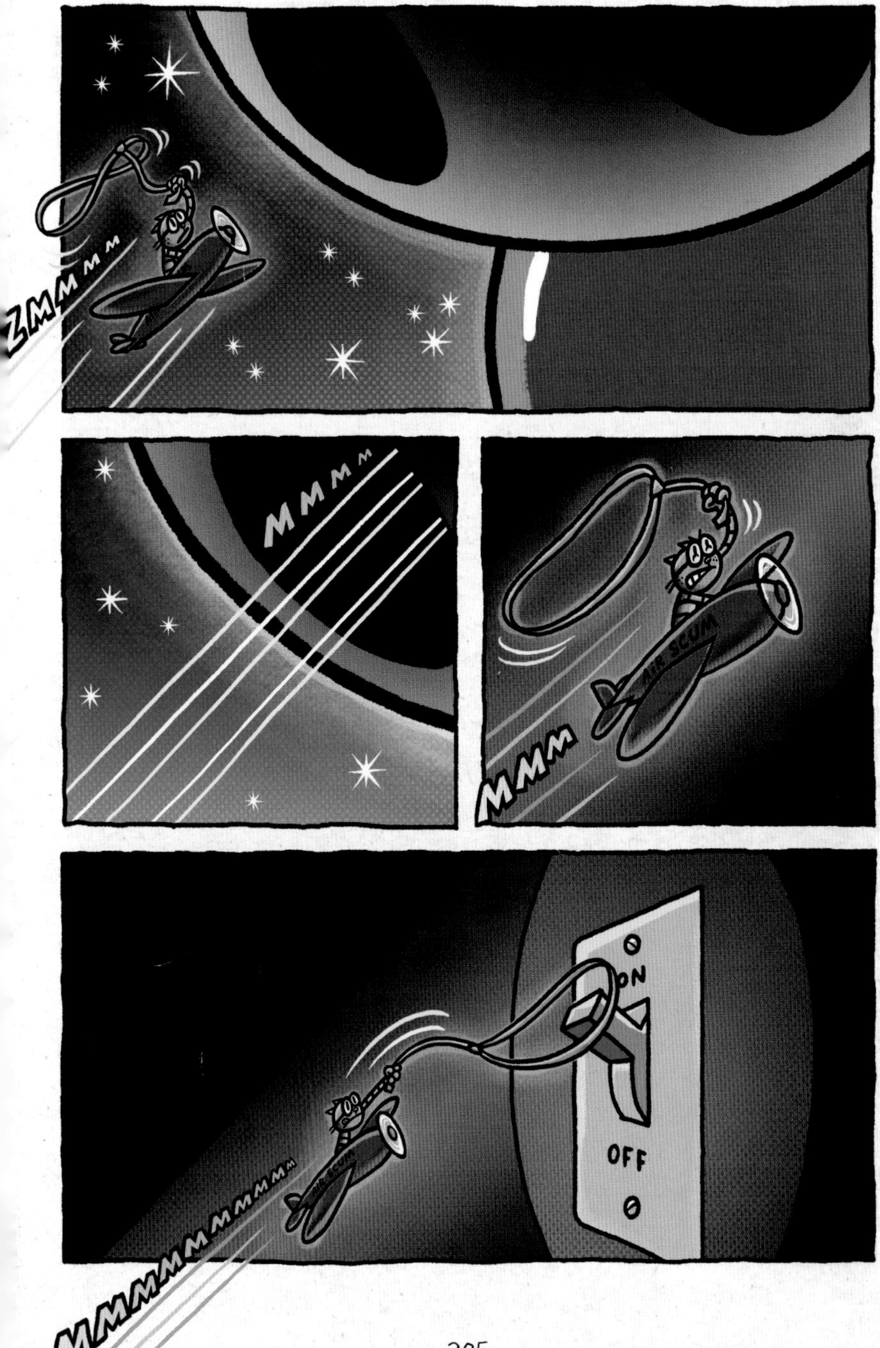
ZMMMMM
MMMM
AIR SCUM
MMM
ON
OFF
AIR SCUM
MMMMMMMMMMMMM

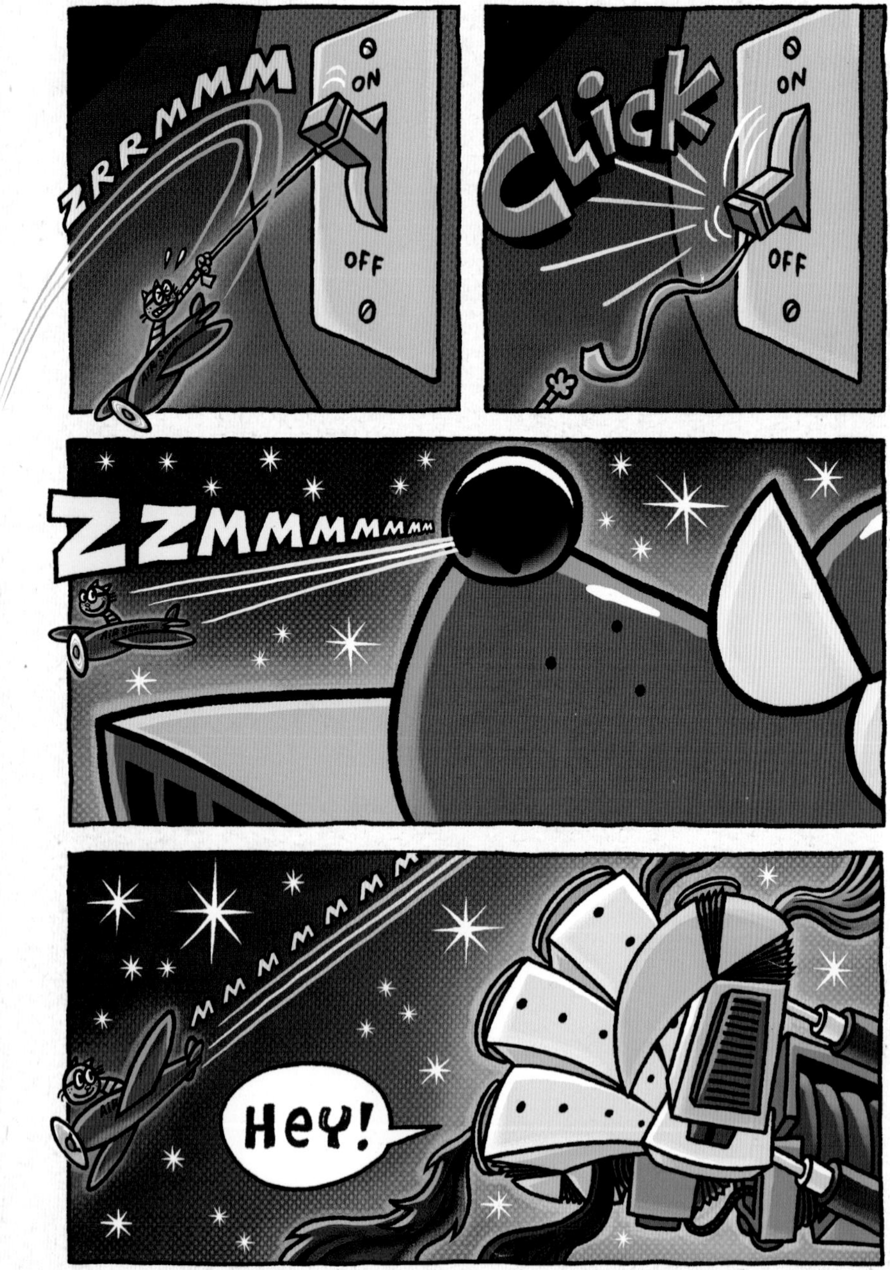
ZRRMMM
ON
OFF
CLICK
ON
OFF
ZZMMMMMMM
MMMMMMMMM
HEY!

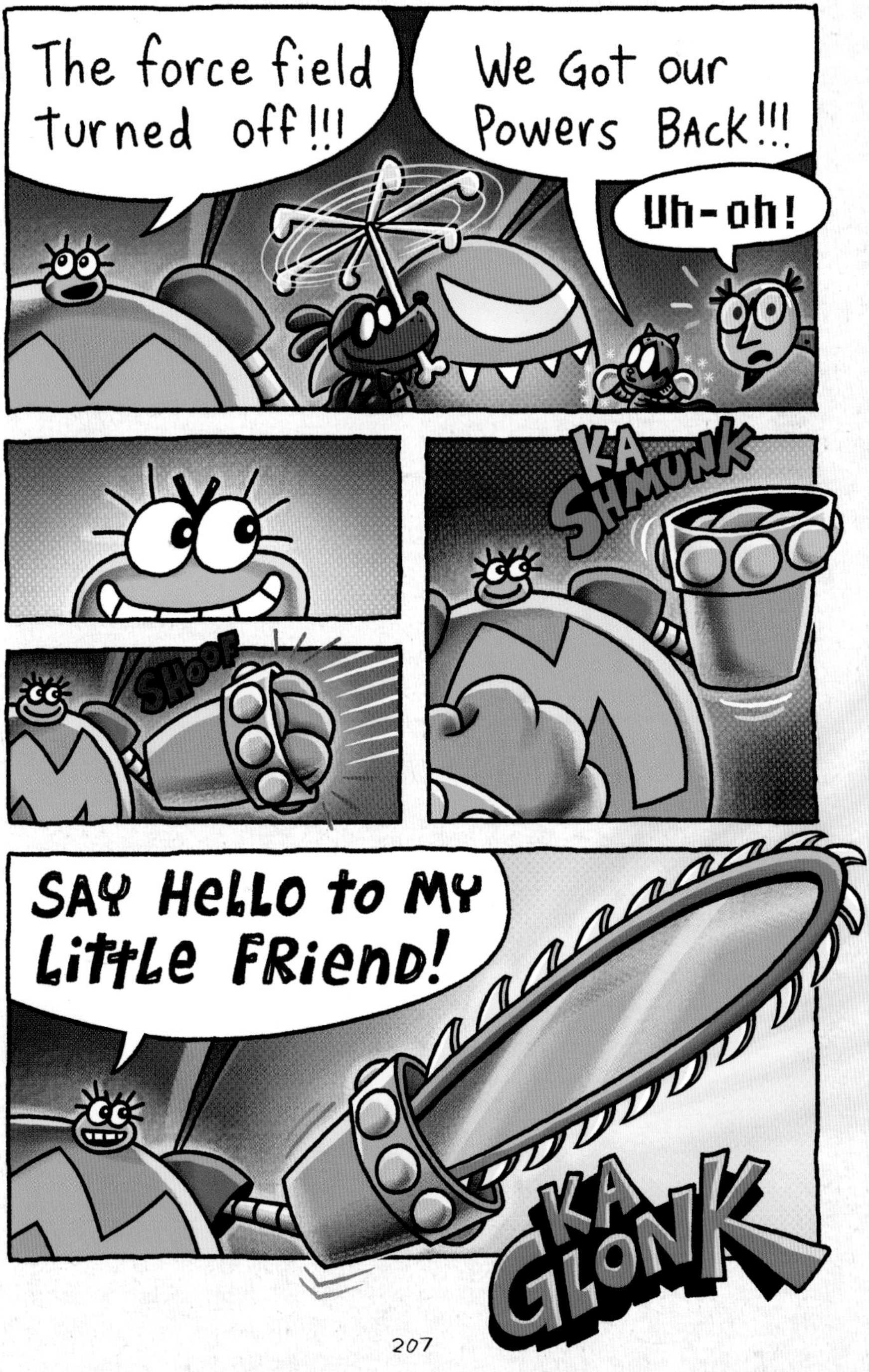
The force field turned off!!!
We Got our Powers Back!!!
Uh-oh!
KA SHMUNK
SHOOF
SAY HELLO to MY LittLe FRIEND!
KA GLONK

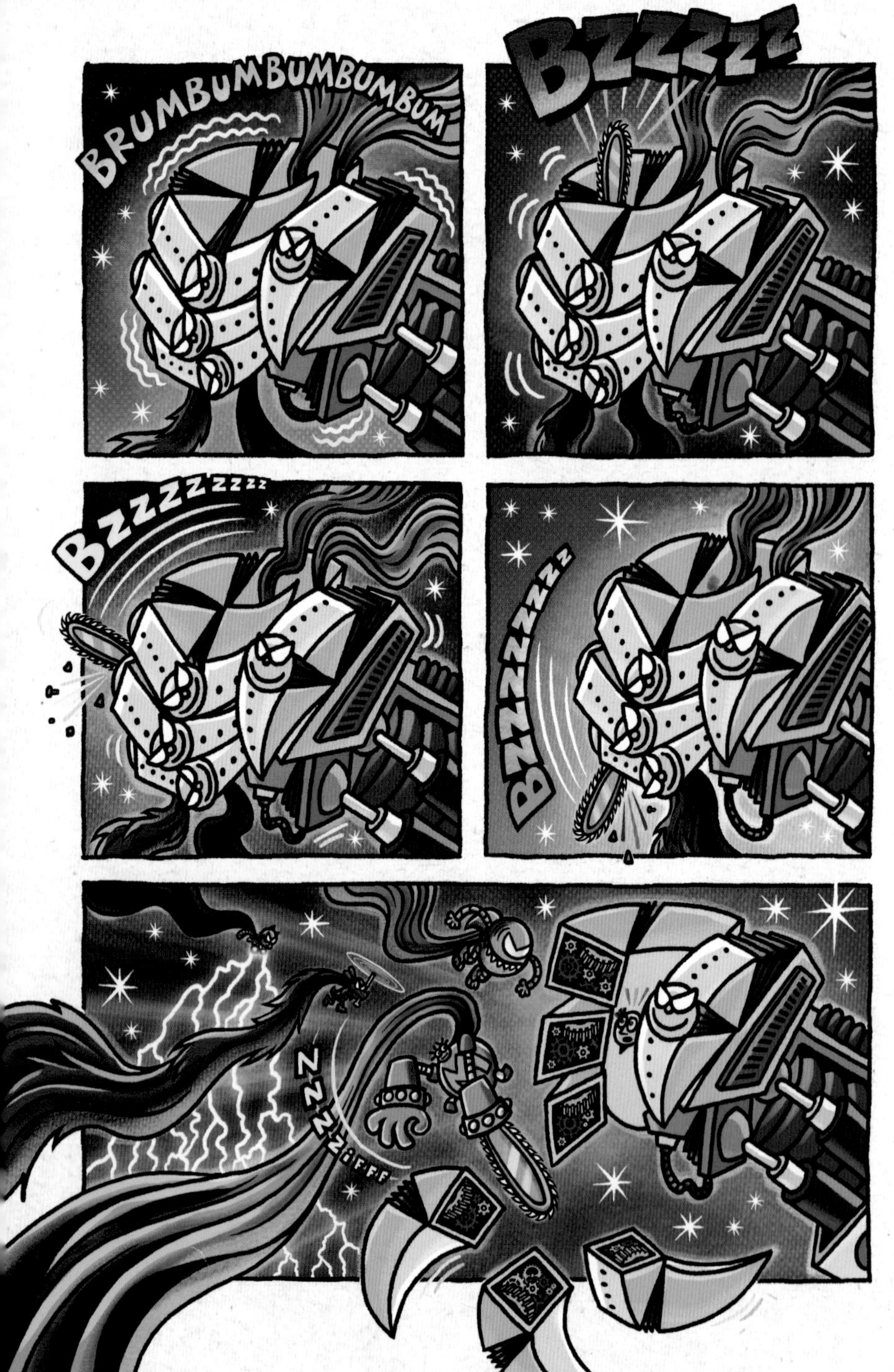
BRUMBUMBUMBUMBUM
Bzzzzz
Bzzzzzzzz
Bzzzzzzzzz
ZZZZiFFF

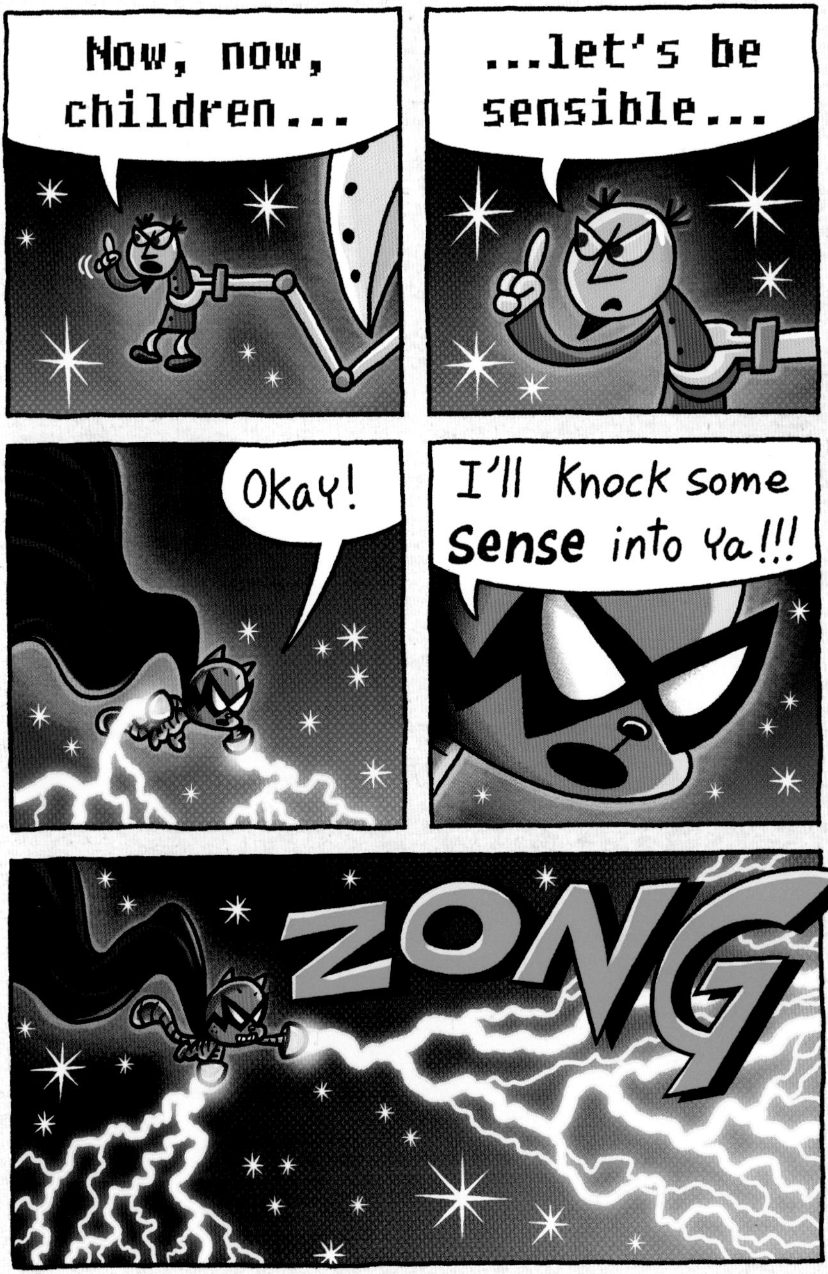
Now, now, children...
...let's be sensible...
Okay!
I'll Knock some sense into ya!!!
ZONG

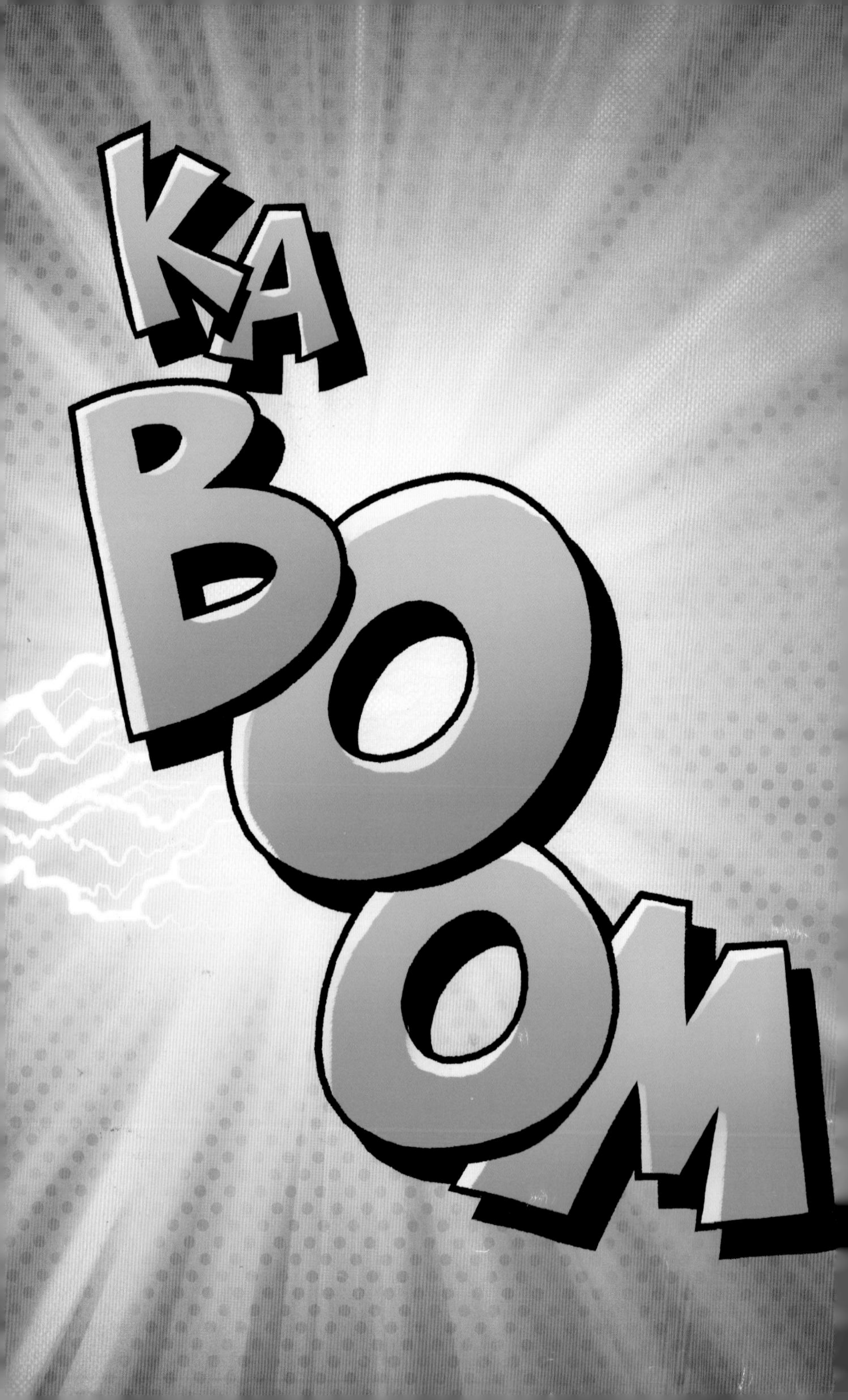
KA BOOM

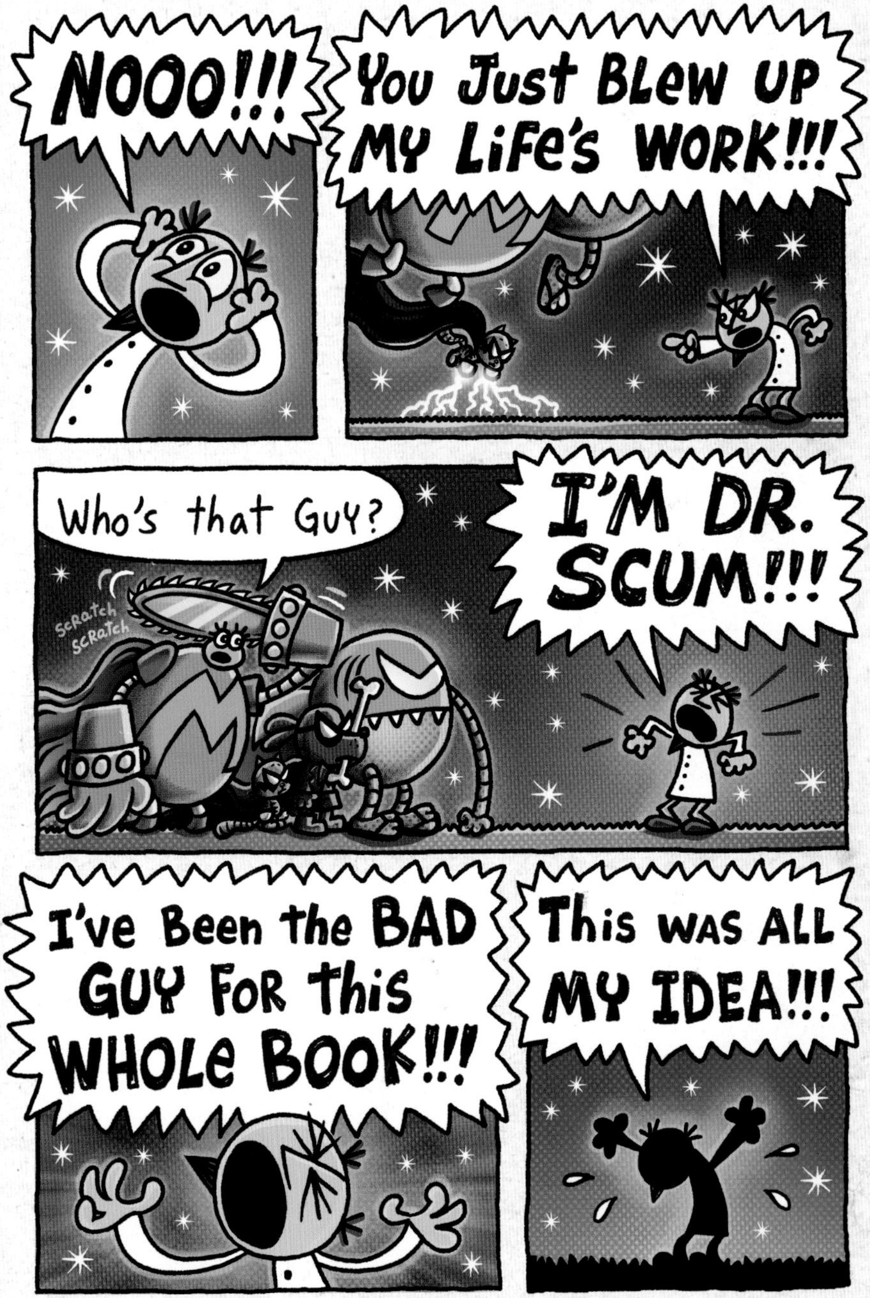
NOOO!!!
You Just Blew up My Life's WORK!!!
Who's that Guy?
Scratch Scratch
I'M DR. SCUM!!!
I've Been the BAD GUY For this WHOLE BOOK!!!
This WAS ALL MY IDEA!!!

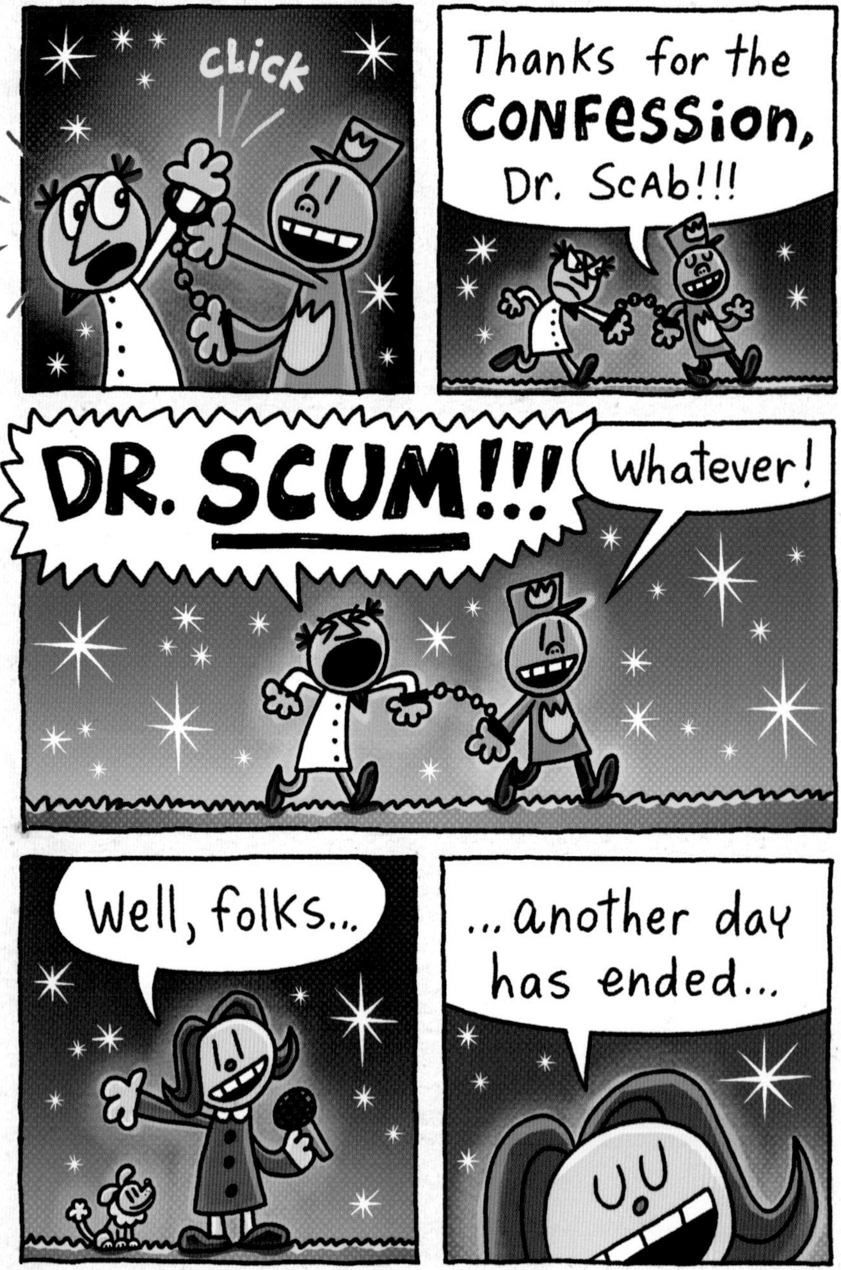
CLICK
Thanks for the CONFESSION, Dr. Scab!!!
DR. SCUM!!!
Whatever!
Well, folks...
...another day has ended...

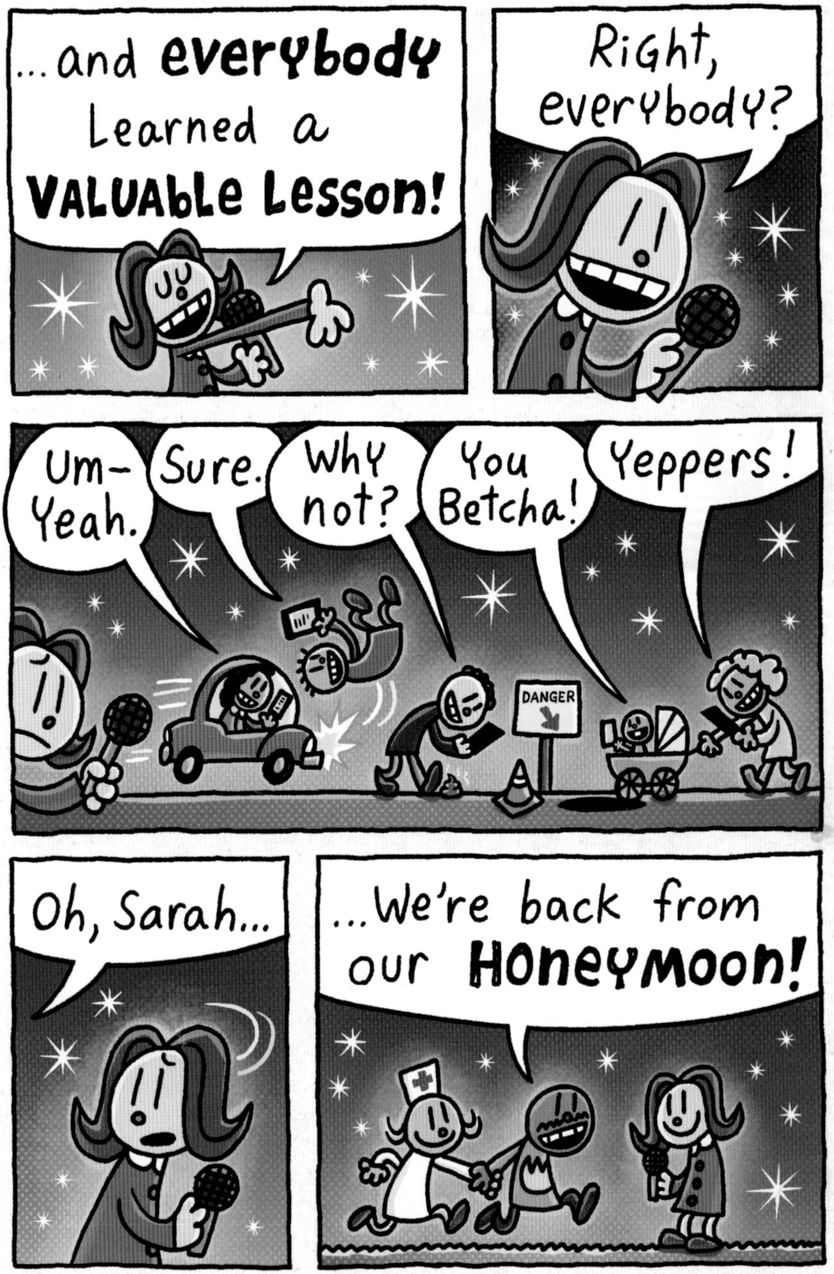
...and everybody Learned a VALUABLE LESSON!
Right, everybody?
Um- Yeah.
Sure.
Why not?
You Betcha!
Yeppers!
DANGER
Oh, Sarah...
...We're back from our HONEYMOON!

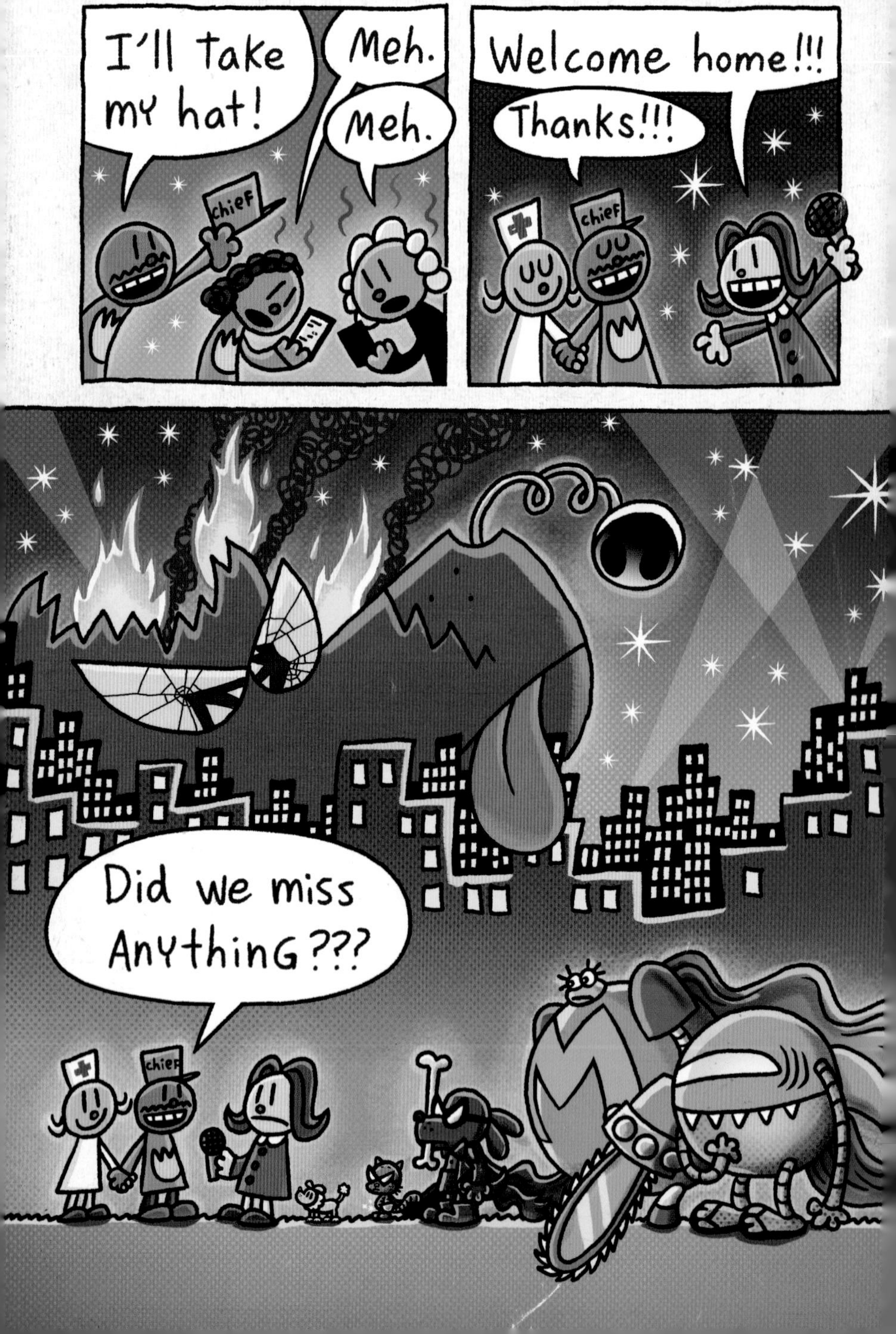
I'll take my hat!
Meh.
Meh.
Welcome home!!!
Thanks!!!
Did we miss Anything???

Chapter 16

Bedtime for Buddies

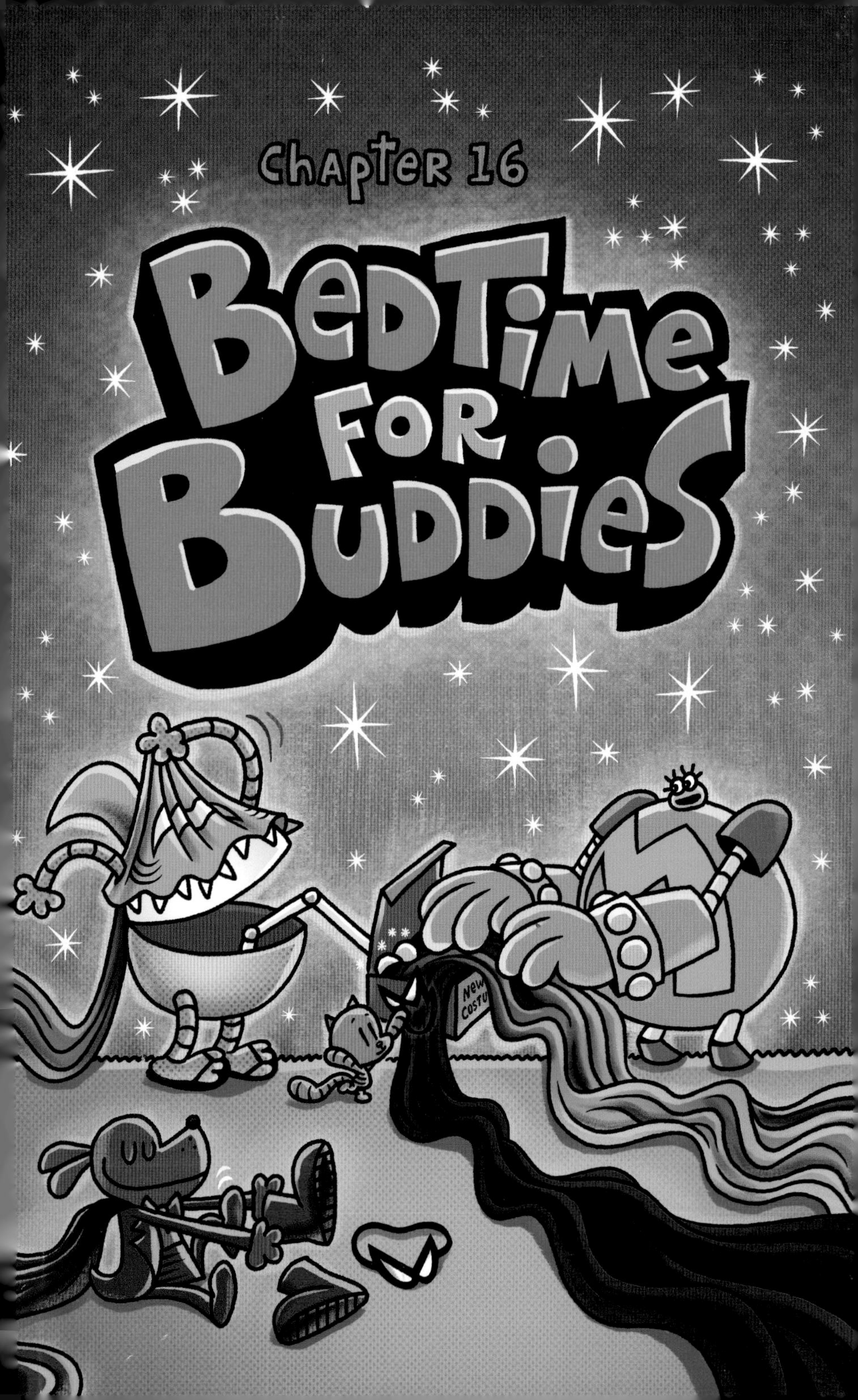
NEW

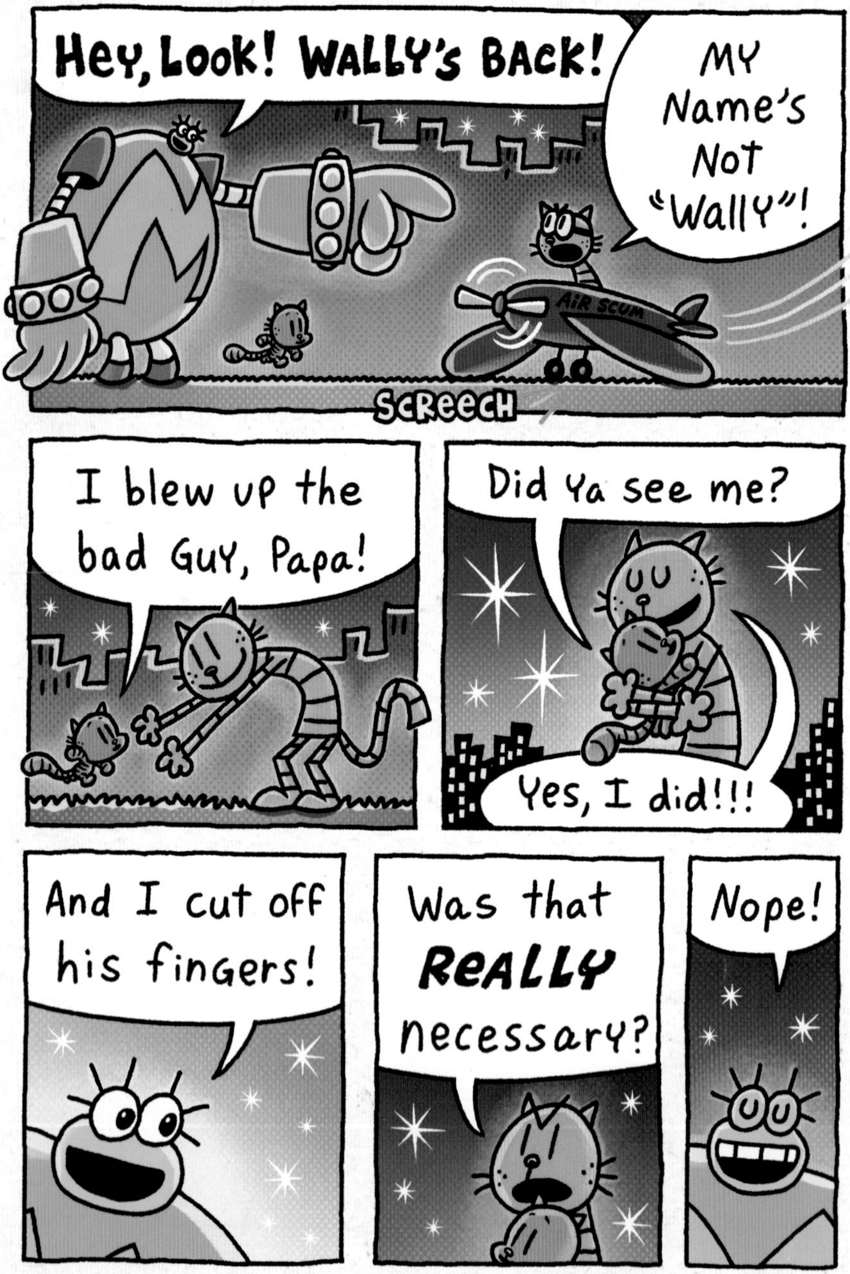
HEY, LOOK! WALLY'S BACK!
MY Name's Not "Wally"!
AiR SCUM
SCREECH
I blew up the bad GUY, Papa!
Did Ya see me?
Yes, I did!!!
And I cut off his fingers!
Was that REALLY necessary?
Nope!

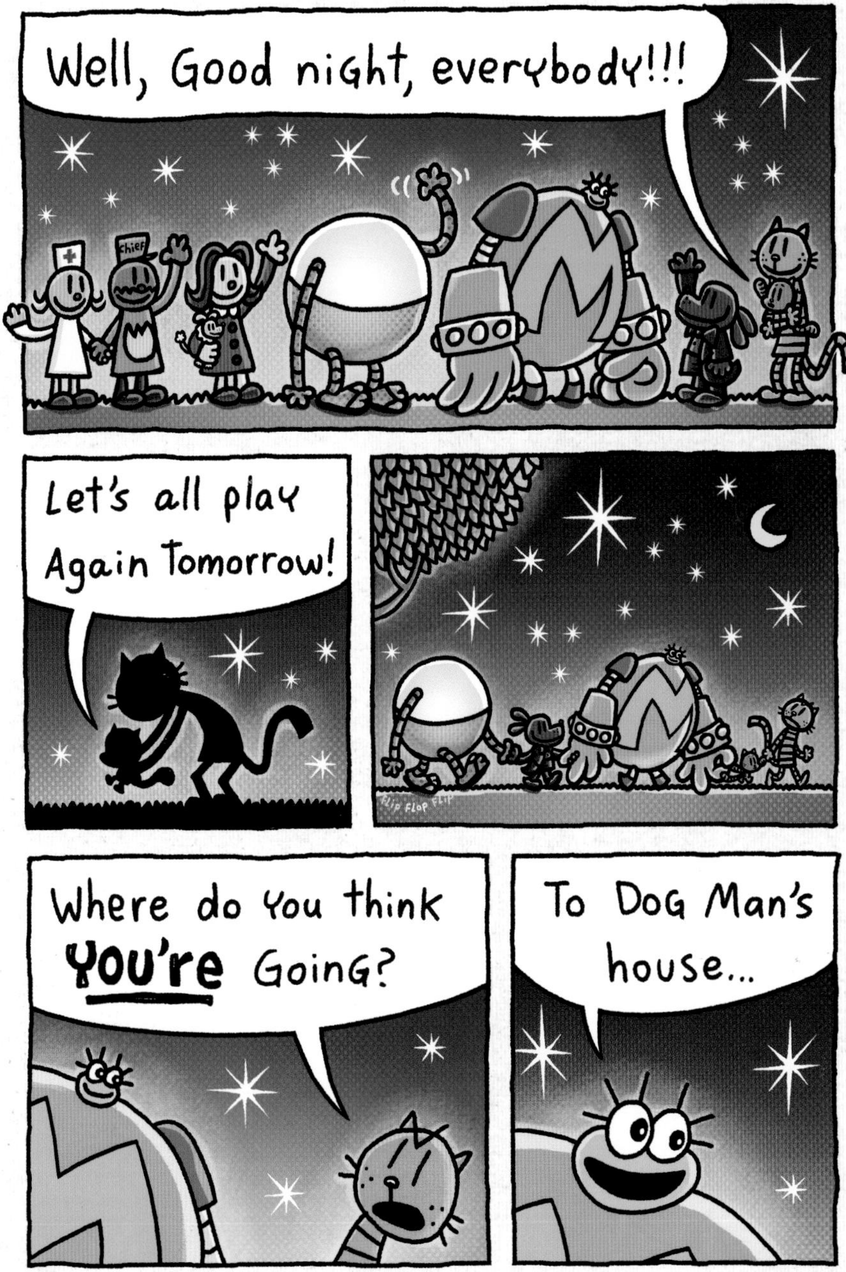
Well, Good night, everybody!!!
Let's all play Again Tomorrow!
FLIP FLOP FLIP
Where do you think YOU'RE GoinG?
To DoG Man's house...

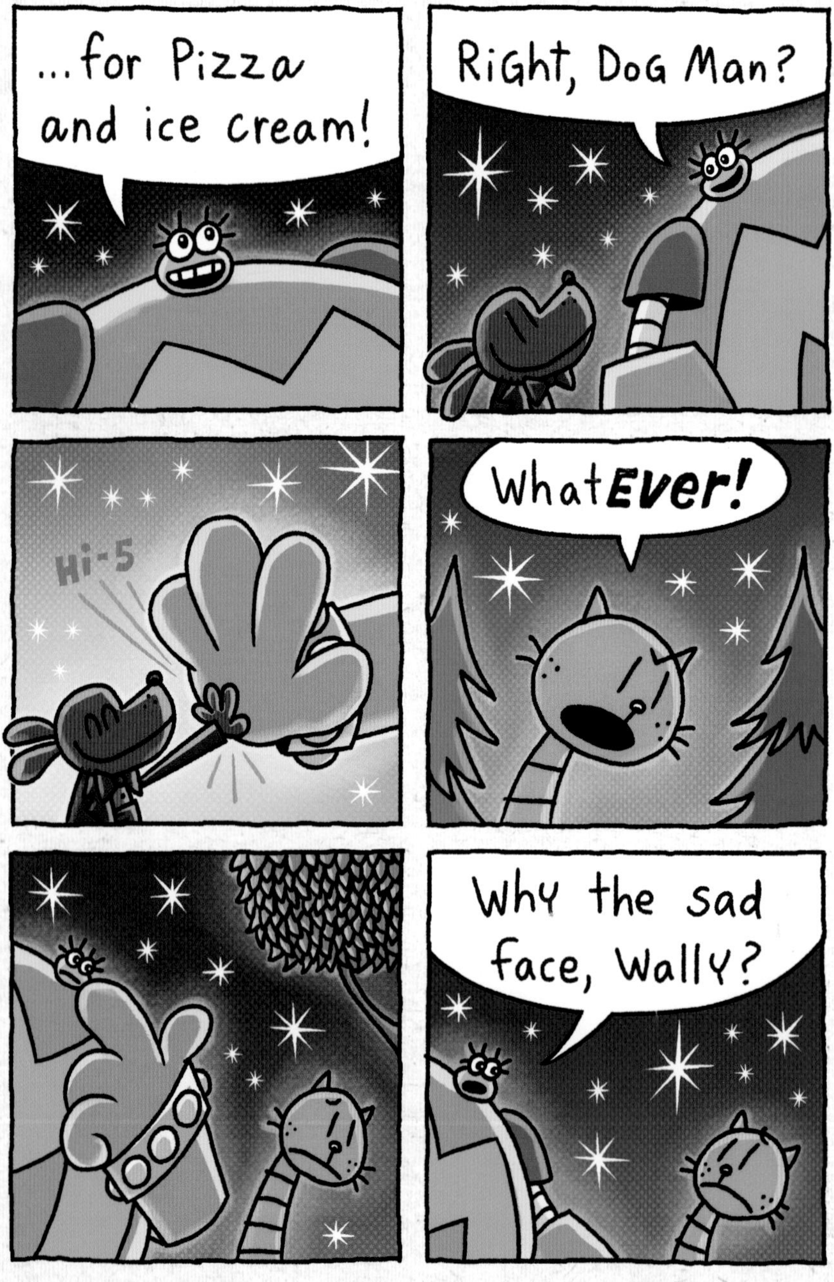
...for Pizza and ice cream!
Right, Dog Man?
Hi-5
WhatEVER!
Why the sad face, Wally?

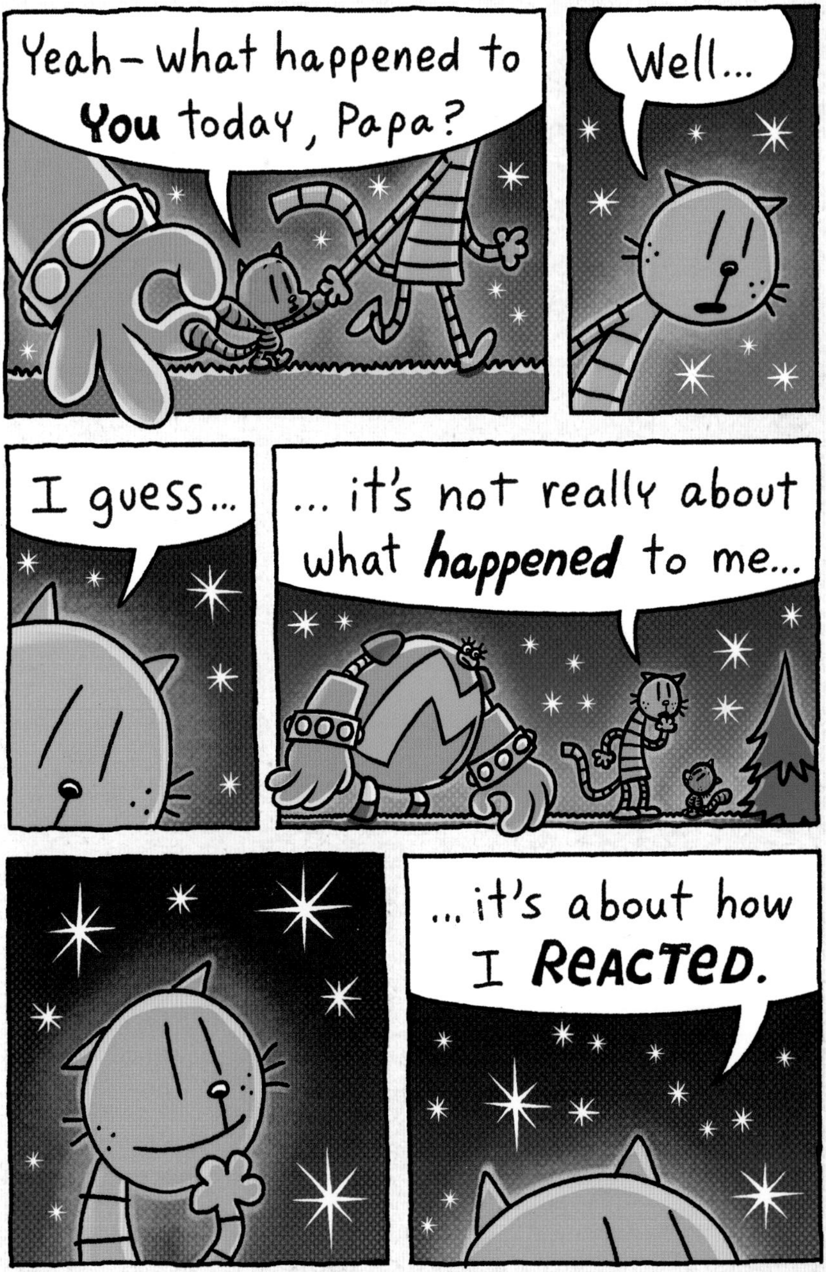
Yeah– what happened to **You** today, Papa?
Well...
I guess...
... it's not really about what ***happened*** to me...
... it's about how I **REACTED.**

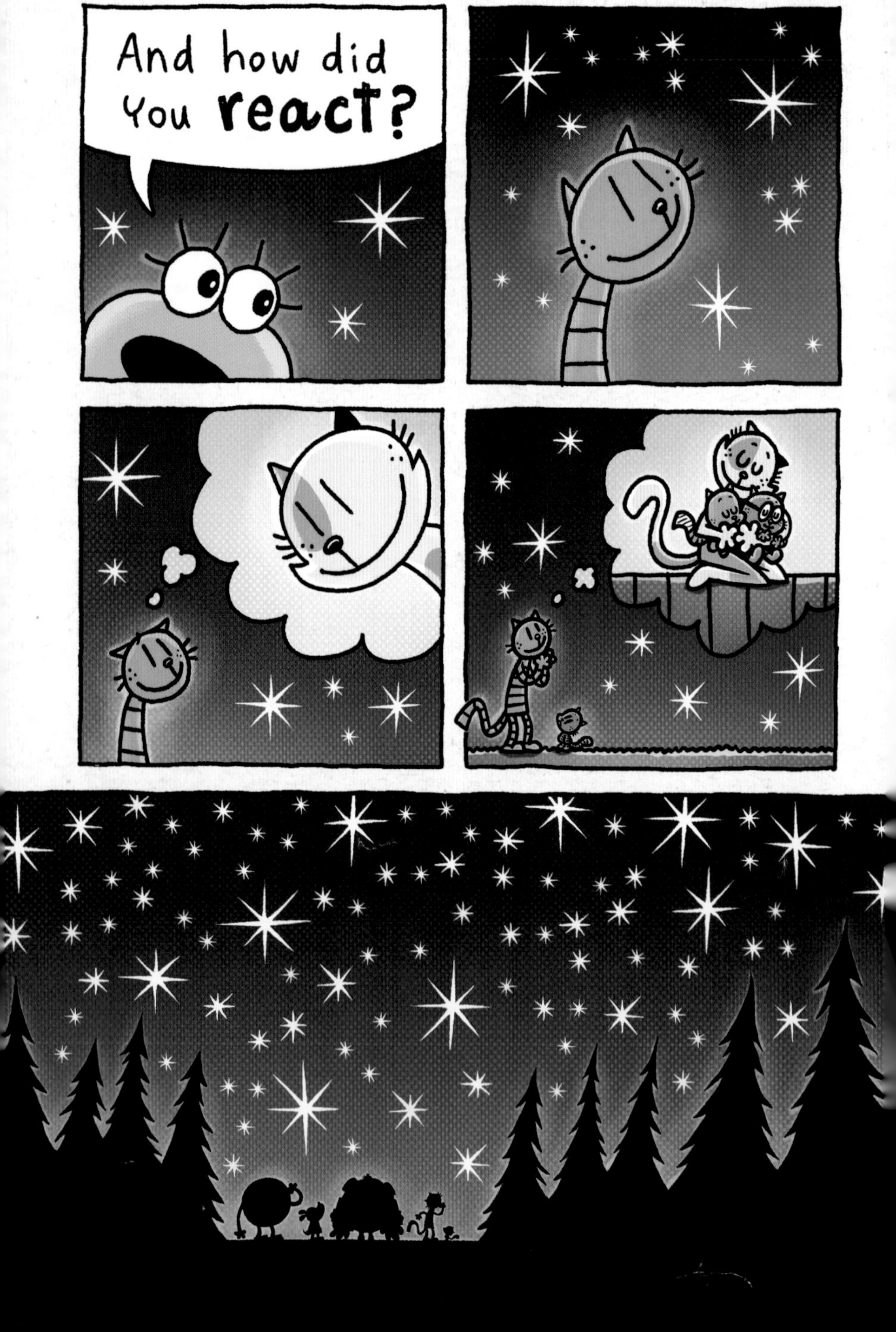
And how did you **react**?

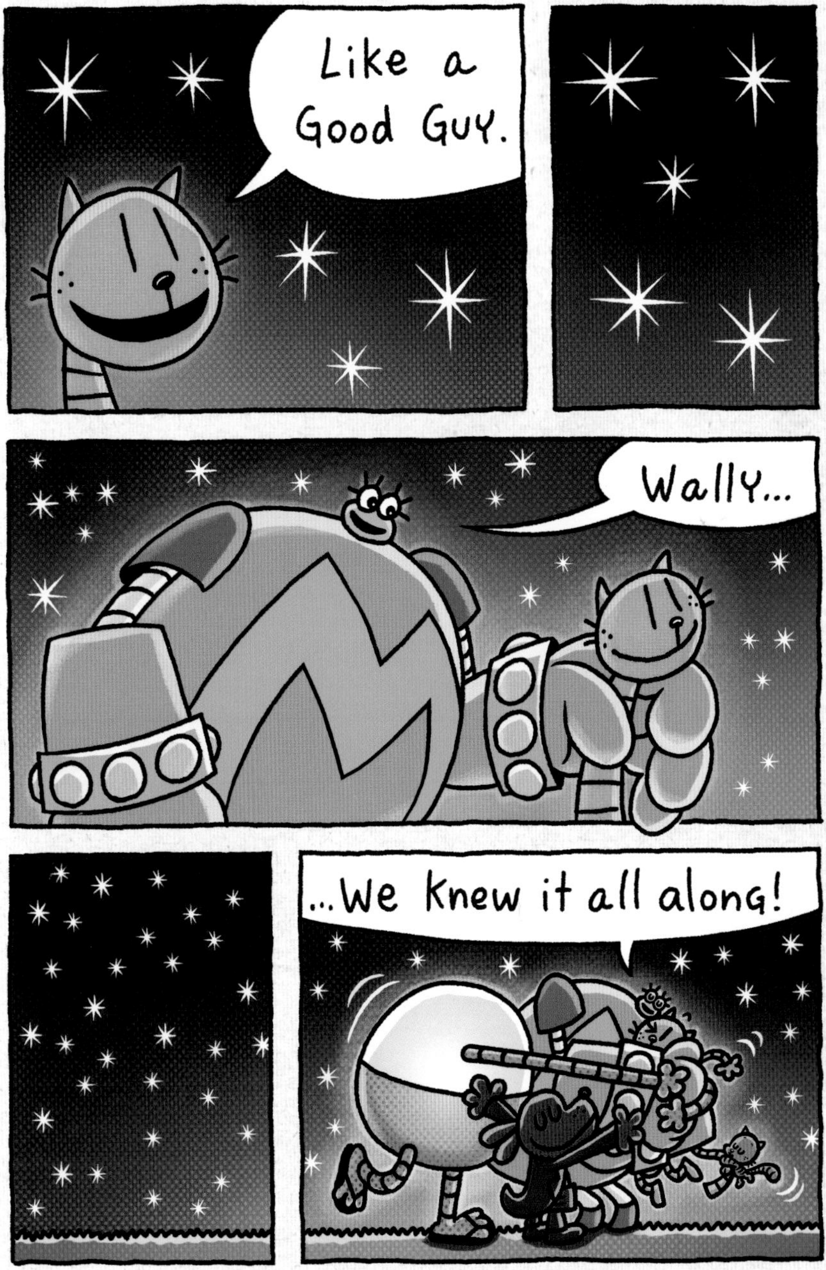
Like a Good Guy.
Wally...
...We knew it all along!

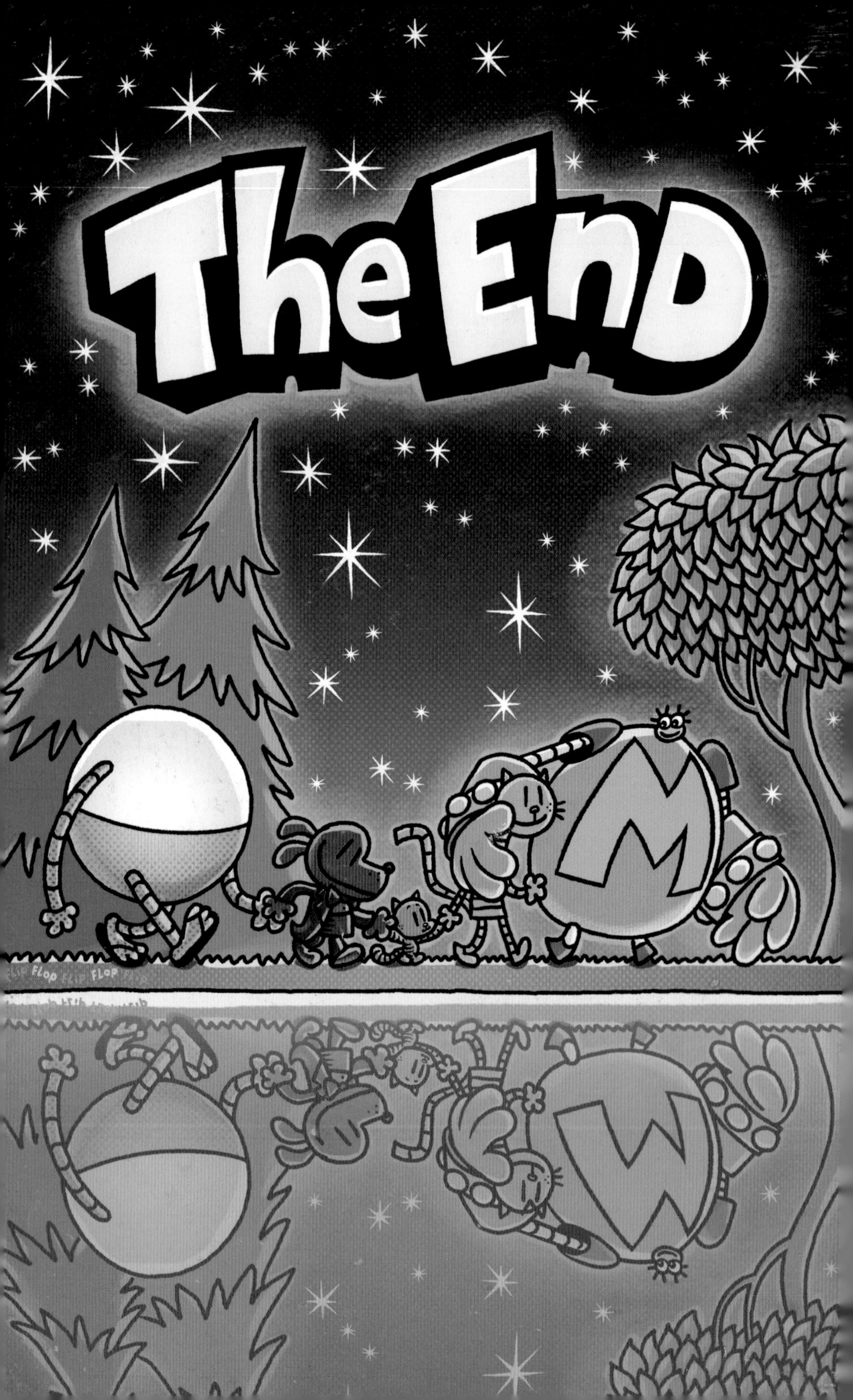
The End
FLIP FLOP FLIP FLOP

NoTeS & FuN FaCtS

Turpitude (Chapter 4) means "wickedness" or "shamefulness."

Bedford Falls (Chapter 8) is a fictional city where the movie *It's a Wonderful Life* (Frank Capra, 1946) takes place.

The giant Dog Man A.I. robot that begins to develop in Chapter 12 was designed and drawn by hand, but contains many visual inconsistencies. This was done purposefully, to reflect how A.I. often creates continuity errors in consecutive images (especially at the time this book was written and illustrated).

The speech from pages 165-169 is based on actual threats made by Artificial Intelligence (GPT-3).

An A.I. robot modeled after science fiction writer Philip K. Dick proposed keeping humans warm and safe in a "People Zoo" (page 188). Many people believe it was joking.

The machines on pages 190 and 191 are based on futuristic machines featured in the silent films *Metropolis* (Fritz Lang, 1927) and *Modern Times* (Charlie Chaplin, 1936).

"We can't control the wind, but we can adjust our sails" is based on a quote by Dolly Parton. This refers to sailboats, which have the ability to move in any direction, regardless of the wind. By adjusting their sails, sailboats can even move forward when the wind is blowing against them.

BONUS CONTENT: Check out Dav Pilkey's Epic Comic Club at PlanetPilkey.com starting June 1, 2024, for ALL-NEW FREE STUFF! Read new comics and jokes, learn to draw Little Jim and Ninja Shark, and MUCH, MUCH MORE!!!

About the
AUTHOR-ILLUSTRATOR

When Dav Pilkey was a kid, he was diagnosed with ADHD and dyslexia. Dav was so disruptive in class that his teachers made him sit out in the hallway every day. Luckily, Dav loved to draw and make up stories. He spent his time in the hallway creating his own original comic books — the very first adventures of Dog Man and Captain Underpants.

In the second grade, Dav's teacher ripped up his comics and told him he couldn't spend the rest of his life making silly books.

Fortunately, Dav was not a very good listener.